REDSHIFT

BY BLOOD OR BY STAR
BOOK 1

TYLER E. C. BURNWORTH

Temple Dark Books

By Blood Or By Star Book 1: Redshift
First Edition
Copyright © Tyler E. C. Burnworth 2021

Cover art by The Structuralist, AKA Eugen Baitinger
www.ebaitinger.de

Cover design & Typesetting by Temple Dark Books
Temple Dark Publications Ltd.
www.templedarkbooks.com

The Author asserts the moral right to
be identified as the author of this work

ISBN (E-Book): 9781838259457
ISBN (Paperback): 9781838259440

For my Lydia

Slumber, my darling, thy mother is near,
Guarding thy dreams from all terror and fear.
Sunlight has pass'd and the twilight has gone,
Slumber, my darling, the night's coming on.
Sweet visions attend thy sleep.
Fondest, dearest to me,
While others their revels keep,
I will watch over thee.

PROLOGUE

It was five minutes before the end of the world, and no one knew. Before Milune became the galaxy's newest asteroid field, it was home to 2 billion people, mostly human. One of them was a nine-year-old boy named Abraham Zeeben...

The obsidian spire loomed ahead of their car as they glided down the boulevard. It lanced the sky like a black dagger, so high Abraham felt dizzy when he craned his neck to see the top. Large glass panes tinted maroon in the soft glow of sunset. His father's latest building stood proudly on the Viridian City skyline, the apex of his career as a locally renowned architect.

Cramped sidewalks between the tower and Terran Ford Spaceport were filled with crowds of stargazers and tourists from far-flung star systems all come together to see The Passing. The wet blacktop smell of recent rainfall was concealed by concession booths stocked with rows of confectionary treats, made fresh on the spot. Most potent were steaming layers of fresh bread doused in butter and crusted with brown sugar, a favorite local dessert called Earth Bread.

Abraham preferred his red bean ice cream.

"It's nice. I guess," his brother remarked. Ice cream drizzled down the tan skin of his hand. His dark hair was swooped to the side, covering one eye. The other eye was fixated on the carpet between his feet.

Abraham was only nine, but he knew David was different from other kids their age. He was a year older and remarkably good at school, but his photographic memory and tendency to correct everyone made it hard for him to make friends.

"That's a fine assessment, son," Father said, his dark, stubbled cheeks pinching with a smirk. "Kellina, you want to remind the boys why we're here? It isn't for a fancy new building."

Mom, holding slack in her seatbelt, turned to lean in between Abraham and his brother. Blonde hair ran in waves down her back, framing a gentle face with kind blue eyes. Her voice was mellifluous, like she was always just on the verge of singing.

"Seatbelt, sweetie." She buckled Abraham in, then pointed over her shoulder. "Any minute now, boys, we're going to see Dajun pass over the sky. The forest moon's passing is a sign of good fortune for the year to come."

1

David snorted. A spattle of melted red bean hit the ground. "Dajun orbits Sadaviridian faster than Milune, Mom. It's just science."

Father kept the wheel steady with one hand, watching the road attentively. He looked strange in casual attire, a simple long-sleeved shirt with no collar and no tie, tan cargo pants and gym shoes. He did something Abraham didn't see his father normally do; he smiled. "It's more than that, son. It's a beautiful sight."

As the words left his mouth a green light flared in Abraham's peripheral vision. The car's visor attempted to adjust to the strange color of Milune's solar eclipse. He glanced up at the sky with wide-eyed wonder.

Cheers broke out from the crowd in the street. Cameras flashed. Shutters clicked rapidly.

Dajun was there, glowing almost neon with the light reflected from the star, Sadaviridian. It was so close, he felt that if he jumped high enough, he could touch the tops of the trees. *I don't remember it being that close last year*, he thought.

David's cone plopped on his lap. "Mom," he said, "is it supposed to be that close?"

She looked to Father. "Obadiah?"

His face hardened. Eyes narrow, jaw set. He reached for the center console.

This doesn't feel right, Abraham thought, but couldn't say. His gut was in a knot. Squealing tires pulled his attention to his window. A red car barreled toward him like a speeding bullet.

Mom screamed.

Glass shattered.

Shrapnel radiated in a hailstorm.

The world spun in a roaring blur and went black.

Abraham came to on the street, covered in broken glass. Something was burning with an odor like oil or ethanol. His head thundered with pain. *Mom? Where's Mom?*

A few meters away, black smoke billowed from the two cars. A man lay on the concrete next to him, bloody face smashed in. It was not his father. *Was he wearing a seat belt?* Abraham thought. *I was. How did I get out of the car?*

Dajun, consumed in flame, barreled toward him like the eye of an angry god. The sky combusted as oxygen ignited in swirling lines of fire. Up and down the street, windows exploded, shards raining from the sky.

We need to get away! Mom! Father! David! Where are you?

Amid the screams and panic of the crowd, he saw something. A man wrapped in strange shadows with a hand outstretched toward the sky.

2

His hand glowed bright red as if holding a flare, but his palm was open. Empty. Abraham didn't understand what he was seeing, not even when the man turned, exposing his face.

It was the face of a corpse. Dark, ashy skin, gray lips in a thin line, a black bar over his eyes like a censor line that covered inappropriate things on television. In the blink of an eye, the swirling shadows expanded, obscuring him from view.

Abraham scrambled to his feet, swaying with vertigo. Twisting metal shrieked behind him. The Interstellar Commerce tower – Father's building – was falling.

A shoulder in the gut knocked the wind out of him. The scent of tobacco and brown sugar washed over him. Father's strong arm held him. David hung limp under the other arm.

What about Mom?

He tried to look for her. The jostling from Father's running stride made it impossible to see anything. *Why are we leaving without her?*

Abraham closed his eyes. A sob wracked his throat. He tried to cry out, but the air was squeezed out of him by his father's iron grip. He heard the hiss of an airlock. Felt a seat cushion under him. Clicking from safety harnesses being secured. The last sound he heard before the shock pulled him into unconsciousness was the thrum of a fusion engine firing at full throttle.

CHAPTER 1

A hissing air vent like a constant whisper above his head. Steady vibrations under him. He was in a starship. He didn't want to be in a starship. He refused to open his eyes.

He wanted to be back on Milune with his mother. Her scream tore through his mind. Inhale sadness. Exhale grief.

Don't forget her face, he told himself. *She can't be gone. She can't be…*

He felt the ghost of her embrace and knew he would never again experience it in waking life.

Gravity was lighter on the ship, but he felt like a lead weight. Something poked him in the ribs. "Hey," the poker said, "wake up."

Abraham rubbed crusted tears from his eyes. Goosebumps sprouted from his skin and he shivered. Space was cold. He felt cold on the inside, too.

"Thanks for saving me. Back there."

She screamed.

The world spun around Abraham in a roaring blur. *I didn't save anybody*, he thought, his throat tightening.

The Interstellar Commerce building was falling.

Abraham blinked. The nightmare disappeared. He started breathing again. It was like sucking air through a straw and his sternum ached. He wasn't surprised when he lifted his shirt and saw a purple bruise.

I lost someone.

The poker was a kid about his age. Dirty blonde hair hung over the sides of his pale face. Weak lighting from the baseboards along the hallway lit his pale cheeks a shade of green where they weren't covered in soot. A miasma of smoke wafted off him.

"You were on Milune, too?" Abraham asked.

The kid nodded, his face scrunched. He sniffed sharply. "My parents…"

Abraham wrapped his arms around his knees and squeezed until they ached. Tears singed his eyes with a heat that felt like his face was melting. He didn't try to hold them back.

"My mother," he squeaked.

A series of beeps sounded from somewhere down the corridor.

"Hey kid," Father called, "you awake?"

Abraham used the wall to help himself stand up. His belly tickled with a tug of low G, but he settled easy enough. The muscles in his legs felt like they were submerged in quicksand. He inhaled a lungful of soot and mucus, coughing as he followed the tall, gangly boy into the crew station.

7

Father was strapped into the seat, harness splayed over him like a spider of belts and buckles. David sat next to him, straps dangling over the sides of the co-pilot's seat, reclined and sleeping with his mouth open.

Abraham's sobs softened enough for him to ask, "What's your name?"

"Larry," the boy said. "Larry Poplenko." He turned to Father and added, "I have...my grandparents...they're on Veranda."

Father laughed. A heavy, low sound that didn't sound like a laugh at all. "That'll do."

He typed on the control pad until a green and brown sphere materialized on the main screen. It made a slow orbit around a large red star. "Maximum velocity is...seven hundred lux, that puts us at...two days out. Strap in."

Abraham shivered. *Father knows how to fly a spaceship?*

His father's voice didn't sound like him at all. The vowels were pinched. The words seemed to crawl out of the back of his throat, like they didn't want to come out at all.

He's scared.

Abraham had never seen his father afraid before today. He strapped himself into the sensory operator terminal, watching Larry buckle into the navigator's chair opposite his own. Obadiah unbuckled himself to get David strapped up. He clicked one of the belts together and cinched it as tight as it would go, but it was still loose.

"Seats aren't designed for kids," he muttered under his breath.

Two days was going to be a long time. Abraham kept making eye contact with Larry. They would both look away, scan the room for a moment, then invariably end up staring at each other again.

"What happened?" Larry asked.

Abraham looked to his father.

A few moments passed in silence. The air felt heavy. The low decibel thrum of the FTL drive and everyone's breathing filled the empty space where conversation would have existed under different circumstances. Only, how could they talk about it? Their home world was gone. Larry's parents and Abraham's mother...dead.

Everything they had to talk about was gone.

The tears returned.

He clamped his teeth shut until his jaw ached. A sob lurched out of his chest. He cried. Through blurry eyes, he could see Larry crying, too.

Father said, "It's...things like this defy all logic."

"I didn't know...accidents could be so...big," Larry said.

The moon was on fire, and it was falling. Abraham's stomach leapt to his throat. The Shadow Man raised his hand, a red glow piercing the air above him.

"You okay?" Larry asked.

Abraham blinked. The nightmare dissipated. "I saw something, Father."

Father's chair squeaked as he repositioned himself. If he heard Abraham, he gave no sign of it. "There's a video log on this ship. It was no accident."

"What do you mean?" Larry asked.

Abraham wiped his eyes and leaned toward his father, hoping he would play the video. Hoping he wouldn't play the video. How did his father know it wasn't an accident? He wanted to know, but he didn't want to see anything. He didn't want to relive it.

Obadiah tapped the panel. The brown and green planet dissolved, replaced by a large spacecraft.

Viridian Square sprawled out over the foreground. The rest of the city district stretched to the horizon. It was carnage and chaos like Abraham had only seen in movies. The city resembled the exposed rib cage of a massive animal; buildings lay on their sides, stripped of windows. People ran between them like flies flitting around with no clear destination in mind but moving fast. The view from the ground looking up made it hard to spot the ship against the background of stars. Small red glows were the only thing that gave it away. The image was a live capture. It moved on an endless loop.

A crimson plume appeared at the nose of the ship, but instead of moving away, the ship followed the plume, tracing its path like a guide through the Milune sky. Across the midsection, slats glowed, swelled, and contracted.

"What is that? Why does it move that way?" Abraham asked.

"That," Father said, "is a riskar ship. They do things differently than we do."

"So, they're the ones who did this?" Larry asked.

"Why?" Abraham screamed.

"Just calm down, son."

Abraham jumped to his feet, but the straps pulled him back down. "Why did they do this? They ruined our home! They killed Mother!"

Father turned to face Abraham. His eyes were bloodshot with tears, but his face was stone cold. The stubble made him look harsh. Angry. "Why does anybody resort to violence?" He covered his bared teeth with his lips in a thin line, staring hard at Abraham. "Because they want what we have."

9

Larry was staring at him, chin tilted down.

He's scared, Abraham thought. *We're all scared.*

The forest moon was on fire. The Shadow Man was there. Mother screamed as the car slammed into them. Father's building was collapsing and –

– and it wasn't an accident, Abraham realized. *The riskar did this. They killed her.*

"I'll kill them!" Abraham shouted through clenched teeth. His stomach churned acid into the bottom of his throat. He was nauseous. He balled a fist and slammed it into the wall.

Larry flinched, but didn't say anything.

Abraham's hand hurt, but he didn't care.

"I'll kill them *all*."

Father shook his head. "It's not that simple, son. Life never is."

Abraham could not tear his eyes from the riskar ship. The way it flexed, swelling and shrinking in the middle, it could have been breathing. Like the whole ship was a giant fish with a red line reeling it in. This wasn't Abraham's first time seeing an alien ship. It wasn't even his first time seeing a riskar.

But it was his first day hating them.

On approach, Abraham decided Veranda looked nothing like Milune. The buildings were squat, small, and spread apart. Most of the houses were surrounded by rolling green hills and flat brown fields. Father talked back and forth with the ground tower as their ship descended. Trees and rows of high-stalked vegetation sprouted from the ground, reminding Abraham of turning pages in a pop-up book.

The temperature inside the ship rose when they landed. Abraham woke David with the same courtesy Larry had shown him earlier – a stiff jab to the ribs. David unstrapped himself with a grumble. The moment his eyes were open, they never left the viewport until Father began corralling them toward the airlock. Abraham was pinned between his brother and Larry.

"Where are we?" David whispered.

"Veranda," Larry said. "My grandparents live here."

The tarmac was a concrete pad with a few dozen spacecraft parked in circular depressions. Trees danced in the distance, a mirage caused by heat emanating from the ground. The sun was red, and about twice the size of what Abraham was used to seeing on Milune. The air was different, here, too. Almost moist.

He hated it.

Abraham shouldered his way between the other two boys and kept close behind his father. They entered the two-story air terminal through a glass sliding door. A wave of cool air puffed down from the ceiling. He could hear the commotion of people moving luggage and making small talk. Abraham blinked several times to adjust eyes to the darker space in the building, and when the white haze finally cleared, they were walking through a corridor marked CUSTOMS/FIRST TIME ARRIVALS.

Coming in with refugee status posed some problems initially with Veranda Customs, but Father was able to prove the escape from Milune with the video loop and the Captain's Log from the ship. The Customs Agent, a bald man in a blue security jumpsuit, put a hand on Father's shoulder. "Obadiah Zeeben, you're a damn hero, far as I'm concerned. As for citizenship, shouldn't be a problem. Veranda's on a 26-hour-day rotation, gravity is point one above standard. Close enough to Milune, for all intents and purposes."

Abraham's ears itched. He hadn't heard an accent like that before. It made the words come out slower than he was used to hearing.

The agent added, "The Navy already got a declaration of war presented to the Senate. If it passes, the Nine Nations will vote on it. Could be war sooner rather than later."

Father stiffened. "War? Since when do the Nine Nations do anything fast?"

The agent shrugged, handed Father a small box and waved him on. When they were outside, Father turned to Larry and put a hand on his shoulder. "Now, kid," he said with a weak smile, "do you remember where your grandparents live?"

The three boys became close, their friendship galvanized by grief and trauma. Larry's grandparents were kind enough to take in Obadiah, David and Abraham for a few months. Obadiah had been a successful architect on Milune, but the local bank and his life's savings were drifting through space in pieces. The demand for fancy skyscrapers and towering apartment buildings was non-existent on the sprawling farmlands of Veranda. Here, the coin of the land was what you could dig out of the soil at harvest.

There was an abandoned plot of land just down the road from Larry's grandparents' house. It had once been a bustling tobacco farm, but the former owner had been an ancient riskar who had mysteriously abandoned the property two months before the Milune incident. The bank seized the property without investigating and promptly listed it on the market. Obadiah broke the news over a family meeting one hot summer day. The Poplenkos sold their spacecraft to front the down payment for Obadiah. The Zeebens moved in a week after the loan was approved. Abraham was relieved to see no sign of the former occupant.

The news headlines were now referring to the destruction of Milune as 'The Collision'.

On Veranda the summers were hot, the winters cold, and the passing seasons were filled with quiet tension and bittersweet memories. Many nights Abraham would lie in his twin bed across from David and cry himself to sleep. Remembering the last time he saw his mother and the terrible end she had faced. Had she known Abraham was nearby? So close to her, but just out of reach? Was she thinking of him when she died? Was she scared? Did she suffer or was it quick, being crushed by a building or burned to a pile of ash in the blink of an eye?

Terrible visions to torture himself with, he knew.

Yet Abraham tortured himself night after night, unable to stop the torrent of feelings and thoughts that welled up inside. As time wore on, he realized he was grateful for the change of scenery. He came to appreciate the shift from a life of comfort to one of endless work presented by the challenge found in a family business. Especially one as 'character-building' as farming. Obadiah constantly beat that drum into the boys. When he could be bothered to speak.

It was a strange, dark shift Abraham saw in his father. On the one hand, Father was remarkably satisfied with the farming life. It put food on the table, kept a modest but comfortable roof over their heads, and occupied their time. The days went by with bruised and calloused hands, cracked and bloody knuckles, weathered skin from sun exposure mixed with the salt-and-onion stench of body odor from long hours in the fields. It was a miserable existence for a child, an emotional vacuum. There wasn't a single bedtime story told. No television to lull the mind into relaxation. Few words of encouragement.

David was the first to crack.

One day when the leaves were falling in varying shades of red and brown, after the field had been tended and the sun was nearly cut in half by the horizon, the Zeeben clan was settling in for supper. The handmade table creaked as David leaned against it, his body quivering with excitement and consternation.

He put forth a very convincing argument, stating the importance of a well-balanced education, for one. And two, that the boys could get their character-building on the farm *after* school, when their minds had already been challenged, and when the idleness of sitting at desks all day would leave them plenty of energy to tackle the near-endless workload that surrounded their home.

Father made a big show of pretending to refuse it, puckering his lips and puffing his cheeks. It was the widest range of emotions Abraham had seen from his father in almost six months. Father thought about it for a minute before allowing David to convince him it was for the best. "Education didn't bring me anything but trouble. Maybe it'd do you boys better. I'm not gonna hold you back based on my personal feelings. You can go."

"This year?" David's face lit up.

Obadiah nodded. "That's right. Starting next term."

David cheered and jumped and pounded his fist in the air repeatedly. It was the happiest Abraham had seen him since The Collision. Abraham hadn't made much of an effort to connect with his brother, preferring to lose himself in the farm work to avoid thinking about that day. Even though they now shared a room, David kept to himself for the most part. The very next week he and David found themselves assimilating into the folds of normal life on Veranda through the public school system.

Abraham's nightmares never went away.

As the years pressed on, he would be haunted by dreams of strange lands and faces, some haunting and macabre, others distortions of people he knew in real life. The dreams never made much sense. They were almost always centered around the death of his mother, but he was never able to gather much meaning from them. Mother would be crushed by the evil moon Dajun; or smashed into smithereens by a falling fireball; or crushed by the Interstellar Commerce building. Every time without fail, he would watch in disbelief. Fear kept him rooted firmly in place. On rare occasion, the dreams would focus on David or his father being killed, too.

Somehow, Abraham seemed invincible in his dreams. The dangers were real, the threat of imminent death so close he could feel it just as tangibly as he could on the day it happened, but there was something out of place about it. Something missing.

He was not afraid anymore.

CHAPTER 2

Abraham stuffed beef stew by the mouthful, grimacing. A delicious explosion of peppered broth was quickly tampered by the sting of salt. Three years of working the farm and his father still oversalted. The simple meals Father made were given the reception a five-star dinner might receive at a fancy restaurant on Parkway Drive downtown, if only because hard work created burgeoning appetites in Abraham and his brother. David chewed with his mouth open, peach fuzz just starting to sprout under his chin. His eyes stared off into space.

Father's chair creaked when he sat in it. Everything inside was wood, carved and assembled by the old man's capable hands. Abraham laughed inside to remember the state of the shed they called home when they first moved in. Water leaked in through the roof. No furniture save a crinkly, crusty mattress on the floor in the upstairs bedroom. No electricity, either. Over the last few years, Father had taken that hunk of shit and made it into a home. It was nothing short of a miracle.

The two-story 'shed' was now officially a homestead. Father's affinity for architecture formed a solid basis for his mastering woodcraft, but unlike the construction projects on Milune, the homestead was improved with a focus on function over art. A simple table for six surrounded by six sturdy chairs, a few flat-faced cabinets, Obadiah's rocking chair, and a rectangular mantle over a fireplace were the extent of the downstairs. The smells of fresh pine, sturdy oak and Father's vanilla pipe tobacco filled the house when it didn't have to compete with hearty meals on the stovetop. Abraham would always associate these scents with the memory of this dining room.

Most evenings under the Zeeben roof passed in relative silence. David was usually reading the encyclopedia collection Larry's grandparents had given them as a holiday gift the year prior, while Abraham was just grateful for the break from physical labor. On rare occasion, the chessboard would be dug out of the closet, and they would play until Abraham and his father gave up – David was the undisputed chess champion of the family. Father spent most of his off time smoking his pipe, seated in his rocking chair by the window with a weary expression on his face and a black box in his hands, always unopened. Abraham inspected it closely as his father's eyelids grew heavy one evening, and discovered the box was actually a book. The strange thing was, he never once saw his father read it.

One night everything changed. Freshly chopped veggies littered the counter. Scalloped potatoes boiled on the stove, wafting a butter-and-green-onion aroma into the dining room. The screen door creaked open as Father entered the homestead. Clutched in his arms was a rectangular screen, like a pane of glass that could be a window.

Father unveiled the latest addition to the homestead: a television.

We must be doing pretty good with the tobacco exports, Abraham surmised at the time.

After a few minutes of tinkering, the screen was installed above the mantle in the living room. Abraham could feel the excitement he shared with his brother at having a TV in the house. They hadn't seen a second of it since the morning of The Collision, instead relying on Father to bring news updates after a run into town for supplies. Father always made those trips alone.

Obadiah hefted the remote and clicked it. The screen crackled to life for the first time. It showed images of war. Spacecraft screamed across the frame, trailing streams of fire. Spacemen carried large rifles that whined with each trigger pull, spewing flashes of light. Jungle landscape erupted in flames.

The riskar most closely resembled bipedal insects with strange bulbs floating over their shoulders, connected where the neck and shoulders met. Presumably, their mouth was nestled beneath the crustacean-like mandibles under their chin. The news clips played, showing lines of light splintering their carapaces like confetti.

All this was backed by a victory fanfare of trumpets and drums.

The boys huddled closer to the set, potatoes on the stove burning as they were caught up in the excitement of the moment.

The images changed from jungle foliage to space. Stars swirled with increasing speed until the screen fixated on a planet labelled DURINGER. It was small. Text popped up beneath it, declaring it a planetoid. The poles were small white smudges bookending a red sphere covered in wavy gray lines. Black clusters were nestled in pockets and geometric patterns across the surface.

Abraham listened intently, his gut in a knot. Father served dinner as a voiceover narrated the progress of the Riskar War.

He recognized the cruel spires of the alien architecture as the image changed. It was the same behemoth ship he had seen flying over Milune. His chest ached. It reminded him of the night he could never forget, the night his mother had been taken from him. Everyone talked about it. Those who didn't talk in the open whispered in their homes.

The Collision. The day the riskar blackened the eye of humanity. The day an evil alien empire started a war they were never going to win. Humans never lose wars.

An old man's face appeared on the television, all hard lines and chiseled features. He had a mole on the side of his face, just behind his temple, and his silver hair was shaved and styled with military precision. A tag appeared at the bottom of the screen – 'Admiral Latreaux'. His voice was gruff and imposing, his mannerisms reminiscent of a bulldog; chest thrust out, jaw clenched. He sounded exactly as Abraham thought he should:

"General Rictor is not fighting a fair war. The riskar have a violent history, rife with terroristic tendencies. The oversight that allowed this to happen was not a military one, but a political one. However, humanity has done a damn fine job of wielding its military might to smash the teeth of oppression and put an end to senseless violence over the last few thousand years. This is no exception. The attack on Milune was senseless violence. It was preventable. And it will be avenged. Milune was not a military target. My official statement this morning is to communicate that our forces have breached riskar-controlled space. The Navy will decimate their spacecraft; the Marines will land on their planets and crush their ground forces. We will locate the enemy home world. And when we do, we will bring a swift end to this war."

The camera zoomed in on Latreaux's hard stare, angling to show his grim resolve in the face of such unbridled evil. Abraham felt he could trust that face, that man in the uniform. He was solving the riskar problem when no one else would. The political bodies that ran the human branch of the Nine Nations had been caught sleeping on the job. They had let these aliens destroy a planet. They had allowed his mother to be murdered. *I'm stuck here, working this farm, when I could be out there, killing riskar.*

Abraham's spoon clinked onto his plate. His chair creaked against the floorboards as he stood up. The commotion pulled the attention of his father and brother from the screen. "I'm joining the Navy," he announced.

The cold calm of his words cracked through the tepid silence. David's long hair flipped with a jerk of his head so he was looking at Abraham with both eyes. Father leaned against the counter and crossed his arms, his brow furrowed.

David swallowed his bite of burnt potatoes with a loud gulp. "But war is abhorrent," he said, as if that should settle it.

"Don't you get it, David? These alien bastards killed Mother."

David flinched.

That cut him deep, Abraham smirked to himself.

David fell into a fit of blinking so intense his head twitched. He didn't move out of this for several moments. When he did, he did it with a groan and a renewed fixation on swirling his potatoes around with his spoon.

Probably pushed him a little too far.

16

Obadiah cleared his throat. "Don't get swept up in it, Abraham. It's not worth it."

Abraham pushed his chair in. He couldn't stand the way his father had become. He was nice, once. Happy. He had made Abraham happy, too. Sure, he had always been a bit more strict, a bit more expecting of certain standards to be upheld by his boys, but on Milune he had been a totally different person.

"*Father*," he used the word like a curse. "They killed Mother. Don't you want to hurt them? Kill them, like I do?"

Father scoffed as he packed his pipe. It was slender, plain ivory, as unremarkable as the man it belonged to. His bushy eyebrows drew together, nearly touching. "No, I don't. Everything seems real simple to you now, Abraham, but that's because you're twelve years old. When you get older, you'll see things more clear."

A riskar soldier, possibly General Rictor himself, appeared on the television. Thick carapace armor covered a tan and gray body. Chin mandibles clicked under three beady red eyes in the center of the face. Two large sacs floated over its shoulders, connected by thin tubes to the base of the neck. Abraham didn't know what those were, but he was repulsed by the alien's appearance. Just looking at the thing made Abraham sick. Knowing that it had killed his mother, killed millions of people, and destroyed a perfectly good planet...his blood boiled.

Abraham said, "More clear? You couldn't save Mom. They took her from us. Maybe if you had been in the Navy instead of designing buildings, you could have saved her."

Father glared at him with a ferocity only his pinched bushy eyebrows and gritted teeth could properly convey. Abraham was pissed. Obstinate. He had lost respect for his father on that day and harbored resentment for years, but that look whittled it all to ash and dust. Father's words were the wind that blew away any remaining dissention. "I understand you're upset, son. I am, too. Devastated. But we have to stick together. Your mother was the center of this family. She loved us all more than we deserved. I miss her just like you do. But what's done is done."

That's it? Mom's dead and that's all you can say?

There was no more discussion.

Father used the remote to cycle through several channels, but they were all similar in content. The television continued to blare shots of the war, of General Rictor firing what could have been a flamethrower into some trees, some shots of the human Navy vessels sailing through space. They looked like floating cities. There was no actual combat footage on most channels, but there were several mock-ups of riskar-looking targets being chewed up by laser blasts, catching fire and melting until they were unrecognizable, or piñata versions of them being beaten with sticks by kids at parties. "Kill the Sackbacks," they chanted. The piñata burst, spilling out mustard yellow slime, while the kids laughed and screamed good-naturedly about it.

Sackbacks? That's a good name for them.

A new clip played. Dajun, angry and wreathed in flame, smashed into the surface of Milune. Fire spread across the sky. Those bodies that weren't crushed or burned were lifted from the surface of the planet, floating through the air between. Obadiah switched the television off. "Whatever happened to cartoons?"

Abraham excused himself from dinner. He sequestered himself in the thin comfort of his twin bed in the room he shared with David. He pulled his blanket over his head and cried. It was cruel of the television to show his mother's last day so casually. He hated being reminded of it. Never wanted to forget it. Couldn't live with it. So many emotions and thoughts conflicting, constricting him, squeezing his chest and not relenting, and he didn't know how he could live through the next five seconds, let alone the rest of his life.

The Navy. Avenging his mother's death.

This was the only thing he wanted, the only thing that could bring some sense of purpose into his psyche. Abraham realized he only had to wait six more years until he could join. Enlist in the Navy, get trained to fly fighter ships. He would get into a massive dogfight and take on the entire riskar Royal Navy by himself. He'd outmaneuver them, outgun them, destroy them. After the battle, General Rictor would be so impressed with his new adversary he would offer a challenge, a duel, and Abraham would kill him. Rip his heart out and smash it on the ground, grind it into mush under his foot.

This is how twelve-year-old Abraham Zeeben comforted himself every night until he could fight back sleep no longer.

18

CHAPTER 3

Years go by. Seasons change and the cycle of life continues at its inexorable pace. This was Abraham's perspective, that every unit of time was meant to repeat itself in some fashion. Especially the units of time in which he lived, at least until his junior year of high school.

Every year was the same. The springs were gusty days consisting of hoeing and prepping the fields after school. The summers were transplanting the tobacco from the hot bed in the barn to the fields, irrigation checks and pest control until the harvest, which was a mad dash to finish before the soil tasted the first frost of winter. Obadiah would cart the tobacco into town by himself, leaving the boys to their own devices for the onset of winter. Abraham looked forward to the downtime of the winter season, even with the one-two punch of the holidays.

He had no escape from the reality of spending time with a family he didn't feel close to, and the constant reminder that his mother would never spend another holiday with them. The time off the farm was rare, which made it more precious to Abraham. Still, he was going to be eighteen at the end of next summer. He was so close to the Navy he could taste the stardust.

The brothers walked the two kilometers to a transit depot, where they caught a bus to Sun Lance spaceport. Sun Lance was smaller than Horizons Gateway where they'd landed all those years ago, but it was also one of the few runways where skiff races were authorized. David spouted facts about the skiffs the whole bus ride, while Abraham stared out the window, doing his best to ignore them.

Forty minutes later they stepped on the tarmac a short distance from the crowd of spectators. Abraham could see the skiffs, the racers, and the markings on the runway. A jolt of excitement ran through him. Today promised excitement, thrills, and things that didn't need digging out of the ground. He couldn't stop himself from grinning.

The mid-afternoon sun shone bright and elated over Sun Lance Spaceport. The light was a pure thing, a soft gold in the sky that transformed into a glittering silver as it descended upon the snow-covered surface of Veranda like a silk blanket. Abraham remembered seeing postcards like this in the shops on Milune. Lively green trees spattered with white powder. Unlike most planets, Milune never had seasons. Now, it was a hapless rock hurtling through space, a limp corpse forever falling in an endless black oblivion.

And so is my mother. He couldn't stop the thought from rising.

To distract himself, Abraham stopped to fix his brother's button-up shirt. David never paid attention to anything much beyond newsfeeds on his Portal or studying for his advanced classes in school. It was up to Abraham to fulfill the role of mother and ensure the boy didn't go out in public looking like a ragamuffin. Obadiah had given the boys permission to leave the homestead for a few hours. Abraham intended to take full advantage of it.

"Don't pinch me," David muttered, half distracted with fixing his hair.

Abraham said, "Remember what Dad always says – 'be a brother, not a bother.' I'm trying to help you. We're going to have fun, trust me. The last thing we want is people picking on us or saying we don't belong there. Because we do."

Abraham fixed the last button and wiped some snow powder off David's shoulders. He looked his brother in the eye, the one eye that wasn't covered by a swoop of dark hair. "If you won't let me cut your hair, you at least need to wear your clothes right."

David shrugged. "Is it going to be fun? Like, for real? I want to see the jets up close." His eyes lit up. "Do you think they'll let us take one apart? I wanna see how they work, inside and out!"

Abraham steered his brother toward the throng of people gathered around the airport site. The last thing he wanted was to waste a beautiful winter's day getting greasy taking apart a jet engine. He loved to see them race but didn't care one iota about their internal workings.

"David, we're here to support Miles. I'm sure he'll let you look at whatever you want, as long as you don't try to take anything apart. Make sure you wait to ask him questions until after the race."

David nodded, and kept nodding. He often did this when his brain was working on overdrive. His physical presence sort of short-circuited. It was part of the reason the Zeeben boys were picked on at school, but Abraham didn't mind defending his older brother over something he couldn't control. It was more the way David talked to people that got them both into trouble, and *that* was something Abraham couldn't stand.

Ever since The Collision, babying David had become the new norm.

As they approached, the crowd erupted in a series of catcalls and shouts and whistles. The cacophony surrounded them as they were immersed in a sea of people, more people than Abraham had seen in a long time. Lined up at the concession stands, a group of farmers in denim pants with worn circles in their back pockets – the shape of tobacco cans – and plaid button-ups shouted back and forth. Excitement lit up their eyes. One of them walked away with a large mug and a foam mustache from his first sip.

I wonder what beer tastes like.

A group of kids chased each other, weaving in and out of the crowd. A few boys chasing a little girl, pretending monsters were after her. She alternated between laughter and high-pitched shrieks when the boys got too close.

"Hey, Zeebens, how's it going?" Larry's greeting wafted out in a cloudy breath. He hugged them both, teeth chattering, his long blond hair parted over red cheeks and chapped lips. The years had seen him grow taller and thinner, his hair now down to his shoulders. He wasn't built for the cold. It looked as if a stiff breeze could carry him away. His normally soft face and hands were splotched with white skin flakes, a sign of wind burn.

Abraham felt bad for him. The Zeeben boys weathered the winters with skullcaps and long-sleeved shirts most of the time.

"Larry," Abraham said, "do you know where the pit's at this year? Miles said he'd let us back there. I'm sure you can come, too. Miles is pretty cool."

Larry heaved a sigh, looking relieved at the invitation. "Okay, yeah, sure. The pit's this way, boys."

Abraham dragged David through the crowd, following Larry on a circuitous route around the spaceport. The main hangar was large enough for four cargo-hauling spacecraft to sit side by side, and it didn't see much traffic on a regular basis. For this small-town event, they had closed it down to off-world arrivals. It was no great loss for the community; space-farers weren't pounding on the gates to land on a backwater like Veranda.

The smell of the pits hit them as they crossed the taped barrier.

The chill of the air diminished in a cloudy miasma of oil, grease, and jet fuel that wafted over Abraham. The vapors were so intense it felt like they clung to his clothes. It was an electric sort of smell that crawled into his sinuses and rested on his tongue. Abraham hated it, but he had to admit the industrial odor was preferable to the smell of shoveling shit in the tobacco fields.

Several single-man craft were parked at intervals along a strip of thick concrete. They were hybrids of motorcycles and aircraft. Fuselages and fairings were covered in elaborate paint schemes like flames or colorful splashes of graffiti, more than a few with patches that had flaked off or been eaten away by rust. It was easy to tell who had money and who was building from scrap parts. The entire scene was a marvel to someone with no mechanical aptitude, like Abraham. He couldn't imagine knowing enough about these machines to build them or even just keep them running.

He also knew he'd never care enough to learn.

Larry pointed out Miles's craft. "Look at that thing!"

"It's a monster!" David beamed.

As far as skiffs go, this one was a status symbol. Chrome pipes gleamed with a perfect polish, blue-marbled fairings painstakingly waxed and wiped until even the smallest speck of dirt wouldn't dare stick to it.

It's a thing of beauty, Abraham thought. *I'd kill to pilot one of those.*

The rider was tall and broad-shouldered. Close-shaved on the sides, his wavy blond hair was swooped back to the nape of his neck in a bastardization of a gentleman's cut. His face was smooth and pale, with piercing blue eyes radiating an infectious passion for racing. He looked at his machine like it was as dear to him as his own family.

Miles Lannam had graduated last year as both head of his class and president of the school racing team. He was, by all accounts, the coolest kid on Veranda. The fact that Abraham even knew him was something to be proud of. It was one shining facet in his otherwise pointless existence on the most boring planet in space.

Miles slammed his foot down on the kick-starter.

A crack tore the air. Abraham could feel it in his knees. He had to steady himself on David's shoulder to keep from falling over.

Miles slammed the kick-starter again, and the engine roared like a savage beast. Chrome pipes belched thick black smoke. The air became saturated with sweet gasoline fumes.

He climbed up on the skiff, which was almost as tall as he was, and plopped down into the seat. The tires barely squeaked as his weight settled. He fumbled with the helmet in his lap, sliding it on and turning to look at the gathering crowd. "Zeebens! Poplenko! Glad you guys could make it out. Make sure you're cheering for me, yeah? I want all of Veranda to know me by name after the first go, all right?"

The group of boys shouted and cheered. Miles pulled away, tires crackling across the concrete from the vehicle's prodigious weight. It trundled toward the track, leaving Miles's skiff pit and crew in plain view.

A large toolbox and blue paint lines sectioned off a pocket of concrete covered in grease stains like bruises. A hasty stencil in yellow declared "LANNAM PIT CREW ONLY".

Behind the line, Abraham saw the mechanic who had unlatched the massive chain, what they called the 'bike-lock'. He was short but thickly muscled, blue coveralls tight across his chest. His shoulders were hunched all the way up to his ears. Ears that were large and awkward on such a small, smooth-shaven head.

This wasn't a real mechanic at all. It was Digger Tacheck, one of the guys who picked on David at school. The one kid Abraham ended up trading punches with semi-regularly in the hallways. Just two months ago, Digger had left him with a bloody nose, a black eye, and two weeks of jeers and sneers from his classmates.

22

Digger tapped a large wrench on the bottom of his boots, laughing. His words came out like poisoned daggers. "What the hell you ladies doing here, huh? I could hear you over the engine rev, pissing your pants and crying over *dreamy* Miles Lannam."

Abraham bristled. "We're just here to watch the race."

Digger swung the wrench, spinning the closed end on a finger, slinging small droplets of sticky black grease over David's shirt.

David flinched, gritting his teeth as if holding something back. He fell into a twitching session.

Abraham wiped him off with a glove, which only smeared the thick clumps into wide black streaks. He slapped the useless glove onto the concrete. It hit with a wet smack.

He turned to hurl an insult at Digger, but his archenemy had already walked off. No doubt chuckling and congratulating himself on being Veranda's biggest asshole. Larry offered to buy a mechanic towel from the pit crew to try to help, but Abraham waved him off. He traded shirts with David instead, not caring if his own shirt had a few grease smears on it. Even though David was a year older than Abraham, they were pretty much the same size. He left the top two buttons undone, feeling a slight tug in the back when he flexed his shoulders, but it wasn't enough to make him uncomfortable.

Fireworks sparkled across the twilight sky like shooting stars. Hundreds of voices cheered in response. Loudspeakers boomed, informing everyone they needed to take their seats or find standing room in short order.

The light display was the signal for the opening ceremony. Abraham hustled his brother and their best friend up to where the pit bordered the apron next to the runway. They watched and covered their ears for the better part of two hours as engines whined, ramped up and lit off. Smoke and heat billowed in wavy lines, causing the skiffs to look distorted. Pit side was the closest non-racers could get to the track. Abraham took in the whole scene with a knot of adrenaline gnawing at his gut.

The drag strip was four kilometers long with white lines placed one klick from the ends. These lines marked the area where the race started and ended. If the tires were still touching the concrete after those lines, it was a disqualification. Skiffs had a short distance to build up as much ground speed as possible, then just before the start line their tires would lift off. At that exact moment they would light their jet engines for a short burst; just long enough to burn a hole in the sky over the runway. At speeds pushing 1000kph, it was an ear-splitting, heart-dropping rush to behold.

Abraham considered himself something of an adrenaline junkie. At least he thought he would be if given the opportunity. It was a fantasy of his to have a rider approach him with an offer to try a race on one of their skiffs. That was about the only way he'd get the chance to ride one. He'd never in a million years be able to afford to build his own.

It would be good flying practice to add to his resume. Something he could use to get the attention of the Navy. This was his greatest dream, he reminded himself – to become a Navy Starfighter pilot. He would destroy hundreds of evil riskar ships. Bomb enemy planets and take *their* mothers away. Assuming those disgusting bug-faced creatures even had family. Assuming they even felt emotions and had connections with each other like civilized people. He doubted they cared much beyond their own interests. As a militarized society, did they even have a home world that wasn't a staging area for war?

Thinking of the riskar began to cloud his mind. It would have stolen him from the excitement of the race had David not tapped him on the shoulder. His brother sported wide eyes and a smile that showed teeth when he pointed at the sky.

Several blue lights appeared above the horizon. Abraham felt his chest tighten up. The sensation was akin to when he had seen the riskar ships above Milune all those years ago. Dread, fear, helplessness. The things he hated feeling more than anything. The things that instinctually morphed into pure, unadulterated anger. Rage.

His knuckles went white, and he ground his teeth.

The lights became larger. In the blink of an eye, they streaked across the sky. Roaring engines cut soundwaves into the emotional tension Abraham felt in his chest. The sound vibrated around him. Through him. He had his hands on his ears, but it was too late. The damage to his hearing had been done. He looked at David and Larry, frantic.

People fist-pumped. Hundreds of arms waved in the air. Some people jumped up and down. Everyone's mouth was open, distorted noises bellowing from their throats.

What the hell was that, and why is everyone cheering?

The announcer explained that those lines of light roaring through the sky were four Navy Starfighters, a combat sortie diverted to perform a simple flyover as a show of solidarity from the inner rim to the outer rim planets. The message was clear: every human life was considered valuable.

They want us to know we aren't forgotten. They're fighting for us, too.

He took his hands off his ears, saw Larry do the same. Soon the sounds around him returned to tones he could recognize. The damage to his hearing wasn't permanent after all. He relaxed his shoulders.

24

Larry shouted, "That was so damn cool, bro!"

David was fixated on the announcer's mini-history lesson, his head tilted to the side like a curious dog.

The boys watched the races with renewed zeal after sundown, cheering and shouting when the engines roared over the runways, red or blue flames ripping across the star-studded sky. Abraham hadn't seen David laugh this much in a long time. He felt it in his chest, warm and fuzzy. He had done a good thing setting this up. He and Larry fist-bumped each time the blue flames crossed the finish line first, showing home team pride. David ritually clapped his hands once or twice, but never more. The evening passed in the blink of an eye. The pulse-pounding races came to an end with another display of fireworks, this one the rapid-fire of a grand finale.

Miles earned first place. He had the best skiff money could buy, and he had been racing since he was eleven. He was the biggest kid celebrity on Veranda, but he had earned the title, something most kids with privilege and money didn't have to. It was a great shock to the entire planet that when Miles got up on the podium to give his victory speech, he instead announced his retirement.

He gave the crowd a winning smile and a wink, finishing with a salute. "My racing career is over now, Veranda. I'm taking to the skies in a whole new way, shipping out to flight school with the Navy in a week. I'm proud to announce I have received a commission as Veranda's newest Navy Starfighter pilot!"

The crowd erupted with voracious applause and cheers.

"Lucky bastard," Larry said, "I want to be in the Navy, too."

Abraham said, "Yeah, me too. I want to fly ships and kill those dirty Sackbacks. They deserve the worst we can give 'em."

David was reading something on his Portal, a tablet he got for Christmas a few years before. Abraham tapped him on the shoulder. "What're you doing on that thing now, David? We're outside. You should put that thing away."

David looked pale as a ghost. "Abraham, I just got an e-mail from school. The holiday dance is in two weeks."

Larry chuckled. "Who're you going with, David? Got your eye on any special lady?"

David shrugged. "I might. If I could find any special ones."

Abraham tousled David's hair, causing a few seconds of nervous twitching. It was more a sign of affection than to piss his brother off. A way of being a brother rather than a mother. David was annoyed by it, but it wasn't enough to set him off.

"We'll help you out. For now, though, it's dark and Father's going to be wanting us home. Let's get out of here. Thanks for coming out with us, Larry. We'll see you at school."

Larry bumped fists with the Zeeben boys and they parted ways, leaving Abraham feeling he had just lived through the first good day since The Collision.

CHAPTER 4

The school was one of the nicer buildings in the slice of Veranda called Stony Ridge. In a town where wood was revered and aluminum siding the undisputed norm, Stony High's marble pillars and floor-to-ceiling windows stood out as a sort of diamond in the rough. Fame and fortune weren't the way for most citizens, but this rural community's devotion to education was something to be admired. Teachers received good paychecks, and a handful of students every year graduated with full-ride scholarships to prestigious universities off world.

Abraham knew it was the desperation to leave Veranda that made those scholarships so competitive. Who would want to go to a third-rate institution on a backwater planet when you could travel across the stars and party in a completely new and exciting place? A place that didn't smell like fertilizer-ridden fields and the sweat that was worked into them. The only decent places to visit were the strawberry fields a few towns over, or Leona Lake to the south. Veranda was a place to seek out simplicity or retirement, the exact opposite of the college experience.

Inside, the school auditorium had been repurposed for the dance. The basketball court was thoroughly scrubbed of both sweat and sneaker stains. A lingering odor of rubbing alcohol or some other cleaning agent clung stubbornly to the makeshift dance floor. Weights, balls, and bats were replaced by tall speakers. Fold-out tables around the perimeter were covered in rows of refreshments in white disposable cups. Several streamers of Stony High red and green were draped over the white walls like floating brushstrokes.

The lights were a little too dim, the music a little too loud.

David and Larry were already pointing out to each other which girls they thought looked particularly attractive. Abraham was checking the collar of his button-up, and he quickly flattened one side that kept popping up. He ran a hand over his spiked hair, smoothed out the front of his shirt and, with a deep breath, finally entered the dance.

Paranoia immediately set in like a drop of acid hitting the pit of his stomach. His eyes couldn't stop flitting to and fro, capturing a dozen images in a single moment.

Teachers stood against the wall, primly dressed with flat expressions. Several girls in a cluster whispered to each other and laughed. A few jocks were bumping and grinding with cheerleaders. Some of the freshmen and sophomores sampled the punch and grape juice from the beverage tables. One kid spilled red juice down the front of his shirt, causing a fracas from his jeering buddies.

In all this chaos, Abraham couldn't shake the building pressure inside him, this nagging, tugging feeling that every single person in the room was looking at him. Judging him. Weighing his every movement, dissecting his facial expression. Even counting every breath he took.

It was unnerving, made more so because he knew it was irrational. He wasn't of any particular interest to anyone here, but he couldn't reconcile that fact with these emotions. He swam outside the common social circle, and he knew it.

Along the sides of the auditorium were lines of kids. The girls seemed to be congregating on the left side where the locker rooms normally were, with the boys on the right at the entrance to the cafeteria. A decent number of kids were dancing and jiving on the floor, but the majority hovered on the borders. Larry steered Abraham and David toward the boys' side of the room.

"So, this is it? We stand here all night?" David asked.

Larry shook his head and flashed a toothy smile. "No, we're going to find some *ladies*," he said the word like it was the name of a dessert he really liked, "to dance with. What did you think, we came here for the punch or something?"

David reached into his jeans pocket and pulled out his Portal. "I'm here because Abraham told me I had to come."

Larry laughed, his long hair bouncing ridiculously.

"Come on, bro, don't give me that! You like girls, right? This is your first real opportunity to get up close and personal with one. If they like you, they might even let you touch 'em, ya know?"

Abraham pulled his eyes away from scanning the crowd to glare at Larry. "You're trying to corrupt my brother, Larry."

"No, I'm trying to *instruct* your brother. You Zeeben boys would be a lot more relaxed if you didn't have to work so hard all the time. But knowing your dad, that's not an option. So, what's the next best thing? A little attention from a female, yeah? Besides, I meant touching like dancing, anyway. If you're gonna slow dance, they let you put your hands on their hips." He raised his eyebrows twice.

Abraham was about to lay into Larry about setting a good example when he saw her.

She was tall and blonde and wore a lavender dress with black sequins at the hem, emphasizing her long, pale legs. Her shoulders were a bit too broad, her long legs carried a bit too much weight, but her face was soft and her smile radiant. She sat close to Abraham in History class. He spent more time studying her than the lectures on Earth civilization prior to the space age. It was an ancient, boring place that all humans came from, but had become a ghost planet long ago.

Larry asked, "Lucinda? You making your move on Lucinda tonight, Abraham?"

He shrugged, not taking his eyes off her. "Maybe."

"You should, bro. I was going to dance with Mylee Draper. They're friends. Look," his voice cracked, "they're taking notice."

Larry slapped Abraham's back, took a deep breath to puff his chest out, and started running his hands through his hair.

Lucinda whispered to Mylee, a shorter, mouse-faced, dark haired girl who was apparently the object of Larry's affection. At least for today. They looked at the boys and snickered, covering their mouths and whispering back and forth.

Abraham didn't know what else to do, so he just smiled.

"C'mon, bro, let's go." Larry slapped him on the back again and started his approach.

Abraham steeled himself with a breath and a tug on his button-up. He was trying to think of how to introduce himself when he realized David was no longer with them. He scanned the room, trying to ignore the sound of his own panic-laced breathing.

David wasn't by the beverage table. He wasn't by the speakers or milling about on the dance floor. He had just up and left, or Digger and his bully squad were up to no good.

Abraham tore through the crowd, moving like a madman. He walked right past Lucinda, who stared at him with something between confusion and disappointment – he hoped it was the latter – and tripped.

His shoes squeaked as he lost his balance and collapsed. His knees burned as they dragged across the floor.

The dancers parted to give him some room, but for the most part the dance continued without more than a few people staring at him. It wasn't enough to stop the heat from rising in his cheeks. Abraham looked up at the crowd wondering, *What the hell?*

Digger was laughing, his arms around the waist of a cheerleader. "Watch your step, Abe. We're trying to dance here!"

His harsh face beamed with hilarity.

Abraham wanted nothing more than to wipe that smirk off on the gym floor, but he had to find his brother. Some things were more important than anything else, and David's well-being was unfortunately more pressing than some petty revenge. He rubbed his knees and stood up.

Abraham flung the door open to the boys' locker room, choking on the humid sweat trapped within. The lights were much brighter in here. The door shut, muting the bass beats of the dance. He had to squint until he saw a dark figure slumped against the maroon-colored aluminum lockers in the back of the room. "David? That you?"

"Yep."

Abraham shuffled over to his brother. His eyes were starting to adjust, but he still had to pinch them nearly shut.

"What the hell's going on? I got nervous when I couldn't find you!"

David shrugged. "I hate this stuff."

Abraham put a hand on his brother's shoulder.

"I know you do. But this is kids' stuff. It's what we're supposed to be doing. Having fun, dancing with girls, making friends. You're graduating this year, David. Even Father has to be proud of that."

David moved the hair out of his one eye. "I know, but that doesn't change the way I feel, Abraham. Mom's gone. She's…just dead. Her body is floating out in space. Forever. And –"

Abraham squeezed David's shoulder. "Stop that. I know Mom's gone. I think about her every day. I know you do, too. But she would want us to be here, to live our lives. That's what she was raising us to do. I know she would have been proud to see you dressed like such a gentleman." Abraham paused for a moment, staring at David's hair. "She would probably have cut that mop off your head by now, but she'd be proud of you."

David slapped Abraham's hand away. "Don't joke like that," he said with a soft voice. He slid his back up the lockers until he was standing. His nervous, thick body twitched rhythmically, fighting total breakdown.

Abraham resisted the impulse to ruffle David's hair. Even a small gesture like that could set him off at this point. Instead, he opted for encouraging words. "Look, David, you're my brother. We both know what we went through. What we survived on Milune. We can't let that stop us. We can't keep living our lives like it just happened yesterday. It's been eight years, bro. It's time to move on."

David laughed. "You haven't moved on. You want to join the Navy. You want to leave me alone and you want to kill people because you can't stop thinking about what they did."

Abraham clenched his teeth. "Sackbacks aren't people."

David spluttered. "Just because their lungs dangle outside their body doesn't mean they aren't people. You calling them Sackbacks is just bigoted. Intelligent life is intelligent life. Alien or not, they're people. And some of them deserve to die for Milune, for…killing Mom. But not all of them. There shouldn't be a genocide."

Abraham shoved David against the locker. It creaked.

He wasn't going to stand for this, not even from his weak older brother, who acted more like his little brother anyway. Forget setting him off, David needed to get this straight.

"There *will* be a genocide, David. If I have any say in it, I'll be the one pulling the trigger and dropping the bombs. The Sac – *riskar* – are monsters and they deserve to be shot and blown up. Every last one of them. Fuck those bastards. Fuck. Them."

David sighed. "I miss Mother. I wish we could go back to that day, just the beginning of it. I just want to see her one more time. Give her a hug. Tell her I love her…and know that she hears me. I hate feeling like I'm talking to myself in an empty room, hoping my words somehow find her…thousands of light years away in a forgotten corner of space."

Tears flowed.

David's shoulders shuddered. Sobs wracked his body until he collapsed against the lockers in a grief-stricken heap.

Abraham locked his knees. His gut developed a chill. He bit his lip, taking a full minute to process his brother's words. They were deep, dark things, those words. They were sharper than they should have been because they were true and when he really thought about it…he felt the same way.

David feels alone. He doesn't know who he is without Mom. I feel it, too. We were too young to lose her. But we did. Nothing we can do will change that, even though we'll spend the rest of our lives trying. Trying to remember, to hold on, to love.

Abraham felt his eyes sting. These thoughts were private, personal things that came from the deep dark of his being, the very core of who he was. He would never share these things with anyone. Not even his brother. David was too close to him. He knew too much about him and the way they both felt was too painful.

Abraham grunted. He punched one of the lockers, denting it.

He didn't know what to do with himself.

He hated the riskar, wanted them all dead. To suffer the way he was suffering. He wanted to comfort his brother. Help him feel safe and know he wasn't alone. He wanted his father to be here for moments like this. They had plenty of paternal guidance in the fields after school. Where was some of that now, when he and David needed help navigating the emotional disaster of losing their mother?

He's at home staring at a book he never opens. The thought skirted his mind like a buzzing fly.

That feeling came back. The one he had when he watched the Navy invading riskar space on TV. The urge to leave Veranda. The realization that unless he joined the military, he'd be trapped here forever. At the age of twelve he had come to realize fighting in a war was the easiest answer to all of his problems. Now he was seventeen, just one year of high school away from realizing that dream.

31

Abraham slammed his fist into the locker again. Pain bit into his knuckles. He went numb up to his wrist. His split knuckles left two half-circles of blood in the dent.

Grabbing David by the underarm, he stormed out of the foul-smelling locker room.

"Are we going home?" David asked numbly.

"Yes," Abraham said through gritted teeth, "we are. This dance is over for us. We never should have come. You were right, David. We don't belong here."

CHAPTER 5

Like a surprise avalanche hits a quiet mountain, the holidays were upon them. There were no real mountains in Stony Ridge, but the snow blanket had been pulled tightly over the surrounding farmlands and valleys. The Zeeben fields were covered an average of five inches. The boys had to team up one afternoon to plow the half-acre walkway between the house and the street.

Abraham did his best to pay attention in most of his classes, but there were a few – especially Pre-Calculus and Earth Literature – in which he struggled to stay awake. These were also the classes he shared with Lucinda Blaylock, but he couldn't bear to look at her after the way the dance had turned out. The two weeks after the dance to mark the holiday break passed with his embarrassment warring against his desire to approach her.

Ultimately, embarrassment won out.

David seemed to be carrying on as if nothing had happened, still his absent-minded, halfway jovial self. Abraham liked that about his brother. Maybe even wished he could deal with his own life in a similar way. The darkness of their childhood would forever shadow them, but David had a way of stepping out from under the dark cloud on occasion. Then again, maybe his mop of hair, finally down past his shoulders, functioned as an umbrella of sorts.

The quiet of the homestead was hypnotic at times. Abraham was enjoying the peaceful stillness until a knock at the door tore him from his reverie.

He got up from his father's creaky rocking chair and opened the door. Sunlight spilled in weak and thin, unable to compete with the winter chill rolling in on icy gusts. The loamy smell of empty farmland was like a fork in the sinuses.

Larry and his grandparents greeted him dressed in puffy jackets, black jeans, and beaming smiles. They had arms full of food platters, heat rising from them in clouds of mist that smelled like turkey, mashed potatoes and gravy, and some kind of casserole.

"Ready to eat, Abraham?" Johnford Poplenko, Larry's grandfather, smiled wider, stretching his thick salt and pepper mustache. He had a full head of hair, but it was withered and gray, like a tumbleweed just waiting on a stiff breeze to uproot it and help it take flight.

Abraham took the casserole tray from Amelia, Larry's grandmother. Her wrinkled nose was red at the creases on either side. She sniffled with dignified effort, followed by a high-pitched *brrr* from her thin lips.

"Yes sir, I surely am," Abraham said to Johnford. "You know Father can cook, but he's the 'eat to live' type. It's been a while since we've had something like this. Thank you!"

David piped up from the couch, "Yeah. Since last holiday."

Everyone laughed politely. David didn't take his eyes from his Portal.

Abraham's stomach grumbled as he walked the tray into the kitchen and placed it on the counter. He removed the tinfoil with excitement. The green beans looked delicious, the onion flakes crisped to a golden brown across the top...it smelled heavenly. Abraham double-checked the fridge still had water bottles while the Poplenkos were sliding their coats over the back of their seats.

"Where's Obadiah?" Amelia asked.

"Out back," David muttered.

Abraham walked into the living room and gave his brother a gentle slap on the back of the head. "Put that thing away, David, it's holiday dinner. Don't be rude."

Larry chuckled. "Don't start like this, you guys. We're supposed to eat, drink, and be merry. How can we do that if you're slapping and bickering? Life's too short to be bitter."

Abraham nodded. Larry always knew how to balance out the relationship between David and himself. It was tough business having an older brother, but even worse when he was like David. Special rules, special treatment, and never really held accountable for anything. It was hard for Abraham to accept, but then he also felt a certain pull to protect him.

Johnford clapped his hands and rubbed them together.

"I'll grab Obadiah and we can get started. Wouldn't want the food to get cold now, would we?"

He chuckled and made his exit.

After a few minutes of awkward conversation between the boys and Larry's grandmother, Obadiah and Johnford came in to carve the meat and set the table. Obadiah gave a brief speech before everyone dug into their food, thanking the Poplenkos for being so helpful to the Zeebens over the years, and for being great, dependable friends.

Johnford took his seat and said, "Obadiah, we owe you everything. You're the best example of what it means to be human. You saved our Larry. I just...we can't thank you enough."

Abraham flinched at the allusion to The Collision. He gripped the edge of the table until his knuckles were white and his wrist ached. *Way to kill the mood, Grandpa*, he thought.

"Truly," Amelia said, "you've given us the greatest gift we could ever receive."

David sat with his hands flat on the table, staring at his fingers. Father took a sip of water with a shaky hand and offered a gracious smile.

Abraham noticed the strange reaction but decided it must be his old man shaking off the cold he'd brought in. His attention was soon divided between small bites of turkey, large bites of heavily salted mashed potatoes and gravy, and flaky, buttery bites of biscuits. It was far and away the best meal of the year, every year. Perhaps the crown jewel of the season Abraham liked the best.

Even David seemed to be enjoying himself. He broke eye contact with his own hands to butter a biscuit with a half-inch thick smear of apple butter. His hair had to be out of his face for him to eat, which made him seem more expressive than usual.

Conversation came in fits, focusing on how great and grateful both families were for each other, until David brought up school. Larry immediately cut him off with his typical braggadocio about the three girlfriends he was currently juggling. Abraham breathed a sigh of relief as the pall of loss seemed to lift from the table the moment Larry started speaking. Amelia made sharp objection to his philandering, but Larry insisted it was innocent. "I'm not taking anything from these girls they aren't perfectly willing to give me, Gramma."

Abraham interjected, "Larry, if you're going to be talking about this kind of stuff, shouldn't it be around the bonfire out back?"

David's eyes lit up. He swallowed a chunk of biscuit and said, "Bonfire! Marshmallows! C'mon Larry, I'll listen to whatever bimbo stories you have if it's outside."

Everyone shared a laugh at Larry's expense. He took it good-naturedly.

Abraham stood to leave the table when Obadiah grabbed his arm. Something thudded under the table.

Obadiah's black book, the one with the two arrows on it, rested facedown under the table. Obadiah picked it up and placed it back on his lap. "Marshmallows are in the cupboard."

Abraham stared at his father, not understanding. He nodded anyway, trying to keep the confusion from his face. The old man nodded and let go of his arm.

Abraham went to retrieve the marshmallows from the cupboard. As he did so, he wondered for a moment why Obadiah was eating dinner with his book in his lap. He was increasingly attached to it, to the point where if he was in the house, he had a hand on that book.

Abraham grabbed the marshmallows from the cabinet. When he did, he realized what the arm-grab had been about.

In the back of the cabinet was a foil-wrapped block with a brown and white wrapper. The smells of holiday dinner had permeated the home, but the sweet aroma of this item had filled the cabinet. It was a pleasant tingling in Abraham's nose, and it started a small shiver down his back. He hurriedly grabbed the block and rushed back to the table to show David and Larry, who responded as one. "Chocolate!"

Obadiah chuckled. "Came all the way from Sila. The Poplenkos were good enough to make us this fine meal, and I'm not much of a cook, as my boys are more than happy to confess for me. I figured this was a small way I could say thanks to everyone for being here."

Abraham and David crushed their father in a hug. Chocolate was only available off world, and the price to import it was exorbitant. This block, notched with portions for ten people, had probably cost Obadiah a month's earnings from tobacco exports.

Abraham separated the chocolate into portions. He got a platter together with the marshmallows and some crackers. In moments, everyone rushed outside to the fire pit.

It was a cluster of wooden chairs encircling a half-sagging tepee of wood, freshly chopped and laid out by the boys that morning. Obadiah joined them and lit the pit. It blazed tall and bright, lighting up the space with a comfortable warmth that was an oasis in the otherwise bleak weather. Both families gathered around, conversation buzzing.

The marshmallows were roasted, the chocolate melted, the s'mores combined and devoured. Even Obadiah, king of bland and simple living, enjoyed one. It was a marvelous time they all enjoyed together, a time of full bellies and warmth from the fire in an otherwise cold and tough world.

Larry pulled out his guitar, fingers slapping against the wood rhythmically. He spent a few moments tuning it with discordant plucks, then launched into song.

Abraham basked in the heat and the music. For the first time this year, he finally felt some sense of peace. David hadn't been too far off the mark with his comment about the food, but the meal was only a part of it. It was the combination of everything; food, music, uplifted spirits…these things made the winter and the holiday season his favorite.

Notes danced by the fire, floated upward from Larry's fingers and his voice, swirled around the air, and settled onto Abraham's psyche. The lyrics of the song were unimportant, but Abraham couldn't help but let their simplicity carry him inside his mind, taking him to an island where it was warm and sunny, a place where there was no future and no past, just an eternal present of contentment. A marshmallow smacked him in the cheek.

He jerked his eyes open to see another one slam into his chest. On the other side of the fire, David was snickering.

That little bastard, he thought, reaching for his own set of fresh marshmallows. Abraham cocked his arm back and let one fly. It twisted through the air for a moment before impacting squarely on David's forehead.

Plop.

David flinched, a second too late, and burst into laughter.

Abraham congratulated himself on a clean hit and reached for more marshmallows. David grabbed a handful. They chased each other around the bonfire. The flames had dwindled to about the size of a campfire, hardly putting off the heat they once had. Larry strummed and sang, the rhythm slowing down, his fingers growing pink and stiff in the cold.

Abraham took a pelt to the side of the head. Ducked another. The marshmallow pattered into the snow behind him. He paused to catch his breath when an idea occurred to him. The marshmallows were soft, but as funny as a direct hit was, they were weak. He scooped up a fistful of snow and packed it into a tight ball. He and David squared off on opposite sides of the fire, two brothers at the height of merriment on a cold winter's night. It was an old-fashioned standoff.

Abraham launched his snowball missile with a crack of his elbow.

David juked left, as predicted. The snowball slammed into his neck with a loud smack and a puff of powder.

Got him! Abraham congratulated himself.

David lost his balance. He tripped over his own feet, arms flung wide

–

– right into the fire.

Abraham felt his body stifle. He became a statue, frozen with fear.

Flames wrapped around David's hands and forearms, coiled around his biceps, and chewed at his shoulders. Skin distorted. White blisters popped up where the fire flashed. The cloth of his long-sleeved shirt wilted and rippled. He threw his head back and screamed.

The sound hit Abraham like a hammer to his kneecaps. He buckled.

Before he knew what was happening, he had his hands at the side of his head, and *he* was screaming. He couldn't look at his brother burning alive, but he couldn't look away. He couldn't breathe but he cried, and somehow his hands on his head were the only thing keeping himself from exploding, and the fire was glowing brighter, redder, deep, deep red, and

–

David rolled out of the fire, sizzling as he spun over the powdery snow. He rolled five or six times. Each time progressively more snow clung to his body. When he came to a stop, he looked like a snowman from the neck down.

A small stream of white smoke, about the size you'd expect from a cigarette, wafted up from the fire pit. The flames had been extinguished. The pile of wood in the center appeared as if it hadn't yet been burned and stood in its half-disturbed tepee.

Abraham blinked, unable to comprehend.

Larry and his grandparents rushed to David's side, their chairs kicked over into the snow. David rolled onto his back, sobbing. Abraham took a step toward his brother, his legs finally feeling like they were unlocked from the adrenaline dump.

Father's hand clapped onto his shoulder. He stopped in his tracks.

The old man looked at him, his face…sad.

Abraham wilted. He knew he was to blame for this. He just hoped David was all right.

"He's okay!" Johnford shouted from the other side of the firepit.

Larry said, "What the hell? He didn't even get burned! Look at this shit, guys!"

"Language, young man!" Gramma chastised him.

Abraham rushed to David's side. "Hey bro, you okay?"

David nodded. "Yeah, I'm fine. I can't believe I didn't get burned. I thought I was going to die!"

David held his forearms out. His shirt was scorched up to the biceps. Burnt threads dangled from what was left of it. Abraham ran his fingers over David's winter-pale skin, amazed. The fire had consumed his long-sleeved shirt, but…not his flesh?

Did I see what I thought I saw?

"Didn't you scream, though?" Abraham asked.

"Let me up." David shoved him back. "Of course I screamed. I fell in the fire and thought I was gonna die!"

Abraham backed up, gave his brother some air. Larry shot Abraham a glance with a raised eyebrow, like, *what are you doing?*

"I thought you were…ugh, I thought I killed you, David."

David laughed. "What? You didn't do anything. I tripped." He brushed some snow off. Larry helped him pat the powder clean. Everyone shared a good laugh at the de-escalation.

Abraham played along with the laughter, but he had a strange feeling gnawing at his gut.

The screen door slammed shut on the porch. Father had gone back inside. That was the signal to everyone that the holiday evening had come to an early end.

CHAPTER 6

Abraham was lying on his desk, deep in the throes of a dream he wished he wasn't having. It was the intense kind of falling that felt like the air around you was rushing up at blinding speed but you were immobile, suspended by some unknown force, unable to catch yourself, the ground rushing up too fast to stop –

He twitched, hard. The desk legs screeched against the floor.

He raised his head, momentarily confused.

The classroom was a bit small, barely wide enough for fifteen bored students to each have their own desk, the walls covered in motivational posters that bordered on melodramatic. A dozen or more books overturned on the teacher's desk, each with several pages dog-eared, told him this was second period. English Literature.

All eyes in the classroom turned to stare at him. Laughter followed.

Heat stung his cheeks. The only person not laughing was the teacher. Abraham scowled to cover up his embarrassment. *Just two more months. I'll graduate and get the hell out of here.*

Mr. Croix was a tall, burly man with slate black hair and a pressed, professional appearance that somehow gave his opinion more weight than the average teacher. He crossed his arms over his chest, stopping his lecture. "Abraham, are you all right?"

Abraham nodded, trying to shrink into as small a space as he could within the confines of his own body. He wanted to hide inside his clothes. To become a ghost and walk right through the walls of the school and never see these people again. He felt most keenly the eyes of Parvati and Lucinda. They were some of the more popular girls in the school, so their share of the laughter cut deeper.

Mr. Croix turned back to the chalk board and in serene swipes wrote the word *PHANTASMAGORIA*. "Anybody know what this word means? Any guesses?"

Abraham shook his head. Relief flooded him when he saw no one else had raised their hand, either.

"Dream-like images or thoughts. The world of literature is one best crafted in your own personal field of experience. We experience something, we take it in with all five senses. When we've chewed on it awhile, really digested it, *then* we are free to express our interpretation of that experience. The only qualifying thing here, class, is that you as the observer must never fail to be honest. Abraham, stand up."

Abraham complied, rubbing a warm spot on his forehead. He could feel the depression of a sleep line on his skin. He sighed.

Mr. Croix stepped up to him, holding out the chalk. "There are two lessons to be learned here, kids. This is normally the part where a teacher would be upset with the student. I'm supposed to ask you, Abraham, if you'd like to teach the class. You feel so confident in the material you find it a better use of your time to sleep than to pay attention. But I'm not going to do that. Instead, I'm going to offer you a second chance. Redemption, if you will. Lesson one, class – humans are a race built on second chances."

A bit of relief flooded his nerves. "Okay, what do I have to do?"

The teacher gave a small, heartfelt laugh.

"Tell us what you were dreaming about, Abraham. And remember, as a literary observer, your account is all we have to go by. Honesty is absolutely sacred."

Abraham felt the vindication immediately. *At least it wasn't a dream about Lucinda or something weird like that…*

"Uh…well, Sir –"

"Oh, don't tell me," he gestured with an open hand, "tell the class."

Abraham glanced over at the other students. They were all staring at him. Expectant. Lucinda turned her head slightly. Was she embarrassed for him? He felt the power of their gaze like a barrier between his brain and his tongue. He needed to say something. Anything. He started rambling with the first words that came to mind.

"It's kind of stupid, but I was falling. Like everything was black, maybe a few white lines like static, and I was falling. Well, the air was rushing upward around me, and I was kind of laying down…like on air, but it felt like I couldn't move and the only way I can describe it is…falling."

Mr. Croix clapped his hands once, smile growing wide. He plopped into his chair and leaned back, steepling his fingers. "And do we accept this explanation, class? Is Abraham telling the truth?"

Murmurs of approval floated around the room.

"Good. So, you are telling us about this raw, undigested experience you had in your dream. Now, digest it. Draw meaning from it. Search deep within yourself and try to understand what your subconscious mind was thinking about while you were sleeping. Go ahead, extrapolate."

Abraham knew where this was going. He didn't want to have to reiterate the source of his nightmares, the dark cloud of his past that he carried everywhere he went. Mr. Croix didn't know any of this. None of the students did. Abraham preferred it that way. He hadn't told a single soul about the things that haunted him at night. The things he couldn't forget even when he tried his hardest. But he was about to unearth everything, right here and now.

"I…when I was younger, I…my mother…"

40

A two-tone beep from the PA system chimed. A velvety female voice interjected, "Mr. Croix?"

He replied, "Yes?"

"We need all students in the auditorium in ten minutes. Mandatory assembly."

"We'll be right there." He stood, brushed the lapels of his suit and smoothed his tie. "Looks like we'll have to hear this interpretation later. Cliff notes version, class; falling dreams are indicative most commonly of an individual feeling out of control in their life. Most of you are seventeen or eighteen years old, and I'm here to tell you that this is a normal feeling. You won't be fully in control of your lives until you're twenty-one, and even then, you won't fully grasp the weight of that responsibility until you're around twenty-five. Your job as kids right now is to learn. Observe the world around you and the people in it. Keen observers will hear the universe whispering to them."

Abraham couldn't help but ask, "What does the universe whisper, Mr. Croix?"

The charismatic man smiled and patted Abraham on the back. "That's for you to hear and interpret, Abraham. Everyone's journey is different. I don't take it personal that you were sleeping in my class. I *will* take it personal if you sleep your way through life. Don't wake up as an old man, working a job you hate, wondering what the hell happened to your life."

Mr. Croix's face tightened for a micro-second, like a bitter taste had entered his mouth. He returned to a wide smile. "That goes for everyone in this classroom. Now let's file out to the auditorium."

Abraham hustled out into the hallway. He weaved in and out of clusters of kids, sliding against green and red lockers as he looked for David and Larry. He caught up with them just as they were exiting the biology lab. "Hey, you guys know what's going on? And what the hell is that smell?"

Larry tucked his books under his arm as they walked. "Nah, man. I heard it was bad news, but no one knows what it's about."

David scowled. "This is interrupting our lab time. I was in the middle of removing the liver from my cat!"

He held up his hands, wrapped in thin white gloves. Bits of pale white skin, rubbery ligaments and a few black hairs clung to his fingers. The thick odor of formaldehyde and death radiated from them. Abraham shook his head. "David, take those things off."

David slapped Abraham on the shoulder – with the soiled glove – and laughed. "I thought you didn't mind getting dirty?"

Abraham exhaled slowly, stopping the tension in his neck from spreading through the rest of his body. Defending David when he was

41

getting bullied was fine; he was his brother, it came with the territory. Putting up with David's peculiarities was fine because it had always been that way. Allowing David to get under his skin was something he just couldn't do.

"Not cool, bro," he said. "Not cool."

David ripped the gloves off and dropped them to the floor, where they squelched under Larry's shoe, who lifted his foot, saw the gloves, and cast a glare at him. David shrugged it off.

Larry kicked a locker, and the gloves slipped from his shoe to the green metal. A thin trickle of clear liquid dripped to the floor.

They took their seats in the auditorium.

The roar of group conversation buzzed around them for several minutes. The open air of the high ceiling made the room feel like an underground cave, especially when the lights began to dim. Whispers rose in the dark. Questions and guesses shared between friends. Everyone wanting to know what was going on. Why they were pulled out of class. A million questions they had no way of answering.

Mr. Croix took to the stage, visibly crestfallen.

"What the hell is he doing up there? Where's the principal?" Larry whispered.

David shrugged. "Maybe she's busy."

Feedback tore the room as Mr. Croix adjusted the microphone, making it too short, too tall, finally getting it to where he wanted it. He tapped it. Cleared his throat. Licked his lips. His head turned as he looked out at the crowd of students.

"All right, thank you all for gathering here so quickly. I have some news to disseminate. Afterward, we will be releasing everyone for the rest of the day."

The auditorium erupted with cheers. One boy pulled his jacket off and swung it around over his head, hooting like an animal. Applause broke out like a surprise rainfall.

"What? That's bullshit!" David growled.

Abraham elbowed him. "Shut up! We don't even know what the news is."

Mr. Croix cleared his throat. His body language stopped like he was frozen in place. He leaned closer to the mic, and when he spoke, his voice boomed.

"We've just gotten word that Mrs. Lannam's son, Myles, has been killed in action on the front lines of the Riskar War."

Everyone stopped.

For a long, uncomfortable moment, the room was like a photograph. Expressions of shock and fear were frozen on every student's face.

42

Abraham's throat went dry. He realized his mouth was hanging open. He looked at David and Larry, saw his own shock reflected on their faces.

Myles was a smart kid. He was the best pilot Veranda had ever seen. The Riskar War had come to overshadow everything. Surprise headlines, both victories and losses, had always been a part of their lives, but this...this was the last thing anyone could have predicted. Abraham felt a weight descend upon the room, as if the loss of such a pillar of the community had collapsed it completely. He knew everyone was thinking the exact same thing he was: *If Myles didn't make it, what chance do we have of winning the war?*

Mr. Croix cleared his throat.

"Now, I'm sure you're all thinking the worst right now, but listen here." His voice softened. He rolled his head on his neck and started flexing his hands to soften his words. "Myles was a hero. Unfortunately, we are in a time of war, and war is unpredictable. Myles is a hero because he stepped up to fight, to keep us all safe. The best we can do to honor our hometown hero is to keep his memory alive. Remember the armor tag player, the skiff racer, the boisterous young man. Everyone, hold young Myles in your memories. In the darkness of this loss, they will be a light that comforts you."

Larry leaned back in his seat, shaking his head. "That poor bastard."

It had happened so fast. Myles joined just before the holidays, and now it was the height of spring. Did pilot training only take a few months, or was Myles just that good?

They must've gotten him on his first combat mission. Poor bastard, indeed.

Mr. Croix carried on with a speech honoring Myles's life on Veranda, but Abraham was only half aware of it. His mind was churning, emotions grinding his guts and twisting them into knots. After a time, he realized he was thinking the same thing on repeat, the words burning into his brain until he could see nothing else when he closed his eyes:

Kellina Zeeben. Dan and Marcy Poplenko. Two billion people on Milune.

And now, one more.

Myles Lannam.

CHAPTER 7

The work was done. The outside of the Zeeben homestead was quiet, a constricting silence where people wanted to speak but no one quite knew what to say. Abraham and David sat on the porch swing, Abraham spitting tobacco into old coffee can spittoons. Father sat on the steps, his back to his sons, spewing pipe smoke into the air like a chimney.

The setting sun spilled brilliant shades of orange across the sky. Smells of fertilizer and body odor were the only detractors from the serenity of the moment, but after years of working with the shit, it was more a reminder of being home than anything. Abraham stewed in his emotions, unsure how to process the latest news.

David, swiping on his Portal as always, announced the newest headline, "Admiral Latreaux confirms humanity has zeroed in on the location of Duringer, the riskar homeworld."

Abraham scoffed. "They better save me some of those alien bastards to kill."

Father tapped his pipe gently against his teeth. "You aren't still going on about that, are you, son?"

"Of course I am," Abraham shot back. "I'm enlisting the day after I graduate."

Father didn't turn around. He gazed at the open skies above, one hand resting on his book. Abraham hated that. It took a magic trick to get his father's full attention. Nothing short of a miracle could get him to look you in the face when you were talking to him. It confirmed to him that his father was a coward.

"Why so eager to go to war?"

"Did you forget what happened on Milune? Father, seriously. How can you expect me not to join? You think I don't want to kill as many of those disgusting freaks as humanly possible?"

The old man rearranged his legs so he was halfway turned toward Abraham while still glancing at the sunset. His silhouette was oddly dark. The setting sun lit a bright red corona over his outline.

It sparked a memory. One that had slipped through the cracks of Abraham's nightmares.

The Shadow Man.

His blood froze.

"The Shadow Man..." Abraham began.

Father raised his eyebrows. "What're you talking about?"

"On Milune. When we all thought we were going to die...I saw this man. He was in shadows, and his hand was glowing red, like magic. It looked like he was trying to push Dajun away. Like he was trying to save

44

us. And you were gone at that time. I remember I looked everywhere for you, but I couldn't find you. Where were you?"

Father popped up to his feet, kicking a nearby rocking chair. Wood ground against wood until the legs caught a gap in the deck. It clattered on its side. The book plopped down next to it.

The old man never does anything fast. What's his problem?

Father stepped close enough to grab him by the arms. Something in his eyes scared Abraham. The intensity of his gaze was withering. His eyes bounced back and forth as he scoured Abraham's face. It was like he was searching his mind.

"Abraham," he said through clenched teeth, "why didn't you tell me about this when it happened?"

Inside, he was nine years old again, scared and confused. He stammered. "Uh, wh-w…I don't know."

His father shook him by the shoulders. Hard. "Is that all you saw?"

Abraham nodded.

Father glanced around, left and right. The open fields provided few hiding spots for anyone trying to sneak up on their conversation. A small blue bird soared overhead, the only living thing within kilometers of the homestead.

Abraham didn't know what to make of this sudden change in his father. Cold sweat beaded on his skin. "The red. You saw the red?"

"Yes."

"You're full of shit." He spat. Tension spread in his neck.

"You saw it, too?"

The old man let him go but didn't take his eyes off him.

"If you saw it, what was it? Who was the Shadow Man?"

Father retrieved his pipe and the book. He did not speak a word.

Abraham felt lost. "What do you know that you aren't telling me?"

Obadiah stared. The side of his neck pulsed.

"I tried to tell you about it on the ship, but you didn't listen. You *never* listen to me!"

David piped up from the porch swing. "Have you been daydreaming again, Abraham? You know the whole school thinks you're an airhead now?"

Abraham loved his brother, but in that moment, if the old man hadn't been standing between them, he could have killed him.

"The *whole school* knows about this?" Father screamed.

"No! David's just being a douche bag."

David replied with dripping sarcasm, "Actually, David is pointing out that two-thirds of the student body knows you were sleeping in Literature class."

45

Abraham wilted. *So much for that*, he thought.

Father paced in a circle, dust billowing with every creaky step. He scooped up his book, tucked it in the crook of his elbow and resumed pacing. A few stomps more and he halted, patted the book once, twice, then nodded to himself. "Two weeks, Abraham. No school. No friends. Just work."

He didn't think it possible, but he wilted more. Two weeks on the farm felt like two months in real life. *Father might as well drag me out into the field and put me down like a lame horse.*

He held up a hand. "And…" he paused to fiddle with his pipe, "you're too young to understand, but someday you will, and I want you to remember it; you don't know shit."

"Really?" Abraham growled his sarcasm through tears and gritted teeth.

Father locked eyes with him and gritted his teeth. "Yeah, really. Think you got life figured out at seventeen? Pfft. Your own family isn't good enough for you? Gonna run off to the military and make a name for yourself? 'Big Bad Abraham' gonna kill a bunch of people and get a bunch of medals for it?"

"Sackbacks aren't people!" he yelled, shaking in his boots.

"Don't believe everything you see on TV, Abraham. And don't talk like that."

Father tapped his pipe on the bottom of his boot, spilling ash onto the grass. It was a signal the conversation was over. He entered the house followed by the slam of the screen door.

Abraham collapsed to the wooden planks of the porch, buried under tides of questions. His insides churned. He felt broken somewhere in that sea of unsettled emotion. He knew, no matter where he was in life, his father's words would forever haunt him.

You don't know shit.

Maybe I don't, Abraham thought. *But I know my life here is pointless. You don't have to tell me what you know, old man. It doesn't change anything. It's still your fault. You let it happen. I will not die a grouchy old prick on this wasteland of a planet. That's more than I can say for you.*

From that moment on, Father became Obadiah in Abraham's mind. He would not allow his old man the distinction of the title he had failed to live up to.

CHAPTER 8

The funeral a few days later was a heavy kind of morbid that tainted the soul. It wasn't remotely close to The Collision, but nothing compared to the day you watched your father let your mother die.

There was a striking similarity between Milune architecture and the construction of the funeral hall. It could have been a homeless shelter on Milune, but here it was the only funeral parlor for hundreds of kilometers. Brickwork shoddily covered in solar panels made up the exterior. Stone steps led up to a heavy oak door with faded stain. The inside had been hastily redecorated in a well-intentioned but failed attempt to project a hallowed atmosphere replete with honors for a fallen hometown hero. The taupe walls were covered in thin cracks. Fresh paint chips gathered on the carpet in the corner of the room.

The utter stillness was sobering. The room was large enough for thirty or so people, but it was stuffed with more than double. People stood shoulder to shoulder, body heat filling every gap. Cherrywood pews were stuffed with pale faces that seemed to float over dark clothing.

At the dais before the pews, a monarch appeared from the anteroom. His wrinkled face bore a sad smile so stiff it looked like a mask. A flowing robe, with a pattern of muted colors that could have been drapes at Larry's grandparent's house, billowed around his wiry frame as he set a photo of Myles on a wide silver plate.

He intoned a few blessings in a distinguished accent, spoke a few kind things of Veranda's celebrity youth and his joy-filled childhood. The eulogy culminated with the celebration of the fierce and noble warrior whose Starfighter flew 64 combat hours and killed 147 riskar fighters, 2 carriers, and led directly to the capture of a dreadnought.

The kids were seated a few rows back from the front, keeping a respectful distance from Myles' father and close friends in the front row. Curiously absent was the principal, Myles' mother.

Larry elbowed Abraham. "Kid was a badass, huh?"

Abraham felt a pang of guilt. "This is a funeral, Larry," he whispered harshly. "Can't you show Myles some respect?"

Larry chomped on some cinnamon bubble-gum. "I'm just saying. Sixty-four combat hours in a month is a lot."

David elbowed Abraham from the other side. "That's not possible."

"Huh?" Larry asked.

David continued, his brow wrinkled. "How did he get through flight training and end up on the front lines so fast? He was only gone a couple of months. That and you figure each combat sortie averages three-point-two flight hours, and they usually do two a day —"

Abraham glared at Larry as David continued with his calculations under his breath. "Look what you did."

Larry cleared his throat and straightened up. Abraham copied his buddy.

David asked, "Where's his honor guard? Aren't they supposed to do a twenty-one-gun salute?"

Abraham didn't see any military in attendance. Did that mean they couldn't be spared from the front lines?

Nothing about this is right, he thought.

Abraham concentrated on the scent of baby's breath and wildflowers resting in glass cylinders at either end of each pew. He needed to take his attention off his brother and best friend, off the war and the mystery that it was. He needed to focus on the reason why they were all here. He took in a deep breath of the floral aroma and slowly let it out.

Natural lighting filtered in through the windows and onto the dais. The picture of young Myles Lannam burst into flames, illuminating the tan wood of the banged-up pine box on which the hot plate rested. The small pyre continued to crackle in the silence.

"No body returned." The monarch intoned.

"Nobody ever returns from the Riskar War," David mumbled.

"Ooh, is this more conspiracies, David? Lemme hear 'em!"

Abraham elbowed them both. "Enough!"

They backed off, but Larry still had a smirk on his face. He had, over the years since seeing his parents die, become more and more of a psychopath, Abraham figured. Everything was a joke to him. Hell, even life itself. Myles was admired by everyone, Larry included, and here he was making light of his funeral. Of his *body* not being returned.

Abraham watched the glow of Myles' smiling face curl in the grip of the flames. It dissolved into flakes of ash that spun slowly down to rest on the silver plate.

Is that how he died? His Starfighter blown to smithereens? His body disintegrated by alien laser weapons? He was a hero; is a burnt picture and a crowded room staring at a plate of ashes and an empty box the best we could do for him?

Abraham sighed. One half of himself believed that to be the truth, knew it as irrefutable fact, and was scared shitless of it.

Even if I leave, I could still end up right back here.

The other half, the more vociferous and primal part, knew it didn't matter. *I'm human. Since the dawn of time, we've always fought fire with fire. An eye for an eye. And now…a mother for a mother, a brother for a brother. If humans die, riskar die. I'll make sure of it.*

The sun had reached its zenith, bathing the surface of Veranda with golden heat waves. A chorus of insectoid chirps filled the air, their song a symphony of violins playing the same note over and over. The heart of summer had arrived. David and Larry graduated with little fanfare. It was a big deal one day, and then just a simple fact the next. Abraham felt his skin crawl, the anticipation of his own graduation building with each passing day.

Hopefully this will be my last summer in this shithole.

The Zeeben homestead had been constructed by calloused hands desperate to carve out a living for a young family. No small amount of pride went into that work. Their struggle made something from nothing in a way that promised to leave an enduring family legacy long after the head of the family passed on.

The siding on the house, once pristine, was now disheveled, the paint cracked and peeled from direct sunlight over many long summers. Rusty chains rattled as the porch swing lifted in a breeze. Grime collected on the windows, offensive to the eye of passers-by, but an effective buffer against the sun.

A few kilometers from the house, two brothers worked the tobacco fields in the blistering heat, sweat pouring down their foreheads. Their skin was sun scorched. Their lips were cracked. They wore cotton shirt and overalls covered in shit.

"It's technically fertilizer, Abraham."

David leaned his back against the wheelbarrow, not looking up from his Portal. Greasy with sweat – induced from the humidity, not from any actual work – his black hair completely covered one of his eyes and fell in waves to his mid back. His fingers scrolled the surface to keep the words he was reading at a steady flow. This one was always reading, always questioning, always lecturing. He was, as the boy's father had finally admitted, an autistic savant. Book smart beyond his years, but morally opposed to manual labor.

"Looks like shit, smells like shit." Abraham wiped a tiny clump from his cheek. "*Tastes* like shit, it's gotta be shit."

"Fascinating," David said, still scrolling the surface of the Portal.

Abraham ripped open the top of one of the many bags in the wheelbarrow and hefted it onto his shoulder with a grunt. His body was taut with lean muscle from many hours put into the farm. "You gonna help? I've been doing this myself for six hours now."

He dropped the bag between rows of tobacco plants, then started dragging it, spreading the shit just as his father had taught him; nice and even. *Because, son, even the simple things need to be done right.* Obadiah's words in his head.

Bullshit, Abraham thought. He was glad the retort had stayed inside his head so he didn't have to hear David's correction – *technically, horseshit.*

"History is important, Abraham. Those who don't know their history are doomed to repeat it. You don't think it's fascinating? Five thousand years ago we hadn't left Earth. Now, we're in charge of all of space," David said.

"Butting into every other alien's business, you mean."

David used the Portal as a talking stick, directing it at Abraham. "No, we're making things better. The Aveo-Torind war, remember that? We ended a two-thousand-year war in *ten months.* Now we all share resources as trade partners. Interstellar civilization continues to advance because of our influence."

By the time Abraham finished dumping the fertilizer, he was panting, muscles burning, mouth dry. He shook the empty bag over the latest streak he'd made, then returned it to the wheelbarrow. He snatched up his water jug, popped the top and chugged a few gulps of warm water. Just enough to soothe his dry throat. The sun was exceptionally hot today, but it was the dead of summer. He shouldn't have expected this day to be any less miserable than yesterday was. Or tomorrow would be. "I hate being a farmer."

David put the Portal down and crossed his arms. "It's hard work, but it's our way of life here. It's what we do."

Abraham threw the water jug at David's feet, splashing him. "No, it's what Dad and I do. You don't know anything about hard work. You just sit there and pet that stupid tablet all fucking day, David. I don't give a shit about history. Or math. Or this bullshit family."

David's face cracked like an egg. He put his hands on his ears and started screaming, "Stop it! Stop it! Just stop it!"

Abraham felt a stress knot develop in his neck. David going into one of these fits was never good, but it would be worse if Obadiah found out. He let out an explosive sigh, struggling not to let his anger boil over. That lasted one long second before he charged David and sent a full-force kick into the water jug. The red and white container skittered across the field, sloshing.

Abraham tried to pry David's hands from his ears.

David hunched over, shouting louder, as if Abraham's touch were burning his skin.

Abraham threw his palms up, shooting his brother a glare, who continued to shout. Abraham heard plants rustling behind him. The knot in his neck tightened.

"Hey, boys, what's all the ruckus?"

Obadiah Zeeben was a simple man, weather-worn and soft spoken, but he was harder than diamonds and brooked no nonsense. Well, no nonsense from Abraham. The glaring exception to the rule was David. His peculiarities seemed to be getting worse as he got older.

Obadiah brushed fertilizer off his overalls as he walked up. He pulled off his wide-brimmed farming hat and tossed it onto the stack of empty shitbags on the wheelbarrow. He put his hands out, palms up in front of David's face, showing them to him.

David immediately stopped shouting. He gripped his father's hands until his knuckles were white. His chest heaved in and out with deep breaths. Obadiah shot a look at Abraham and jerked his head toward David. *Get over here.*

Abraham marched over to them. He tried patting his brother on the back.

Obadiah's eyes never left Abraham. The weight of that look was like the whole world resting on your shoulders. He felt himself wilting on the inside. He wondered if the old man could tell he was feeling guilty.

Obadiah said, "Alright, son, come on now. What's going on?"

David seemed to catch his breath after a moment but didn't let go of his father's hands. He looked over at Abraham and shook his head. "Abraham said history isn't important. He said...he said he doesn't give a *shit* about it. Or about us, either."

Obadiah nodded. "That true, Abraham?"

Mortification darkened his already sunburnt cheeks. Abraham just nodded, not looking at his father. He meant what he said, he just wouldn't have said it if he knew David was going to react like this and get him in trouble. This had become the circle of life in the Zeeben family. *That's what* Obadiah's *cowering on this forsaken planet all these years gets us. Hard work and no reward, until one day you go crazy and run away.*

Unable to bring these words to bear on his father, Abraham looked down at the ground, soiled hands burrowing into the pockets of his fertilizer-covered jeans.

"Abraham, you look at me when I'm addressing you." Obadiah's voice was stern.

Sensing the potential for a dangerous outburst from the restraint in his father's voice, Abraham clenched his stomach and looked up. It took everything he had to keep his eyes from watering. Obadiah was a hard man to please. Unless you were David, whose fits garnered sympathy.

"That's better, son."

David was still holding onto Obadiah's hands. The old man turned him so he was facing Abraham, carefully sliding his hands out of the older boy's grip. He patted David on the back, then nodded toward Abraham.

"You know the rules, now. No crying in the field, either of you. David, hug your brother. Abraham, stop being an asshole."

David's face wrinkled. He sniffled back a few tears. He wrung his hands.

He couldn't help it. He hated seeing this kid that was supposed to be his older brother acting very much like the younger. Abraham always had to set the example, to show David things, look out for his feelings. He had to keep the bullies away at school, earning him detentions in class and scoldings at home. The only edge his brother had over him was a bunch of useless book knowledge that came from spending countless hours on the net while your younger brother wasted away in the field.

He pulled David into a hug, just for a moment, then gently pushed him back. David made eye contact, the eye that wasn't hiding behind a wave of hair glaring at him. Abraham laughed. The hair-over-one-eye thing was so dorky, so uncool, so weird. He just didn't get it. Abraham had always kept his own hair short. He hated the feeling of his hair touching his ears. He turned his attention back to the fertilizer chore, leaning in to start wrapping it up now that the family talk was over.

"What're you laughing at, ignoramus?" David growled.

Heat rose inside Abraham's chest. He stared daggers at David for the remark. He turned his attention back to his father, but the moment had passed. Obadiah was already halfway back to his own area, almost completely obscured by the waist-high tobacco plants. A cloud passed over the sun, staving off the heatwave momentarily. When the light broke through the other side it started beating down on Abraham again, chewing up his skin some more. He turned back to spreading the fertilizer on a new row. Sweat dripped down his back. When he wiped it off his brow, it felt like smearing rather than drying.

David sat huddled under what little shade the wheelbarrow provided, hunched over the Portal, fingers flipping. He nodded to himself, lips quivering as he muttered under his breath. It was as if the altercation between brothers had never even happened.

Same shit, different day. Graduation didn't change anything.

This was when he made the decision to leave Veranda before his eighteenth birthday.

52

CHAPTER 9

The walk was long and the night dark. Veranda had very few streetlights and no moon to light up the night sky like the fairy-tales of humanity's old home planet. Tales he had heard as bedtime stories from his mother. The only guide he had was the bonfire blazing in the backyard. The place he was going wasn't exactly friendly territory. In school, Abraham had made more enemies than friends, but he knew that alcohol tended to blur those lines.

At least, he had heard the kids at school talk about it often enough, so he suspected it was true.

The thought of his father's face floated into his mind. Obadiah would be sorely disappointed to know his boy had snuck out and was up to no good.

Abraham shrugged it off as he trudged across the gravel driveway.

I don't give a shit. I'm not working the farm another day.

He was already seventeen. In three months, he'd be old enough to enlist without his father's permission. At this point, he didn't care about sticking it out another year to graduate high school. Abraham was sure he'd heard stories of kids as young as sixteen getting in. He was reasonably sure he could figure it out. Tomorrow he would leave the shithole farm and become a man. No reason why the latter had to wait till exactly tomorrow, right?

The homestead was a far cry from Abraham's.

The house was a sprawling ranch-style, with a rooftop balcony. Encircling it, a wraparound deck was covered in fold-out tables and chairs. Hundreds of neon-colored drinks in clear plastic cups were everywhere, and a few tables had strange hors d'oeuvres Abraham had never seen before; but they looked divine and smelled gamey enough to make his mouth water.

The thought of one family possessing such opulence would have seemed an impossibility if he weren't witnessing it for himself. *Would we be living like this on Milune if The Collision had never happened?*

Several generators circled the house. Light towers rose above them about five meters high, beams angled down at the ranch-house grounds. Abraham estimated around a hundred kids dancing in the lawn. Most had plastic cups in hand. Some were dancing or just bumping into each other. They were all smiling or laughing.

Abraham had always thought himself better than this sort of thing, but he had to admit his curiosity would never be satisfied until he indulged himself. Just this once.

Waves of grungy punk music assaulted the place, vibrating the grass on the lawn, rattling the floorboards of the deck. Abraham entered the house through a cloud of smoke. The journey was like a descent into the maelstrom. Dancing kids on the outside of the house transformed into boys and girls straddling each other on couches, faces smashed together. Some couples were against the walls, lips and tongues connecting as hands roamed across bodies. On the couch, one boy had his hand completely inside a girl's pants.

That sight alone gave Abraham a stab of embarrassment.

They were so…blatant. Nonchalant. No one cared who saw what. Maybe this *was* too much for him.

"Abraham Zeeben?"

The gravelly voice snatched his attention away from the surrounding debauchery. *Of course it would be you.*

The kid who had picked on David mercilessly for years. Abraham remembered swapping punches with him just last year after he had sat on David's desk in study hall and ripped a loud fart right in front of him.

"Digger." Abraham offered his hand.

The bully took his arm from around the back of a girl much taller than himself to take Abraham's hand. A plastic cup half-filled with green liquid sloshed in his hand, millimeters from spilling. As he approached for the handshake, his alcohol-laced breath filled the air.

Digger was a brutish sort of kid, a year older than Abraham and built like a bodybuilder. Abraham still hadn't won any of the fights they'd gotten into. When he crushed his hand with a tough grip, Abraham knew two things; Digger was still much, much stronger than him, and he was completely smashed off his ass.

"Shipping out for the Marines, tomorrow. You come to celebrate my last night? I didn't figure you for the type."

He eyed Abraham up and down, swaying on his feet. He inhaled deeply and puffed his chest out. His bald head and surprising amount of facial hair made him appear much older than nineteen.

Abraham wasn't the type, had never considered the possibility of being the type, but tonight he was. It was the first time he remembered ever making a conscious decision to disobey his father's wishes. Somehow, that little act of rebellion strengthened his resolve. It gave him a sense of bravado at stepping outside the rules.

"I haven't been, not till now. I'm leaving tomorrow, too. Navy."

Digger's jaw dropped. He turned to the girl next to him and handed her his drink. She took it with a fake smile. Abraham, not being drunk at all, picked up on that immediately. Digger seemed not to notice.

"Abe an' me gotta have a talk, babe. Why don't you piss off for a minute?"

She flipped her head, hair swishing with attitude. She sauntered off with raised shoulders, arms pinned at her sides. Whatever curses she muttered under her breath dissolved into the backdrop of the party. Abraham took one last look at the chaos around him before Digger wrapped a small, muscled arm around his neck and squeezed.

Abraham stumbled. Digger dragged him a few steps and threw him into a corner.

Abraham's back hit the wall. *Is this a fight? Already?*

He was about to raise his fist when Digger turned his head and shouted over his shoulder, "Hey, Schust, get this man a drink!"

Abraham unclenched his fist. The gnawing in his gut started again. Did he want that drink, really? The idea of it, sure, but he had never done anything like this in his life. Was he really about to get drunk? To carouse around with a bunch of girls, the likes of whom had never set foot on his own homestead, not even to sell cookies? It wasn't like the concept was foreign to him; Abraham had been noticing girls ever since middle school. Even had a crush on one or two of them. Somehow, those feelings had always seemed too impossible to be real, though. The life he'd lived up to this point was scripted by his father, and he had faithfully played his part without a single major deviation.

Schust was taller and wider than Digger, his jaw like a brick. The kind of guy who had to turn sideways to fit through a door. He lumbered into the room with a toothy grin, sloshing beer from two plastic cups. He bumped a shoulder into the wall, smiled as if to himself, then held out a cup toward Abraham.

Abraham took it. The plastic was wet on the outside. It smelled of chemical and…something like wheat. He stared into the neon yellow liquid for a moment. *This is it.*

"Go on then, Abe. Or ain't you man enough after all?"

Digger laughed and slapped him, way too hard, right on the back.

Abraham lurched forward, spilling beer onto the floor. He shot Digger a glare.

Digger tilted his head sideways and threw his arms out. The gesture reminded Abraham of a dog, unsure of the commands it was being given.

Abraham took a swig. Then another. He downed the whole cup. It was supposed to taste like piss, but it just tasted like wheat, with a metallic kind of bite to it. He enjoyed it. Beer wasn't as bad as his father had made it sound when he was a kid.

"Not bad, Digger. I think I'll have another." Abraham coughed. A sense of bravado swelled in his chest. He headed for the kitchen.

"Hey, Abe!" Digger shouted to be heard over the music. "Focus more on the hoes than the brews. If this is your last night in town, make it a good one!"

Abraham stepped into the unfamiliar sea of music and boys and girls, making several trips to the kitchen, where he drank several beers. The room was getting blurry the more he drank, like he was looking through heat waves. He felt a tickle in his gut that made him want to laugh. Posting up in a quiet corner of the room, he kept up his observation of the party without getting in anyone's way.

The smell of sweat was different in a scene like this, he realized. In gym class, people smelled like effort and angst. Here it was a different scent, like desperation. After a moment of glancing around at several couples in various stages of romantic entanglements, Abraham laughed at himself.

There's all these kids making out and feeling each other up, and here I am analyzing different scents of sweat. David would be proud of me.

"Hey! Abraham?"

The shout was nearly lost against the backdrop of punky guitar riffs bouncing off the walls. Abraham turned around just in time to be crushed in a hug. He hadn't been able to recognize who was hugging him, but they were soft, warm, and definitely female. He returned the hug, careful not to spill his drink. All he could see was a tuft of red hair. It smelled of strawberry perfume.

When the hug was broken off, he saw Lucinda Blaylock. A flash of her in class ran through his mind; the way she would twirl her hair and sigh. Instead of taking notes she drew intricate unicorns and fairies on her notebooks.

If he were honest with himself, his attention always lingered more on the artist than the artwork.

Lucinda said, "I've never seen you at a party before. What're you doing here?"

Abraham said, "It's my first time. And my last time, I guess. I'm leaving tomorrow. For the Navy."

Abraham couldn't tell how drunk she was until she exaggerated her disappointment by puckering her lips and pouting. Just like girls he used to pick on in kindergarten. It started to taint the sanctity of those observed doodle sessions in history class. Abraham made to head outside, where he could finish his drink under the stars.

Lucinda grabbed his wrist. "Hey, where're you going?"

Her eyes fixated on his with intensity. Her voice had a tone to it, one that Abraham recognized instinctually. She didn't want him to go, which was odd because he hadn't heard that from a girl before. This had to be the alcohol talking. Abraham didn't consider himself a dud, but he knew he wasn't film star material, either. Did she actually have feelings for him? If she had been watching him the way he had watched her in history class, she would have seen droopy eyelids and the occasional finger sweep of his nasal passages.

He decided it must be the alcohol.

"Uh...I was just going to step outside for a minute. Get some fresh air. You know, hang out," he stammered, heat rising in his cheeks.

Lucinda playfully slapped his chest, which caused her to sway on her feet, which caused her to laugh. It was a noise that Abraham could only connect to a braying donkey he'd seen wandering a neighboring field a few weeks ago. That, combined with a noisome wave of tobacco and alcohol on her breath, was enough for Abraham to pull his wrist from her grip. Gently.

"Lucinda, what's up?" Abraham placed his hands on her shoulders to steady her.

Her round cheeks shook with more laughter. Long eyelashes fluttered.

Abraham leaned back as she shouted, "I'm going upstairs. Digger's got a few rooms open up there, if you wanna...come?"

He shook his head. He was about to launch into a lengthy explanation. Throw out a bunch of excuses. Anything to cut this short. He wasn't fast enough.

Lucinda shook his arms off her shoulders and slid her hips up against him. He grabbed onto her lower back to keep himself on his feet. That's all it was. Just to steady himself.

He felt her hips in his hands, her hair in his face. The strawberry perfume was enough to distract from the odor of stale cigarettes. The feel of her soft body against his numbed his mind. In the span of a second he short-circuited. Somewhere up in the distant night, the rational part of his mind was lost in the clouds.

The alcohol had made its presence known.

Lucinda's lips touched his with force.

Wet and soft, she pressed into him, her mouth opening against his. The reality of all those daydreams shattered. Abraham panicked.

He had never kissed a girl before, never been to a drinking party, never done anything like this before. He knew teenage boys were supposed to like this sort of thing, that dozens of his classmates would be clamoring to be in his position right now, but something about it didn't feel right. Even with his physical state changing from numb to heated, he still felt a pit developing in his stomach.

He opened his lips in response, and that's when it happened.

Lucinda's tongue brushed against his, full of tobacco and alcohol. And *heat*.

He vomited.

All around him, dozens of kids stopped in the middle of what they were doing.

To stare. At *him*.

Abraham stepped back, wiping chunks of chicken stew from his button up shirt. He glanced up at Lucinda in disbelief.

She was huddled in the corner, crying and swatting at her face, round cheeks covered in...chicken stew.

I just threw up in Lucinda Blaylock's mouth.

His cheeks burned.

Two girls appeared in the hallway, fashionably overdressed in sequin dresses and very high heels. One, a large and plush brunette in purple, the other a freakishly tall and thin blonde in pink. Abraham recognized them as Parvati Hanson and Sarah Lymar. They were, as far as Abraham knew, Lucinda's closest friends.

They rushed up with wide-eyed faces and dropped jaws. Hands fanned the air. Hair whipped with gestures of disbelief. Collectively, the three girls' vocal cords shrieked like violin strings out of tune as they gestured in confusion to each other. It looked like they had just witnessed a murder and couldn't understand the kind of person who would do this.

After several moments of girl talk, the party resumed.

Lucinda was hunched over, one arm draped over the couch, fingers scraping at her tongue. Whether it was the alcohol or the shock at the unexpected turn of events, Abraham felt his legs were like cement pillars. He was unable to move a muscle.

Mortification burned his skin, but he felt a deeper sting for Lucinda.

He marched over to check on her.

"Lucinda, holy shit, I'm sorry. Are you all right?"

Parvati, the brunette, flung a glare at him with a flip of her hair.

"What the fuck were you doing? You puked on her. You hilljack!"

Sarah, not to be outdone, rubbed her ailing friend's back while she shouted, "Yeah, *reject*, what the fuck?"

Abraham put his hands out and shrugged his shoulders. "She just kissed me, and I –"

Parvati charged him. Abraham felt his head swimming. He couldn't stop her. Didn't even realize she was on him until it was too late. A plump finger jabbed three, four times into his chest.

She growled, "She kisses you and you throw up on her? You a faggot or something?"

Abraham couldn't believe she said that. "What?"

A guttural bellow shook the room. "What the HELL is going on in here?"

The music stopped. Time itself was arrested.

Abraham saw couples in varying states of undress diverting their attention directly to him for a second time. Lucinda sniffling and crying was the only sound in the room. It felt like a furnace had been switched on. Sweat ran down the back of his neck. He stood there, stammering, looking around at familiar faces. Wishing they weren't so familiar.

Everyone here knows me. Everyone in this town knows I just puked in Lucinda's mouth. I'm never living this down.

"Abraham, did you do something to this little lady?"

The voice was Digger's.

Abraham felt his heart sink. He should have known this night wasn't going to end well. He hadn't pictured it ending with his face beat in by his arch-rival for the third time.

At least bruises heal.

"He threw up on her, Dig!" Parvati said.

Digger slammed his fists together, cracking his knuckles. He growled like an animal. "Abraham, that ain't no way to treat a lady." He cast a furtive glance over at Lucinda, then looked back at Abraham. "Even the ugly ones don't deserve that. You got to go, Navy boy."

Lucinda buried her head in her arms, coating them with fresh tears. Parvati and Sarah hugged her, rubbed her back, and whispered encouraging words.

Abraham's head swam. He felt like he was underwater. His thoughts were drifting down a fast-moving river and he couldn't get a firm grip on any of them. He knew Digger was bigger than him. Stronger, too. Part of him knew he stood no chance. This was Digger's home. Digger never lost a single fist fight.

Working on the farm day in and day out and missing school for two weeks to pull long shifts of manual labor had graced Abraham with a good deal of muscle mass. Sweating his life away on the farm might make him look like a bodybuilder compared to his lazy sack of a brother, but here, facing a behemoth like Digger, Abraham felt outclassed.

A spike of adrenaline hit his gut. The hair on his neck raised.

It might have been the alcohol. It might have been the rising tide of emotion brewing in him over the last ten years. It might have been from being trapped in a life he didn't want, or it might just have been his fight or flight response kicking in.

Whatever it was, Abraham knew he wasn't going to back down, win or lose. He curled his fingers into a fist and stared right into Digger's eyes.

They fought.

59

Abraham swung for all he was worth.

Digger retaliated.

Digger hit hard.

Abraham saw stars.

Flashes. Swirls. Blinking dots of light and darkness. His eyes closed.

He opened his eyes with the knowledge that he had lost the fight thundering inside his skull. He could feel the swelling on his face like a hot iron resting against his cheeks and jaw. His blood pumped hard, pulsing against his brain, chewing on any rational thought that dared try to rise to the surface.

Smells of freshly cut wood. Sweaty sheets that stuck to his skin. It took another few minutes of shaky breathing before he could think.

He was lying on his bed at the homestead. Sunlight beamed through the window. Too bright. He raised a hand to block the angry glare, noticed bruises on his knuckles. He must have landed a few good hits on Digger before he had his face pulverized.

Realization hit him. The sun was up.

He was supposed to be out working in the field. How had he gotten home last night?

Obadiah receiving a phone call in the middle of the night, carrying his son's drunken, fractured body back to the homestead…was it a dream, or had that really happened?

In any case, Father would have to be the most pissed he'd ever been to leave Abraham inside. He was losing out on the family workhorse for an entire shift.

Abraham groaned. His stomach cramped.

He threw the thin sheet off himself, swung his legs over the bed and sat up. Instinctually, his hands flew to his head, trying to hold his skull together, to stop the pounding hangover. It felt like he couldn't reach it. The pain was inside his head, protected by his skull. He could do absolutely nothing to assuage the discomfort.

"Well, Obadiah's gonna kill me," he grumbled. "Unless he already did, and I just woke up in hell."

There was a shuffling outside his door. The handle turned, stopped, turned, stopped. When it finally opened, David peeked inside. His expression said it all: *You're dead, Abraham. Dad is going to kill you. As a matter of fact, he went out to the shed to get the switch, and he's going to flay your ass for hours. He'll beat you until he gets too tired to discipline you anymore.*

"Father, he's awake!" David shouted.

Abraham puked between his feet. Hardly anything came out the first time. The second time scorched his throat. It was all bile. Brown, acidic, stringy bile. He retched again, coughed, tried to clear his throat but couldn't. He was sitting there with phlegm and bile dangling from his lips like an umbilical cord when Obadiah finally stepped into the room.

Bare feet, calloused as most of his skin was, creaked against the floorboards. The old man wore his soil-covered overalls. His expression was characteristically flat, but his eyes spoke volumes. As the old saying went, they were windows into the soul, and Obadiah's soul burned with something like retribution.

"You have fun last night, Abraham?"

Abraham grabbed the string of spit from his lip and flicked it onto the floor. He couldn't even look up at his father.

Please, just let me die. I don't want to have this conversation. Not right now.

"You're taking the day off. Come tomorrow, you're gonna have to make up for it. Double-duty."

Abraham nodded.

David said, "Father, what's gonna happen to him, for real? Missing work isn't a punishment to Abraham. That's like *rewarding* him!"

Abraham managed to look up enough to cast a glare at his brother. How could David be so childish? How could he just throw him under the bus like that? Sure, Abraham didn't want to work the farm. He doubted he could spend much time out of bed in his current state, either, but damn it, he didn't need this. No one could stand to live like this. Not forever.

"I know, son. But when people make mistakes, they gotta make up for it. And he will. Your brother's not a bad kid. He's just gotten confused about who he is."

David patted the old man on the shoulder. "I know who we are, Father. The Zeebens are farmers. We make our living by working harder than everyone else."

Obadiah shrugged. "That's enough, David. It's getting late, and we still have to finish up rows double-X through double-Z. I'm gonna be needing your help until tomorrow when your brother can return to work."

David crumpled like he'd been stabbed in the stomach.

"Ugh, but Dad! I still have to finish reading about the Pathfinders! They're a secret society –"

Obadiah placed his hands on David's shoulders and looked him in the eyes. "This is a family, David. You're a part of that family. Abraham decided to go out and get drunk and get into a fight, so he can't do his job right now. There's two lessons to be learned here, son. One, you're responsible for your own actions. And two," he turned to look at Abraham, one eyebrow raised, "your actions always affect more than just yourself."

David fell apart but didn't quite go into a fit.

Abraham felt it. The same thing he had felt last night just before the fight with Digger. The feeling that had been brewing inside him ever since The Collision.

He stood up on shaky legs, steadied himself with a hand on the wall. He forced himself to look right into his father's face. Eye to eye. It took more courage than anything he'd ever done before. He knew it was a moment he couldn't take back once it was over. The feeling intensified. For the second time in his life, he let it. "Dad, I'm not doing this anymore."

Obadiah put his hands on his hips, staring hard.

Abraham took the pause as a small victory. He pressed on, not giving himself a moment to let the fear take hold of him. He didn't need to wait for graduation. It was now or never. He had waited for this too long. He wasn't going to let it go now. "I know why Myles Lannam left. He couldn't stand by and watch the war just happen. He wanted to do his part. Well, so do I. I'm leaving, too. Even if it means I'm never coming back."

He bent over, holding back the urge to dry heave, and slipped on his boots. He ripped off his puke-stained shirt, replaced it with the shirt he had worn the day before. Quickly ran a hand through his hair, fingers coming back clean. He stood straight, intending to march past his father and brother. To walk right through the door and onward to his new life.

Father stood stock still in the doorway, blocking his exit. He said, "Is that so?"

Abraham snapped. "'Is that so?' That's all you've got to say? Yes, *that's so*, Dad. I'm not working this bullshit tobacco farm anymore. It's against child labor laws, first of all. Second, I'm going and you're not going to stop me. You *can't* stop me."

Mustering up his courage, Abraham took a deep breath, squared his shoulders and walked toward his door. All his life, Abraham had looked up to make eye contact with his father, but now he realized they were the same height.

Obadiah stepped aside.

Abraham walked past him.

In the moment, Abraham couldn't believe that his father would give in so easily. But then, this was the man who had let his own wife die. Maybe he shouldn't be surprised that he'd let his son go so easily, too.

Abraham reached the front door. He yanked it open with a rusty creak and stepped out onto the porch. The yellow sun was high in the sky. No clouds. It was going to be a hot one for David and Obadiah. Abraham shrugged off these thoughts. The only thing he cared about was getting the hell out and never coming back. The screen door slammed shut behind him, porch floorboards creaking under his feet.

David was crying, louder now.

"Father! You're just gonna let him go?"

David burst through the screen door, shouting, "Abraham, you can't just walk out. We're a *family!*"

He shouted back, "You and Dad are. I don't belong here."

Abraham turned his back on his family. His old life.

He started walking toward his future. One that he would make for himself. As the sun beat down on him and he started sweating, a light breeze picked up. A chill crawled down his spine. He shivered, a mixture of nausea and anger.

"I never did."

CHAPTER 10

The red sun beat down on him as the hour neared noon. Gravel crunched beneath his feet for several kilometers before it became asphalt. It wasn't until he hit sidewalk that Abraham realized he had left his ID back at the homestead. He didn't care. He would get a new one if he had to. Buy a fake one if he couldn't do that. Nothing on this planet could convince him to turn around and head back home.

It's not home.

He didn't know where home was. What that would even feel like. He had felt different his whole life. Out of place. A third wheel in the family dynamic. Even when Mother was there, Abraham hadn't really felt connected. For years he had convinced himself it was normal. That kids helped their parents when they went through hard times. Hell, David referenced similar situations he had learned about in history class. The cycle of hard times forcing kids to grow up fast or drop out of school altogether to help provide a living for the family wasn't a new concept.

Abraham walked by a waist-high mailbox, idly noting the stamp on its face: PROPERTY OF STONY RIDGE.

I'm never coming back.

Going to that party last night showed him the truth. The mansion full of kids, their families doing so well that they had the opportunity to go to college…that was what normal looked like. The kids worked jobs if they wanted a little extra spending money, not to ensure the survival of the family legacy. They cared about getting drunk, getting laid, having fun. Father had always told him these things were foolish. Irresponsible. If that were true, why was the family Zeeben the only one on Veranda that seemed to know it?

Buildings of gray brick and dust-covered glass loomed ahead, drawing nearer with every step. Soon they surrounded him, casting long shadows over the asphalt and sidewalks. Gone was the smell of the farm, swept away by the pungent odor of grease-covered onions and the hot blacktop of the street. He passed several fast-food restaurants on his way to the recruiting station. Here in downtown, Abraham saw people from all walks of life, not just simple farmers like the community in which he had grown up.

People from many few different races, humans among them, hustled by in business attire, some carrying briefcases or talking to their Portals. The humans wore big sunglasses. Expensive analog watches adorned their wrists. Fancy shoes reflected the smallest glimmers of sunlight. Cars trundled by, rubber tires screeching as they wove paths between buildings. An elderly gentleman was standing at one intersection, plucking a stringed instrument that might have been a mandolin, fingers flashing with a little too much precision for a street performer. A wrinkled beanie rested at his feet, within which were two crumpled credit slips and a modest assortment of grimy coins.

A group of kids about Abraham's age were huddled at an intersection, handing out flyers. One of them, a short and plump female with a dark bob cut, shoved a flyer into Abraham's hands, all but screaming in his face. "Do you support Veranda separating from the Nine Nations? Of course you do, you're young and smart. Not like the old, decrepit, douche bag politicians we let dictate our lives! Spread the word, brother! Veranda does not support the alien murderers! We farm our own food, fight our own wars, we don't have any ill will toward the riskar!"

"We don't?" Abraham asked. He glanced down at the flyer.

It was a picture of Admiral Latreaux, the highest-ranking officer in the Human Naval Fleet. He looked like a despot in this picture, different from his TV spots. Eyes crazed, lips a straight thin line but somehow looking like a frown, too. The headline underneath said, "Warmonger Latro Still Can't Find Duringer!"

"I don't understand. I thought we found Duringer?" Abraham asked.

A tall kid with a big head leaned over and shouted, "The Navy wants control over Cortz and Diome. They're two ghost planets in the Adirondi Sector where the riskar mine eighty percent of their natural resources. That asshole wants the resources, and when the riskar told him to eat shit, he gave a press conference asking the Guardians to designate them as military targets. It's classic human imperialism."

"We've already been fighting the war for almost ten years!" the girl said. "Ten years and we still haven't found their home planet. Ten more is just going to get us more dead humans. This war is a joke!"

The big-headed guy added, "We only went to war with the riskar for their gravity tech, anyway. They hid their home planet. It's already confirmed on Alternative News Underground."

Another girl spat on the concrete and shouted, "Latreaux can suck my asshole!"

The kids were directing their ire at a building across the street.

It was a two-story building with four large white pillars in front. White letters on the brickwork denoted it as City Hall. The windows were dark, preventing pedestrians from seeing the people working inside. The quiet stillness of the building gave the impression it was empty. It remained indifferent to the kids' shouting.

Abraham sighed. This wasn't his scene. He just wanted to sign up for the Navy and get the hell off this rock.

The plump female with the bob cut shoved Abraham. "Do you even watch the news? We learned all about Admiral Latreaux in ethics class. He's the worst kind of politician."

Abraham frowned. "I thought he was in the military. How's he a politician?"

The girl let out an explosive sigh, eyes rolling back in her head. "Oh my god, dude, really? High-ranking officers *are* politicians. Doesn't matter they're military. If you don't know anything, why are you even *out here*?"

Abraham shrugged.

Deciding he'd had enough, he marched across the street. When he felt like he'd gotten past the crowd, he let the flyer fall to the ground. It was quickly snatched up in a breeze and carried out of sight. He walked away from city hall and the disgruntled college kids, trying to remember where the recruiting station was. He'd only been in the city a handful of times, mostly for school field trips. He had a half-formed memory of seeing the Navy Recruiting Center somewhere downtown but couldn't remember the cross streets.

He turned a corner between a Mandarin food place and a bookstore, still unsure of his sense of direction.

There's gotta be someone here who knows where this place is.

Down the street, he finally saw it.

Two young men stood guard outside what looked like a brownstone residence. They wore baggy red and brown fatigues that looked a size or two too big. Red berets adorned their heads. Rifles were slung across their backs.

Abraham had seen enough movies to recognize soldiers when he saw them. They were not the pristine blue and white uniforms of the Navy, but it was a step in the right direction. He approached them with a certain level of caution, eyes not straying far from the rifles.

"State your business," one of the men spoke, voice cracking.

Abraham waved a hand. The guard didn't wave back.

"I'm looking to join the Navy. Is this the right place?"

The guard snorted. "This is the Veranda Militia Headquarters, idiot. You're in the right place."

"Jay-on!" The other guard reached out and slapped his arm.

Jay-on stood up straighter. "Apologies, citizen."

A moment passed in terse silence. Abraham stared at the guard. The guard stared back at him. A few seconds passed by with neither one speaking until the tall oak doors of the building thundered open. A thick wave of marijuana vapor spilled out from within.

A man with a thick, curly black beard stumbled onto the landing. He held a large clear bottle in his hand, brown dregs swirling inside. Four large medals the size of Abraham's fist clinked on his chest, resting at a forty-five-degree angle to accommodate his rotund midsection. His uniform was stained with food residue Abraham couldn't identify. It was in his beard, too. The man swayed and took a long swill, draining the bottle. He tossed it, shattering glass into the concrete at his feet. He kicked the shards onto the street, right past Abraham.

"Damn fascist pricks!"

The two guards pivoted on their feet and popped salutes.

"El Capitan!" They barked.

El Capitan waved his hand angrily at the two men. He gestured to the glass fragments on the porch, shouting all the while. "No, no, enough of that. Clean this shit up, dingbats!"

The two men promptly shouted, "Yes, Sir!" and stooped to pick up the glass fragments with their bare hands.

No, they aren't men, Abraham realized. They were about his age. The one he'd spoken to, maybe even younger.

The fat man watched for a moment, arms crossed over his large belly. When one of the boys cut his finger on the glass, El Capitan groaned loudly and slapped himself on the head a few times. "Dingbat! Dipshit! Shithead! How can my militia overthrow –" He stopped speaking as his eyes caught sight of Abraham, and he cleared his throat and straightened his uniform before jabbing a finger at him. "You there, boy! You here looking for glory?"

Abraham put his hands out. "I don't know. Look man, I'm lost. I'm just looking for the Navy Center. Can you tell me where it is?"

El Capitan heaved a laugh, loud and deep, releasing alcohol vapors. The fat man stepped over one of his 'men,' holding out a hand. Abraham shook it, uneasy.

An unsettled feeling developed in his gut. He wasn't sure what to do. You had to work hard to meet someone you didn't already know on Veranda. Most of the people Abraham went to school with, he knew their entire family history – who worked where, what their parents did, what they wanted to be when they grew up. This was different.

El Capitan eyed him steadily, sizing him up. Or perhaps he was just staring at the bruises on his face. Abraham felt a shudder run down his back. He wondered if the man would mistake it as a sign of weakness instead of just being creeped out. Over the man's shoulder, Abraham peered inside the house. He saw a young boy, maybe twelve, walk by with a drink platter. He was barefoot, wearing an adult-sized t-shirt that came down to his knees.

El Capitan buried a hand in his uniform pocket, pulled out a cigar stub and shoved it in his teeth. He said, "You look like shit. But I bet you clean up nice, don't you?"

Abraham clenched his jaw. This was wrong. "I'm in the wrong place," he said and turned to leave.

A meaty hand slapped onto his shoulder and spun him around like a rag doll. El Capitan's face was close enough his cigar stub nearly slapped Abraham in the face. It stank of saliva and damp smoke. Like a campfire that had been rained out.

Abraham coughed. *Or pissed on.*

"How old are you, kid?"

"Old enough. I'm seventeen." Abraham stood straighter and took in a breath, puffing his shoulders up. *This man thinks I'm too young, but he doesn't know me. Doesn't know what kind of shit I've put up with my whole life. He's in for a surprise if he thinks he's just going to kick me off his porch like a broken bottle.*

"Seventeen's too old." He patted Abraham's shoulders and chest, a little too gruffly. Abraham felt his knees jolt with each pat. "But I might be able to work out a deal for you. You're running away from home, right?"

"Don't you mean too *young*?" Abraham asked. "Why would you think that?"

El Capitan snorted, sending his cigar stub flying. He reached out two flailing hands, barely managing to catch it before it hit the ground. Abraham doubted the quality of the tobacco would have been affected much, given its miserable condition. El Capitan slid the stub between his fingers, gesturing with it as smokers often do. His tone was suspiciously like that of a salesman.

"Veranda Militia sees this all the time. What, you think you're the only kid whose dad put hands on him? The only teeny bopper on this rock that's dreaming of stars and spaceships and killing aliens? Come on, kid, you're not that naïve."

Abraham looked over at the two soldiers he had mistaken for men. A closer look at their faces told Abraham that one of them might be seventeen or eighteen, but the other was definitely younger, maybe not even sixteen. A clearer picture of this El Capitan character, and the Veranda Militia itself, started to form in Abraham's mind. One that explained the kid waiter he'd just seen.

He wasn't liking the way this was going.

"Come on, kid. Let me walk you through the place. You'll fit in good here, I guarantee it."

El Capitan put an arm around Abraham's shoulders and guided him a few steps toward the door. Abraham felt a sudden jolt that excited the hairs on his neck. He knew beyond the shadow of a doubt that going through that door was a one-way trip. The uniforms had been convincing enough, but El Capitan's demeanor was a dead giveaway; this militia was not the Navy that Abraham was looking for.

He had to get out of here. Fast.

"Don't you need to check my ID?"

El Capitan guffawed, pushing the front door all the way open. "IDs aren't necessary."

"You haven't even asked me my name."

The fat man's face wrinkled, changing from plastered smile to a darkened scowl.

Abraham saw the opportunity and took it. He shrugged himself out from under his assailant's arm.

The situation escalated into territory Abraham was familiar with. He slapped El Capitan's hands away with his forearms, followed with a one-two to his face. The fat man stumbled back, jaw hanging open.

Abraham leaped over the two kids still bent over picking up glass and tore off down the street. His wrists ached from the impact of the punches.

Air rushed around him. He ran as fast as he could, not daring to take even a moment to look back. He ran until his lungs burned and his muscles ached, until the blood churning inside him felt like acid. He crossed several intersections, throwing out a hand several times to narrowly avoid being taken out by approaching vehicles. He wasn't running from the fat man, from the brainwashed kids, or from what was surely a hellish existence in the Veranda Militia.

He was running from his brother. His father. His home.

He ran until he bowled headfirst into a teenage boy. The two somersaulted across the sidewalk, landing in a heap of skinned knees and elbows.

"Hey, fuckface, what the hell!" the kid shouted, rubbing his bloody elbow.

Abraham stammered a sorry between labored breaths. He looked into the kid's face and smiled. "Larry?"

"Abraham? What're you doing here?"

Larry Poplenko hadn't changed much over the summer. He was still tall and lanky, and his blond hair flowed wildly from his head in waves. He had a small bag in one hand and picked his guitar up off the street. Larry was the only other kid in Stony Ridge that was also from Milune. He also lost loved ones in The Collision and lived to talk about it. He was Abraham's closest friend.

Larry leaned down and offered a hand.

Abraham let his buddy help him up. He brushed his pants, stifling a sigh at the scuffs in the denim. All he had were the clothes on his back, and they were now perilously close to being rags. That and the small plug of tobacco in his back pocket. This and a thousand thoughts flew through his mind – how was Larry doing, where had he been since graduation, what was he doing downtown, nobody ever went downtown – but he could ask none of them as he gasped for air, trying to recover from his mad dash.

Larry patted him on the back. "Shouldn't you be on the farm, dude? Where's David? Bro's always been like your shadow, even though he's the older one."

"I'm…looking for the…Navy Center."

"Whoa, dude, you're enlisting, too? *Sick*, man. You found the right dude. I'm headed there now. I'm gonna be a paid serial killer, bro!"

Larry struck a pose and flexed his muscles. The wiry frame of his body seemed about to snap. His cheeks flushed with the effort. Abraham was glad he hadn't caught his breath yet, or he would have burst out laughing. It was a ridiculous sight.

"Sweet, man. I'm just trying to get the hell out of here."

Larry looked over his shoulder as an elderly couple approached. They walked close together, hand in hand. The woman was dainty, dark gray hair, wearing a simple blue and white dress. The man wore a collared shirt and tan pants, his body too thin everywhere, except an extra twenty pounds collected solely at the stomach. It was a beer belly if Abraham ever saw one. He recognized Larry's grandparents instantly.

Johnford said, "Larry, don't get into a fight before you even sign up. That's not very gentlemanly."

Larry rolled his eyes. "Gramps, come on. In two months, I'm going to be getting paid to slaughter alien pricks on their own home planets. Don't baby me!"

Amelia said, "Language, young man. You're not in the army yet."

Larry crossed his arms. "*Navy*, Gramma! I'm joining the Navy!"

Abraham had caught his breath enough to laugh now.

It sent endorphins racing through his supercharged heart. It was a great moment. The sun didn't feel so hot. The danger of El Capitan seemed distant. For the first time in a long time, Abraham thought it was going to be a great day.

He patted Larry on the shoulder. "Come on, man. Show me the way. I got a little lost on the way over."

CHAPTER 11

The office was a box with modest gray walls covered in posters of starships and officers saluting with smiles. One image, a spaceman in a bulky S-skin brandishing a rifle in a dramatic pose stated, "*Securing Our Future.*" The suit made the man look much bigger than he probably was; thin black lines divided his body like grout in tile flooring, the spaces between a dark blue flecked with white. All the images looked too clean, too embellished to be real. They were the Navy's image seen through the eyes of outsiders and the naïve.

"It's an absolute 'No'. To either of you." The words stained the air with a whiff of cinnamon gum.

The recruiter was a bald, round-faced man with a pissy attitude, and a sharp nose that made him look hawkish. His piercing eyes struck a chord with Abraham. Everything about the man was an unsettling reminder of his father. Except the bloated stomach on which the man's hands rested, just as they would on a desk.

Larry spluttered. "Come on, bro. We're of legal age. We're ready to sign our lives away on the dotted line, here. What makes us not good enough?"

The recruiter slapped his polished boots up on the oakwood desk. The leather chair gave a refined sigh as he leaned back. He sucked his teeth, eyed the two of them again, then leaned forward and pointed at Larry.

"You're of legal age. But, son, you're a toothpick, and dumb as a box of rocks. I can tell by your country twang." He pointed at Abraham. "I don't care what your story is, you are *not* of legal age. You want humanity's Navy to give you guns and teach you how to fly starships that cost more than this godforsaken planet? You don't have pilot's licenses *or* experience with firearms. Try the Veranda Militia. I hear those guys will take anybody. Maybe even you."

Abraham frowned. "Don't you get a bonus for every recruit you enlist? How are you saying no to money right now?"

"I *lose* money if you don't fill out your commitment. You two are likely to get me docked six months' pay by failing out of basic. Trust me, I'm not a gambling man. And you two would be a *big* gamble. Now get the fuck out of here before I break my foot off in your asses."

Abraham felt his hopes die in that moment. He sure as shit wasn't going back to the Militia. He had half a mind to turn El Capitan in to the police. He was surprised, thinking of it, that no one had investigated that organization yet.

Once the boys had stepped outside into the blazing red sun, Larry said, "All right, come on, Abraham. Let's go get some lunch. We'll come back when he goes on break. Maybe another guy will be nicer."

Abraham didn't have money for lunch. He didn't have anything but the torn jeans, sweat-stained shirt, and ragged farm boots to claim as his own. He worried right up until they met with Johnford and Amelia at the local café, a hole-in-the-wall place specializing in 'hearty human fare', according to the sign dangling on its door.

Larry's grandparents treated him to lunch, which they ate on the patio outside; a couple of hot dogs and a bag of wasabi-flavored chips. Abraham wasn't into spicy things, but his stomach was still churning from hurling bile all morning, so he didn't complain. The meal came and went with hardly any discussion, aside from how they were going to circumvent the first recruiter to enlist in the Navy. Larry suggested everything from straight up bribery to stopping by a magic shop and picking up some disguises. Abraham shot those ideas down quickly, instead offering a new approach. "We have to go in with some confidence. Like we've been planning this for a while. Like we're fulfilling our destiny by enlisting."

Larry slid his plate away. Scraps of half-eaten nachos slopped onto the ground. Abraham winced, thinking of the waiter who would have to come by and sweep them up. As if nature had heard his thoughts, a few sickly birds landed by their feet. They scuttled over, heads sideways, large eyes blinking cautiously as they crept. They scooped up their prizes and took flight, leaving barely a stain on the concrete.

The grandparents headed off to do some shopping, leaving the boys time to discuss their plans in private.

"I like my idea better," Larry said. "You can get a fake beard so you look older, and I can get a muscle shirt. Like the ones in superhero costumes, you know? We'll check all their boxes. They'll sign us up before we even say hello."

Abraham shook his head. "I don't know..."

The street was still bustling with people. The individual energies pooled to create a tangible vibe of industry. Despite the frenetic pace, everyone moved purposefully and in an orderly fashion. Businessmen walked without looking where they were going, eyes glued to Portals. Cars zoomed by, trailing clouds of smog that billowed into the air. Parents held little hands, guiding their children through the tangle of civilization, not even looking before they crossed the street. They all knew this place, these streets and these buildings, like Abraham knew every stalk and row of tobacco on his farm. It might be new and foreign to him, but navigating this dense block of city could become second nature if you lived here long enough.

What had kept his father from living here, he wondered? Why had he chosen a simple life on the outskirts of civilization, rather than embedding the family in the heart of it? Why choose relative isolation when there was so much to be seen and done downtown?

He snapped his fingers. "That's it, Larry." Larry looked up from his moping, hopeful. "Family legacy. That's what it's all about, here. So, I'll be your brother."

Larry laughed. "Abraham, I'm a foot taller than you and about fifty pounds lighter. I'm pale and you're...not. That idea's never going to work."

Abraham slid his chair back and stood. He rubbed his hands on his pants, then started pressing and rubbing them on his face. When he could feel the grit sliding under his fingers, he walked to the floor-to-ceiling window of the restaurant and looked at his reflection. The shit and dirt that stained his pants had transferred to his face well enough. It looked very much like a five o'clock shadow. He just needed one final touch, something that screamed adult. He knew exactly what it was.

"You ever dip before, Larry?"

Larry smiled. "No, but I see where you're going, and I like it."

Abraham pulled out the small tin from his back pocket. It was the one thing he had on him besides his raggedy clothes. The last of his possessions from home. He cracked it open, scooped a pinch of leaves and packed them into his lip. He offered the tin to Larry, who hesitantly dug his fingers in.

"Not too much, bro, it's your first time. You don't wanna throw up on the recruiter's boots."

"Don't tell me how to be a man, Abraham. I can handle it."

Larry packed in a huge cluster of leaves. His lips barely touched when he was done, his face contorted in discomfort. After a few moments, he spit a huge loogie onto the concrete. His scowl was permanent. "Ugh, this is disgusting."

"You'll get used to it." Abraham spat a stream onto the ground. He coughed a few times, trying to lower his pitch. "Let's get moving, sailor."

"Don't do that. It just sounds like you're constipated. Maybe just let me do most of the talking, yeah?"

Abraham and Larry shared a laugh as they headed back to the Navy Center. They were shooting the breeze, pointing and laughing when they saw the college protesters shouting and throwing their posters at passing cars. A few apples and a head of lettuce exploded on the windshield of one car, but it didn't even slow down. They were just coming up to the block with the Navy Center when they saw the recruiter leaving the building. They had to duck into a side alley as he passed. Abraham hated the smug look on his face, the way his shoulders were pulled back, his chest thrust out as he strutted by. He clearly thought the whole planet beneath him.

"What a douche," Larry said. "You ready for this, Abraham?"

Abraham held out his fist. Larry bumped it with a grin.

"Let's do this."

Larry led the way into the office.

Abraham was surprised to see the replacement recruiter was a woman. She swiveled in her chair when they entered, long black hair dark as midnight, her expression much the same. She eyed them with a scrutiny that put the man they'd dealt with earlier to shame.

"You punk-asses looking to sign up?" she asked, chomping on bubble gum obnoxiously.

What's with the Navy and cinnamon bubble gum?

Abraham gave her a slow nod. He looked to Larry for him to do the talking. Larry put his hands on his hips, turned his head, and spat right onto the carpet.

The woman recoiled in disgust. "If you're gonna do shit like that, step outside! What the hell do you think this is, the Marines?"

"Sorry, Ma'am," Larry mumbled.

Abraham stepped forward, trying to stand how his father did. He set his shoulders back, raised his chin and set his jaw. Seeing how she reacted about Larry spitting, Abraham wished he could take the tobacco out of his lip. Since he couldn't without making a bigger scene, he abandoned the brother angle.

"Ma'am, this is our time. It's a tradition in our families to join when we turn eighteen. We want to carry on our family legacies, to serve humanity and space's greatest navy. We're not here to waste your time or to get you docked pay for failing out. We don't give up. Never have, never will."

"You two aren't fit to clean the shittiest shithole in *my* Navy. You might as well march your asses out of here and join your little bullshit Veranda Militia. The basic requirement is being *human*. I don't know what farm you guys escaped from, but animals don't make the cut."

The boys were promptly escorted out by security and thrown onto the curb.

Abraham felt the high noon sun beating down on him. Tasting the sandy heat of the concrete, it all started to swirl inside his mind. He got up, brushed himself off, then held out a hand for Larry.

Larry waved him off, turned to the side and vomited tobacco and nachos onto the sidewalk. He looked paler than usual. Pale as a ghost and sick as a dog. Abraham tried to help him up again, but Larry swiped his hand away and threw up again. "Leave me alone, Abraham."

"Come on, Larry, we'll find a way to get in. Just because these two recruiters are assholes isn't any reason to think we're not going to be able to enlist. Remember Saria Jacobs? She joined two years ago, and she was a dainty little thing. Maybe this is all a test. Just to see how bad we really want to join, you know? If we keep coming back, showing our persistence, then maybe they'll change their minds."

"They're not changing their minds. They're pricks. Pretentious, hoity-toity pricks that think that uniform means they're better than everyone." He sat up on the curb, looking ruefully at the pile of puke on the street. "Maybe they're right to be that way. They've probably sailed across space, fought wars and killed aliens, and they know what it takes. Maybe we don't have what it takes, Abraham."

"Of course we do!" Abraham protested. "I know we do. I'm not made to be a farmer. You're not destined to stay stuck on this shithole of a planet either, Larry. We can do whatever we set our minds to. We just have to prove our worth."

"How do we do that? You heard them both. We're not fit."

Abraham stammered. He knew he was fit. He knew Larry would be a good sailor, too. Larry was smart. He graduated close to the top of his class. He had a knack for math and science, Abraham's two worst subjects besides history. Larry would be a good navigator, maybe even a good ship pilot. The Navy was making a mistake. He told Larry this, and by the time he was finished building up his friend, the two resolved to try again. They just needed to find out how to convince the two biggest assholes on the planet that they were worth enlisting.

Someone shouted from down the sidewalk. Abraham turned to see where the noise had come from, and when he located it, his gut churned.

A large man was hulking his way down the street, strutting like he was the richest man in town. He bore a smile, huge and full of bravado. A stubbly beard clung to his chin; a real one, not one made of smeared shit and dirt like Abraham's.

I just can't escape him, can I?

Digger, with two towering brutes by his side, his cronies walking in his shadow as they always did. They were smiling, too. Big grins full of pride that showed tobacco stains on their teeth.

"Hot damn! Abraham Zeeben and Larry Poplenko, two biggest dorks to ever walk the face of Veranda."

Abraham felt his cheeks flush. He was grateful – actually grateful! – for the dirt smeared on his face right then. "What do you want, Digger?"

"I didn't believe you last night when you said you were leaving Veranda. I thought you just wanted to crash my party, but I gave you the benefit of the doubt. Sorry about that rough shake. But you know you can't go around puking in young ladies' mouths, right? I had to teach you a lesson. Had to."

The two cronies snickered behind him. One puffed a cigarette and slung his ash onto the sidewalk. The other picked his nose, completely uninterested in the conversation.

Larry looked sideways at him. Abraham just shrugged. "So, the Navy already let you sign up, then?"

Digger spluttered, unintentionally wetting Abraham's face. "Hell no, man. Navy's for bitches. Anybody who's ever done anything worth a shit has been in the Marines. I'm going to sign my papers right now, and they're shipping me out tomorrow. They already got a shuttle lined up and everything. This time tomorrow, me and the boys are headed to Juno for basic!"

Abraham locked eyes with Larry. He nodded.

The process was much simpler than getting into the Navy.

A quick DNA sample and a signature was all it took for Abraham to end up in the Human Marine Corps.

PART 2: JUNO

A blazing fire makes flames and brightness out of everything thrown into it.

- ***Meditations***, Marcus Aurelius Antoninus

CHAPTER 12

When Abraham was fourteen, he and David had traveled, on foot, over fifteen kilometers to go spelunking in the caves at Leona Lake. Abraham was vividly reminded of the bittersweet memory – he nearly drowned in an underwater cavern – because of the cramped space in the ship. It looked big on the outside but was a sardine can on the inside, barely large enough to accommodate the hundred or so kids piled into seats without armrests. Every so often he would see the brown and red camo of a Marine uniform, hustling kids into seats and helping strap them in. Most kids had never been on a spaceship. For them, it would be the first time to leave Veranda. The sheer number of kids his age was surprising. They looked like a bunch of high schoolers, jeans and graphic t-shirts, farming boots or gym shoes. Idle chatter, all the breath being shared back and forth, was heating up the inside of the ship. Something shifted, slamming their bodies up against one another. A girl screamed. Several people laughed.

The Verandan sun was pouring out some sweltering heat. The skin to skin contact of forearms and shoulders with the other kids was a sticky, slippery kind of gross that Abraham really wished he could forgo. He glanced across the aisle, seeing Larry sandwiched between Digger and one of his goons, a tall, pale, broad-shouldered guy with a blank expression. The Marines hadn't allowed for time to choose seating. The mass of kids had just crammed into whatever open seats were available.

Mercifully, they hadn't even asked to see his ID.

Abraham smelled piss, sweat, vomit and tobacco wafting through the cabin. He could hear the boot stomps of the Marines moving frantically. A few yells and shouts at the back of the cabin. He couldn't wait to get into the actual corps. To wear the uniform and do things far greater than shoveling shit and providing thankless, backbreaking labor to a family business he didn't care about.

Larry whistled at him. He gestured to the towering buffoons on either side of him and rolled his eyes. "One smells like shit, the other smells like beer farts. This is going to be a *long* ride."

Digger bristled at the comment. "Just feel lucky I don't fold you up into the overhead bin, Larry."

Larry's already pale face grew paler, even though the insult was metaphorical. He snorted with derision. Abraham could tell he was blustering.

"There are no baggage bins. We're not allowed bring anything. I had to leave my guitar with my Gramps. He doesn't know the first thing about caring for a musical instrument. The old man better take care of it. That damn thing cost me four hundred bones!"

Abraham nodded, sharing his friend's pain. He knew Larry was a great guitar player. Actually thought he was going to be a musician before bumping into him on the way to the Navy Center. But now, he was going to be a Marine. *Some turns in life you just can't predict.*

A tall, dark, and thickly muscled brute of a man stomped his way down the aisle, silencing the snippets of conversation with his presence. He was easily the biggest human being Abraham had ever seen. The red and brown camo pattern of the uniform seemed like it could barely hold itself together around his monstrous shoulders. His huge head was shaved clean. He stopped at the end of the walkway, standing in front of the bulkhead that led to the cockpit. A large black flag was painted above the door with the red insignia of the Marine Corps at the center.

The shout that burst from the Marine's chest was all bass. And it was loud. "SHUT THE HELL UP!"

Silence reigned.

"That's better. Now listen up, pissants. Y'all are here to become Marines in the Human Marine Corps. Anybody here by mistake? Anybody not sign their papers? Raise your hand."

One hand went up that Abraham saw.

The Marine pointed and shouted, "Corporal Johnson, get that fuckface off my ship. Now! Move-move-move!"

Corporal Johnson was a short but stocky Marine who responded with alacrity. He unbuckled the unsuspecting kid with one flick of his hand, hefted him up by the collar and tossed him a full meter down the aisle. Abraham heard a thunk and a whimper, followed by the corporal shouting obscenities.

"I am Staff Sergeant Demarius Hinton," the other Marine continued, "and y'all are prospective Marines, right?" He held a hand up to his ear. "I could hear a mouse fart right now. When a Marine asks you a question, you sound off. Now!"

The cabin erupted with kids shouting, 'Yes, Sergeant Hinton!' and the man smiled. He lifted his leg and slapped his thigh before slamming his boot down. It was a movement like Abraham had seen in a musical dance number on TV.

"That's right, you sorry sons-a-bitches. This is your first minute in the corps. From here on out, you are no longer little Johnnies and Sallies from Veranda. This ship is going to take you to Juno for Marine Corps basic training. You *will* follow instructions. You *will not* back talk, joke around, or fuck up. If you do, your ass will be on a ship right back to this godforsaken shithole. Do you understand?"

They shouted, a discordant chorus of mixed replies.

The big man kicked the bulkhead. It rang like a gong.

"What a clusterfuck," he said, shaking his head. His eyes nearly popped out of his head they grew so wide, and he screamed, "SOUND OFF AS ONE VOICE!"

Abraham's throat burned as he screamed along with the other recruits. His vocal cords knotted painfully. It was no small effort to produce that much noise. The shouts had a tone of urgency in them, but they still came off as a bunch of raw, nonsensical noise.

Digger's buddy, the large bald kid on the other side of Larry, could be heard over everyone else. "Sir, yes sir!"

Sergeant Hinton flew over to him, the deck rattling with each heavy stomp of his boot. "Who the fuck are you, tubby?"

The kid froze.

"I asked you...WHO THE FUCK ARE YOU? ADDRESS A MARINE WHEN YOU ARE SPOKEN TO, DUMBASS!"

"P-p-Piebold, sir. A-A-Alan Piebold."

Sergeant Hinton knifed the air with his hand, fingers centimeters from Piebold's nose. "You will address me as Staff Sergeant Hinton. You got that?"

Piebold swallowed. He nodded.

"IS THAT CLEAR TO ALL YOU PUKES?"

The recruits yelled, mostly as one, "Yes, Sergeant Hinton!"

He scowled. "Don't give me that Navy bullshit. In the Marine Corps we do shit right the first time, every time. We *do not* take shortcuts, we *do not* kiss asses, and we *do not* give up. My name is *Staff* Sergeant Hinton, and you will address me by my full rank. Understood?"

"Yes, Staff Sergeant Hinton."

"Sir," Piebold added.

Hinton exploded, arms flailing, bass booming from his chest.

"DO NOT CALL ME SIR. I WORK FOR A LIVING! IS THAT UNDERSTOOD?"

"Yes, Staff Sergeant Hinton."

Abraham took a deep breath and massaged his throat. He hoped they got the response right that time. A part of him wondered if he hadn't made a huge mistake taking the Marine Corps over the Navy.

Sergeant Hinton crossed his arms and nodded. He scanned the recruits with a critical eye for a few moments of tense silence. When he spoke, his voice was harsh but not quite a shout. Abraham took that as a good sign.

"That's right, boys and girls. You are about to leave whatever life you think you had behind. Whatever hopes and dreams and family you have here, they're staying. You're going. You're doing something with your lives, and that's commendable. But if you don't *bring it*, you will fail. This is the best advice I can give you. Prepare to have your guts ripped out, your asses flayed, your minds effectively fucked. You didn't join the Navy. You didn't go to college or get jobs with mommy and daddy's bullshit businesses. You joined the Human Marine Corps. The first thing you're going to do is keep this in the forefront of your minds."

He threw a fist in the air and shouted, "As Marines, it is our sacred and hallowed duty to tear the universe a new asshole. Now, Marines. What. Is. Your. Duty?"

"Tear the universe a new asshole!"

Sergeant Hinton transformed in that moment. He erupted in a furious blitz of movement, kicking and flailing his arms like he was possessed. Or doing a dubstep version of the robot. His voice scratched and cracked as he screamed at the very top of his lungs. "What the fuck is that? Address me properly or I'll throw you off my ship right fucking now. And sound off like you've got a pair! Yes, even the females, I better fucking hear you!"

"Tear the universe a new asshole, Staff Sergeant Hinton!"

"That's better. Not good enough, but better." His voice dropped to barely a whisper now. "All right Captain, we're ready."

Hinton stomped down to the back of the ship.

The captain's voice echoed over the speakers, "All right ladies and gents, make sure you're strapped in for the FTL transition. We'll be traveling at about a five hundred lux for most of this trip, so limit your time out of your seat, and if this is your first FTL trip, you're in for a treat."

What the hell is a lux?

The unpainted metal of the ship's interior was a blur. Abraham's head spun from all the shouting. His throat felt raw. Screaming that loud strained his vocal cords. It was not something he was used to. He could go three or four days without uttering a single word back at the homestead. His father wasn't much of a talker, and David talked enough for all hundred or so kids on this ship.

The engines spooled up with a cough, a shrill whine, and a contained explosion that shook the seats against the deck. Abraham regretted wasting his tobacco on the failed ruse with the Navy recruiters. Consternation gripped his gut as he stared out the window next to him. The city was close, buildings clustered together almost like the people in the ship around him – close and rigid. Beyond the skyline, he could see the sprawling fields. Somewhere out there his father and his brother were working, sweating, carrying on with their lives like he had never left.

He couldn't know it for sure, but he had a strong feeling about it. Obadiah hadn't shed a tear since Abraham left. David had probably cried enough for them both, but not over Abraham leaving. He was crying from getting blisters on his hands for the first time, sweating in that field, smearing shit on his clothes, probably lamenting his loss of time with his Portal.

It'll do him good. Teach him that snitching and throwing your family under the bus isn't the way to be.

Even still, as the ship shuddered and his vision blurred, Abraham felt the tiniest stab of guilt. He was finally leaving, but not on good terms. He was doing something that couldn't be undone. He could die. Was he doing it for the right reasons, or was he being selfish? Just a spoiled kid who didn't want to work anymore?

The ship took off with a roaring rumble. Abraham watched the city and the fields disappear beneath them, watched as the dust ball that was Veranda became very, very small in the empty ocean of space, watched until the place he had called home his whole life, the only familiar thing he knew, was swallowed up in the darkness he left behind.

He knew this was what he wanted. He just hadn't counted on being this scared.

CHAPTER 13

If Abraham had thought Staff Sergeant Hinton was a rough man, he was in for a rude awakening once they landed on the surface of Juno.

The Marines in uniform didn't seem to be rattled by anything. The only time they bothered getting up was to kick the lavatory door and hurl a stream of curses if a recruit was in there longer than five minutes. Abraham didn't have a watch to know how long the flight was, but it felt like an eternity.

A sharp round of turbulence woke him. The vibrations shook him until he thought his limbs would tear off his body. Visions of his teeth grinding into powder flashed through his mind. He glanced out the window to catch a glimpse of Juno from space, but the fires of atmospheric re-entry obscured the view.

Abraham had slept most of the ride. It wasn't a comfortable one by any means, not even as comfortable as his twin-sized bed back at the homestead, but it was time free and clear of any obligations. Something Abraham hadn't really had much of. He awoke several times during the flight to catch glimpses of Larry grumbling and throwing a shoulder into Digger, who was doing a great impression of a bear in the deep throes of hibernation. Drool caught in his beard while he snored like a hacksaw cutting through a redwood. Larry would struggle for a moment to force Digger's head off his shoulder only to have Piebold, Digger's righthand man, slam his forehead onto Larry's other shoulder. It was a mild form of entertainment on a ride where the slightest whisper would raise the ire of Staff Sergeant Hinton.

Once, Abraham had been jarred awake by the bulky Marine berating two female recruits who were whispering to each other. He got right up in their faces, spittle flying as he asked them if this was a fucking knitting circle or the motherfucking Marine Corps. When one of the girls stammered and whispered a reply, he slammed his boot up on the back of her chair and leaned over her until their noses nearly touched. He howled obscenities until she burst into tears.

The straps pulled tight, cinching his back flat against his seat. Excitement coursed through Abraham's veins. They were touching down now. He was about to be a Marine. He couldn't believe just last night he was at his first party and now he was about to land on another planet. This was exactly the adventure he had been missing in his life. No more endless fields to work. No more school to be teased at. No more fistfights with preppy jocks and popular kids. He was about to be a real man. A Marine.

Everyone was plastered into their seats, waves of G-forces rippling over their faces. The blazing red of re-entry fire cast a pallor over the aisles and the stretched faces. Abraham had to squint his eyes. He felt like he was in a microwave. A large sweaty kid next to him slammed the window screen shut, but the light flared through the cracks like a solar eclipse. The seats rattled. Abraham's eyes bounced and his teeth ground tightly against each other. He didn't allow himself to wonder if this were normal landing procedure, didn't take a moment to question if the fires were going to chew through the window or if the landing gear would fail. None of these concerns were given any weight. The only thing he could think about was how much better his life had gotten in the few hours since he'd left home.

Maybe I'll come back someday, Obadiah. When I'm a Marine. When I've earned medals, saved lives, toppled alien regimes, and finally added some true meaning to the family name. When people think of us, they'll think of heroes. Legends. Anything's better than being a forgotten farmer on some backwater shithole.

"Hey! What the hell are you doing? What's your name?" Staff Sergeant Hinton's face loomed large, and too close for comfort.

His stomach tightened. "Abraham Zeeben, sir."

"WHO THE FUCK ARE YOU TALKING TO, RECRUIT?"

Flecks of saliva pelted his cheeks. The sheer air pressure from the shout in his face made his eyes water. He was about to stammer a reply when he heard a commotion stir up toward the rear of the plane. The hiss of an opening airlock. Bright light flashed into the cabin, glaring on every metal surface and beam, sending forth a shower of sparkling sunspots. Abraham blinked, trying to clear his vision. When he finally did, he saw the Marine's attention had been diverted.

We landed already?

"Get out," Sergeant Hinton said.

No one moved.

"GET OFF MY MOTHERFUCKING STARSHIP, NOW!"

He spun on his heel and jabbed a thick finger in the air.

"MOVE YOUR COW-FUCKING ASS, ZEEBEN!"

Everyone was unstrapping themselves in a frenzy and jumping to their feet. Abraham's hands shook with nerves. He unclicked and tossed his straps off, saw Larry fumbling with his own. He wasn't sure how any of this worked, but maybe if he could get to Larry, could just stand next to him, maybe they'd put him and his buddy together in the same group. He needed to get to Larry, and then the two of them needed to get as far away from Digger as possible.

The shouts at the rear of the cabin grew louder, more intense, but Abraham couldn't make out what was being said. He saw people streaming into the aisle, headed toward the back exit. It was like someone had pulled a fire alarm. All the kids were moving so fast, nobody paid attention to who they bumped into or stepped on. Larry toppled under a stream of them, crying out. Abraham shoved a kid twice his size out of his way and threw out a hand to Larry.

"C'mon, Larry, let's move!"

Larry managed to catch Abraham's wrist. He hefted him to his feet, but not before a boy jumped over him, boot swiping across Larry's face. Larry growled at the kid, hand flying to his face, fingers working to assess the damage. Abraham didn't see any blood, just a red spot in the shape of the boot print on Larry's left cheek and forehead.

"You're good, man. Come on, we don't want to be the last ones out of here!"

Abraham led the way, dragging Larry behind him.

The light grew dim as they stumbled through the cabin. The pathway was clogged with too many bodies trying to do the exact same thing at the exact same moment.

Something hard scraped against his elbow.

He turned to observe a young girl, probably the same age or even younger, trying to wriggle between him and Larry. The scrape he felt became clear when she stumbled ahead of him, and a boy hefted her up by her arm, lifting her shirt just enough to expose a knife tucked into her waistband. The handle was shaped like a diamond and colored a deep ocean blue.

"What the hell? I thought we couldn't bring anything?" Abraham grumbled.

He had no less than a dozen knives back in his room on Veranda. He wouldn't be half as uncomfortable if he had a blade on him to deter people from smashing his face into the seats as they hurried to disembark.

After an eternity of dodging elbows and knees, of being sandwiched up against too many people, his face squeaking against polished metal walls as they were pushed along, Abraham finally stumbled out of the spacecraft, down the stairs and onto the tarmac. He breathed his first breath of air on another planet. It was equal parts hot blacktop and rocket fuel.

It was *heavy*. He didn't know what gravity was like here, but he felt like a lumbering oaf as he trundled across the tarmac. The ship had landed on a runway at the outskirts of a major city, and it wasn't alone. Marines marched up and down the tarmac, screaming and shouting with wild hand gestures, corraling three additional streams of kids to merge with the Verandans. Abraham saw the other three spacecraft beside the one in which he rode.

I wonder where these people are from.

The recruits were hustled into lines four wide and marched toward a destination Abraham couldn't see above the heads of the taller recruits in front of him. Relieved to see Larry still by his side, he looked over his shoulder, excited to see this new planet.

Juno had a flat, barren landscape that stretched for kilometers until it merged with a red and brown mountain range to his left. On his right, perhaps half as far as the mountains, a city shimmered in the sunlight.

It was a massive assortment of buildings. Some of them were so tall he couldn't see their tops. Others were a few stories high but sprawled out for kilometers, as if they were once skyscrapers but had been laid to rest on their sides. The architecture was beautiful. An abundance of glass with silver struts that caught the multi-colored sunlight and split it into a million glowing, spinning facets. The city looked like a painting, the sky above colored like an oil spill. Abraham blinked a few times, trying to adjust to the light so he could properly absorb the beauty that lay before him.

He was shaken from his reverie by Staff Sergeant Hinton.

Screaming and cursing with renewed vigor, he gestured at Abraham and Larry like a madman. At that volume, Abraham couldn't understand a word the man was saying. Behind the Marine, Abraham saw most of the recruits had already started lining up on a concrete pad against a brick wall behind Hinton. Some were standing tall and proud, some with quivering lips or shaking knees. But there they were, a bunch of young people nervously awaiting their transformation from civilians to Marines. Abraham patted Larry on the back and pointed. Larry led the way to the formation. They stood next to several boys and girls their age. Maybe a handful were older.

Staff Sergeant Hinton approached Abraham and Larry with all the fierceness of a charging bull. A thick vein broke out on his forehead. Try as he might, Abraham could not look away from it as the Marine bellowed with the voice of a thousand trumpets, right in his face.

"That's it, you disorganized band of ass-clowns! On your faces. On your fucking faces! Push ups. Go!"

Abraham looked up and down the line of kids. Almost none of them moved. They instead glanced at each other, sharing confused expressions. Abraham saw two boys further down the line drop to their hands and begin doing push-ups. He then dropped and started doing the same as fast as he could. The concrete was hot on his palms. The grains ground small depressions into his skin.

"Push-ups. Now, recruits! Y'all think you wanna be Marines, but all I'm looking at is a bunch of tobacco-chewing animal fuckers. Push-ups! Now!"

Immediately, the rest of the kids fell to their faces and started knocking out push-ups.

"Count them out," the burly Staff Sergeant boomed, drawing the last word into two syllables.

The shouted counting was more cohesive than the reporting statements had been on the spacecraft. Abraham was appreciative of that. If they could start coming together as a group, it might mean less attention from the drill instructor.

A girl cried out from somewhere down the line. He wondered if it was the same one that got scared on the ship prior to take off. Corporal Johnson took off in a flurry, presumably to yell at the girl for her weakness.

Abraham breathed deep and slow, keeping his pace measured. He was surprised to hear he was one of the few still counting reps. He felt good, despite all the screaming. Some of the recruits were groaning already. Larry was sucking air, sweat accumulating in his eyebrows. Without stopping his motions Abraham glanced up, trying to gauge the time of day.

The sky was a haze of oranges and reds, almost like sunset on Veranda. Very few clouds hung in the sky, and the ones that did were deep purple blots with gray linings. It was a strange view for a kid who had only ever seen blue skies with white, puffy clouds his whole life. Something in Abraham's gut told him it was close to noon here on Juno.

"Enough!" Hinton screamed. "Company, atten-hut!"

Abraham saw the two boys on the end rush to stand stiff and tall with their hands at their sides. They were the only ones.

"Larry, c'mon!" He tapped Larry's shoulder and pointed at the boys.

They imitated the pose. Abraham flattened his palms against his pants.

"Oh, no." Sergeant Hinton marched over to stand in front of him. "Oh, hell, no. Everyone STOP!"

The push-ups stopped. Recruits froze in place.

Sergeant Hinton grabbed Abraham's hand and crushed it into a fist. He placed the fist, roughly, against his leg. When he made eye contact, Abraham shivered.

He shouted, "Keep those dick-beaters closed." He glanced down the line of recruits and said in a normal speaking voice, "The position of attention is this; chest out, belly in, stand tall and keep your hands closed, touching your legs."

The recruits took the hint. In moments, they were all at attention.

The chaos of arrival quickly became a long, drawn-out blur.

Abraham sweated more than he ever had a single day on the farm. They were grilled by Sergeant Hinton like a record being played on repeat. One moment they were berated for being too slow or repetitions lacking form, another they were going to be motherfucking Marines and they had better do the corps proud, and then again with some kind of physical punishment for failing to meet Hinton's demand for standing perfectly at attention, or ridiculously high numbers of push-ups, sit-ups, burpees and flutter kicks.

Abraham's arms failed him and he collapsed onto the hot concrete. He had lost count somewhere in the thirties for this round. He was certain he had already done five sets of fifty. The screams and shouts of Marines running to and fro echoed over him. He wondered for a moment between breaths if he really had what it took. Was a seventeen-year-old farmer with no knowledge of the military capable of becoming a Marine? He seriously contemplated the thought before shrugging it off.

Of course he could do it. As long as he didn't quit.

Just don't give up.

"All right, shitheads! Calisthenics are over," Hinton announced.

Abraham rolled over onto his back, heaving and gasping.

The concrete scorched the sensitive skin of his back, preventing him from resting in the same position for too long. He glanced over his shoulder at Larry. His friend was red in the face, grimacing, air whistling between his teeth. He locked eyes with Abraham and shook his head. It seemed like he was feeling much the same way as Abraham himself at that moment.

Larry's expression seemed to ask, *What did we get ourselves into, bro?*

Abraham shook his head in return. *I really don't know. All I know is I belong here. We belong here, Larry. Just don't give up, bro. Don't leave me here alone with Digger.*

"Form up!" Sergeant Hinton shouted. "Officer entering the area."

The recruits vaulted to their feet. They slammed shoulders together, standing tall and stiff as boards. Abraham knew enough about the military to know that when you stood at attention you weren't supposed to move a muscle. He couldn't help feeling like his racing heartbeat was causing him to tremor. He imagined his heart bursting through his chest like an animal escaping captivity. Wet, red meat splatting on the concrete, pulsing and flopping about like a fish out of water. He would have laughed if his muscles weren't burning profusely, his chest feeling like he'd smoked a pack of cigarettes over the last thirty minutes.

Sergeant Hinton snapped to attention, shouting, "Ten-shun! Officer in the area!"

"At ease, Staff Sergeant."

Abraham craned his eyes as far as they would go, trying to catch a glimpse of the officer in question. He didn't have to wait long.

A gray-haired, pale-faced man stepped into his field of view. The first thing Abraham noticed about him was his uniform; it was a display-type outfit. Blue and white and gray triangles of Navy camo fell in an endless cascade down the man's body. It didn't seem rated for space travel, which meant it was a C-skin, or civilian uniform. The second thing was his rank; a golden eagle gleamed on the center of his chest.

This guy's definitely a big deal.

Two other Navy officers approached, taking positions on either side of the old man. They, too, wore the digital fabric, but their shifting display was in the red, black and brown of the marine camo pattern. Each had a single gold bar on the center of their chest. One was a tall man with a significant tan, maybe nineteen or twenty years old with a thin moustache and chiseled features. The other was a woman.

Abraham's breath caught in his chest when he saw her. She was short and fit, and looked not a day over sixteen, which of course was impossible. The smooth skin of her face held a soft darkness that surrounded the two bluest eyes he had ever seen. Her hair was brown on one side, blonde on the other, the two colors split exactly down the middle. The opposing sides were braided individually, then together at the nape of her neck.

Abraham wondered for a moment if that were allowed by military regulations, or if officers just made their own rules.

The eagle-bearing officer in the middle spoke with a gravelly voice.

Abraham was surprised to hear it did not come out as a shout or a guttural bellow. He almost leaned in to listen better but caught himself at the last moment. He dared not break the rules that blatantly with so many eyes on his formation.

"I am Captain Pendleton. Recruits, welcome to Juno." He gestured with both arms, indicating the city of splendor shimmering behind him. "You are all here for different reasons. I know that. Some of you come from a very humble existence. Farming or industrial trades. Some of you are carrying on a family legacy, taking up arms and serving humanity as your fathers and mothers have before you. Many of you are here to escape the trappings of whatever was tying you down on your home planets. Maybe you couldn't get into college or are tired of working dead-end jobs. Maybe your family let you down. Whatever your circumstances, whoever you are and wherever you've come from, none of that matters anymore. You're here now to be a part of something bigger than yourself."

Abraham felt his breath slowly return, though his lungs still felt flat.

As Captain Pendleton's speech carried on, it became more than words to Abraham. Everything seemed to spiral inside his chest until his hair stood on his arms and neck. He had to fight the shiver that tried to course up his spine. It felt like the officer was speaking directly to him.

The oranges and reds of the mid-day sky spilled their colors over the glass-covered city, sunlight shimmering over buildings like it did on the calm waters of Leona Lake, all the way back on Veranda. It was pristine. It was clean and futuristic and everything Abraham had dreamed of since he was a teenager.

The captain was right, Abraham thought. He had never seen a more beautiful view.

"Now, ladies and gentlemen, I have some golden nuggets of wisdom for you. If your heart's deepest desire is to become a Marine, I need you to understand three things right now. One, your life belongs to the corps. You knew that when you signed the dotted line. Two, there are customs and courtesies in the military, and you will abide by them. Ours is a culture rich in heritage, bought with the blood of courageous men and women who have earned our eternal gratitude and respect." His eyes narrowed and he glanced harshly down the line of recruits. "You will not dishonor their sacrifice. You will not dishonor the corps."

Abraham's knees started to quiver. His mind was fully engaged but his body was starting to feel the pressure. The strain of the last hour of constant motion followed by the prison of attention his body was locked into pinched his hip flexors. He hoped they would be allowed move about freely in a few minutes. Standing still as a statue was beginning to make his calves cramp.

There was a long pause during which something flashed across the captain's eyes. Abraham wasn't sure if it was ghosts of the man's past or perhaps a rush of emotion at imagining these young kids going to war, dying on hostile alien planets. The glint in the old man's eyes faded as if it had just been a trick of the light.

"Third." He held up a hand. "Third and final nugget of wisdom is this: you look to your left, you look to your right, you will see men and women, not unlike yourselves. These are now your family. I don't care where you came from or who you were, and they don't either. When bullets tear the sky and bombs descend from on high, the only shelter you will find is the bonds of brotherhood. The only thing keeping you alive is the people next to you. Don't ever forget that."

Abraham felt a trickle of adrenaline drip into his gut.

Of course, he knew Larry and he had each other's back, but having to go out of his way to help Digger and his goon squad? That didn't sound like what he'd signed up for. Then again, human versus alien, Abraham imagined the choice was pretty easy in a combat situation. An image of Digger asking Abraham for help halfway materialized in his mind, but it was such a ludicrous thought it dissipated quickly. Some things just couldn't happen in real life.

Captain Pendleton slammed a boot heel and shouted, "Company, at ease."

Abraham and the rest of the recruits breathed a deep sigh, finally allowed to relax from their stock-still stances. He shook his feet, trying to smooth out the stiffness in his joints. He felt strange, standing in a group of kids, wearing his farming clothes and sweating his ass off. Muscles burned with fatigue. He felt a deep, cheek-stretching smile bloom on his face. Whatever challenges awaited him here, he knew beyond the shadow of a doubt he was ready to face them.

CHAPTER 14

"Line it up, now!" Staff Sergeant Hinton shouted.

The recruits looked like concertgoers after an all-night rager. Dark sweat stains on their t-shirts, droplets on the concrete as if it had been raining. The captain walked off the scene, leaving the two junior officers behind. They stood aloof from Sergeant Hinton and Corporal Johnson, not speaking to each other.

I get the impression they don't get along too well.

Abraham scurried through the line, desperately hoping for a break from physical training for a few more minutes. He took his place against the brick wall and resumed his statue-like attention. He stared straight ahead at the beautiful city of glass, the same as everyone else. Someone stumbled behind, shoving him forward. He quickly resumed his position, but not before casting an angry glance at the offending elbow that had jabbed him; it belonged to the girl with the knife.

She was short. Maybe five feet tall, and her pale arms were barely the thickness of handrails on a staircase. She glared back at him with dark eyes. The blue-diamond dagger was still on her belt. He could see the outline of it under her shirt. Abraham huffed and turned his back to her, taking his place in the formation. He wondered what her problem was, whether a need to compensate for her size or she was just a bitch.

Still, he wasn't about to give her an excuse to pull that blade on him.

Sweat collected at his brow. He struggled against the tickle. It took everything he had not to wipe it off. The burning spread from his wet eyebrow to the top of his head. Abraham hoped if he focused on his breathing, he could distract himself long enough for the sensation to subside.

Sergeant Hinton flexed his muscles at the head of the formation. A recruit sneezed, drawing a cloud of obscenities from the marine. After the tirade, he took a deep breath as if to gather himself, clicked his bootheels together and pulled a Portal from his leg pocket.

"You will be divided into two platoons. Eagle Platoon, you're with Ensign Lechero. Raven Platoon, you're with Ensign Seneca. I don't want to hear any noise whatsoever except for an acknowledgement. Is that understood?"

The recruits shouted an affirmative.

Sergeant Hinton nodded. "That's right. Now," he swiped across the screen, touching a few spots on it, then said, "Denton Tachek, Raven Platoon."

Abraham's jaw nearly hit the ground. *Digger's real name is* Denton?

Digger shoved his way through the crowd, shouting an affirmative. He trundled over to stand behind the female officer, Ensign Seneca...and she made eye contact with Abraham. For a moment, their eyes stayed locked. Abraham felt awkward and had to look away.

She must have been staring off into space. Not paying attention. It just felt like she was looking at me.

Since they weren't exactly in a position of attention, Abraham leaned his head forward to look down the line at Larry. Larry's questioning gaze found him, and the two shook their head in disbelief. They shared a small, quiet laugh at discovering Digger's real name.

Sergeant Hinton read off more names.

The lines were filling up behind both ensigns.

Abraham felt a pang of anxiety. He was at a disadvantage now. He had wanted to be in the Raven platoon with the captivating Ensign Seneca, but now that Digger and his oversized sidekick Piebold had been selected for it, he wasn't so sure. Sharing classes with the brute on Veranda had been torture enough; having to live in the same quarters would push Abraham over the edge.

"Lucas Schuster, Eagle Platoon."

That was one of Digger's buddies. He bellowed his affirmative and stood behind Ensign Lechero, disappointment written on his face.

"Larry Poplenko, Raven Platoon."

A dagger to the gut, Abraham watched his friend hustle over to stand next to Digger. Now his mind was made up; Abraham desperately wanted to be in Raven Platoon. He would have sold his brother to make it happen. The air felt constricted as he fought the urge to just run over there without having his name called.

"Amory Eilson, Raven Platoon."

Abraham took an elbow to the back. The blow knocked him to his knees. He looked up to see the usual suspect, the girl with the dagger, step over him and shout, "Yes, Staff Sergeant." She looked down as she passed and whispered, "Girls weaken the knees, asshole."

"Zeeben, get the hell up," Sergeant Hinton shouted.

Abraham felt his cheeks blister with heat. He hustled back to his position.

He was raised to respect women, to hold open doors for them and consider them the 'weaker sex,' but right now, this girl...Amory. Abraham was heavily considering tripping her down a staircase.

"Abraham Zeeben, Eagle Platoon!"

Damn it. Abraham couldn't hide his disappointment.

He muttered his affirmative, stumbling over to stand next to Ensign Lechero, Schuster, and a bunch of other names and faces he did not recognize. Lechero gave him a half-grin, his angular face emanating something like disgust and an air of superiority. Abraham got the feeling this man was the third kind of person Captain Pendleton had referred to in his speech – rich and snobbish. Lechero seemed the type used to having his ass kissed. Abraham groaned inwardly. He already knew this was going to be a disaster.

"Staff Sergeant, a word?"

A shoulder brushed past Abraham's, carrying a strong scent. Vanilla and honeydew. It was a welcome change to the sweat and stale breath he'd been smelling since starting this journey on the interplanetary starship. Abraham watched intently as Ensign Seneca conferred with Sergeant Hinton.

He couldn't hear what she was saying, but the expression on her face…she was cold as ice. Abraham had never in his life been afraid of a female, but there was something in the officer's eyes that cut right to the bone. After Sergeant Hinton nodded to her a few times, he said, "I understand, Ma'am. It's your platoon, anyway."

Abraham felt his pulse quicken.

"Zeeben, change of plans. Eagle Platoon has two extra recruits, so you're relocated to Raven Platoon."

Digger huffed and cast a glare at Abraham.

It took everything he had to keep his face neutral, to remain still and not jump and shout at the top of his lungs. Fate had smiled on him like never before. Maybe now that he had struck out on his own, things were going to be different. Maybe he could leave the dark cloud of bad luck that was his life behind and start something new, something that would earn his family name some real respect.

"Zeeben, stop standing there like a dipshit and fall in. Now!"

Abraham shivered back to reality.

He slammed into the ranks of Raven Platoon. It was the happiest moment of his life. On his left was Digger, his biggest rival. To his right, Larry, his closest ally. And behind him, Amory. She might be a bigger rival than Digger, but right now, they were familiar. They were names and faces he knew. He wouldn't have to face the rigors of basic training on his own. For now, that was enough.

Up ahead, Ensign Seneca locked eyes with him.

Her expression was flat. Perfectly neutral. Her eyes were oceans of fathomless depths, the darkest blue Abraham had ever seen. If eyes were windows into the soul, Abraham figured hers was made of the same stuff as the rings of Saturn.

Digger piped up next to hi, and Abraham wished he hadn't.

"Bet you'd like to throw up in *her* mouth, huh, Zeeben?"

Several recruits snickered around them. Abraham elbowed Digger in the ribs, but the brute was laughing so hard he barely grunted. Larry was covering his mouth with a hand, but his shoulders were shaking with laughter. A superficial pang of betrayal knifed at Abraham's gut. It dissolved when Sergeant Hinton screamed for everyone to shut up and snap to attention, which they did with quickness.

Limbs flattened against his body, standing stiff as a board, Abraham's attention fell upon the mysterious Ensign. He watched her while trying to avoid being noticed. This amounted to stealing glances for one or two seconds at a time, before flitting his eyes away to stare at a window-covered skyscraper in the distance.

At Sergeant Hinton's barked command, the push-ups started anew. This time the officers were watching.

Staff Sergeant Hinton drilled them, berated them, and insulted them, ground them into the dirt when they couldn't keep doing push-ups, but the only thing Abraham could think about was his officer. Chest and arms burned, palms tingled on the rough concrete, but he remained distracted.

She studied the ranks with a keen interest, marching between the rows of recruits and glancing them up and down. Sizing them up, it seemed. She knelt next to one recruit a few rows over and whispered. Abraham strained, but couldn't hear over the wheezing and coughing and hacking of the kids around him.

Something wet slapped onto the side of his face. Abraham wiped it off with the back of his hand. Thick strands of saliva stretched between his fingers. He wiped them off on the concrete. Knowing who the culprit was, he tried to shoot a glare at Digger, but his arch-rival was suddenly doing push-ups with renewed vigor.

"Zeeben, Abraham?"

Her voice was sharp and insistent, but not unkind.

It was miles from sounding like anyone else Abraham had seen wearing a uniform. Without thinking, he flexed his chest muscles and started doing his push-ups faster. His heart was racing, but he knew better than to think it was from the physical effort alone. The sweet scent of honeydew all but flew off Ensign Seneca's uniform. It tickled his brain, that smell. It made his blood feel a little bit warmer.

What the hell is wrong with me? I've never been so affected by a girl before.

"You will speak when spoken to, recruit." Her tone flexed just enough to sound both annoyed and composed.

Sweating profusely, breathing heavy from the exertion, and possibly drunk on pheromones, Abraham managed to exhale a breathy, "Yes, Ma'am."

She pulled a Portal from her back and tapped the screen. "You are eighteen years old, hailing from Veranda? There's a lot of you Veranda boys here, today."

"Yes...Ma'am..." Abraham grunted. The muscles in his arms were burning.

"Flutter kicks!" Sergeant Hinton shouted.

Abraham immediately flopped onto his back, grateful for the break his arms and chest desperately needed. He started swinging his legs to keep the sergeant from screaming at him, but his gaze never left the ensign's face.

She tapped at the screen on her wrist, frowned, then looked down at him with cold eyes. "I need to see you in my office tomorrow morning."

Confusion slammed across his brain like a lightning bolt. "Uh, what?"

But the ensign was already headed toward the front of the formation. She hadn't heard Abraham stammer his reply, probably didn't care what he had to say anyway. Abraham was getting the impression that officers didn't care much for the enlisted. At least not enough to give them a clear picture of what was going on.

Digger and his henchman started making gagging sounds and laughing. Abraham sighed as he continued to swing his burning legs. Somehow, he had the feeling the rest of the recruits were going to hear about his encounter with Lucinda Blaylock before the night was out. Digger rolled onto his side and acted like he was throwing up. Abraham took the opportunity to shove him. Digger was in the moment, fully embodying a kid throwing up; the shove took him by surprise. He tumbled into two other recruits.

Sergeant Hinton bellowed, "Zeeben! Tachek! Since you two lovebirds seem to get along so well, you just won the award of the day. Y'all have been designated Latrine Queens. Duty to begin at twenty-two hundred hours. Understood?"

"Yes, Staff Sergeant."

Hinton gave a mischievous grin. "You know what, just so you're not lonely, why don't you take Poplenko and Piebold with you? Camaraderie keeps morale alive, and those shitters are gonna need some spunk to defunk."

Beside him, Larry and Piebold groaned in protest.

Abraham was too embarrassed to draw any more attention to himself. He kept his legs pumping, kept his breathing in time with the motion of an endless train of flutter kicks. He had lost count long ago when Sergeant Hinton allowed them their next respite.

"All right, that's enough. Stand up and fall in," the burly marine growled.

Sluggish, spent, sweating and wheezing, the recruits struggled to comply.

Abraham staggered into his line, bracing himself on the recruit in front of him. The kid shrugged him off with a curse, leaving Abraham to suck air on legs that felt like jelly in a microwave. He heard a couple of kids grumbling at each other behind him but was too tired to pay any attention. His lungs were on fire, the balmy climate of Juno scorching him in a different way than Veranda's sun. He could feel this heat like cat claws dragging on his skin. An image of the skin bubbling and blistering came to his mind. It didn't seem farfetched given how he felt.

Sergeant Hinton bellowed like an angry bear, bringing the recruits to attention. "This is Juno, as you all are well aware." He made a sweeping gesture. "That behind you sorry pricks is the city of Chevalier. You will, under no circumstances, enter the city. That is a direct order from Captain Pendleton himself. The locals do not want their clean city streets desecrated with the footsteps of filthy degenerates who aren't even true Marines. That means each and every one of you." He jabbed a finger at them, swiping it up and down the line, making eye contact with each of the recruits.

"Eagle Platoon, form up with Corporal Nichols. Raven Platoon, form up with Corporal Johnson. Big daddy Navy has decided to try something new with this class at boot camp, and you all get to be the lucky lab rats to test it out for headquarters at NavCom."

A little voice whispered, "Human Naval Command. That's the congregation of the gods who run the Navy."

It took Abraham a moment to realize it was Amory's voice.

He didn't even know the tough little girl could speak like that. He was surprised to hear the awe, the reverence almost, in her tone when she spoke of the Navy. She was odd anyway, but her soft voice contrasted her prickly exterior in the most striking way. Abraham almost shook his head in disbelief, only stopping at the last moment when he remembered they were still at attention by Sergeant Hinton's command.

A vein rippled across the sergeant's forehead as he commanded with a shout for the recruits to form up in their now separate ranks. Abraham hustled to comply, finally feeling he had caught his breath. His legs felt like they had been chewed on by one of the zombies in those cheesy late-night horror movies he and David used to watch on Milune, a lifetime ago. He desperately needed an ice bath and a nap. The thought came to him unbidden: *When's the last time I slept? Hell, I don't even know what time it is. Feels like we've been on Juno for two days already.*

Once the formations were complete, Sergeant Hinton clapped his large hands together. His knuckles turned white. A smile baring large square teeth spread across his face. He bucked his shoulders once, twice, then locked himself up into attention. Abraham was dizzy just watching a man of that colossal size move with such alacrity.

"We are currently five kilometers from Camp Butler. Unlucky for you, the Navy is all out of transportation. This is a way of life for Marines. We are the grunts of the military; you all knew that. That's why you're here. You *will* get used to this, and you *will* learn to love it. You will eat, sleep, and breathe every aspect of this training until your parents can smell it on you back on your home worlds. When shit hits the fan, you get to shoveling."

Abraham's chest heaved at the thought of running five kilometers. He had never been much of a cardio person, even though it was an area of fitness he excelled in. It was more mental than physical, but he always found it tedious and maddening.

"You ready for this shit, Zeeben?" Digger whispered.

Abraham took a deep breath and gritted his teeth. "Shut up, *Denton*."

Amory chuckled behind him. "I thought it'd be at least a week before the dick measuring started."

Abraham bristled at the comment but didn't make a rebuttal. He didn't want to chance getting caught talking in formation and risk more end-of-day punishments. He certainly hadn't planned on scrubbing the shithouse on his first day at boot camp.

Digger just smirked. Abraham smiled inside. *I can get under your skin, too, asshole.*

Sergeant Hinton shouted, "Recruits! Double time. March!"

Abraham started the run, sidling up next to Larry. He and his buddy could pass each other glances as they suffered over the next five kilometers. It wouldn't stop the pain, but it would be a small comfort to help see them through.

CHAPTER 15

The city receded behind a range of towering red and brown mountains, the sky slipping into a deeper orange. Purple-lined clouds faded to black. Heat became more than a smell. It could be tasted in the chest, like car exhaust.

There were several times when the fatigue almost got the best of Abraham, but Larry was there to motivate him, to pick him up if he tripped over a rock in the road, or to shove him forward if he started lagging. Abraham was able to reciprocate once when Amory tripped Larry as she passed, sending him into a tumble through the dusty gravel of the road. Larry brushed pebbles out of bloody gashes on his arms, cursing. "That little *bitch*, dude. What's her problem?"

Abraham wheezed his reply. "Fuck her, man. Let's go."

Larry snickered. "I wouldn't. Not even with your dick."

"Shut up, bro, let's just go."

Digger kicked a cloud of gravel-strewn dust as he passed, pelting them.

Abraham was reaching breaking point. On every level. If it wasn't the torturous physical training, or the mental assaults of large marines screaming in his face, it was Amory or Digger – people who were supposed to be on his team! – kicking him when he was down. Up until this point, the memory of losing a half dozen fistfights to Digger had been enough for Abraham to realize his situation was futile. The fatigue added to it, and he could do nothing but shrug it off.

I hate feeling like a wimpy. I want to be a marine already!

Larry brushed gravel out of his thick blond hair. He looked every bit as worn as Abraham felt. He caught a glance at Larry's watch, immediately wishing he hadn't. It was two o'clock.

They still had eight hours until the day was over.

Until everyone else's day is over. Thanks to Digger, we'll have at least an extra hour of disciplinary. Probably the old toothbrush as a mop thing I've seen in a dozen movies…that bastard.

The glimmering, shining vista of splendor that was Chevalier had fully departed beyond the horizon. The recruits pounded dirt and gravel and asphalt that seemed to stretch forever, following their fearless leader Sergeant Hinton into the unknown. Sure, they knew they were headed to Camp Butler, but after several minutes of glancing around, Abraham was not convinced there *was* a Camp Butler. By his admittedly poor senses, he estimated they had run about three kilometers in the past twenty minutes. Surely there should be some sign of the base nearby?

He could only see the darkening purple sky overhead, the strange light spilling onto the recruits in front of him. A mountain range in the distance, the base of which was perhaps thirty kilometers away. Off to the west he could see what looked like a shooting range, where dilapidated buildings riddled with bullet holes barely managed to stay standing. They looked like they'd survived a few fires, too. Out in the distance to the northwest, Abraham could just make out a silver glint. It seemed to be about ten kilometers up ahead. Could that be the base, and Sergeant Hinton had lied about the distance?

It wasn't meant to be.

Sergeant Hinton angled to the southwest, steering the columns of recruits toward the torn apart buildings. A few minutes later they were being shoved inside by the dozens. Abraham realized he had forgotten one key aspect of the boot camp experience.

Inside the building, he felt claustrophobia for the first time since nearly drowning when he was a kid. Mirrors lined the walls. Below them on shelves were hair clippers, scissors, and straight razor blades. Small bundles of cords were strewn about the cracked white tile floor. He had to kick his feet frantically to maneuver toward a chair. The room emitted a stale odor, one that reminded him of a horse stable. After slipping through the sea of recruits, Abraham managed to secure a seat.

He was greeted by a tall, thin lady with a pleasant face that reminded him of Larry's grandmother. She curtsied in her sundress, the pattern mostly obscured by her white apron. Abraham nodded at her as he plopped down into the chair. Several clippers engaged, sounding like miniature skiff engines. Myles Lannam crossed his mind, but Abraham was too exhausted to dwell on it. The lady swiped a layer of his hair with the clippers. He watched it fall to the floor. Somehow this event had seemed more dramatic in the movies.

All around him boys and girls were taking their seats while clippers were chewing through hair with the efficiency of an assembly line. Abraham couldn't believe the women were having their heads shaved, too. It seemed very Spartan-like. They had to be more traumatized than the boys. Abraham didn't know much about girls, but he did know the importance they placed on their hair.

It's going to be hard to tell the girls and guys apart.

Obadiah's face flashed through his mind, expression blank.

Abraham shrugged the thought away, refusing to engage with it.

The haircut lady bristled and snapped at him with a harsh accent, her grandmotherly demeanor suddenly switching to be more like a drill instructor. Abraham winced, his fingers rushing to feel his head. They came away with a tiny streak of blood on them and he cursed his inattentiveness.

After he suffered through the remainder of his cut, Abraham was rushed out of the building to stand in formation, made more difficult by the itchy, loose hair fibers that clung to his neck and collarbone. He wanted so badly to scratch himself, but after seeing individual recruits being forced to drop and knock out push-ups for similar infractions, he decided against it.

Larry came out after a few minutes, looking glum. Abraham barely recognized his buddy without his flowing blond locks tucked behind his ears. He had to stifle a chuckle, seeing Larry's near-bald head shaped like an egg. Abraham shuddered to think what strange food item his own head resembled. He had never had his hair this short in his life; it was like having a five o'clock shadow on his head. Sweat collected and trickled down his forehead and into his eyes. He risked a glance down the line of recruits and saw many of them blinking sweat out of their eyes, too. Hair that normally might have trapped it was gone. They were all having to adapt.

Joining the military was supposed to be thrilling and rewarding. Abraham was starting to think of it as a strange kind of torture. Less than a full day and he was already second-guessing his decision. The thought of heaving shitbags on an oversized farm plot brought him back to reality. He didn't care how miserable this was; he was going to do it, and his desire couldn't be tempered by a few uncomfortable workouts and a forced haircut.

After the haircuts were completed, the recruits followed a bellowing Sergeant Hinton across a gravel alley and into another rundown building, this one the size of a warehouse. They entered single file, walking through an assembly line of workers who wore billowy cargo pants and black shirts. Abraham wasn't sure if they were military or not. The room smelled of moist laundry detergent. Across the entire length of the place, uniform items were folded and stacked high. A few stacks nearly brushed the ceiling. They were marched through, handed a few pairs of uniform pants, shirts, outer garments and under garments, as well as two pairs of boots and a large duffel bag to throw everything into, then hustled out the back door and onto the gravel. Abraham noticed a blood-stained bullet hole in one of his uniforms. He was about to turn around and request another when Digger slammed into him. "Move it, punk ass."

Abraham gritted his teeth but said nothing.

He scooped up his clothes, along with a few handfuls of gravel he didn't bother trying to shake out, and stuffed it all back into the bag.

Amory's duffel bag, filled to the brim, smacked him on the back, spilling his bag open again.

Thin and small, she looked like a little boy with her haircut.

Again, Abraham gritted his teeth and said nothing.

He quickly finished packing his things and clipped the bag shut.

"All right, recruits. This is your first step toward being a real marine." Sergeant Hinton said. "We're going to arrive at the barracks in a few minutes. At that time, you are to don your uniforms and report for inspection. Men, you will shave. Ladies, you will remove any makeup left on your face. If you fail inspection, there will be consequences."

Sergeant Hinton called double time. The recruits slung their duffel bags and hoofed it. Abraham couldn't stop himself trying to steal a glance at any kind of watch worn by nearby recruits, but everyone was running, arms swaying, and he couldn't see what time it was. Not that it mattered. The monumental pace of the day didn't show any signs of slowing down. Not for a while. Not for an eternity.

The barracks Sergeant Hinton had referred to rose out of the desert like a mirage. They were two identical tents on a patch of sand, one red, one blue, both very close to the busted-up buildings they had just left. A few wood picnic benches rested either side. Abraham was relieved to catch a peek through the door flap and see cots with pillows situated inside. He didn't care what the sleeping arrangements were; at this point, if he could steal just five minutes to lie down and close his eyes, it would be worth his entire first paycheck.

"Recruits, halt!" Sergeant Hinton called out.

He took his customary place a few meters in front of the recruits. After a moment of walking up and down the line, eyeing everyone with what had become his trademark glare, Sergeant Hinton stomped his boot on the gravel. "Inspection in five minutes. Get your asses inside, claim a cot, and get dressed. Time starts now."

Abraham rushed inside, dodging shoulders and elbows, ducking low to avoid most of the flailing recruits who were taller than him. He grabbed a cot toward the back of the tent, slammed his bag on it and dumped out the contents. After a few heart-pounding moments where he could feel the clock ticking in his veins, Abraham was dressed. He opted for the uniform without the bullet hole in it, but it still smelled like someone else's sweat. He hurried over to the side of the tent where four sinks stood with tiny mirrors above them. A bag of razors rested under the sink. There was no shaving cream in sight.

He snatched a razor, ran a trickle of brown water, and started swiping the stubble off his cheeks and chin. He got two swipes in before the mass of recruits bowled into him. It was chaos. Dozens of guys trying to use only four mirrors. Abraham ran a hand over his face, decided he was close enough, and hustled out of the tent.

The sky was all inky blackness now. A spotlight from somewhere deeper within the camp provided just enough light to see a few meters in any direction.

Larry rushed out right before Abraham, looking presentable enough. Another couple of seconds passed in terse silence. More and more people rushed out of the tent. Abraham held his breath, hoping against hope his team could get this right on the first try, if only to spare them all more push-ups and flutter kicks.

"Time's up!" Hinton barked. "Everybody out, out, out! What the *shit* is taking y'all so damn long? You braiding each other's hair in there or what?"

The stragglers filed out, looking miserable. One man, tall and lanky, only had one boot on, the laces dangling like frayed wires. The other, a heavy-framed girl with brown hair, stumbled out in just her brown undershirt and pants, bare feet slapping against the gravel. Both recruits wore faces like they'd just wet themselves in front of a crowd. Abraham let out a breath, disappointment creating phantom pains in his muscles. He knew what was coming next.

Sergeant Hinton stalked up and down the line of recruits, his head bobbing in and out of the ranks, eyes critically examining faces and uniforms. He shouted and yelled, raised his hands threateningly, but never once did he strike a recruit. Abraham was relieved that, even in a branch of the military as hardcore as the Marines, there were no true physical reprimands.

"Recruit Poplenko! What the hell is this?" Hinton stroked Larry's face with the back of his fingers, the motion emitting loud scraping sounds.

"That's my face, Sergeant!" Larry's body was tense, neck muscles twitching. Abraham's heart raced for his buddy being thrust into the center of attention.

"Naw…" the instructor mocked his tone, "…that couldn't be. The Marine Corps is shocked as hell to find out a recruit has arrived at our prestigious Camp Butler *with a face*!" His expression darkened. "That's pube fuzz clinging to your cheeks, Recruit. Everybody back inside, and I want all hairs off your faces, or we'll be doing this shit all night. You have sixty seconds, now go."

The recruits hurried back into the tent, fixing up their uniforms. Larry hurried over to the sink, razor in hand. Abraham rushed over to stand guard, making sure there was mirror space available for his friend. After about thirty seconds, Abraham turned to see what was taking so long. His heart nearly fell out of his chest.

"Larry, bro, what the hell?"

"What?" Larry turned to look at Abraham, his face totally shaved. Pale, smooth skin from chin to forehead.

Abraham scoffed. "Never mind."

They rushed back out for inspection with a solid four seconds to spare on Hinton's countdown. The animated sergeant began his inspection again, and when he stood in front of Larry, he started up his twitchy, jerking, overreacting behavior, jabbing a finger a centimeter from Larry's face. "Poplenko, what the fuck is this?"

"I shaved my face, Sergeant."

The sergeant shook his head. "Who the hell told you to shave your fucking *eyebrows*? You defaced government property. That's vandalism, Recruit Poplenko. *Please* tell me no one else was stupid enough to do this?"

The recruits stood silent, but they all turned their eyes toward Larry. Abraham felt the mortification reeking off him. He could feel it on his own shoulders, too. Larry had always been such a cool guy in school. Abraham didn't understand how the popular kid could make such a simple but huge mistake.

The moment came and went. Hinton's ire faded, Larry's blush returned to normal, and the torturous hell that was Marine Corps basic training continued without a hitch.

After several rounds of push-ups and flutter kicks, the gravel on the ground was starting to leave impressions on Abraham's hands and ass, he could just feel it. Worse was the growling that had started in his stomach. He heard more gurgling stomachs from the recruits next to him, too. They had to be feeling the same hunger pangs. He barely managed to think of his last meal, the hot dogs and chips Larry's grandparents had bought for him on Veranda less than 24 hours ago. More than a week ago, it felt like.

He caught a glance at Larry's watch.

I haven't eaten a single meal on Juno yet and I've been here for twelve hours.

The drilling continued. The push-ups and flutter kicks, too.

Abraham lost track of time. It felt like a couple of hours, but it could have just been thirty minutes later, he wasn't sure. The number of times he ran back into that tent, battling for mirror space to shave his face again, elbows knocking into ribs, kids falling and getting stepped on, even Abraham himself at one point…it was insanity of the highest order.

Abraham's muscles had failed him long ago. His push-ups were really just spurts of holding himself off the ground, his flutter kicks wagging his feet on his ankles, knees bent and full of spasms. Sometimes he would risk a pause to look around, usually when he'd fallen face first onto the gravel. He'd take his time wiping the debris off his face, eyes roaming the sea of recruits around him.

The platoon was like a vehicle that had run out of gas and coasted its last kilometer.

Larry was struggling to stretch his long legs out for flutter kicks. He could barely keep them off the ground. There was no way he was going to knock out any more reps the state he was in. Digger huffed and puffed, spit flying from his lips. His lack of form made him look like a lame dolphin. Amory and Piebold were taking a break, gasping for air and holding their sides. They were both out of shape, Abraham thought. One was too fat, the other too skinny. He wasn't sure which was a worse state to be in for boot camp.

Sergeant Hinton seemed to catch on that the repetitions had come to a standstill. He kicked some gravel off to the side and spat.

"Y'all had enough, then?" His voice was a whisper, barely audible over the sounds of an exhausted platoon. "You have not managed to pass inspection. Now, I'm going to cut you a break and give you until tomorrow. Maybe a good night's sleep will motivate you sacks of shit. Ravens, dismissed!"

Abraham turned to limp his way back to the tent. His knee was on fire. His back cramped. He had a severe urge to piss that stung all the way from his bladder to his diaphragm. Several other recruits around him looked in similar condition, either limping or supporting each other with arms slung on shoulders, bemoaning their pain. Abraham found Larry and they limped side by side toward the tent flap.

Sergeant Hinton's voice struck like thunder. "Zeeben! Poplenko! Tachek! Piebold! The hour is nigh. Latrine duty begins in five minutes."

Dammit.

He saw the same sentiment on the other guys' faces. They were too tired to fight with each other, or even look on each other with disapproval. Now they were going to have to spend the next hour scrubbing shit-stained floors because they had fought earlier.

Amory's innocent voice sang from inside the tent. "*Bo-ooooys.* Don't forget your cleaning supplies!"

A bucket bounced out of the open tent flap. Toothbrushes still in the package crinkled and spilled out of the bucket as it rolled. It came to a stop against Digger's knee. He looked down at the dozens of toothbrushes, followed the trail up toward the tent, then glanced back at the bucket. Abraham could see the wires in his brain tangling up.

Sergeant Hinton shouted. They moved.

Digger scooped the toothbrushes back into the bucket, then carried it to the latrine area. It was about the size of the gymnasium in Abraham's school on Veranda, with one exception; it was outdoors. No illumination aside from a few weak rays of spotlight managing to cast a gray pall over the steps. An overhang of wood planks designed to stop the sunlight from beating in on the occupants, but other than that, the air was free and clear around the structure. Abraham got a whiff of that air, decided to himself it was free, but not clear of the worst stench he'd smelled in recent memory.

Digger dropped the bucket against the cement floor, spilling toothbrushes everywhere. He walked over to a long bench and sat down on it, letting out an exasperated sigh. He made no motion to begin cleaning.

Abraham couldn't believe it. He tapped Larry on the shoulder and nodded his head in Digger's direction. Larry fumed, crossing his arms and jutting his chin out with as much attitude as he could muster. Without eyebrows, he looked sort of like an Aveo, or something else not human. "Yo, Digger, what the hell, man?"

Digger's cheeks spread in a wide grin. "I'm on break, Poplenko. Get started, I'll catch up."

Abraham stepped closer to Digger, fists clenched by his side. "Digger, we've all had enough of your shit. Your attitude got us into this in the first place. Get up off your ass and help."

Digger chuckled, ran a hand through his hair and said in a mocking voice that was supposed to be Abraham, "I don't like your attitude, Digger. You beat my ass all the time, but I think I've got big balls because I've been at basic for a few hours."

He turned his stare to Abraham. "Piss off," he said, laying his head on his elbow and closing his eyes.

The only sound was Piebold scrubbing a particularly large dark stain off the wooden floorboards. He either didn't hear the exchange thanks to his vigorous scrubbing, or he was just too tired to care. Abraham wondered momentarily if there wasn't more to the lumbering giant after all. He dropped the thought and grabbed a few toothbrushes.

He unpacked one, then chucked it at Digger.

It bounced off the toilet seat next to Digger's head. He didn't move.

An idea formed in Abraham's mind as he and the others scrubbed and spit and scrubbed some more. His back was aching, his joints creaking as he crawled on hands and knees, cleaning the shit and grime stains from the floors, benches, and toilet seats. The idea was likely to get them into more trouble, but he thought it was a risk worth taking.

107

When Abraham whispered his plan to Larry, they both chuckled under their breath. Piebold acted like he hadn't heard them, but Abraham could tell the big man was feeling left out. It didn't make sense, but then, nothing had made sense since the moment Abraham walked away from his family to start this crazy journey. He still couldn't believe he'd begun this whole thing only twenty-four hours ago.

Piebold listened to the plan eagerly, stifling laughter. Even though the plan was against his own buddy, he whispered enthusiastically, "He deserves it."

The plan in motion, Abraham moved to where Digger was resting his head and started scrubbing the toilet seat. Digger grumbled something but didn't seem too concerned. Abraham lifted the seat, exposing a hole and unsealing a rank odor that blasted up out of the latrine in a sick wave. It was nauseating. It made Abraham's eyes water.

It made Digger lift his head up and open his eyes.

Piebold made his move. He was twice Digger's height, and easily twice his weight. Digger was a tough bastard, but even he could do nothing but scream as his buddy shoved him into the hole headfirst. His muffled cries were music to everyone's ears.

They understood the meaning of side-splitting laughter as they watched one of their own swinging his legs helplessly in the air, struggling to escape.

Abraham and Larry bumped fists. Piebold added his fist to the gesture. The three shared another round of groaning, painful, rolling laughter.

For once, Digger got what he deserved.

CHAPTER 16

Raven Platoon passed inspection in the morning for their first time. Abraham had been ambivalent about his meeting with Ensign Seneca; on the one hand, he wanted to be in her presence as much as possible because she was interesting, but on the other hand, he feared she may have somehow discovered he wasn't really eighteen. The knot in his gut eased as the hours went by and he didn't see her. None of the drill instructors mentioned her, and no one came to order him to report to her.

Was that just a scare tactic, or what?

He forgot about it after the first day.

The Ravens spent the first week marching to classrooms, where they were taught how to properly address officers and higher-ranking enlisted members. Customs and courtesies, the military called it. They had to learn the ranks and responsibilities of the Navy and the Marines, as well as Earth military history. It was a struggle to stay awake in these classes, but Abraham found frequent sips from his canteen helped keep his eyelids from drifting and his stomach from growling.

If they weren't in a classroom or at their tent being taught how to properly roll, fold, and store their uniform items in their bunks, they were in a medical office, going over medical history and being poked and prodded for blood samples and an endless series of immunizations. Abraham wasn't sure which he hated more, but he was starting to feel like he was in a laboratory more than in the military.

They had one day off a week, but still had to maintain their quarters and stay in line with military customs and courtesies, which was easy enough because Abraham slept a solid twelve hours. He barely had time to get dinner at the chow hall before it was time to get back and prepare for the next week of training.

The beginning of the second week, Abraham started to become familiar with Camp Butler. He was never comfortable, always holding on to a certain level of paranoia and bracing for the next tirade from a drill instructor, but he began to understand what was expected of him.

The morning came early, as it always did. They were jostled awake by Corporal Johnson screaming and kicking bunks, letting them know they had five minutes to be shaved, dressed, and in formation.

This is one hell of an alarm clock.

After forming up within their allotted time, they made a brief fifteen-minute stop at the chow hall.

It was the single largest building in Camp Butler, a squat brick and mortar construction that took up a sizeable portion of the center of the base. After filing in, stuffing a few mouthfuls of powdered eggs and a bite or two of flaccid French toast (Larry affirmed, in his expert opinion, that they were microwaved rather than cooked on a griddle), they were rushed outside to stand in formation. Locked constantly in the position of attention, the urges to yawn and scratch became increasingly difficult to ignore.

The sky was a lilac purple, like an overcast sunrise. Spaced like heavenly freckles, pale orange spots shone through the inkspill cloud-cover. Juno's skyline was the most inviting thing about it. Camp Butler itself wasn't much to look at, which solidified the validity of first impressions in Abraham's mind. He glanced with just his eyes – careful not to move while at attention – and searched the horizon for any signs of civilization. Even Chevalier, the city of splendor that had greeted them when they landed, was completely obscured by the mountains.

Corporal Johnson made sure to remind them that this boot camp was different from any other boot camp in history. This was a competitive boot camp. Ravens versus Eagles. The Ravens were already behind. The Eagles had passed their inspection after only the third try last night, earning themselves an extra hour of sleep. The Eagles were the favorites to win the Distinguished Platoon award, and to get first pick of duty assignments.

Abraham scoffed when he heard this. He wasn't here to win awards. He was here to become a Marine. Why should he care what the other recruits were doing?

Digger piped up next to him, his voice a muted whisper, "Eagles ain't shit."

Amory said in her soft voice, "We'll kick their asses."

Larry chuckled. "You're too busy kissing Digger's ass, small fry."

Amory raised her eyebrows. Abraham thought it was a weird response, but he had decided to leave the girl alone and hope her attention would divert toward another recruit.

Sergeant Hinton arrived, strutting up and down the line, eyeing the recruits, inspecting their uniforms, staring them in the eyes. He was checking their resolve after yesterday's antics, Abraham thought. His subgroup hushed up as the man lumbered by, evil eye bulging as he scanned for infractions. He passed by after a tense few moments, finding nothing to get pissed off about. Then he froze mid-step.

The drill instructor's demeanor softened just a bit. When he spoke, his voice was a little hoarse, but still carried an edge.

"Last week was the easy stuff. This is where shit starts getting real. To be a marine is to know that tomorrow is *not* guaranteed. Never forget these words, for they are wisdom personified. Words by which marines live and die. Here at Camp Butler, you will experience some of the toughest shit you've ever endured. It is not my intention to break you for the sake of breaking you. I have watched too many marines get killed by their own stupidity, their own lack of training and discipline, to let any of you suffer that same fate. That said, loss is the catalyst for growth. Your bodies are in physical pain right now because you are bags of shit being beaten into plates of iron. Physical pain is superficial. Wounds you acquire in training will heal. The wounds of war..." the big man ran a finger across the purple scar on his throat, "sometimes those don't heal. That's why it is incumbent upon each and every one of you to look out for the marine beside you. When it's you against the enemy, all you have is your weapon and the man or woman standing next to you."

Sergeant Hinton leaned in on bended knee, about to share a great secret. "The best tactical advice I can give you is to face threats head on. Kill the enemy before he kills you."

Abraham did his best to suppress a shiver. The totality of what his instructor was saying cut through his gut, burrowed right to his core. He hadn't so much as killed a chicken on a farm. Abraham couldn't help feeling an innate responsibility to care for beings weaker than himself. He imagined it was a trait inherited from his mother. That, or constantly having to look out for David – bully-magnet that he was – might have been conditioning enough.

Still, Abraham knew he would kill when it came down to it. It was a fool who joined the military expecting to never have to kill. There were so many societies outside the influence of the Nine Nations floating around space that 'enemy contact' was truly unavoidable. It just made sense.

Sergeant Hinton snapped to attention. "Recruits! The mission for today is weapons familiarization and base sanitation. Form it up!"

Piebold laughed. "That's what I'm talking about." A blank look crossed his face and he turned to Digger. "Is sanitation like latrine duty again?"

Digger scoffed. "It's about time we got to something useful. I'm sick of all this lecturing and cleaning bullshit."

Abraham chuckled, remembering Digger stuffed halfway down a toilet. "Guess you've put up with enough shit for a while, huh?"

Digger gritted his teeth but didn't press the issue.

Bodies slammed into bodies around Abraham. The bumping and shifting were starting to become second nature. He squeezed his shoulders in, sifting his way through the sea of recruits to take a place next to Larry. Amory wriggled her little body between them. Goosebumps rippled across Abraham's arms when her tiny hand brushed against his. He almost whispered a derogatory comment to her, but the look she flashed him was just as threatening as the illegal dagger she carried in her belt.

Abraham settled for cursing her out in his head.

"Recruits. Double time!" Sergeant Hinton called.

The run began. He tried to look up at the sky, to the beautiful vista of oranges and purples that were so new to him, but sweat dangled from his eyebrows. A gust of wind shook the droplets free, like rain from leaves on a tree in a hurricane, stinging his eyes.

The smell of Camp Butler was a mixture of burning grease from the chow hall area commingled with the locker room smell of many sweaty bodies confined into a tight space. Abraham had grown up farming, literally spreading shit across dirt, and even he felt the odors here were particularly ripe.

I suppose there are advantages to growing up simple. Namely, that I'm used to being uncomfortable.

Boots pounded. Gravel crunched. The recruits of the combined Raven and Eagle platoons hustled through the desolate space that was their home base. Eyes were puffy, foreheads shiny with sweat, and the heat of the early morning was already sweltering. The fatigue was palpable, the sense of adventure muted, but a sense of resolve teemed on the air. Abraham could feel it like a collective consciousness, hear it in the heavy breathing of the recruits around him. Probably not everyone here was going to become a marine, but he could tell they were a tougher cut of humanity than the average person. The thought of an office worker trying to complete even this jog made Abraham smirk.

Obadiah had always told him there were two paths in life. One, the college route, where you did well in school, earned a degree and moved on to a high-paying job. Two, the working route, where you learned a trade skill and worked it until you mastered it, then continued to work it until you died. Abraham hadn't been interested in either, even as Obadiah would push him to be more and more available on the farm. David always got the encouragement for the college route, mostly because he had an uncanny ability to retain and regurgitate information. Abraham had never seen David read the same book twice, not even textbooks. David was good like that, good with school and facts and numbers.

"Comes with the territory of autism." Obadiah's voice in his head.

We never confirmed that. We could be babying him for no reason.

It was a weird thing, having a conversation with someone who wasn't there. His brain just formulated words for Obadiah and even managed to sound like him. Abraham made a mental note to ask Larry if this was normal.

The jog took them further into the desert wasteland of Juno, but still within the wall that surrounded the base. Ten minutes later, the recruits were standing outside an isolated building. It was covered with cold-rolled steel wall panels, held together by bolt heads as big as Abraham's fist, and a single, heavy blast door on the front. It looked like it could shrug off a direct hit from a nuke. Abraham admired the building's structure, seeing it as the only aesthetic in this deserted no man's land.

It took him a moment to recognize it as the source of the glint he'd seen on his initial approach to Camp Butler.

Sergeant Hinton motioned his hands, slapping the air a few times. Corporals Johnson and Nichols took positions at the head of the two platoons. Abraham was glad to see Johnson was still the corporal for Raven Platoon. Aside from his ear-splitting wake-up calls, something about the man's composed demeanor gave Abraham a sense of stability to cling to, a sort of balanced counterpoint to Hinton's constant hijinks.

Ensign Seneca and Ensign Lechero exited the reinforced structure and stood beside Sergeant Hinton. It was hard not to be distracted by the dizzying cascade of shapes on their C-skins. They both had shiny silver rifles slung over their backs, gleaming pistols on their hips, and seemed comfortable carrying them. Ensign Lechero's face was smug as he looked favorably upon his Eagles' platoon. It shifted into a darkened glare when his eyes roamed toward the Ravens' side of the formation. Abraham felt the man was too petty to be an officer. Of course, he didn't know much about the military aside from what he could remember from last week's lectures, but it was just a gut feeling he couldn't let go of. Lechero, in Abraham's mind, was an asshole.

He unslung his rifle and hefted it in the air. He moved it about, showing all the angles of it to the recruits. After a moment, he shouldered the stock, pulled back a lever and fired into the ground at his feet. A high-pitched hiss tore the air as blue light like a tiny lightning strike bit into the ground, sending miniscule pieces of red-glowing gravel skittering.

"I'm sure I've got your attention now, recruits. This is the backbone of the Marines offensive arsenal. This is your basic CLR. This weapon has served humanity in conflicts across space for over a thousand years. The design has changed since its inception, but the core principles remain the same. You will each be given a CLR during your stay here at Camp Butler. You will, each and every one of you, be expected to clean, maintain, and secure your weapon at all times."

Ensign Seneca kicked a glowing rock off her boot. Her face betrayed no emotion, not even the slightest hint of annoyance at her counterpart's rash demonstration. Abraham was equal parts confused and impressed with his commanding officer. Was she in possession of a great deal of self-control, or was she a one-track mind, just focused on the moment so that she didn't allow herself to be distracted by anything else? He wasn't sure why, but he felt like she was as annoyed with Lechero as he was; she was just better at hiding it.

Maybe that's officer training, Abraham thought.

Ensign Seneca stood up straight and tucked her chin. She took a long, tense moment to look at each recruit, making eye contact for a solid second before moving to the next. After what felt like an eternity, she spoke in her soft but edgy voice.

"You may or may not know anything about firearms. Rest assured, recruits, that you will become experts by the time your stay at Camp Butler is over. It is our job as instructors to convert you from civilians to the finest fighters in humanity's arsenal. You may not know this, but history shows that wars are fought – and won – by the youth. Do not think yourselves too young, too weak, too fragile to fight. You are here for a reason, and that reason is not to simply collect a paycheck and travel to the worst environs in space. You are here to protect and defend humanity and its interests across the cosmos."

Ensign Seneca pinched her lips for a moment.

Is that emotion she's holding back? Who is this girl?

"War is hell. It costs too much. But this is the price we must pay to spare the many from the imperialistic aims of our enemies. Take this training, and all of the training you receive here, as literal and complete as you can. You never know when even the smallest, most esoteric fact you learn here can be the difference between you coming back to your family or dying on an austere planet far from home."

Abraham stood a bit taller upon hearing these words. He wasn't a typical kid – at least he didn't feel like he was – but he hadn't really understood much about politics or intergalactic news. Nothing beyond the Riskar War. The snippets he could really remember were anecdotes and facts thrown out by David as he scrolled through stories on his Portal. Stories Abraham found it difficult to care about when he was slugging away at the farm work. Part of him wished he had paid more attention. A base knowledge of the universe, alien cultures, and the climate of humanity's intergalactic relations would have given him some context, here.

Just a week ago he had his first brush with a political protest in downtown Veranda, with the college kids handing out flyers about Admiral Latreaux. Abraham still didn't understand how an entire planet could be missing; he was just glad to have escaped El Capitan and the Veranda Militia. As far as he was concerned, the protest was some college bullshit that didn't concern a Marine-to-be like himself.

Lechero barked, "Fall into the armory and grab yourselves a CLR, recruits. One per customer, then fall in at the back of the house. We'll jump right into target practice."

Abraham's stomach grumbled. As he followed the other recruits into the armory, he wondered when the next chow hall stop was going to be. Somehow, he figured the base sanitation was going to be in lieu of his lunch, and he'd have to go half a day without a meal. He and his cramping stomach just knew it was going to work out that way.

The inside of the armory smelled greasy but clean, the scent of unburned oil. It was the most beautiful thing Abraham had ever seen. Camp Butler didn't have much to offer in terms of aesthetics, but this was a true marvel to behold. Ceiling-mounted fluorescent lights coated the space in a soft glow.

Blue and silver walls were inlaid with glowing lines of data. Clear glass panes rose from shiny white desks, displaying images of various firearms. Some of the images shifted into an exploded view where the weapons slid apart into pieces, showcasing the exact breakdown of their parts. The CLR seemed to be extremely complicated, Abraham noted as he passed one of the screens; it was listed as having fifty-four total parts. Other than the rifle, clip, and trigger, Abraham didn't know anything about guns. He wanted to know about guns, wanted to be confident around them, knew he would have to be if he was going to be a Marine, but the learning curve seemed steep from this first glance.

The recruits marched through the ornate room, boots scuffing and squeaking on the floor. Two doorways at the end of the room with an exit sign of orange glowing letters awaited them. Just off to the side of each door was a floor-to-ceiling rack of CLRs. They gleamed in the soft, fancy armory lighting.

No wonder our camp looks like shit. They use all their funding on the armory.

Two boys were ahead of him, small but wiry muscles on their frame. They each brandished a rifle, laughing to each other. They were the boys that knew how to stand at attention on the tarmac when they first arrived on Juno. Their accents were thick and tight, the kind that reminded Abraham of movies about exuberant islanders getting into silly situations that always made him laugh. Aside from one being a bit taller than the other, they looked like twins. Abraham was about to shove them aside so he could grab his own CLR when one of them tapped the barrel of his weapon against Abraham's chest. "Halt, riskar scum, 'fore I blow ya ballsacks off ya back!" He laughed.

The other boy slapped him on the back of the head. He blinked but didn't flinch. "That's they lungs on the back, Tar! Don't point that ting at nobody. Ya gonna get us kicked out!"

Tar lowered the rifle, but his smile widened in response to the slap. "Ya better keep ya hands to ya'self, Juke. Momma's Golden Rule, bubby."

Juke grabbed Tar's shoulders and spun him on his heels, then gave a shove that propelled him out the door. He muttered a slurry "Sorry 'bout dat, man" to Abraham and followed his twin outside. Abraham couldn't stifle a feel-good laugh at them.

The rest of the recruits piled up at the racks, claiming dozens of CLRs until there were but a dozen left. All high, high up on the racks.

Abraham stretched himself, painfully, and managed to unseat a rifle from its perch. The damn thing was heavy, much heavier than it looked. He paused for a moment just to look down at the weapon in his own hands, feeling a rush speed through his veins. Something about holding this weapon felt right, like he was born to –

– have it snatched right out of his hands.

He was about to pounce on the thief, fists flying, when Amory shoved her face right up against his. The thought of her dagger flashed through his mind, and he backed down. Her eyes were a deep brown, almost black, and this close he saw her olive skin was flawless. She had to be younger than him.

"Thanks for the rifle, Zeeben. Don't make a big deal about it, and neither will I."

"Sure, whatever."

She gave a self-satisfied huff, pushed her lips out with some attitude, and walked away with the CLR slung casually over her shoulder. With all the theatrics, she could have just conned her boyfriend into buying her a new purse.

Abraham stretched, trying to reach one of the few remaining rifles. He almost let himself fall into a tirade of thought about why everything in basic training had to be so difficult, but the sudden quiet made him realize he was the last one in line.

He jumped, swiped the rifle off the top rack and hustled outside.

The sky was a swirling mix of shades of orange. Two yellow orbs peeked through the purple cloud cover. The sand pit that must have been the firing range was just a few meters ahead. The gravel crunch under his boots became soft patters on sand.

I didn't know Juno was in a binary star system.

Sergeant Hinton was speaking with the officers, and Abraham breathed a sigh of relief. He shouldered his way into the formation without his tardiness being detected, glad to avoid another session of push-ups or whatever new tortures his instructor always came up with at a moment's notice.

The officers and instructors continued to whisper to each other.

That's unusual. What are they talking about?

Abraham and the other recruits began breaking protocol by glancing around at each other, expressions quizzical. The air had suddenly taken on a harsh scent, as if it were mere seconds from exploding with a rainstorm. It was the kind of feeling that Abraham got right before a sweltering migraine showed up to ruin his day. Come to think of it, he was surprised he had yet to experience a migraine at basic. *Guess I haven't had time for one*, he thought with an inward smile.

Sergeant Hinton walked, slowly, to stand at the front of the formation. He didn't seem to mind that the recruits were moving when they weren't supposed to. Something was going on. Abraham didn't know what it was, but he hoped it was going to cut their day short. He desperately needed more sleep. Some food. Maybe even a private shower. His burning muscles ached at the thought.

Hinton's face looked broken.

It reminded Abraham of Mr. Croix, the day the news about Myles Lannam had dropped. The Marine collected himself quickly, turning his gaze intently on each of the recruits.

"This isn't easy to say, men and women of the Eagles and Ravens. The Navy has decided you need to be informed right away, so that's what this is – a briefing. There's been an incident –"

Larry raised his hand.

"This isn't a classroom, Poplenko. There are no questions until I give you per–"

Larry couldn't contain himself. He was shaking so hard sweat droplets were flying off him. His face looked strange with no eyebrows. His CLR clattered against his utility belt as he asked, "Sir, are we going to war? Has there been an invasion?"

Ensign Seneca stepped forward, her expression harsh. Much harsher than Hinton's had ever been. It was scary, like a dark cloud had descended with the intent to shade her face a proper hue of pissed off. It was made to sharpen the effrontery she was about to unleash, Abraham thought.

She took a small breath and shook her head.

"If you are from the Adirondi Sector, we will need to speak with you after this class. Immediately. There has been an intergalactic incident in the region."

"Another collision?" Piebold asked.

Ice formed in Abraham's gut.

Adirondi was the sector of the outer rim he knew best because he had just left there. It was the pocket of space that held Veranda and a handful of other sparsely populated settlements. Up until his decision to leave, it had been the place he called home.

"Ma'am," Abraham spoke out of turn, "what kind of incident are you talking about? Is everything okay back...there?"

Ensign Seneca took a few steps toward him. Her eyes seemed as though they carried the weight of many decades, although he suspected she was only a year older than him. She presented herself with such quiet dignity it was almost haunting. Her resting face was tough, but as she talked it softened in a pleasant way.

She leaned in toward Abraham, her face centimeters from his.

"There has been an incident that we cannot talk about in express detail. This incident..." She sighed. "This incident has the potential to pull humanity deeper into enemy space. At the moment there has been no word from NAVCOM on whom exactly perpetrated this incident, but there will be. And the moment there is, we need to be ready to prove ourselves."

Beside Abraham, Digger chuckled. "So, does this mean we're marines now? You fast-tracking us to the front lines?"

Lechero marched up, one hand forming a knife shape and stabbing at Digger's face.

"You will address officers with respect, Recruit! What backwater planet are you from where they teach you your manners in a barn? And the answer to your question is hell no. As far as the Marine Corps is concerned, you don't know your ass from your elbow until I say so."

Ensign Seneca turned to Ensign Lechero with a dark expression but said nothing.

Digger acknowledged the officer with a weak affirmative, perhaps feeling a bit sheepish about his cheeky response. His normally stony countenance had shifted over the last week. For one, his beard was shaved off, which made his skin the smoothest marble, but his features were still very harsh, like a statue that had been chiseled with hard angles, no roundness to the texturing. Abraham thought he looked like a Neanderthal freak.

He wisely kept this thought to himself.

118

Ensign Seneca stepped back to her former position and hefted her CLR.

The oil-spill sunlight shimmered over the body of the weapon. It was a thing of beauty. A thing of death. Most of all, it was the one thing that could ensure survival on the battlefield. The reality of the universe had started to become a bit clearer to Abraham since arriving at boot camp. These civilian kids were being transformed into a cohesive unit of adult fighters.

The truth was that the universe was a big place with lots of shadows, and what lurked within the shadows was hidden for a reason. The temptation to open Pandora's box was not so easily avoided. Nothing would ever stop mankind from piercing the veil of the unknown.

That's what marines do...where others shy away from the endless dark, we rush into it.

Abraham stewed on these thoughts until the officers led them to the range.

The shooting range was pretty much how he had seen it in movies. The lanes were tall and boxed in, the range itself a long expanse of sand and gravel. A few meters in, several targets swaying in the breeze were affixed to floating squares with glowing red corners. Abraham hustled into an open lane where he found three triangular clips of ammunition on a narrow wooden table. One side was long, the other two smaller and identical in size. He looked at the clips, then at his gun in confusion. He had no idea where to slide the clip.

"It's a *sink*, not a clip," Lechero corrected him, nose touching Abraham's cheek.

Abraham had to bite down a sarcastic retort at the dopey looking man. David, his brother, had said things that made him feel far dumber than this guy ever knew.

I need to stop thinking out loud.

Abraham hefted a clip – *sink* he corrected himself – and slid the cartridge forward along the slot in the left side of the upper receiver. It locked into place with a click. He couldn't help but wince; it was much louder than he expected. He was used to the sounds of the tobacco farm, of a sparsely populated planet where he lived on the opposite side of civilization. For a brief moment, the thundering of the rocket ship that brought him to Juno came to mind, steamrolling into the shouts and bellows of angry drill instructors, finished by the angry buzzing of hair clippers.

The click of a new sink locking into his weapon brought him back.

Abraham stared down at his weapon in amazement. The damn thing weighed a ton with a sink on each side of the rifle. It took effort to hold it upright with two hands. Abraham felt the muscles in his arms bulging but not straining. He kept his face smooth as ice. It was a new skill he was learning, always shielding his emotions. He wasn't going to give Digger and the others any sign of weakness. Especially not Lechero.

"And there, kids, is why you don't try to be a Billy Badass."

He slapped the release, dropping one sink – right onto Abraham's foot – and prattled on in his holier-than-thou tone. "You can affix up to four heat sinks on each CLR. These sinks do not contain bullets. These weapons do not shoot bullets unless you install a magazine into the lower receiver. CLR is short for Compact Laser Rifle. You get me, shitheads?"

"Yes, Ensign Lechero!" The united response erupted from both platoons.

"That's what I want to hear. Sounds like y'all put some ass into that response. I love that. We are supposed to be learning the innards of these bad boys. Figuring the disassembly and reassembly of them prior to learning to shoot. However, I think seeing and feeling these things in action will give you a clearer understanding of how they work. For now, you just need to know that each sink can diffuse heat for one hundred shots. Kinetic rounds are ten mil, with a depleted-uranium alloy tip."

Lechero unslung his CLR from his shoulder. He held the barrel down and away from his feet, off to the side. He slowly spun a dial on the side of the weapon, producing a shrill whine.

"That sound, boys and girls, is the laser intensity. You can take it from standard all the way up to a solid beam for cutting through an airlock, or for armor penetration." The whine died down as he spun the dial back. "Drawback is your sinks can only handle about ten trigger pulls at max intensity."

Lechero grabbed the front of his rifle, almost at the end of the barrel, and yanked.

The barrel telescoped out to almost a full meter from the stock to the end of the barrel. The rifle whined just like when he had spun the intensity dial. He shouldered the weapon, looked through the scope, and pulled the trigger.

A blue streak of light and heat screamed overhead.

Abraham almost fell to his knees. The lancing light was as beautiful as it was deadly. Lechero's face lit up from the muzzle flash. Sunbursts caught in his eyes. He seemed, in a brief span of time, like a crazed madman. Someone who was envisioning shooting into a crowd of innocent people rather than a sky full of innocent clouds.

"The CLR allows for three primary modes of fire," he continued, "rifle, marksman, and scattershot."

Yanking the barrel again, Lechero collapsed the weapon to almost a solid rectangle. He fired it from the hip, spraying ten laser blasts with one shot. They arced out in a triangular pattern from the barrel.

Smoke billowed from the bottom of the CLR. The sink now had twenty short red lines across it, glowing with heat. Lechero slapped a lever on the side of the rifle, shouting, "Heat sink release!" The sink hit the dirt at his feet and sizzled. Lechero moved faster than lightning; almost as soon as the expended sink hit the ground, he slid a fresh one across the receiver and locked it into place with the heel of his hand. He grabbed the lever at the top, yanked it back and shouted, "Charging handle!"

Lechero's mustache twitched as he lectured them on the absolute importance of pulling the T-handle with each new sink. Apparently, the heat sinks on the cartridges weren't open until you charged the handle…something about them exploding if you pulled the trigger before pulling the T-handle…Abraham's growling stomach and heavy eyelids started to take precedence over the officer's lecture.

A moment later, Ensign Lechero fired off another hundred rounds, this time at a boulder in the distance. It took about fifteen seconds. The brown and gray surface remained immobile against the assault, but it began to take on an orange glow as the blasts of heat slammed into it.

Ensign Seneca stepped forward. She looked directly at Abraham.

At least, he felt like she was looking at him. He wasn't sure why he felt that feeling – that creepy, eerie sense like someone was looking right through him, but he couldn't deny his instincts.

Ensign Seneca hated his guts. He could tell.

But then, why would she have pushed for him to be in her platoon if she hated him? Was it a woman thing? She wanted to keep a close watch on him because she expected him to screw up? Abraham knew grown men always grumbled about women, but he wasn't sure if this was a thing like that or something more serious.

His mind continued to race as Ensign Lechero's weapon clicked empty. Thoughts continued to steal away his attention as the smoking heat sink fell to the ground and the officer slung his rifle across his back, making a grandiose pose in front of the platoons.

"Raven Platoon, take your positions on my side of the range," Seneca called out.

Lechero grinned like a madman, baring his canine teeth.

He said, "Eagles, form it up on my side. Prepare for your first rounds of target practice."

Abraham was slightly chagrined about the whole proceeding. He expected military life, especially basic training, to be uncomfortable and demanding. He hadn't expected every little aspect of his life to be a competition. The biggest weapon Abraham had ever wielded was a rake, the closest thing to a gun he'd ever touched was a slingshot. He didn't think he'd fare too well this first go at the range. He could already feel the insults being hurled at him from the other members of his platoon.

Ensign Seneca's voice took on a unique quality. One Abraham hadn't heard from her thus far. It was the voice of command.

"Ravens. Positions!"

CHAPTER 17

Abraham went through the exercises with Corporal Johnson, trying not to think about the incident that could possibly be another disaster. For all he knew, the Sackbacks could have found a way to destroy entire planets, and his second homeworld was ash and asteroids. As remote as the possibility was, he had to bite his lip to keep his mind off it.

Aiming, holding his breath, squeezing – not pulling – the trigger, dropping the sink, sliding and locking the sink, charging the T handle...it couldn't have been more than an hour of his life, but Abraham was already running through the drill without thinking, mumbling the order of things as he did so. Whatever the CLR was made of, it was heavy enough to make his shoulders and arms feel like overstretched rubber bands.

He was pretty good at remembering the sequence, but his shots always seemed to go wide, and he wasn't sure why. He sighted in on several targets, periodically switching to closer ones, but he missed far more than he hit. He ground his teeth in frustration, body twitching with every trigger pull. If this had been a video game back at Larry's house, he'd have already thrown the controller against the wall until it shattered.

"You're not exhaling slow enough."

A full two meters behind him, her voice caressed the back of his neck. Her blonde and brown braids framed the sides of her head, reminiscent of a crown.

Abraham said, "Ensign Seneca, I've never shot a gun before. A rifle, I mean. I understand the concepts, but I'm just not sure why –"

She stepped up beside him, nocking her own rifle into her shoulder. The blue hue of the scope lit her right eye as she breathed, her finger flitting over the trigger. Fire emitted from the barrel. Abraham watched her shot slam dead center on a target three times further than the one he had been aiming at.

"It's your breathing for one, and your trigger pull, for two. Put your hand on my back."

Abraham looked at her dubiously.

"That's an order, Recruit. Place the palm of your hand between my shoulder blades."

"Yes, ma'am." Red-faced, Abraham hastened to comply.

He felt her sharp intake of breath, the slow fall of metered respiration...and the jolt as she fired another direct hit. Abraham was amazed. It looked so simple when she did it. So *elegant*.

"Okay, I think I get it now."

"Put your weapon in the firing position, aim down the sights. Meter your breathing. Good, now squeeze...no, not like that." She stepped up close to him, pulled his finger almost completely off the trigger. She adjusted it so just the center of it rested on the trigger. It reminded Abraham of when Larry had tried to teach him guitar for a week, the precise placement of the fingers on the strings.

"That's it," she said, stepping back. "If you pull the trigger with the tip of your finger, the barrel is pulled to the left. If you put your finger too far in, it moves to the right. Center part of your finger, full exhale, *then* gently pull. Marksmanship is about proper technique and lots of practice."

"Yes, ma'am," Abraham said, squeezing off a shot.

The target lit up with a hit on the upper right corner. It wasn't a deadeye shot, but his aim had drastically improved. He felt a surge of adrenaline. So far, this was the part of basic training he liked the best. He had a feeling if he practiced the techniques enough, he could become a very good shot.

"Better. Keep at it, Recruit."

Abraham paused to watch her walk down the line. The way the C-skin material moved over her body was interesting, but the landscape on which those shapes slid kept his eyes fixated. Her shape was athletic. Muscles toned but not bulky. Abraham had never seen a female with a body type like that in real life, and it shocked him.

She was checking the technique of other recruits, stepping in and helping them just as she had with him. He didn't know what he was really expecting her to do, or if he had thought her helping him was somehow special.

Either way, he grinned to himself, *she's got my attention.*

After pegging several targets, he was becoming more comfortable with the CLR. Abraham was happy to see Larry doing a bang-up job with his, and even Amory and Digger were pretty good shots. He felt a wave of confidence build within him.

We got this. We can take on any threats that come our way.

Ensign Lechero started shouting, signaling the end of weapons training. Everyone packed back into the armory to hang up weapons. They quickly formed it up outside the armory, where Sergeant Hinton announced their next stop.

"Recruits. Chow time!"

A collective breath of relief escaped the Ravens.

"Except for Recruits Poplenko, Zeeben, Tachek, Schuster and Piebold. Report to the officer's quarters immediately. That is all. Ravens, dismissed!"

124

Abraham's stomach folded in on itself with an audible growl. He was beyond hungry. Basic training took a lot of energy out of him. Even more than the farm life had.

Larry blew a sigh, shoulders sagging. "This is bullshit that they're not telling us what happened. Do you think everything's okay back home?"

Digger kicked at a small pile of gravel. "Who cares? It's not gonna stop me from being a Marine."

Abraham said, "I care. I want to know if my family's still alive."

Digger laughed. "Didn't you join to run away from them?"

"Doesn't mean I don't care about them."

Piebold scratched the back of his massive head, his heavy boots pounding the ground. "I haven't heard you say anything about your family here, Zeeben."

He didn't bother replying. What could he say? They were right. Abraham hadn't given much thought at all to his family. He had his own busy life going on. When did he really have time to think about his father and brother?

The thought chewed at his conscience all the way to the officer's tent.

Entering this side of the base was like entering a different world. The tents were twice the size of Raven Platoon's. Everyone on this side of the base wore a C-skin and a fake smile. Abraham saw displayed on chests ranks that he had never seen before, all of them shiny and regal. He marched into the cluster until a young man with blond hair and a gold bar on his chest waved them over. He was standing in the threshold of one tent near the end of the alley, a stone's throw from the fence bordering the base.

"You the Stony Ridge boys?" the man asked, looking down at his Portal with half-opened eyes.

"Yes, sir," Abraham said with a salute.

Gold Bar whipped a half-hearted salute in return before mumbling, "Stand at attention in the hallway until you're called."

Abraham led the way inside and did as he was told. His stomach grumbled, equal parts hunger and consternation. He stood at attention in the hallway. Ignored Larry's attempts at whispering. He stared at the same discolored stain on the wall fabric until Gold Bar's boots drew his attention.

"Recruit Zeeben. Ensign Seneca will see you now."

"Yes, sir."

Abraham did a rough salute before spinning on his heels and marching into the office. He didn't bother waiting to see if he got a salute in return. He was happy to leave the hallway even though his skin felt electric with nerves.

125

The office was impressive in size and filled with trinkets that immediately made Abraham uncomfortable.

A hairbrush on the desk rested on a dark oak pad, as it might have in a museum. Several photos moved across a wall-sized-display, showing Ensign Seneca in civilian clothes and doing normal things –curtsying in a ballroom dress; boarding down a modest hill blanketed in snow; a violin between her chin and shoulder, bow held with elegant but precise fingers, her gaze serene and focused. One thing he noticed, a bit embarrassingly, was the absence of anyone else. No boyfriends, no friends…not even a family photo. Abraham felt like he had gotten to know her by the time he took his position in front of her desk.

He popped a sharp salute. "Ensign Seneca, Recruit Zeeben reporting as ordered."

The woman was an enigma. Her crisp blue eyes studied him, roaming his uniform. She was searching for the slightest imperfection, he knew. After a moment she seemed satisfied and returned the salute.

"At ease, Recruit."

Abraham relaxed, wiping a drop of sweat from the back of his neck. He struggled not to gaze around at the incredible aeronautical decorations and knick-knacks throughout the room. Each model or toy or whatever they were fascinated him; having never seen things like this before, they emitted a vibe that was damn near magical. Miniature airplanes and spaceships floated gently through the air, orbiting the desk in the center of the room.

He was pulled out of the wonder of the moment by his commanding officer's voice. "Recruit Zeeben. You know why you're here?"

Her flippant tone got under his skin. Abraham couldn't stop the instinct to argue building inside him. He had been bullied by Digger his whole life, defended his weak older brother from bullies and put-downs for just as long. It could have been the uniform, the training he'd received in the last few days, or just the accumulation of farm life angst finally blowing through his moral safeguards. Whatever it was, he couldn't hold it back anymore.

Abraham bared his teeth and hissed. "Of course I do. Do you?"

His vitriol must have caught her by surprise. Raised eyebrows, a small but sharp intake of breath. "Careful, Zeeben. We may both be new to the Marine Corps, but that doesn't mean I don't have the authority to send your underage ass home at my sole discretion."

He stammered.

She nodded. "That's right. I'm aware that you conspired with Recruit Poplenko to enlist in the Marine Corps underage. Your presence in my office is proof positive that you are the worst sort of liar. And, to make matters worse, you're good at it. I didn't detect any hints or suspicions from you since your arrival."

A pause. An eternal moment of measuring passed between them. Abraham struggled to maintain a flat effect while searching for any sign of intent on the ensign's part. He could feel the electrical tension between them, like he was standing in a sparking gap between power lines. Her smooth face betrayed no emotions. There was no raising of a brow, not even a twitch at the corner of her lip, just…nothing.

Abraham couldn't help but feel powerless standing in front of her. It was a feeling he was used to, but not from a woman. It was a feeling he hated more than anything. Being helpless, unable to change an outcome in his life that he did not desire…it was a phobia he endured.

"Say something, then," Ensign Seneca snapped. "You've got some explaining to do."

He searched his gut, wracked his brain, but he was numb.

"Is…is everything okay on Veranda?"

Her eyes softened. She contemplated him for a moment with a sharp intake of breath.

"No, it's not. Something happened on the outer rim. We believe it was a retaliation by the riskar for invading their territory. Four planets in the outer rim of our territory have been completely destroyed."

Abraham's jaw dropped. His worst fears realized.

"Destroyed?"

My father…my brother…dead?

His eyes swelled with tears. Pressure built in his sinuses. He felt like he was breathing through a straw.

It can't be. It's not real. This isn't real.

What was that thing his old teacher had said?

Phantasmagoria. This couldn't be anything but a dream.

"What the fuck is going on?" he spat.

The ensign did something he didn't expect.

She smiled.

A sad, comforting smile accompanied by compassion emanating from her eyes. She could feel his pain, and she was letting him know. There was a connection here, something that transcended the officer-enlisted dynamic. She was human, just like him.

His rage and confusion fizzled away.

"I'm not sending you home," the ensign sighed. "Partly because you have no home to go back to."

The silence was deafening. Abraham felt like he was floating in it.

"Devastating as this news is, there is something more curious I want to inform you of."

He was ready for anything now. "More curious than the death of my family…er…Ma'am?"

"We're still waiting on confirmation of that. We don't know the exact circumstances. How thorough the destruction was." She folded her hands together and leaned forward, eyes boring into him. "Abraham, I have been…ordered…to allow you to continue in the Marine Corps."

The room spun. He almost staggered on his feet. These revelations were crushing him under mounds of devastation and curiosity. The edges of his vision crawled with darkness. His head spun.

"Ordered by who, if I may ask?"

Her knuckles were white. "You may not."

A full minute passed in silence.

"I have just one question for you, Recruit Zeeben."

"Yes, Ma'am?"

Ensign Seneca stood and saluted. Abraham quickly returned the gesture.

"Who are you?"

When he didn't answer, she dropped the salute, reached over the desk, and placed a hand on his shoulder.

"Dismissed, Recruit. I want to see you in my office again in a few days. I'm going to be personally checking in with you until you can answer my question."

Abraham nodded.

"Now get out of here and send in your co-conspirator, Poplenko."

The second week of training went by in a blur.

Corporal Johnson informed them they had reached their day off. Abraham was shocked to realize he was two full weeks into boot camp. He couldn't stop thinking that he'd slipped through the cracks; the Marines knew he wasn't eighteen, but they were letting him stay.

He considered himself lucky beyond measure.

The recruits cheered at the corporal's news, excited for a chance to sleep in and have some down time.

Digger howled like a wolf at the moon and pounded his puffy chest like a gorilla. Abraham chose to ignore this, instead taking the opportunity to try drifting off to sleep. He was relieved that despite the late-night shenanigans between the fifty or so recruits in the tent, sleep came quickly.

When he woke several bliss-filled hours later, sunlight had just started spilling in through the tent flap. He woke Larry, who popped right up, face beaming, and asked, "Breakfast time?"

Abraham started pulling on his uniform pants. "I'm starving, bro. Let's get there before Digger's fat ass eats all the French toast."

"Y'all have room for one more?" Piebold's booming voice found them from a dark corner.

Abraham chuckled. "Sure, Piebold, why not. Where's your boyfriend at right now, anyway?"

"He's probably already at the chow hall. He doesn't sleep much."

That surprised Abraham. "Really? I thought rich people slept like twenty hours a day."

Larry was pulling on a sock, tripped and fell flat onto his bed, sock stretched between the ball of his foot and both hands. "Ugh. Yeah, aren't Digger's parents like billionaires? My gramps said the Tacheks inherited a bunch of money from their inner rim relatives."

Piebold stepped into the sliver of light, his frame slightly less pudgy after a couple of weeks of constant physical exertion. He smiled. "I'm hungry. Let's talk shit about Digger *after* we eat, yeah?"

"Hell, yes." Abraham buttoned up his uniform top. The red and black camo was the coolest damn thing he'd ever worn. He wondered if Marines actually wore this in combat, or if that was just for the movies.

It was strange that they didn't speak of their losses. Veranda was gone, to what extent they couldn't know for sure. For the second time in Abraham and Larry's lives, their home did not exist anymore. In the blink of an eye, the riskar had reached out and wiped away the last remnants of their lives before the corps. Larry didn't utter a syllable about his grandparents. Abraham threw himself more into the training, trying to distract himself from thinking of a Collision incident from which his father and brother didn't escape.

After Larry grunted and complained about his soreness for another five minutes, they were all fully dressed and walking through the sparse, dust-covered area of Camp Butler. There were no sidewalks, no paved streets, no signs. Everything was fabric tents or gravel and brick, broken and run-down. Abraham looked for five straight minutes in every direction and saw not one green living thing in the vicinity.

Even other Collective *planets can look totally alien.*

They followed the scent trail of grease and syrup to the chow hall, a large one-story building near the center of the camp. Larry led the way. He was getting fewer weird looks from people now that his eyebrows had started growing back. Abraham was surprised to see Larry struggle so

129

much in adapting to the training, but he was glad to be able to help his buddy out. It felt like reciprocation for all the times Larry had helped David and himself in school.

The three of them entered the chow hall, grabbed trays, and made their way through the line. The sweet, pungent smell of cooking…well, it wasn't clear *what* was cooking, but something was, and they were hungry enough to want to eat it. They shoved their way into the line, grabbed trays and made their orders. Abraham pointed at the French toast, hardboiled eggs, and charred bacon. Piebold was practically cheering when he was able to get biscuits and gravy (the gray and white concoction they called gravy seemed like dried concrete to Abraham, so he skipped it) and Larry helped himself to the cereal bar area.

Trays loaded with food and several dozen packets of condiments, they made their way through a field of tables filled with recruits until they saw a few empty spaces at the end of the aisle where Tar and Juke were finishing up their breakfast.

"Mind if we join you, boys?" Abraham took his seat before waiting for a response.

Tar started laughing right away. "Ya boys are hungry this mornin', huh? Fatboy over here tryin' ta stay fat, yeah man?"

Piebold's part of the bench creaked as he settled in. "I'd break your skull with this biscuit if I wouldn't regret not eating it, Tar."

Larry leaned in almost conspiratorially. "Hey, you guys been checking out Ensign Seneca lately? I swear her ass is about the size of a small planet."

Juke's face went stiff. "Poplenko, you can't talk like that about our commanding officer." He glared at Larry, then turned to Abraham and smiled. "But I wouldn't mind seeing her full moon, ya get me?"

He burst into an obnoxious round of laughter, slapping the table repeatedly.

Everyone at the table laughed, caught in hysterics. Abraham rolled his eyes, heat collecting at his cheeks. He didn't disagree with them. He just wasn't used to people talking so blatantly like this.

Welcome to the military, I guess.

The conversation eventually got past their commanding officer's appearance and ended up in the exchange of backgrounds and personal histories. Abraham and Larry shared a glance at this, both not wanting to go there.

"Aspinos was a shithole, I ain't goin' ta lie," Juke was saying, "but it got a little easier when I found Tar. Poor kid was caught shoplifting by a doughnut cop."

He moved his hands wide around his waist to show just how fat the cop was.

Larry spluttered. "You couldn't outrun him, Tar?"

Abraham started chomping down his bacon, enjoying the greasy deliciousness. Even if it was a bit burnt, he hadn't had real bacon in well over a year. He swallowed a bite and asked, "Wait, I thought you two were twins?"

Tar started peeling a banana, not looking concerned with all the questions. "Hell nah, man. Ya think, a looker like me, *I* could be related to this man? I'm here to tell ya, if ya seen Juke's face, ya seen a baboon's ass. Save ya'self the safari, I promise ya."

Abraham was shocked at first, but the more he studied their faces, he did see Tar had a big nose. Juke's eyes were a bit too close together. It must have been the uniform and the haircuts that had thrown him off. Hell, most of the men looked similar when you put the same dress and appearance standards on them.

I get the feeling that is entirely intentional on the military's part.

Tar had finally gotten his banana peeled and opened his mouth to eat it when Amory and Digger approached. Amory slapped the back of Tar's head. He choked on the banana.

Digger burst out laughing. Amory plopped down on the bench next to Abraham, her elbow sliding him and his tray into Piebold. The hulking brute of a man was nearly finished with his breakfast. He hardly noticed.

Juke hustled up halfway to his feet, anger directed toward Digger, but he was quickly muscled back into his seat. Digger sat next to him, wrapped an arm around his neck and rubbed the top of his head with his knuckles. The friction produced loud scraping sounds.

"Hey, kiddies, is it story time? I wanna hear some good shit. Tell me, tell me!" Digger laughed, finally releasing Juke. The top of his head had a shiny streak where his scalp had been burned from the noogie.

Tar finished coughing and glared at Amory. "That's no way to make friends, Eilson."

She crossed her eyes, her cheeks stuffed with oatmeal. The sight was so ridiculous even Tar had to laugh.

"We're talking about where we're from, Dig. It's not very exciting." Piebold leaned back and belched.

Digger picked up a strip of bacon, eyeing it suspiciously. "Ah, that's some boring shit." He dropped the bacon to the plate. It was so brittle and overcooked it shattered. "This food sucks, by the way. Haven't eaten shit this terrible in my entire life."

Abraham asked, "Why don't you start us off, then, Denton?"

131

Digger ripped a chunk of biscuit off with an overly aggressive bite. "I don't have nothing to prove, Abe. Why don't you tell everyone about your last night on Veranda?"

Larry groaned. "Are we really bringing up this old shit, Digger? Don't you have anything *real* to throw at us?"

Amory piped in with a full mouth, "Y'all are a bunch of crybaby bitches. I joined to be a hardened fucking killer."

Everyone stopped mid-bite to look at her.

"What?" She mumbled before swallowing. "I wasn't gonna stay on Halzenti. It was the Marines or the gangs, and I know what kind of a life a female gets in a gang. I'm not about that shit."

Larry said, "Holy shit, you're from Halzenti? How the hell did you get out?"

Abraham looked at his buddy. What the hell did he know about this strange planet, and where had he heard it? Amory's home must be on the inner rim. Abraham was half convinced she was making it up to make herself sound tough.

Amory's whole demeanor changed. She stopped eating, for one, her spoon making endless circles in her oatmeal. Her shoulders hunched up a little and her eyes stayed closed for a beat. When she opened them to look at Larry, her lips were pursed with emotion.

"Yes, I'm really from there. Between the beorn and the riskar gangs, even the government can't do anything. But I had friends. We helped each other." Her eyes grew moist. "Leaving them back there is the only thing I regret."

Larry nodded, eyes never leaving Amory.

Looks like he found a new target.

The rest of the day was spent with Larry caught up in Amory's gravity, asking her a thousand and one questions about Halzenti. They walked over to the outside of the tent and took over the four picnic benches in the sand pit. Old, splintered wood creaked as they sat down on the tables, feet on the benches. The surrounding base was dead quiet. The sun lazily perched on the horizon, casting small, curved rainbows between dark purple clouds.

For reasons Abraham couldn't figure, the seven of them seemed to be turning into an inseparable collective. Each of them was so different, even just the four Veranda kids. None of the differences seemed to matter at all right now, though.

It was interesting how immediate the acceptance had been. Barely a week, and Amory was suddenly halfway less hostile, her shell starting to fall away as she bonded with Larry. Digger was even starting to be less rude, like he was saving his energy for the hellish training they would have to resume the next day. Juke and Tar never stopped bantering back and forth, which could have been emotionally exhausting if it wasn't a constant source of entertainment.

"The beorn are wolf-like humanoids," Amory was explaining to Larry. "They're always howling and barking at anything that walks by. Pretty scary if you haven't seen one before. Their fur is beautiful. Eye-catching, even. But there's evil in their eyes. Thing about them is they eat *any*thing, and they have a real bloodlust for living meals. I always preferred the riskar to them, honestly."

Tar whispered to Juke, loud enough for all to hear, "Alien's an alien. Ya get me, man?"

Juke laid down on the tabletop with an explosive exhale. "Alien's an alien. Shoulda killed 'em all in the first contact, if ya ask me."

Tar said, "Ya, but then we're out of a job, man."

Larry scooted closer to her on the bench, trying to make it look casual. Abraham saw right through it. Amory's emerald eyes were glossed over with a strange kind of recall. Abraham was sure she hadn't noticed his buddy's move.

"I can't believe the riskar would be so...I don't know, easy to live with?" Larry asked.

Amory snapped her head toward him, big eyes narrowed dangerously. "They're not what people say they are. One of my best friends was a riskar. The local gang, they called themselves the Three Bleeding Eyes, they were actually decent to me. Not like the beorn, those animals."

A shudder racked her shoulders. Abraham couldn't help but interject.

"You say the Sa–...erm, riskar, aren't what we think they are? How well did you know them?"

"I never fucked one, if that's what you're asking."

"No, I mean...you don't think they're behind The Collision?"

Amory stood up and stomped her boot in the sand. Her lips bunched like she was gritting her teeth. "I'm not saying there couldn't have been a handful of psychotic aliens that killed millions of humans. I'm just saying that a handful of psychotic aliens doesn't make the entire race terrorists!"

Larry looked at Abraham, shaking his head.

"What the fuck are you shaking your head for? You were there! We were both there. We saw the riskar ship, I saw them, I...my mother, your fucking *parents*, Larry. Those Sackbacks fucking killed them. Right in front of us."

Amory shouted. "Don't call them that, you fucking xenophobe!"

"They do have ballsacks on their back, though," Digger said.

"He ain't wrong." Juke snickered.

Larry wilted. "Abraham, look, I'm not trying to get into this. I'm just feeling like Amory's making sense, bro."

Piebold chimed in from his bench, "You guys. It wasn't the riskar. Anyone paying attention knows that."

All eyes turned to the fat kid.

Piebold deflated slightly with everyone staring at him. He gathered himself with a breath and leaned in close, face lighting up with a huge smile.

"It was the Ghosts," he said, a tremor in his voice.

Digger started laughing hysterically, slapping his buddy on the back.

"Piebold. That's the biggest load of shit I've ever heard in my life. We got the best technology in space! Our race is on *top*, bro, and you're telling me you still believe in paranormal shit? My fucking dad used to tell me ghost stories before bed when I was nine. That shit ain't real."

Piebold's face constricted. He blinked a few times, then turned and shoved Digger off the bench.

Digger was caught by surprise. He landed on his back, dust billowing around him. He shouted a few obscenities and brushed sand off his arms, glaring at his old sidekick.

"And just what the fuck do you think you're doing?"

Piebold, to his credit, didn't flinch. "Had enough of your shit-talking. The Ghosts are real. I know because I've seen one before."

Abraham couldn't help but roll his eyes. He had no stomach for ghosts, banshees…really any paranormal things. He didn't even like watching movies like that on TV, let alone considering these things to be real.

"Oh, this is gonna be great." Digger flapped his arms in exasperation. "Go ahead, Piebold, bore us to death with your bullshit conspiracy theories. Not like you have any interesting stories to share, anyway. Your dad was a janitor, and your mom was fucking a janitor, and here you are obsessing over some dumb shit."

Piebold did flinch at that.

He hunched his shoulders and lowered his head. The fabric of his pants made scratching noises as he tapped his thigh. Digger had just betrayed his buddy's insecurity in front of everyone, crossing the line in a way that Abraham could tell Piebold wouldn't forget. Piebold seemed to debate something internally for a moment, then nodded to himself.

134

"I'm not an only child. I had a little sister. The reason we moved to Veranda in the first place is because she got abducted by a Ghost. We never saw her again."

They all stared, not speaking.

Then they laughed.

Juke and Tar made boo noises at each other, accented voices quaking for maximum effect. Digger slapped the bench several times, tears streaming down his red face. Amory put her forearm on Larry's shoulder, wheezing between peals of laughter. All the while, Piebold's face grew deeper shades of red.

Abraham was the only one who managed not to laugh.

He felt bad for Piebold, but the story was just too ridiculous. Especially coupled with the big man's morose voice. As he tried to ignore the awkward discomfort that gripped him, Abraham saw something no one else did.

Piebold was tearing up. He had actual moisture collecting in his eyes. He must have felt it at that exact moment because he quickly wiped it away and grunted. When the laughter had died down, he cleared his throat.

"That's nice, guys. I didn't make fun of Amory for getting raped by gangs when she was a kid. I should have expected you dumb assholes wouldn't believe me. My kid sister *was* stolen from our house, and it happened *right in front of me.*"

"I never said anything about being raped," Amory said defensively.

Digger guffawed. "Bro, it ain't about your sister, man. You say you saw a ghost? Convince me, then. What did it look like? What did you see?"

Piebold cleared his throat again, eyes flitting between each of them. His nerves were clearly getting the better of him, but Abraham could tell this was important to him. In Abraham's mind, that tendered some measure of credibility to the big man's story.

"I was sleeping in my bed, and I heard a noise. It woke me up. This was when we were living on Vatican."

Amory held up a hand. "Wait a minute, you're from Vatican? Capitol of human space? No way."

Piebold sighed. "Can I tell the fucking story, or not?"

"Sorry. Go ahead." Amory rolled her eyes.

"We had a two-bedroom flat, because my parents were janitors and couldn't afford much. So, my sister and I shared a room. I heard this noise, and I woke up to this...this shadow standing over my bed. Only, when I looked at it long enough, I realized it wasn't a shadow, it was a man. He was reaching for my sister's bed. I was scared, I didn't know what to do. I tried to get up and scream, but nothing came out."

Larry held up a hand. "Uh, time out. You saw this freaky looking dude diddling your sister in the middle of the night and you didn't do anything about it?"

Piebold's face was pale. He looked like he was about to throw up. It was a genuine display of fear. "You don't understand, man. This guy was *scary*. I can't really describe it, it was just...I was scared shitless. Before I knew really what was happening, they were both gone. I ran to my parents to tell them what happened..."

Piebold's voice trailed off. The atmosphere had gone from dubious to heart-breaking. Abraham became fully convinced of Piebold's integrity the longer the story went on.

Digger said, "And? What did they say?"

"My dad said there was nothing we could do. My mom was crying, of course, and she wouldn't let me go for hours that night, but...I guess my dad said he knew something like this was going to happen one day. He said that he wished he never had kids."

Larry said, "Damn, bro, that's fucked up. What happened after that?"

Piebold just shook his head. The sky was growing dark, and the hour was getting late. He seemed to be feeling the fatigue of the last week most acutely in the last five minutes of conversation.

"I think I'm going to bed, guys. It's gonna be a long week. I'm getting some sleep while I can." Abraham stretched his sore muscles and stifled a yawn.

"Sounds good to me. I've heard enough stories for one day," Digger said, standing and scratching his ass.

Digger, Larry, and Amory entered the tent. Abraham was taking a step in that direction when Piebold grabbed his shoulder.

"Hey," he said, face somber, "thanks."

"For what?"

"For being the only one not to laugh. You're a good dude, Zeeben."

A thought occurred to him just then. A burning in his gut that wouldn't go away until he asked Piebold about it.

"Hey, Piebold...you never said what the Ghost looked like."

Piebold's grip on his shoulder tightened. "I didn't think you guys would want to know."

Abraham pressed him. "Was there any kind of glowing lights or anything around him?"

Piebold shook his head. "No."

Abraham sighed with relief. He nodded and turned to head into the tent. His hand was on the flap, but his blood froze when he heard Piebold's next words.

"But he did have a weird black line over his eyes."

CHAPTER 18

The siren tore through the night like the tormented wail of a banshee. It was a wavering tone. The kind that inspired fear and dread in the bowels of every soldier, sailor and marine since the twentieth century of human warfare.

Automatic fire erupted, loud, fast, hard. It scarred the air with heat and the odor of burning oil.

That would be the Guardians – large, automated turrets set on great swivels that watched over the base like faithful sentries of old. The unbelievable noise was like physical blows inside their skulls. The tremoring earth shook them out of their beds. Shouts and screams reverberated outside the tent. They were echoed by the recruits inside the tent. Abraham rolled off his bunk, still more than halfway asleep.

He reached for his CLR, fingers fumbling in the darkness. He brushed across a face, an armpit, a few other places he regretted, but he found his weapon. Hoisting it, Abraham slammed a heat sink onto it, slid it across the receiver until it clicked, yanked the charging handle. It was instinct. Fatigued as all hell, he didn't know up from down right now, but none of that mattered. When a Marine, even a simple recruit, heard the wavering tone of the siren call, he immediately prepared to defend the base and his fellow recruits with his own life.

It meant enemy attack was imminent.

Abraham flipped his light on, pointed the barrel of his weapon around frantically, trying to assess the situation of his fellow recruits. What he saw was about what he expected. Like waking the dead, overtired recruits were slinking up out of their bunks in varying states of undress. Abraham's light passed over a particularly flabby mass of flesh as it bounced over toward the wall lockers. He flicked the light up, shocked at the immodest sight, only to feel a wave of disgust wash over him.

Why couldn't it have been Amory?

It was Digger.

More precisely, Digger's bare ass.

"Digger! What the fuck, man?" Abraham asked.

Digger's response was classic. "What, you never seen a man's bare ass before?" His face changed from confused to smug. He pivoted to a full frontal with his hands on his hips. "Never seen a meat sword this big, either, huh?"

Tar piped up from his bed, "More like a button on a fur coat, Dig."

Juke burst into a fit of laughter. "Is it cold in here, or what?"

"Fuck you," Digger grumbled, pulling on his skivvies.

Abraham scoffed and turned his attention to finding Larry.

Several of the Raven recruits were well on their way to dressed. He saw Juke lacing up his boots, uniform ruffled but otherwise put together. Piebold was staring into the mirror, shakily holding a bloody razor up to his face. Abraham stepped over a few recruits that were seated or full-on crouching in the aisles, the fear becoming too much for them.

The automatic fire tore away any levity the recruits had raised. It could have been an eternity. It could have been thirty seconds, Abraham didn't know. When it finally eased, his ears were ringing. He continued his search for Larry.

As he stumbled into the shower area, he inhaled a breath of rank humidity. In his rush to find his buddy, Abraham's boots slipped on the wet linoleum. He threw his arms out in a vain attempt to steady himself.

At that same moment, recruits appeared on either side of him, trying to rush past. Abraham's eyes darted from left to right, and his jaw dropped in utter amazement. It was Amory and Larry.

Abraham's desperate search for a handhold found both towels and ripped them off. He slipped right onto his back with a wet smack. The impact set his head spinning. He could see the already sparse lighting in the tent growing dim. Standing over him was the very naked forms of a psychotic young girl and his best friend.

Abraham's eyes were about to roll into the back of his head. There was nothing he wanted more than to pass out right at that moment. Except maybe to die of embarrassment. As had been the case since arriving at basic a few weeks ago, Larry had his back.

Amory shrieked, snatched up her towel and darted away. Larry offered Abraham one hand, appropriated his own towel with another and covered his sensitive area. Abraham reluctantly took his friends hand, suspicious of the appendage's purity.

"Dude, what's going on?" Larry stammered.

Abraham scoffed. "We're under attack. What're you and Amory –"

Larry shook his head and steered Abraham toward the wall lockers. "Later," was all he said.

Abraham took the older boy's words as good advice and followed him. They stomped through the maelstrom and ended up at Larry's wall locker. Larry quickly donned his undergarments and his pants. Abraham helped him with the shirt part of the uniform, and they each laced up a boot of his, hands shaking with adrenaline.

We're under attack. Real attack from who knows what, and I'm helping Larry get dressed for the occasion. Who knew this is what military life would be like?

"You cut yourself shaving." Abraham patted the half-inch long cut on Larry's chin with a clean sock, collecting the already clotting blood.

"What? Oh, thanks." Larry took the sock and patted his chin a few times.

Silence fell. The breathing of the recruits, heavy, panting, panicked, could be heard like a passing tropical storm. Abraham felt like holding his breath. The silence seemed unsafe. Foreboding, somehow. He tried but failed to keep a relatively low sound profile, but his breathing continued to sound like a hacksaw trying to cut through a redwood.

After several minutes of strained silence, two figures burst through the tent flap, CLRs gleaming in their grips. They were both wearing a strange form of body armor that glinted even in the weak interior lighting of the tent. Abraham knew without looking too closely that they were Ensign Seneca and Sergeant Hinton.

"What the hell's going on in here? Are we a bunch of cowards or are we Marine recruits?"

"Marine recruits, Staff Sergeant Hinton!" the Ravens shouted.

"Fuckin'-A right!" Hinton grinned. "The aliens are officially here. This is a combat briefing. Congratulations, recruits. You're about to get your first mission."

A shudder ran through the ranks.

The recruits looked at one another, sharing glances filled with emotion. Some were fear, others shock. Abraham shivered when he saw Amory's face twisted in a sick look of excitement.

She would *be the one happy that we're going to have to kill. Psychopath.*

Abraham paused for a moment to hope that he would never end up like that. The eagerness to deal death from his own hands. To kill simply for the sport of it, or some twisted idea of fun. He wasn't afraid to do it if he had to, he just wasn't looking forward to it. Perhaps some of the innocent farm boy still clung to his persona. Childhood innocence not so easily uprooted.

Isn't that what I want to do to the riskar, though? Kill them all?

No, the riskar are different. They're not people, they're Sackbacks. Animals. And I'm going to slaughter them like animals.

Sergeant Hinton spent the next few minutes explaining the plan. He pulled out a Portal and set it on the ground. A light-map filled the empty air between him and the recruits, a holographic representation of their camp. Abraham saw just how sparse Camp Butler really was; there couldn't have been more than twenty-five buildings enclosed within a ten-kilometer radius. There were a few blue dots in a tent with the marker "RAVENS" above it. Next to it, green dots denoted "EAGLES." Abraham suddenly had an overwhelming suspicion that this was a war game. An exercise.

He let himself relax a little, but when he looked around, everyone seemed to be on the brink of either pissing themselves or jumping for joy. Digger couldn't stop smiling, an expression that always looked wrong in the absence of his beard. Amory tapped her fist against Larry's arm and pointed at the map. Larry nodded, the light of the map filling his eyes, revealing his panic. Several recruits were kneeled over, hands resting on knees. Abraham knew by now the classic signs of light-headedness, and that was a big one.

Ensign Seneca stepped up, squared her shoulders, and began the briefing with a perfect storm of decorum, military bearing, and...zeal.

"You all heard the Guardians just now. When those go off, that means we're in serious trouble from airborne combatants. This is a drill, but I want you all to treat it as real world. Outside the tent you'll find practice magazines. If you already charged your heat sinks, give yourself a pat on the back and drop them. We're doing this with training rounds only. I will repeat myself to emphasize the importance of this: you are to treat all aspects of this – weapons, tactics, the lives of your fellow recruits – as real world. No horseplay."

Abraham felt a greasy tingle in his stomach. It might be comforting to know that he was right about the exercise versus real-world nature of this, but he wasn't so sure how serious his 'fellow recruits' were going to take this thing. Tar and Juke were clowns. Amory had already pressed her illegal dagger against his ribs, and Digger had made a career of punching Abraham's face at every opportunity. At least he had Larry in his corner.

Although, now that he had accidentally seen them leaving the showers together in the middle of the night, stark naked with nothing but towels, Abraham wasn't so sure his buddy was still his buddy. Sleeping with the enemy was generally frowned upon in most alliances. Abraham couldn't lie to himself – he felt betrayed.

Digger made a face at Abraham that said, *What're you looking at?*

Abraham rolled his eyes and shook his head. He couldn't wait to get out of basic, to be in the real Marine Corps, and to never see Digger's face again. Whenever he did, it would be too soon.

Abraham and the other recruits fanned out across the base, starting their first patrol. The wavering siren had died down once they'd left their tent, leaving the sounds of boots on gravel and crinkling uniforms. They walked in a formation four columns deep, weapons slung but held at a low ready. The cool night air was a welcome reprieve from the normal sweat sessions of daytime bootcamp. The smell of baked concrete and hot sand lingered on the air like a bitter memory.

The otherworldly colors of the sky were starting to become familiar. This early in the morning they were muted, but still visible. Pale greens and dark blues, almost like aurora borealis but without the shimmer, painted the night. Abraham decided, as he slugged his way across the harsh terrain of Camp Butler, that he liked the planet of Juno just fine.

Could you call it home, though? If Veranda's gone, if Dad and David are –

Amory shouldered past him. "Watch it, asshole."

Abraham felt his adrenaline spike for the hundredth time that morning. At least this time, it hadn't been a knife against his ribs. Still, he was tired of getting picked on. Especially of getting picked on by a girl almost half his size. The comradery they had shared on their first day off had all but evaporated over the last few days of brutal training.

Abraham decided it was time to make a statement.

Keeping his CLR to the side with one hand, Abraham reached out with the other, grabbed a fistful of Amory's uniform and gave a gentle tug.

Her head rocked back, then snapped forward.

In a blur, she was standing on her toes, nose-to-nose with him.

"What the actual fuck do you think you're doing?" she growled.

"I'm done playing games."

He grabbed Amory by the collar of her uniform and dragged her out of the formation.

Her hands clawed at his wrists, her CLR dangling from the sling, forgotten. Abraham dragged her into an alleyway between two buildings. It was cramped, more like a crevice than an alley. He already knew he was going to have to deal with her dagger, but he wasn't prepared for the veracity of the fight in her.

Amory kicked him square in the crotch.

Abraham collapsed into her, groaning. Their rifles clattered to the ground.

Amory shoved him, hard.

He bounced his shoulders against the brick wall. Skin scraped against brick. Abraham wrapped his arms around her small body in a bear hug and squeezed. The tough little thing wheezed, trying to cry out, but he held her too tight to get out more than a cough.

Abraham lifted her up and brought her down to the ground, hard.

Amory smacked her head on the pavement, and her eyes rolled. Abraham wrestled the dagger out of her white-knuckled grip, then stabbed it into the dusty ground with a thud. Just out of her reach.

"Listen to me, little girl." He gritted through clenched teeth. "I don't know what your problem is, but I'm over it. You're gonna start picking on Digger, or Piebold, or somebody else. I don't care who it is. It's just not going to be me. You want that dagger back? I want you to leave me alone. If you don't, there's going to be problems. You understand?"

Amory nodded, but refused to look him in the eye.

Her lips were tight, her jaw clenched.

There was something in her expression that gave Abraham pause. He felt, for a fleeting moment, a stab of remorse, but he couldn't for the life of him figure out why.

She must have gone through more than she told us.

Abraham watched Amory breathing heavy for a moment, a trickle of blood curling on her bottom lip. He didn't like seeing her like that, even though she'd been nothing but hateful toward him since he'd first met her. There was a quality to her suffering, something he couldn't exactly identify. Her diminutive size was one thing, making her appear more on the frail and helpless side, but her rough and gruff exterior trounced that idea as a façade.

She pushed herself up, swatting her chest and stomach. Dust billowed off her uniform like a beaten rug.

"I don't care that you outmuscled me, Zeeben. But don't you *ever* touch my Pontcha again."

"What? I didn't —"

She bent down and yanked the dagger out of the ground, then hurried out of the alley.

"Oh," he said, cheeks burning.

Someone patted him on the back. He shouldn't have been surprised it was Larry.

"You did it, bro. You earned her respect."

Abraham laughed. "Whatever, bro. Let's get back to the formation before they notice we're gone."

Larry nodded. "I'm serious, bro. Amory's a tough bitch. She appreciates learning things the hard way, ya know what I mean?"

Larry's forehead wrinkled twice. It took Abraham a moment to realize Larry was raising his stubby eyebrows suggestively.

Abraham asked, "Is that what was going on last night?"

"No, actually. I, uh…well, I don't know how to say this, but…for the first time in my life, *I* got manhandled." He rubbed the scab on his chin. "You know why she carries that dagger? It's not for nothing, I'll tell you that."

Abraham burst out laughing. "She's got a cutting fetish or something?"

143

Larry shook his head. "No, dude! Well, kind of, yeah. Look, she hasn't told you everything there is to know about her. You can't say anything, obviously, and I'm only telling you because you're my bro and I trust you. Amory was raised by riskar parents."

Abraham stopped walking. "What do you mean?"

Larry sighed, exasperated. "Just what I said. Her parents – her biological parents – sold her to the riskar the day she was born. She's got a step-brother that's a straight up alien, bro."

Abraham spat onto the gravel. Three weeks into basic and he still hadn't gotten used to having no chewing tobacco. All the stress had him regretting leaving a field full of the stuff back home. He didn't know how to respond to what Larry was telling him. Amory's adopted parents were aliens? Was that even legal? And the riskar, no less?

I guess those demented bastards do have a family structure. They get less and less alien the more I learn about them. But why would they buy a human child?

Abraham stammered. "Larry, bro, what the hell?"

Shame crept onto his friend's face. "I know, man. I don't know what to think. I like her. She's twisted and exciting and she's got an amazing pair of…uh, well, you know. And her hair will grow back. You saw her, man. I *like* her. A lot. Even if she's got alien parents."

"Even if those aliens killed your parents. And my mother."

Larry deflated.

He had a look in his eyes like he knew he was wrong but wasn't about to change his mind. It was strange for Abraham to see such ambivalence from his best friend. Larry, the popular kid, the guy everyone wanted to be like, the guy every girl threw herself at. Larry, the one who had life figured out and always coasted by with a devil-may-care attitude.

"Her parents didn't do that, Abraham. You know I feel the same way you do. I want to hurt them for what they did. I think they deserve payback. Hell, it's why I'm here in this training right now instead of playing guitar on the porch at my grandparents' house back on Veranda."

A moment of silence passed between them. It was the sting of remembering a home they no longer had.

"I know," Abraham sighed, "but I think you're getting blinded by the female anatomy, Larry."

"No, this is different," he insisted.

"They're all different, until you're bored and you move on. You always do, Larry. It's who you are."

Larry's words were biting. "Thanks for the encouragement, douche bag."

They marched together without another word between them. In moments, they had blended in with the rest of Raven Platoon with no one noticing their absence. Just when he felt like he had Amory under control, he felt like his friendship with Larry was falling apart. Part of him didn't want to bother trying to mend it.

The other piece of himself added Larry's name to the list of casualties at the hands of the riskar. His blood boiled. Another thing they had taken from him. Another person he had lost.

He would make them pay.

CHAPTER 19

The next few weeks went by so fast it seemed like one never-ending day.

Raven Platoon learned how to patrol properly after failing their first exercise. They spent endless hours under the blazing Juno sky, sweating and cursing, while running and doing push-ups, flutter kicks, pull-ups, dips, tire flips and sandbag carries. They learned to use communication equipment, to assemble and disassemble radio transmitters, and how to rig small explosives. Punishment for failing to meet goals established by officers was rewarded with extra duties, extra workout sessions, and occasionally extra threats about being sent to the mines on Diome for the remainder of their enlistment.

Abraham tried to pass the time in his own mind by ignoring Larry's and Amory's obnoxious displays of affection, although this was fast becoming a monumental task. Every night one of them would creep into the other's bunk, and even in a tent full of fifty other people, they would slink off to the showers, running the water in the middle of the night as a privacy curtain.

One surprising development was his budding friendship with Piebold.

The giant of a man was actually very intelligent. It was a fact Abraham was ashamed he had never considered. Piebold's first name was Alan. He was originally from Vatican, the city-planet capitol of humanity in the Vorpal sector. What most intrigued Abraham about his talks with Piebold, between classes on alien anatomy, space travel, and battlefield tactics, was the shared experience they had as kids. They had both seen a Ghost.

Before leaving for the military, Abraham had no idea what he saw on Milune beyond a mysterious Shadow Man with a hand that glowed a strange red as the moon of Dajun fell from the sky. Piebold disagreed, shaking his head and waving his hands excitedly.

"Look, Ham," he would say when the conversation steered this direction, "I know you saw some crazy shit, too, but I'm telling you. The Ghosts don't have superpowers, they're not magic or anything. They're just really twisted, brainwashed people. They have to be to do the kind of shit they do."

"But why was he on Milune? One person out of millions who just happens to be a Ghost. What the hell was he doing there?"

"They're Nine Nations. Maybe some kind of super-secret agent types that do the kind of shit the government doesn't want people to know about. It's in the movies, constantly. That kind of shit happens in real life, Ham."

Abraham wasn't convinced, but he let the topic die. He wished Piebold would stop calling him 'Ham,' too, but he didn't want to make a thing out of it.

Their sixth week was coming to an end and the sixteen-hour days had become the norm. It wasn't a happy normal, but it was a satisfying one. Abraham hustled in and out of the shower as quickly as he could, just enough time to clean the sweat and dust off his skin before he collapsed onto his cot, exhausted.

The lights were switched off, leaving only the shower light at the end of the bay to filter into the bunk area. Abraham saw Amory crawl out of her bed, but she walked past Larry's cot and wandered into the showers.

Larry turned over and looked in Abraham's direction. It was too dark to see if he was looking directly at him, but Abraham closed his eyes anyway. He wasn't in the mood to talk to his old best friend. He just wanted some sleep, and to enjoy a huge, lazy breakfast free of screaming instructors, endless classes, and push-ups.

"Abraham?"

"What, Larry?"

"You still pissed?"

Abraham rolled over so his back was to Larry. "Just leave me alone, bro. I'm trying to sleep."

Digger piped up from his cot a few bunks down. "Ooh, lovebirds in a quarrel, everybody!"

Jeers went like a wave through the tent. Just like that, Digger had managed to turn a tent full of tired recruits into a jungle. Abraham despised his ability to work a crowd, especially when it was used against him. He didn't bother saying anything. It would only provoke him to talk more shit.

Larry said, "Look, I'm sorry about...you know, about everything. We've been friends our whole lives, Abraham. That doesn't have to change just because I'm in...just because things with me and Amory are getting serious."

Abraham laughed. "What, you think I'm jealous or something? I don't care who you're fucking or who you hang out with, Larry. I just can't stand how she's making you sympathetic to the riskar. Honestly, it's disgusting, and I can't help but think less of you for it."

Larry sat up with a quickness and threw his blanket off. He stood up in his underwear. Newly formed muscles flexed under his pale skin in the dim lighting. He wasn't the same Larry he had been, Abraham thought. None of them were. Their whole lives had been upended, and here they were trying to sort through a mess of physical and mental exhaustion, sifting shards of emotions endlessly lost in the wake that moved at blinding speed in basic training.

"Get up, Abraham, so I can punch you in the face."

Abraham got up, blood boiling. He slammed his chest into Larry's chest, knocking his old buddy back a few steps. If there was one thing Abraham was good at, it was fighting, and Larry should have known that. Of course, Digger had been the only kid that Abraham couldn't beat, but Larry had never been in a fight at all. Never even thrown a single punch.

"Larry, what the fuck are you doing? You know I'll crack your cranium on the floor in two seconds."

Larry approached him again, chin out, eyes narrowed. His shoulders rose and fell dramatically. It was a tell-tale sign of adrenaline.

He actually wants to fight me over this stupid bitch?

"You think I'm gonna let you talk about me like that? That I'm gonna let you talk about *her* like that? We've been through the shit since Milune, Abraham, that's true. But you're dishonoring the memory of your mother by being so hell-bent on genocidal vengeance. Would she really want you to die on an alien planet? A monument to her memory, her beloved son, a human corpse crowning a pile of alien corpses. What does that solve?"

Abraham felt it in his gut, the lightning bolt of adrenaline that he always felt before a fight. He didn't want to fight Larry, never wanted to harm his best friend. But the guy standing in front of him right now wasn't Larry as Abraham knew him. He had changed. He was something totally different now, something…

…alien.

Abraham stepped into him, gritting his teeth. "You gonna do this, or what? I'll fucking break your pansy ass in half."

Larry didn't back down. "You better take this back. All of it, or you'll regret it."

Larry and Abraham were nose to nose, neither willing to back down.

Several recruits were perched on their bunks, watching the exchange with fervor. A low chant of "fight, fight, fight" started up, until Digger sat up, cupped his mouth and changed it to, "Kiss! Kiss! Kiss!"

Abraham was making a fist with his right hand, his muscles tensing, when a shout split the scene.

"Stop!"

Amory was standing in the light with water seeping from her shaved head to her bare shoulders and a white towel covering the middle of her body. Water dripped down her smooth calves, collecting at her feet. She looked ridiculous.

"You two dipshits stop this, right now! We're not in high school. This isn't Mommy and Daddy's house. We're adults and we're in the *fucking Marine Corps!*"

She walked over and stood next to Larry, leaned in to him and looked into his eyes. "Larry, be calm. I'll take care of you."

She turned to glare at Abraham. "*You* need to calm the fuck down. I'm not an alien. I bleed red like every other human. Having adopted parents doesn't change that."

"Whatever." Abraham shrugged it off. He slipped his pants on, threw on the black undershirt and boots, then stomped off to catch some air outside. He hadn't made it three steps when he heard Amory talking to the rest of the platoon.

"See that, everyone? My man's got brass balls."

A chorus of laughter. Digger hooted like a dog and pumped his fist.

Abraham slapped the tent flap open, inhaling the musty air. He stomped his way through the gravel until he found the picnic table in the sand pit. He planted his ass on the tabletop, rested his feet on the bench and just stared at the sky.

It took him a moment to realize why he was doing this. The lump in his throat, the sting behind his eyes. He was fighting the urge to cry.

What the fuck is wrong with me?

This thought compounded the emotion, swelling a tide of electricity in his belly that he was not used to dealing with. His shoulders tremored, but he looked up at the stars, jaw clenched, refusing to let a single tear fall.

For the first time since he got the news from Ensign Seneca, Abraham didn't try to suppress the feelings about his family. What would David be up to if he were still alive? Probably nothing interesting. Would his father and brother have expected that he could make it through boot camp? He was halfway through, now. Would Dad have managed to complete the harvest without his workhorse?

Would the school have forgotten the boy who puked in Lucinda Blaylock's mouth? Would they have already added my name to the list of casualties, just like I did with Larry?

Thinking about his school, the hundreds of lives lost there, cut him deeper.

The more he thought about it, the more he realized the Sackbacks were single-handedly responsible for ruining every aspect of his life. There was nothing left untouched, nothing they hadn't corrupted or taken from him.

Larry stumbled through the darkness, boots crunching on the gravel. Abraham slinked away from the bench as quietly as he could, wincing every time his boot scuffed the sand. He made five steps out before Larry called out to him.

"Abraham?" he whispered hoarsely. "Come on, bro, let's talk this out. We need to settle this for good."

Abraham stayed silent for a moment. He was conflicted. To talk it out now would feel like backing down from a fight, and he couldn't have that. It went against every piece of his nature. He didn't necessarily pick fights, but he damn sure didn't back down from them.

"Look. I know you've got your feelings, and I've got mine. We can agree to disagree on those. But we have to work together, bro. We can't get through basic, we can't fight a fucking war without having each other's backs. It may look different, but I promise you I've always had your back, and I always will. That's what I came out here to say."

"Larry, I'm not –"

A light flashed over them, like someone snapping a photograph. Abraham's breath caught in his chest. He saw his own fear reflected in Larry's calm eyes.

It was red.

The camp was quiet. Not an alarm was raised. No one shouted or cried or pointed at the sky. One second it was the bright red of daylight. The next, it was as if the light had never been there.

Abraham and Larry sprinted to the other side of the camp, trying to agree on whether they had really seen the strange bolt of lightning. Larry insisted there was nothing but followed him anyway. Abraham knew what he saw. He was more concerned with where it touched down. It was somewhere in the vicinity of the officer's quarters, but he couldn't narrow it down much more than that.

The thrill of the unknown and the nagging curiosity kept them going when fear of being caught should have been at the forefront of their minds. Two recruits in black tank tops, cargo pants and combat boots, outside their tent after lights-out...they would lose their day off for sure. Abraham half wondered if this is what war was like: you would fight and bicker with your brothers and sisters in arms, but as soon as shit hit the fan, you were best friends again.

Abraham sidled up to a tent in the shadows, peering around the corner. A lamppost at the fence spilled bright light onto a wide alleyway between several tents. The only way to get deeper into the tented area was to walk right down the street, several meters in full exposure. A few moments of waiting and watching told Abraham there weren't any patrols in the area. How long it would stay that way was anyone's guess. Abraham leaned forward on his haunches.

Larry pulled him back. He pointed at a large tent three spots down the alley. The door flap billowed slightly in the breeze. A crack of red light blinked once, twice under it.

"Somebody left the flap open? Or are we under attack or something?" Larry asked.

"I don't know. But we need to find out before something happens."

Larry had a change of heart. "No way, bro, we've come far enough. We need to raise the alarm. We need to alert somebody!"

Abraham clenched his jaw. "That light is the same color as the Ghost I saw on Milune, Larry."

"What light?" Larry asked.

"You didn't see it?"

Larry shook his head.

"Why'd you follow me over here, then?"

"I thought you might need my help. I knew you weren't going to listen to me telling you to stop."

"I can't stop. Not now. So, you can help me, or if you don't want to, then just go."

The lanky recruit considered this for a moment. Only a brief moment, then nodded. "All right, all right, I'll help you. But you're leading the way. I'm not getting snatched by one of these freaks."

"Cover me. I'll get up to the tent. You watch and signal me if someone's coming."

"With what? We're grunts, Abraham, not special ops. We don't have computer interfaces or fancy A.I. bullshit."

Abraham held back a laugh. "Just whistle."

Larry blinked. "Oh. Yeah, okay. Just hurry back, all right?"

It was a nerve-wracking sprint to the side of the tent. His body was fully illuminated for about fifteen seconds as his boots slapped on the gravel. His leg muscles cramped from trying to minimize impact on the ground without sacrificing speed. He made it to the safety of the shadows without hearing a whistle from Larry.

He allowed a sigh of relief to slip through his lips.

Being this close to the tent flap entrance, Abraham recognized it as the ensign's office building. He had been here every few nights to have pseudo-friendly conversations with Ensign Seneca about his mental state. When he peered at the tent flap, the red glow was gone. Had it been a trick of the light, or had he really seen it coming from inside?

Abraham took a deep breath to steady his nerves. He was about to do something crazy. Something that could possibly end his military career. He didn't want to think about that, but he couldn't hold back the deluge of fear that welled up. Everything in his body was screaming for him to stop, to go back, to not be a dumbass and just get the hell out of there while he still could.

Hand shaking, he reached for the tent flap.

The fabric billowed sharply, slapping his hand. Abraham flinched back, immersing himself in the shadows. His heart beat so loud it hurt his chest. He took in a sharp breath and held it. Two pairs of boots crunched on the gravel just around the corner.

"I'll do my best to comply," Ensign Seneca's voice came from within the tent.

"Your father will be informed if you don't." It was a male voice, gravelly and strained. Like this was the first time he'd spoken in years.

"What does he have to do with this?" she asked.

"You don't have clearance for that. Tell no one, and carry on. The war will end soon."

Abraham risked a slight shift in his neck to get eyes on the pair. Ensign Seneca stood facing him, her eyes showing something he had never seen from her before – discomfort. Her arms were crossed over a white tank top, her foot pivoting on one ankle. It was a very strange, almost girly sort of pose.

Holy shit. She's terrified. *I didn't think anything could scare that woman.*

Standing in front of the tent flap was a swirling mist of shadow. Within, Abraham could see a muscular body and a pale face, like that of a corpse. His chin and the top of his head bore the slightest dusting of gray stubble.

His eyes were covered by a black bar.

The red lightning bolt came down from somewhere far up in the sky and illuminated the Shadow Man. There was no sound, no visible effect on the gravel-paved street. No rustling of Ensign Seneca's hair or clothing. Just like that, he was gone. The sky was clear. Not a single cloud for a spacecraft to hide behind.

Where the hell did he go?

Ensign Seneca shuddered, her shoulders sagging. She collapsed onto the gravel, head in her hands. Abraham wanted nothing more than to comfort her in that moment. Walk over to her, put a hand on her shoulder and let her know that she wasn't alone. He almost did it, until he heard a high-pitched warble from down the alley.

It was Larry's whistle. Abraham's blood froze.

Ensign Lechero stomped down the alley, CLR at the ready. He sauntered up and grumbled, "Ensign Seneca, everything all right?"

She stood up, brushed gravel off her bare legs and tapped a loose piece out of her running shoe. "I'm fine, Ensign Lechero, thank you."

"What're you doing up at this hour? Don't you have a meeting at zero seven?"

She bristled. "You must have me confused with a recruit, Lechero. I'm an Ensign, the same as you. I don't report to you, and I don't have to divulge my itinerary or my off-duty dealings if I don't feel the need." Her eyes narrowed dangerously. "And I don't feel the need."

Lechero stood in the street, stammering for a moment, jaw open but no words coming. He gathered himself for a second, then said, "Sure, Ensign. No disrespect, just checking on the well-being of a fellow officer. Enjoy your midnight stroll, then."

He fired off a salute and trotted down the street before she could return the gesture.

"Needle-dick prick," she muttered under her breath, disappearing into the tent.

Abraham stifled a laugh. Hearing her be so venomous, especially about another officer, gave him a warm feeling in his chest. She was more human than her icy exterior suggested.

He glanced down the street. Larry was waving frantically at him.

Abraham peered down the street to make sure Ensign Lechero was out of sight, then high-tailed it to Larry's position. Once they met up, Abraham shushed his friend, who was bursting at the seams with crazed excitement.

"Talk back at the tent," Abraham said.

The jog back only took ten minutes, but it was the longest ten minutes of Abraham's life. He plopped down on the bench, breath coming in ragged gasps. His skin was slick with sweat. The physical exertion of the run hadn't phased him at all. It was the adrenaline dump from the sneaking and spying that had his heartrate up.

Larry and he shared a huge round of laughter.

"I can't believe it, bro."

Abraham playfully punched Larry in the shoulder.

"Believe it, asshole."

Piebold and Amory came out of the tent. Amory with her arms crossed, Piebold rubbing sleep out of his bleary eyes. It must have been the boys' laughter that woke them up.

"What the hell's going on out here, Larry?" Amory grumbled.

Larry laughed again. "You'll never believe it, Amory. We just saw a Ghost."

Piebold's jaw dropped.

CHAPTER 20

The next week of training came and went without incident. Abraham wanted desperately to figure out what a Ghost was doing at Camp Butler. There just wasn't a whole lot of time to skulk around camp in between classes on alien anatomy and CLR breakdown procedures and the inner workings of fragmentation grenades. Abraham got to pull the pin and chuck a few of them into a pit, where they exploded as designed. It was the most satisfying thing of the entire week.

The status of his friendship with Larry was basically back to normal. Abraham figured the shenanigans with the Ghost had been serious enough to erase whatever trespasses they had been holding against each other. Abraham didn't ask him about Amory, and Larry didn't volunteer any information about their relationship, which by all accounts was still going full steam ahead.

It wasn't until they were doing patrol practices in the middle of the week that Abraham had his first real chance to talk to Piebold about it. It was the first time the recruits had been given the chance to wear B-skins, the 'B' for Battlefield, so there was a general feeling of excitement in the air. That had been hours ago, when first putting on the heavy armor plating, knuckles to toes, made them feel like gladiators.

Now they were patrolling a paper town, a mock-up the Marines made to look like it had been taken over by aliens. The buildings were pockmarked with bullet holes and hairline slices where lasers had cut into the drywall. It was a cluster of mostly single-story boxes spaced out to resemble a suburb. If the cheap buildings were fabric walls instead of particle board it would have been indistinguishable from the recruits' living accommodations. Their job was to find the hostiles hiding amongst the residents. Kill the aliens. Save the civilians. Standard Marine Corps job tasking.

"It's crazy that you both actually saw him," Piebold was saying.

The gray and blue B-skin amplified the already giant kid's size to make him look like a creature that walked off the page of a comic book. Digger was a burly bastard, but Abraham had to give it to Alan Piebold; he was the biggest Raven by head, shoulders, and a good forty pounds.

The big kid passed by a half-melted car chassis that was parked halfway on the sidewalk. Smoke rose in lazy curls from under the hood. He wrinkled his nose in disgust.

After peeking around the trunk of the car, he said, "Clear. And you're sure you heard him say the ensign's father was involved in something?"

Abraham kicked a pile of gravel with his boot. The sky was throwing some exceptional heat his way. He felt like he'd forgotten the last time he had a drink of water. His throat croaked as he talked.

"I'm sure, Alan. You would have shit yourself if you were that close to him. He was as real as I am walking next to you right now. And I know you said the one you saw didn't have any lights around him, but I saw the red lightning bolt. Clear as day this time."

Piebold squinted. Abraham couldn't tell if he was dubious, or just wished his helmet actually fit, so he could slide down the sun-visor. Sweat collected at his brow, slid down his face and hung like a stalactite from the end of his nose. Long walks weighed down with equipment were taxing for anyone, but Piebold seemed to take the physical exertions as a personal affront. It was the one thing Abraham didn't understand about the gentle giant. Even Amory, who weighed less than half as much, didn't complain about the patrols.

This is probably going to be our daily lives. Might as well get used to being uncomfortable now.

They were entering a suspicious section of the town. The last time they ran this drill, Abraham had taken two sim rounds to the chest. It would be the last time he let a child get his guard down in any kind of patrol. The kid had run up to him, fear etched on his chubby face, and when Abraham knelt to try to ascertain what was going on, the kid pulled out an L-pistol. Blasted him right off his feet.

The embarrassment hurt worse than the sim rounds, but they had left lesions on his chest and ribs. He rubbed at the bruises under his B-skin with one hand, flicked the safety off his CLR with the other.

"Up there." Piebold indicated an intersection up ahead.

The cross streets were filled with people laying in the dust, pretending to be casualties. Some of the people had make-up and fake blood to simulate wounds, others were lying flat, pretending to be dead. Upon seeing Abraham and Piebold approach, a few of them started moaning and groaning, holding their fake injuries and putting on a show.

"I'll assess, you cover?" Abraham asked.

Piebold jerked the T handle on his weapon. "Sounds good to me."

Abraham checked the screen on his wristwatch, the thing the Marines called a 'Pulse.' Digger and Amory were fifty meters west, Tar and Juke fifty-five meters to the east. So far, the mission had progressed with nothing out of the ordinary. Abraham knew that was going to change, he just didn't know at what point the instructors would spring whatever trap they had laid for the recruits.

An overturned car rested on a corner, a smoke machine spraying small clouds from the ground by the front end. A dark-haired, pale-skinned young woman lay beside it, screaming bloody murder. Several bodies were around her, their chests rising and falling, but clearly meant to be dead for the purpose of the drill. Abraham approached the lady, CLR pointed to the ground but still at the ready.

"Help me, sir, please! I'm hurt, I'm shot, I'm blown up, I'm dying!"

Abraham knelt in the gravel five meters from her. She glared at him with dark, beady eyes, through a splotchy mask of smeared dirt. He knew she had rubbed the dirt on herself because the smears were the size of her fingers and looked almost like a botched attempt at a warpaint pattern.

"I'm Recruit Zeeben with the Human Marine Corps, ma'am. I'm going to make you safe and get you out of here. Before I do that, I need to know what your injuries are."

The lady's eyes rolled, hard. She made a dramatic flourish as she collapsed onto the gravel. She must have been instructed to pass out once the recruits arrived. Abraham went through the motions of checking her pulse and breathing, then dragged her under the shade of the overturned vehicle.

"Ouch!" she cried. "You don't have to drop me so rough, asshole."

Abraham said, "Aren't you supposed to be unconscious?"

"Isn't a man in uniform supposed to be a gentleman?"

He spat onto the gravel at his feet. When she scowled and said nothing further, he assumed the conversation was over. He resumed his patrol, heading deeper into the paper town. CLR in his shoulder but kept low, he spoke into his Pulse as he moved.

"Raven Patrol, this is Raven 5. One wounded." He counted the 'bodies'. "Seven casualties. Incident unknown. No sight of the enemy."

One by one the other recruits responded with their call signs. Everyone reported similar findings. After seven straight weeks, the sweltering heat was starting to become their biggest obstacle in these training missions. Between the forty pounds of gear and the taxing terrain, every mission was a difficult one. The cracked concrete sidewalks were a nice relief. Even gravel roads weren't terrible. Any time they had to transition into the brush it was uneven footing, tons of roots to snag your ankles on, and prickly bushes like cacti that stuck to uniforms and bit into the top few layers of skin.

Abraham was glad this particular day found him in an urban setting. These were the ones he liked best, when the environment wasn't much of a factor beyond temperature. It was difficult to keep his mind focused on the patrol, on the rundown houses and the state of mock destruction that he traversed. The Ghost kept returning to the forefront of his thoughts.

Ensign Seneca seemed to have no problem acknowledging the existence of that Ghost. Her surprise, Abraham felt at his core, wasn't rooted in seeing his physical presence. It was something else, something more along the lines of the message and the implications of that message.

Which meant the message was important. Double that for her father being involved. Who was her father? Abraham wondered. In all their talks in her office, she had never once mentioned anything about her family. Ensign Seneca was simultaneously one of the most interesting and frustrating people he had ever met.

"We've got something. Stand by for –" Piebold's transmission dissolved in static.

"Raven 6, Raven 5. Say again, you cut out." Abraham tried for several moments to raise Piebold on the radio. It amounted to nothing.

"Raven 5, Raven 4," Digger's voice, "we're seeing some activity on the east end. Maybe make your way…shit! Eilson, look left!"

Abraham heard the CLR bursts through the radio and echoing from further into the city. He needed to check on Piebold, but he needed to assist Digger and Amory, as well. He opted for Piebold.

"I'm not letting you die, Alan. I'm headed your way."

Abraham hustled along the gravel street, right up onto the sidewalk of a nearby strip of storefronts. He had his CLR before him, safety off, heat sink locked in. He made sure to move quick but careful, observing the road in front of him, the ground he walked on, and the sky above. If there was a threat, he wanted to spot it early enough to react in time.

He came to a corner and immediately hit the deck.

White-hot blazes of light scorched the air where he'd been standing. Abraham hustled on his back, crawling to the cover of a parked car. His muscles felt twitchy, his brain fuzzy. He hadn't been around the corner long enough to see what was shooting at him, but he had seen Piebold sitting on the ground, fuming. He knew this was a very different encounter than the last time.

"Raven 5, taking fire. Source unknown," he reported. "Confirm Raven 4 KIA."

"They're circling up. Boxing us in!" Juke called out.

Abraham spared a second to glance down at the map on his Pulse. There wasn't much to this town in terms of fortifications. Just a few storefronts, some detached family homes in a small grid to the north and west, farmlands and barns to the south, open fields to the east.

"There's nothing. No cover. We're sitting ducks out here," he radioed.

Tar called in, his blasting sim rounds making it hard to hear. "Guerrilla warfare, man. Center of town, spread out."

Abraham nodded, realized Tar couldn't see that from his position a hundred meters away, then tapped his radio. "Got it. There's a schoolhouse with a water fountain in the center of town. Rendezvous there, ASAP."

Abraham hustled down the street, his senses keenly alert. The streets were quiet. Deserted. He had seen things like this a million times in movies. The quiet atmosphere, the only sound a tumbleweed bouncing against the street, and then out of nowhere a dozen guns go off and somebody dies.

It's not gonna be me this time.

"Contact! Contact from the east!" Digger shouted into the radio.

Abraham reached a concrete alley between storefronts. He was thirty meters from Digger. He could hear the gunfire on the other side of the alley. The schoolhouse was sixty meters in the opposite direction. He weighed the options, deciding it would be best for him to link up with Digger. Two guns were better than one, right?

Even if one of the guns is a self-aggrandizing douche. Sure Digger, I'll come save your ass.

Abraham was halfway across the alley when the lasers started flying at him.

He tried to get low like he'd been taught, to crouch and run at the same time, but with his arms swinging his heavy CLR, he lost his balance and tumbled headfirst to the ground.

Porous concrete chewed at his wrists and hands. Dust flew up into his face and burrowed down the collar of his uniform. He heard the snap of his sling breaking. His rifle clattered on the concrete behind him.

A hand grabbed the collar of his vest and yanked. Abraham struggled against it, prepared to go fisticuffs. Before he could get his feet planted, the hand let go. His head smacked against the ground. Stars exploded behind his eyes. When his vision cleared, it was Digger's smiling face standing over him.

"Thought *you* came to rescue *me*?"

Abraham panted from the adrenaline. "I did. Enemy...coming our way. Dropped my...weapon."

Digger's CLR clicked against his shoulder. Suddenly boot stomps sounded from both sides of the alley. Digger alternated sighting in on both sides, but it was to no avail.

Two burly kids in gray and red B-skins blocked the same entrance Abraham had stumbled through. When Digger turned to check the other entrance, two tough looking females were blocking it. There was no escape, no way out except through four CLRs and the enemies wielding them. The larger of the two boys was Schuster, Digger's old buddy.

"All right, this is over. You guys are prisoners now. Drop the weapon, Neanderthal, and we'll let you live."

Digger chuckled. "Schust, long time no see."

The burly Eagle recruit shook his head, smiling. "Dig, you're such an asshole."

Abraham stayed lying on his back, risking a glance at his CLR. It was two meters away, far out of reach. He put his hands out, palms open. "You're taking prisoners?"

Schuster shrugged. "This is a war game, and we're playing riskar. They're smart bastards. They take prisoners to torture for intel. So, drop the fucking rifle and *let's go.*"

Digger was still standing over Abraham, still holding his rifle out and pointed at the two boys. He flicked his eyes down to Abraham, who blinked emphatically.

"You want prisoners?" Digger asked. "Marines don't surrender."

The CLR fell from his hands, dropped a half-meter down.

Right into Abraham's hands.

Abraham did a sit-up as he pulled the trigger, lighting up the two Eagles in front of him.

Digger grabbed him by the shoulders and lifted him up, using Abraham as a shield for himself. Abraham's finger never left the trigger until the heat sink popped off, smoke hissing.

He felt the electric sting of sim rounds bite into his legs and stomach.

The two women collapsed to the ground, groaning. They were peppered with hits, enough to put them out of commission. After a minute of whining about the pain, they sat up to grumble about their failure.

Digger dropped him on his ass. "You're finally good for something, Abe."

He assessed his wounds. Three shots in his left leg and two in his stomach. If those had been real laser hits, his intestines would be cooked, and his left leg would be blown off. Zero chance of surviving those injuries.

"You used me as a shield?" Abraham growled.

"It worked, didn't it? Gimme my weapon back."

Digger snatched it away. Abraham rested his back against the wall, holding his cramping stomach, trying to catch his breath.

"I know this is practice, but you know they say you should practice how you play?"

Digger slid a new sink into the open slot and slapped it to lock it in. He cast a look at Abraham, one eyebrow raised.

"I did. You fuck up, so I'm supposed to die so you can get another chance? You'd probably fuck that one up, too."

159

"What is your problem? Why are you always such a douche bag?"

Digger glanced down at his Pulse. He called in Abraham as KIA and reported the 'dead' riskar. After an acknowledgement from HQ, played by Corporal Johnson, Digger was told to standby for orders.

"Aww, fuck. It's probably gonna be an hour." Digger groaned. He picked up a pebble from the street and chucked it at the two female recruits. It bounced off an armored leg plate.

"What do you want?" she growled.

"No telling when word's coming down. Y'all got anything to eat? Protein bar or something?"

The two girls shared a look of incredulity.

The one he hit with the pebble spat, "You're not getting shit from us."

Digger shrugged. "I should have picked you out for a grazer based on your size." He held his hands out to indicate a fat belly. "Believe me, all I wanted was food. I'm from a farming community, but I've never been one for cow-tipping," he gave her a once-over with his eyes, "and I ain't into bestiality."

"Fuck you," she retorted.

"Pervert," her companion spat.

Digger slid down to sit with his back against the wall, laughing to himself.

Abraham watched the whole thing in amazement. He thought about it for a minute, then decided he had to figure this guy out. Digger was one of his oldest enemies, but also the person he knew the least about. Abraham felt like he knew more about Tar and Juke than he did about Denton Tachek.

"How do you do that, bro?"

Digger picked his nose. "Do what? Win all the time? Someone has to."

"No. Automatically piss off everyone you come in contact with. It's an art form."

The short, muscled kid flicked whatever was on his finger.

"It's not me. Most people can't take a joke if it's about them." He chewed his bottom lip. "But I sure as hell miss tobacco, eh, Zeeben?"

Abraham nodded. He could feel the burn in his lip, a memory-induced tingle, like a tickle on the brain. "It always came in handy when shit got too real."

Digger spit. "If we had tobacco here, I wouldn't ever wanna leave."

Abraham felt a tightness in his chest. It was a good feeling, talking about something they had in common. It made Digger seem less like an asshole with a big mouth attached to it, and more like an actual human being.

"You hear this shit about what Larry and I saw the other night?"

Digger scoffed. "Yeah. What a coincidence, right? Piebold starts bullshitting about it, and you two limp dicks just happen to see one the next day?"

Abraham bristled. "It's true, man. I know what I saw."

Digger balked. "You know what you *wanted* to see. If you really saw it, how's come your butt buddy Poplenko didn't see the corona?"

Abraham flinched. "The what?"

Digger shook his head. "Corona. You know. Like a silhouette? You said he had a red silhouette?"

Abraham had to pause for a moment. "Where did you learn a word like 'corona'?"

Digger stared, eyes nearly going cross-eyed.

"I'm just saying," Abraham shrugged, "I never heard you talk like that before. You were always clowning around in school, so I thought you never really paid attention."

"Of course I never paid attention. I had two hours of private tutoring every day after school. The fuck do I need ten hours of school a day for?"

"Tutoring? What for?"

Digger swallowed, memories burning behind his eyes. "I'm not having a heart to heart, life-changing discussion with you, Zeeben. I don't want to be your friend. I don't want to get to know you."

The radio crackled. It was Corporal Johnson with more directions for Digger.

"Aight then. Gotta move, Abe. Don't go anywhere, now."

He hopped up, dusted himself off and flipped off the two ladies on his way out of the alley. Schuster stuck his foot out. Digger kicked the boot so hard the kid flopped onto his side and his face hit the ground with a meaty smack.

"Eagles are punk bitches," Digger muttered as he charged his rifle.

Abraham was left with even less of an idea of just who Digger really was.

CHAPTER 21

Abraham was laughing at Juke's dirty joke when the evening sky caught fire.

A thunderous crash splintered the air, sending shockwaves through the Ravens' platoon. Some recruits fell to their knees. A few lucky ones remained standing, using the barrel of their weapons as crutches. Abraham and Larry leaned on each other for support, staggering at the head of the formation, searching for any kind of cover.

The thing about this patrol was that cover was very sparse. All roads were gravel, which made it impossible to be stealthy to any extent. Buildings and other hardened structures were few and far between. The strange colors in the darkening sky were throwing everyone off. There was no sense of direction but what was offered by a few weathered landmarks and dilapidated buildings, and that wasn't much to inexperienced recruits.

The Ravens huddled up, fifty of them, each with their own ideas on how to figure out their position. Hands swatted at the map. Tar and Juke were on guard duty; to Abraham's complete lack of surprise, the two were chest-slamming each other and making barking noises.

"Look," Abraham said, "we need to figure this shit out, quick."

"Oh, really?" Larry fumed. "I'm trying. Everyone, back off!"

The tension snapped. Collectively, the platoon seemed to take a deep breath and focus. Abraham smiled. Larry had actually stopped the entire platoon from losing their nerve. He was taking charge. It was a good thing to see.

Larry was center of attention as he tried to read the map, a crumpled piece of paper with crude drawings on it. Trees looked like upside-down Vs and water looked like a string of zigzagging Ss. It was, in Abraham's estimation, a map of a fantasy world. One that had been drawn in crayon by a child.

Larry gritted his teeth, alternating between turning the map upside down and right side up, eyes squinting. "There's no fucking way this map is of Juno." He glanced around, almost frantic. "There's not a single fucking tree in sight. According to this, we're in the middle of a forest right now."

Larry flinched as Digger tried to swat the map away.

"Don't need directions. We just need to look for the aliens, numb nuts."

Amory laughed, resting the butt of her CLR on her hip. "We'll find 'em and we'll fuck 'em up! *I'll* fuck 'em up. My safety's already off. Finger's on the trigger. I'm the best shot in the unit. Just point me in the right direction, babe."

Piebold snorted, elephant-sized shoulders bouncing heavily.

He boomed in a deep voice, "You have a very large ego for such a little lady."

Clouds of heat and light puffed up in the sky. It looked like a cluster of giant bubbles. The hair on Abraham's neck stood with static cling.

Streaks of fire slammed into the ground around them, spraying white-hot chunks of gravel in every direction. One blast tore into a two-story building less than a block away. The decaying structure creaked, flames flickering through shattered windows. It collapsed like a delicate sandcastle.

Shouts and screams surrounded Abraham.

A din of catastrophe.

All around him his fellow recruits were ducking, falling to their faces, or gripping their weapons and shaking. Larry crumpled the map into his leg pocket, dropped to a knee and brought his CLR up. A few other Ravens were sighting down range with their CLRs, scopes over eyes, fingers on triggers. Digger was one of them, until he started waving his left hand in the air. Some recruits began to follow him as he marched toward the incoming fire with his weapon up.

Abraham knew *that* wasn't the right choice.

War was desperation and chaos, but it could be controlled chaos to some extent. As far as they knew, these aerial strikes were randomized, the enemy probing through the fog of war, shooting in the dark and hoping something would pop up. He wasn't an expert on military tactics, but he had seen enough cinema and played enough video games to know that knee-jerk reactions were most often the quickest path to death.

"Digger, hold up!" Abraham shouted, running to catch up.

The burly kid swung around to acknowledge him but didn't lower his rifle. "What the fuck are we waiting for, Zeeben? Let's fucking *go.*"

Abraham swatted Digger's barrel.

"Don't point that thing at me. We don't know where this shit's coming from. We need to take cover. Hunker down. Send out a scout team."

Digger guffawed. "That right? Who made you platoon leader?"

Several lines of flame tore through the air. The sound was deafening. The fiery streaks slammed into two recruits, setting them ablaze. Abraham watched in horror as two lives were snuffed out of existence right before his eyes.

It happened so fast.

One moment they were standing in formation, the next they were piles of ash and bone.

"Whatever we're doing, we need to do it quick!" Larry shouted. He shoved Digger and Abraham both, his expression grim. "We just lost two people and you're standing around arguing like we're in fucking high school! This is war, jackasses!"

Abraham wilted under Larry's stare. Larry was the best friend he had here, but the look he was giving him...he considered Abraham and Digger on the same level right now. Anger and resentment swelled in his gut. It took a solid moment. A clenched jaw, an exhaled breath. Abraham collected himself.

He *was* being like Digger. Digger was a brute. A shoot-first-and-ask-questions-later kind of guy. Abraham had never been much of a planner, but he knew how to break down a colossal amount of work into smaller pieces and tackle the pieces one at a time. That summed up the entirety of his childhood on Veranda.

"Cover!" Abraham shouted, waving a hand for the recruits to see. "That building!"

It was a pile of rubble that wouldn't defend against air strikes in the slightest, but it was something to stop any potential small arms fire from ground forces. Abraham reminded himself to think tactically, to think things through before committing to a decision. They had already lost two recruits. He wasn't about to lose any more if he could help it.

The recruits pounded gravel, hustling across the street and piling themselves up against crevices in the damaged foundations. After the briefest moment of contact, their black and red camo tops came away smeared with gray dust from the rubble. Abraham watched Tar and Juke patting each other down, small clouds of dust wafting around them.

Abraham brushed himself off, trying not to choke on the dust.

The deafening roar of incoming hellfire shook them.

Abraham wiped a line of sweat off his eyebrows, breath coming in deep and ragged. A tingle had developed in the pit of his stomach. Something primal. Something much bigger than himself that made him feel out of place. He was in a state, a mind-warp. Whatever it was, it felt like he was standing still while his soul was being slowly compressed.

Amory scooted her back along the wall until she came up beside him, shouting, "What do we do now, genius?"

Abraham opened his mouth to respond.

An explosion tore through the air. The ground shook, bringing them all to their knees. Flames crawled over the barricade, licking the tops of their uniforms. The heat stung. For the flash of a second Abraham was reminded of Veranda's sun on his skin.

He shook the memory as he peered around the corner.

The aliens had arrived.

Ten or twelve little beings, each maybe a meter in height, marched down the roadway in formation. Gravel and glass crunched under their tiny feet. Smooth white armor covered their bodies. A single black oval on each of their faces. Presumably their visors. On their backs they wore large black backpacks from which a hose ran up to the bottom of a kid-sized rifle. Hovering an inch in front of the barrel was a small flame.

Abraham thought they were flamethrowers, like old videos he'd seen of humans burning up jungle foliage. It wasn't until one of the little bastards leveled the weapon and pulled the trigger that he finally understood.

A globule of blazing red plasma erupted from the weapon, screaming through the air like a banshee. It slammed into a building across the street. Glass shattered. Steel girders melted and slowly twisted like barber poles, deforming from the intense heat. A few more blasts crumpled the building in on itself like a stick of butter in a microwave.

Abraham turned to his team. "Everybody ready for some action?"

Digger slapped his CLR. "Hell, yes!"

Abraham pointed to the street and called out, "Half of you follow Digger up the west corridor, the other half with me!"

The recruits broke cover, boots stomping concrete, rifles up.

A few steps out into the street they opened fire. Thin blue beads of laser blasts lanced outward, peppering the aliens. The shots bit into the armor, tearing streams of blue blood through the back. The blood quickly flashed from blue to red once it hit the air, confirming they were dealing with aliens. Human blood was always some shade of red, regardless of where in the galaxy you lived. A fact he remembered from boot camp biology class.

When did I graduate boot camp? He couldn't remember.

Abraham charged a few paces up the street, adrenaline soaring through his veins. He had never been more excited, more scared, more…alive.

A fiery plasma shot the size of a car bellowed down the street, headed right for him. He dove off to the side, landing on a pile of gravel and dirt.

The missile streaked by, narrowly missing the other recruits.

Abraham smiled. *This is so much better than being a farmer.*

He drew up to his secondary firing position, laid the barrel across his left elbow, elbow on his knee, rifle butt in his shoulder for stability. He scoped in, just how Ensign Seneca had taught him.

He could almost feel the softness of her hand on his shoulder. He could hear her words in his mind, echoing softly: *Steady, breathe, aim…*

Fire.

He pulled the trigger.

165

A hole blew through an alien's chest piece. It dropped its rifle and fell to the ground, small arms twitching. The recoil against his shoulder was less forceful than a shove from Amory. Abraham aimed down the line, noticing another stream of aliens approaching in formation, four lines across and perhaps twenty deep. Lines of blue light struck them. One by one they fell in flashes of light.

Out of scope, Abraham saw the Ravens were unloading from both sides of the street, peppering the incoming surge of aliens with indiscriminate fire. They were doing a good job of holding their positions.

Practice like you play.

Abraham went back in-scope, lighting up the enemy with vigor. Each pull of the trigger was an electrical thunderclap in his ears. The recoil was a friendly slap from a buddy. A new heat sink, a breath of fresh air. Every dead alien was another of his friends kept safe. What had started off as a firefight became a slaughter.

It couldn't have been five minutes later when it was all over.

Abraham hustled up to the center of the street, waving for his team to hold off. He examined the bodies of the aliens, not sure what he was looking for. The need to observe the damage he had inflicted on these beings was instinctual.

The bodies had fallen just as they'd marched, in a fairly organized fashion. Abraham felt like he was walking through a graveyard, the shattered white armor pieces like ravaged headstones. The strangest thought found its way to his awareness, like a voice surfacing inside his head, crawling up from the depths of his subconscious unbidden: *I just killed – and I didn't feel a thing.*

Did that make him a psychopath? Sure, these were aliens, and they were shooting at him. They had killed two of his own recruits. But what if they had been humans? Abraham felt a spike of uncertainty. He hated himself for it.

I'm a Marine, dammit! Or at least, I will be, and soon. I shouldn't be feeling this conflicted over doing my damn job.

Glass broke behind him.

Abraham raised his weapon and spun on his heel.

Amory stood over one of the aliens, the butt of her CLR dripping blue-turning-red blood. The visor of the small creature was smashed in, glass shards everywhere. The disturbing thing wasn't Amory's action, or the brutality of it, either. It was what Abraham didn't see inside the visor that he felt he should have.

There was no face. No head. Nothing organic at all.

Instead of flesh and blood, a dozen bundles of wire were routed inside the headspace of the 'alien', varied in color. Abraham, being a simple farmer, had no idea what he was really looking at.

The color-changing blood must not be blood at all. It's some kind of chemical.

"That confirms it. This is a simulation, bro." Digger's always-puffed chest actually deflated.

Larry nodded. "Bastards! I was scared to death for no reason. The alien invasion is just an exercise?"

Amory slapped Larry's shoulder. "You pissed your pants for nothing, Larry!"

"Hey, I did not —"

A screaming banshee of flame slammed into the ground, blinding Abraham with a quickness. He didn't have time to cry out or shield his eyes. Heat waves buffeted him. The lightning strike faded, taking him with it.

Abraham patted down his uniform, breathing slow and full breaths. He was standing outside Ensign Seneca's office, and he knew beyond the shadow of a doubt that she was pissed at him. Being out of the simulation, he now remembered being marched into the testing room, injected with something, and the lights going out. He remembered waking up in his tent to a wavering tone, the panicked hustle of Ravens gearing up and marching out to find half of their camp destroyed.

He hated disappointing anyone, but the thought of letting down this girl – this *woman*, he corrected himself – made his gut twist. Not only was she his commanding officer, but he had an undeniable affection for her, one that transcended any kind of little boy crush he had on any girl back on Veranda. When there had been a Veranda. This failure made the rigors of the past few weeks suddenly seem like minor inconveniences rather than the greatest trials of his young adult life.

Okay, it wasn't your fault. Larry and Digger were distracting you, Amory was threatening you, and you had just neutralized a heavily armed enemy squad. That's excusable, right?

Sweat dripped down the back of his neck. The world seemed no bigger than the hallway he stood in. He was afraid his failure had doomed him to never see the stars, to never experience combat. If Ensign Seneca kicked him out, he would never make a name for himself and his family…

Larry and Amory, Tar, Juke, Piebold and Digger…they'd all move on, fight in wars, and defend peace and justice in the galaxy. And when the fighting got to be too much, their backs against the wall with no recourse…Abraham wouldn't be there to help them. Protect them. Die for them if it came to it.

It would be better than dying a slow death on Veranda would have been. After another year working for his father, Abraham pictured himself looking just like him. A teenager with a ninety-year-old body, gray beard stubble, wispy hair, and a personality like an itchy asshole.

Except…Veranda was dust and ashes in the solar winds. There was no father, no brother. Nowhere to go. If he didn't make it in the corps, he didn't know what he would do.

Dying on a faraway alien world seemed like a privilege.

He knocked on the door.

"Enter," she called.

He moved swiftly to his place in front of her desk. They swapped salutes.

"Recruit Zeeben reports as ordered, Ma'am."

She had her hair down, creating an interesting symmetry to her face. The brown half of her hair seemed the angry side, the blonde the gentler. Her C-skin's shifting pattern of red, black and gray triangles didn't distract him at all from her physique; he had gotten used to the moving patterns over the weeks of boot camp. Her glacier-blue eyes pierced him with accusatory barbs. He could feel her anger radiating like microwaves.

His stomach gurgled in response.

"You didn't know it was a simulation." She said this matter-of-factly. "Why were you so careless? You got yourself and your team killed."

Abraham stiffened. He could see the death play through his mind's eye, that flash of fire, the fade to black. It was as real as waking life. He never wanted to experience that in a literal sense, not unless it was for something more than a war game. Something actually worth dying for.

"I don't know, ma'am. That may sound like a bullshit excuse, but it's the truth. I'm still new to the corps, to battle tactics. I've had no experience in war other than what I've learned over the last few weeks."

He saw a sparkle in her eyes. Like she hadn't expected him to be so honest with her. That was strange, since he'd been talking with her every few days about his feelings, hopes and dreams for his military career. She had to know he was an honest person by now. Abraham took her silence as permission to continue.

"Yes, I'm only seventeen. But I'm a mature kind of seventeen. The kind the Marines need. I'll be eighteen in a few days, anyway. It's not an excuse, it's just a fact. Up until I got here, the only things I knew about the military were what I saw in movies. I didn't make high marks in school. I definitely wasn't going to college. But I'm learning here. Really, truly learning. I'm interested. Engaged. And prepared to do what I have to do to keep my fellow marines safe. Up to and including laying my life on the line for each and every one of them."

Ensign Seneca stood, hands gripping the edge of the desk, white-knuckled. She shook her head, flipping her shoulder length hair to one side. The motion cast a wave of vanilla and honeydew over Abraham's face. The smell was a soft caress on his cheek. A silk blanket draped over his brain. The tingling was delightful under his skin.

Wow, I'm a creep. Who cares what somebody smells like, even if they are good looking?

The officer-in-training said, "Do you know that I've seen combat, Recruit Zeeben?"

"No, ma'am, I did not know that."

Ensign Seneca walked around her desk. "I was, regrettably, an infant at the time, so I have no active memory of it. Still, traumatic events tend to linger in our subconscious long after they occur. My mother was killed protecting me from certain aggressive aliens that had paid us a visit one evening. They razed half the planet. Killed many of us. Bloodthirsty, not so much. They just wanted us dead. We presented a certain biological threat to the infrastructure and natural equilibrium of the planet's biome."

She laughed, more of a snort than a chuckle. "Exterminated us like we were vermin."

Abraham could hear the emotion in her voice. He knew what this felt like. Unlike her, he had been old enough to remember The Collision with unfortunate clarity. Up until now, he had been vague on the details. He gained confidence at their shared pain, and for the first time since he'd been having these counseling sessions with her, Abraham allowed himself to open up completely.

"I was on Milune when the riskar crashed Dajun into it."

She was the first person he told every detail of what he could remember. Every thought, every feeling he ever had about it. He fought back tears, recounting the story through clenched teeth. He had to stop at the death of his mother, but he stared up at the ceiling until the tears dried enough for him to finish telling it with some kind of dignity.

Ensign Seneca approached Abraham, clasping her hands behind her back. She leaned in toward his face, eye to eye, staring hard. She was a few inches shorter than him, but her constant sizing him up set him on his heels. What the hell was she so curious about him for?

"Perhaps," she said, her voice trailing like her mind was elsewhere, "perhaps you do know." She snapped her fingers, producing a wince from Abraham.

"That might be why they're interested in you. I've been looking at you like you're a case study in broken nuclear families. To them, you're a survivor of The Collision."

"They? Them?"

She ignored him. "Did you have siblings?"

Abraham couldn't hide the shock in his voice. "Uh, yes. I have…had…an older brother."

Ensign Seneca rushed over to the desk, took out her Portal and began slapping her fingers across it, apparently taking notes.

"So, older brother." She drummed her fingers on the screen, then looked at him with glassy eyes. "But he didn't act like the older brother, did he?"

"No, he didn't. How did you know that?"

Ensign Seneca leaned over the table and held out her hand. Abraham glanced at it, amazed to see calluses adorning the palm and underside of the fingers. She was no stranger to hard work, herself. Was she telling him she had siblings, too? He was confused. The ensign was far more than she appeared to be. Abraham was sure he was going to leave here with more questions than answers about his commanding officer.

And that, too, bothered him. He didn't want to leave. Now that he had shared his childhood trauma with her, he felt a sense of comfort. It was the comfort of connection with another human being. It felt even stronger than his connection with Larry, his old best buddy. He still needed to find a way to con Digger into agreeing to a truce of some kind.

It was impossible, he knew. Officers and enlisted couldn't fraternize. Ensign Seneca was older than him, her looks were several rungs up on the ladder, but he couldn't help the way he felt. It was equal parts enamored with her presence and embarrassment at the intensity of his feelings having developed in such a short time.

This wasn't like him at all. Practical was the way he liked to live his life. This emotional tempest he held within himself was excruciating. And intoxicating.

I can't hope for anything to happen between us, he thought, *but I do.*

"Oh, I'm sorry, let's do this a different way." She cleared her throat, coughed into her fist. "Okay, in this office, once I've put you at ease, you're no longer Recruit Zeeben. You're Abraham. Got that?"

"Yes, ma'am. What do I call you, then?"

She slumped into her chair and leaned back, hands thrown out from her sides. An 'arms wide open' kind of pose.

"Pleasure to meet you for the first time, Abraham. My name is Vase."

"Come on, dude, you gotta tell us!" Larry was elbowing him in the ribs. Digger was slapping him on the back and the ass, hooting and barking like a dog. Amory was standing off in the corner, rolling her eyes and scowling. Was she actually jealous that Abraham, a hated enemy of hers, had gone in for a private meeting with Vase?

Ensign Seneca. Don't fuck up a good thing, Abraham, he reminded himself.

"What's there to tell? She just wanted to let me know I fucked up the training exercise, and not to do that again. She didn't have a meeting with anybody else...for real?"

"Fuck no," Digger grumbled, plopping himself on his bed. "She didn't do shit with us. And you're a *fuck* for not sharing the deets, man. You at least gotta cough up something, Abe. Did you puke in her mouth?"

Abraham threw a water bottle, hard, but Digger swatted it away like a harmless fly. It burst on the ground between everyone, showering knees and boots. It did no more damage than splashing in a shallow puddle might have.

"Fuck you, man. She's an officer. That's against the rules."

"Happens all the time, though." Amory spoke up from her corner.

Digger's voice shrieked in a high-pitched, mocking tone. "That's against the rules, guys. I'm Abraham, a big bitch that's scared of girl tongues." He stuck his tongue out and wagged it for maximum effect.

Piebold chuckled from his usual spot as Digger's shadow. "Don't stick it out too far, Dig. Abe's turning green!"

"Whatever," Abraham muttered. "I don't know why I bother telling you assholes anything." He jabbed a finger at Amory. "And that goes double for you, lady. I'm supposed to be getting some advice on women from a woman, and you're huddled over there while the conversation's going down over here."

Amory said nothing. A silence descended over the tent, Abraham's words falling flat. What he intended as banter suddenly transformed into what felt like a barbed insult right for Amory's core. He felt his cheeks heat a little.

She turned her back to him, head down, arms crossed tightly in front of her; not like she was pissed, but like she was hugging herself, consoling. After a moment, she stood and walked into the showers. Abraham felt like he'd just experienced whiplash with her mood change, and then a thought occurred to him.

Is this what a period does to a girl? Should I ask her if she's...doing it? How the hell do you even say that?

Thankfully, Larry took it upon himself to chase after her.

171

They were seated on his cot a few minutes later, Larry's arm over her shoulders, his face inches from hers. The two were locked into deep eye contact. The creepy kind that always annoyed Abraham with how intense it was. They murmured slightly under their breath. Abraham couldn't hear a single word of what they were saying.

"Hey, Amory, I'm sorry if I said something –"

She flipped him off, then put a hand on the back of Larry's head and stuck her tongue down his throat.

"– to offend you…"

Piebold chuckled. "She is very aggressive. I like that. Tough woman. Good in combat, good in the bedroom, too."

Digger leaned against the lockers, picking his teeth with a toothpick. He stared at the kissing recruits for a moment, then shook his head. "Never thought I'd want to be a dipshit weakling like Larry Poplenko. But then, every dog has his day. Right, Abraham?"

Abraham shrugged. "I'm not into public kissing."

Digger said, "You're not into *kissing*. You're allergic. Tongue to tongue contact induces vomiting."

"Hasn't that gotten old yet, Dig? Really?"

Digger laughed. "Nope. You being a limp-dick virgin will entertain me for a lifetime."

Tar ambled by, bare feet smacking on the floor. He marched up and down the aisle between bunks, calling cadence in his loud, accented voice.

"*Hut*, two, *tree*, four!"

Juke started shouting from the end of the aisle.

"Tar! How many times have I told you? You have to wear pants in public, ya great baboon!"

Sure enough, Tar was stark naked. He wore only his web belt and canteen, which had been strategically placed to cover his nether region. He stopped in the middle of the aisle, popped the lid on the canteen and shook it vigorously. Water sloshed everywhere.

"All trainees must hydrate!" he shouted.

Abraham rolled his eyes. Crude jokes were a way of life for oddballs like Tar and Juke. Right now, he had a hard time relating. Just because they had killed some aliens on their first drill was no real reason to celebrate. Especially since Larry and Amory had been the only two to technically survive.

Still, he couldn't take his mind off Vase – Ensign Seneca, he corrected himself – couldn't take his mind off Ensign Seneca and the strange out-of-regulation conversation they had shared. A million questions flooded his awareness. They hovered inside his mind's eye like pop-up balloons filled with text.

Why am I so drawn to her? Is it just because she's beautiful, or is it something else? What's her interest in me? Why is she such a different person in her office than she is during training? Will she ever tell me about the Ghosts?

He didn't know the answer to any of them, but he vowed to figure it out. Even if he had to skirt the edges of military regulations to do so.

CHAPTER 22

Ensign Seneca's office started to look different after the third time he visited her since their relationship became more personal. The pictures on the wall became familiar, the chair opposite her desk inviting. Airplanes and starships that soared around the room changed from distracting to charming. He had even noticed a chessboard on the end table behind her and was astonished to learn it wasn't hers; it had been left behind by the previous ensign. The game quickly became a fixture of their time together.

Teaching Vase how to play chess was a distinct kind of torture. She was smart, sassy, and a sore loser. After two or three games, she would usually get frustrated and put the board away. At this stage, the conversation would change to a more business-like interview. Vase seemed to want to know as much about him as she could dig up.

Still, Abraham came to appreciate their talks on a very different level than he expected she intended them to be. He couldn't shake the impossibility of the situation in his mind, that a woman of her level of importance, her station raised so much higher than his own, could possibly find him interesting. And yet, each hour they spent together was full of laughter and insightful conversation, even to the point of secrets being shared.

The transition from Ensign Seneca to just Vase was an immediate one, as quick as a change of clothes or the pulling back of a mask. Abraham managed to maintain his professionalism during training, keeping his distance from her and addressing her properly. They had, over the course of the last few weeks, been able to keep their meetings secret.

Abraham felt slightly guilty that he hadn't told Larry, whom he'd told everything else thus far, but he didn't know how much he could trust his old buddy anymore. That ship had sailed once he'd gotten in bed with Amory, and there was no telling if he were chartering a return course any time soon.

It wasn't just the fact that she was beautiful, or nice, or interested in him and his simple existence prior to the corps. There was something much deeper at work here, something he could feel in his veins, like a different kind of blood flowed inside him when he was around her. He could breathe in her scent, the vanilla spice or whatever it was she used for her hair, and he was totally changed. It was the first time in his life he ever felt this deeply about anything. Or anyone.

"How do you think your father would have responded to an attack on the homestead?" Vase asked. "If he knew about this Shadow Man you're talking about, I mean?"

Abraham had added this critical detail to his recounting of The Collision on his second visit. Vase had immediately unloaded a dozen questions, none of which Abraham was really able to answer. They had gone over it many times since.

"If my father knew about the Shadow Man, it would mean two things. One, he'd be completely responsible for the death of my mother. Two, he's lied to me my whole life about who he was. So, I have no idea about anything, at this point."

Vase nodded. She used her feet to rotate her chair side to side, her bottom lip puffed out as she mulled over what he said.

"Do you think he lied?"

Abraham snatched a starship nicknack out of the air, examined it close up. "I think he lied, I just don't know what about. Or if it even matters."

Vase put a hand on his shoulder.

"It matters. Truth is the most important thing in life. Without it, we aren't really living in reality. We're living in an alternate dimension crafted by a liar. It cripples us. Stuck in a state of dreams or delusions, where we make life-altering decisions based on logic dictated to us by…"

She drifted momentarily, voice trailing away.

"Vase?" He put a hand on hers. "We spend all this time talking about me. I see this affecting you, and I…don't like that. What is it?"

A soft sheen of tears fell over her harsh blue eyes. She stared right through him. He saw her face up close, closer than he knew was appropriate, but he couldn't help himself, couldn't douse the flame burning in his chest. Vase had a gravitational pull on him he could never shake off. She might as well have been a black hole, he a passing star caught in her event horizon. He stood no chance of escape. It seemed she wasn't about to let him go, either.

So close now, the air sparked between them. He smelled her skin, the honeydew part of her scent that always snared his senses, and he threw all caution to the wind.

He leaned in to kiss her.

It was a millisecond. It was quicker than that. It was the smallest measurement of time possible to record, but Abraham felt it. She did not pull away. She hesitated. She was possibly even turning into it, so close they were nearly touching when –

– a shrill beeping came from her monitor.

Abraham sheepishly pulled back, rubbing a hand on the back of his neck. He broke into a sweat. The nervous kind where his back felt heated but the perspiration felt cold.

"I have to...I have to take this, Abraham. Would you like to meet again tomorrow, twenty-three hundred?"

Abraham nodded. "Yes, ma'am, I'd like that."

She nodded, all business. Just like that, the phone call had pulled her Ensign mask back on, and the soft human side of her was buried completely beneath the façade.

"Dismissed, Recruit." She saluted from her chair.

Abraham fired back a crisp salute. "Yes, ma'am."

He spun on his heel, placed a hand on the door, and before it opened, he said over his shoulder, "You have a good night, Vase."

It was the first time he'd been so casual in his departure.

When she didn't correct him, he couldn't help but leave with a smile on his face.

"Vase, I've been meaning to talk to you about something, something that's been bothering me for a few days now."

She was staring at the chessboard, her eyes roaming the pieces, mind working. It took her a moment to respond to him, a moment he didn't doubt was filled with a dozen ways for her to destroy his pieces on the board.

"Yeah, so, go ahead and out with it."

She moved a bishop over a few spaces, putting his knight in a precarious position. If he moved it, he'd expose his king to a potential checkmate. If he left it, he'd be out a knight and in a bad position. Abraham weighed his options, then chose to castle.

He picked up the king and the rook.

"Hey, what the hell? We're not done."

"I know, Vase. I'm not breaking any rules. I'm castling."

Her eyes narrowed. "That sounds made up."

Abraham finished moving the pieces so his king was in the corner of the board, safely guarded by a sea of his own pieces. He tapped the king for emphasis, to show her.

"This is a move you do when your enemy has you in a bad spot. There's nowhere left for you to run, but you have this one option to hopefully shift the fight in your favor. It's defensive, but it has the benefit of making it very difficult to get checkmated."

"Really?" She stared at his arrangement, puzzled. "Castling...hmm. You know, I think this is what the riskar are doing to us. My...uh, I mean, I've been hearing that the war is almost over, but we've been having trouble finding General Rictor."

Abraham let his incredulity show on his face. "What? Isn't he on a capitol ship, or on their home planet? How is it possible we can't find him?"

Vase shook her head. "I don't know. But this move you pulled has me thinking. What if they're hiding him?"

He laughed. "Hiding him? I thought the riskar weren't as technologically advanced as humanity? They can't hide from us. Not for this long. No one could."

She slammed her fist on the table, but her face was twisted in a wild, happy grin.

"They could do it if they had technology we don't know about. Which would explain why we're in this war in the first place. New technology makes us nervous. This makes too much sense not to be true."

"What did the Ghost want with you?"

Vase's demeanor changed. She grew deathly serious, and her eyes bored into him.

"Abraham, what are you talking about?"

He forced himself to ignore the shriveling feeling brought on by her glare.

"I've known you for eight weeks, Vase. I've really only gotten to know you an hour a day for the last couple of weeks. How long have we been doing this? Three, four weeks? That's not a lot of time, really, but I feel like it's been enough for me to know you. So, I think we should play a game. Stand up and come here, face to face with me. I'll tell you something about you that I've noticed. If I'm right, you explain why that is."

She shook her head, her half-blonde, half-brown hair swishing. "No," her voice dropped to almost a whisper, "I'm not playing that."

Abraham decided she was, and didn't give her a moment to back out of it. He placed his hands over hers and pulled her up. Her icy eyes looked up at him, nervousness emanating from them. It was a different nervous to what he'd seen in her eyes when she encountered the Ghost. It was the kind that caused her voice to stretch when she talked. Her pale, slender hands seemed to tremble in his.

"You were raised by a single parent. One who didn't have a lot of time for you but was still there for you whenever you needed them."

Tears filled her eyes. "My mother...in childbirth. Father raised me...but he was busy with his career."

Abraham squeezed her hands, gently.

"You took a commission with the Marine Corps to separate yourself from your father, but also to follow in his footsteps."

Her lower lip quivered. "I wanted to be just like him, it's all I ever wanted...but I want to be *better* than him. To still be a person outside the uniform."

He brushed a tear off her cheek.

"You are. Trust me, Vase, you are."

Resisting the urge to clear his throat, to lick his dry lips, Abraham pressed on further.

"You know that, in the time you've been psychoanalyzing me, you've started to feel something. Something like you haven't felt before. And I feel it, too."

"I don't know what I feel."

She pulled her face away from his hand.

"I do."

Abraham moved a stray lock of blonde hair from her face, slid his hand to the back of her neck. When she turned to look at him, the nerves were gone, replaced by...fear? He slipped his other hand into hers, interlacing fingers. He gently placed his lips against hers.

Vase inhaled sharply, almost as if in pain, but he couldn't hesitate any further, couldn't stop the fireworks exploding inside his chest. He kissed her, full on.

She froze.

He could feel her hesitation. Her body pressed against his. Her fingers flexed in his grip.

His legs went weak at the knees. He was jelly from the stomach down.

The slap cut right through the bliss.

He blinked several times, hand flying to his cheek. It was red hot, stinging like a son of a bitch.

"I'm sorry, Vase, I didn't..."

She had her back to him, head resting on her forearm against the wall. Her hair covered her face. It was impossible to tell what she was feeling.

He went to put a hand on her shoulder, stopped himself at the last moment, deciding to just stand there, silent. He watched her for several moments before deciding she had regretted the whole thing.

The sting of embarrassment hurt worse than the slap.

He felt sheepish. Couldn't help wondering if she thought of him as no different from all the other male recruits that gawked at her and whispered debaucheries as she walked by.

He palmed the door panel. When it slid up with a hiss, he spun around to fire off his departing salute, but she was right behind him.

Her hand slapped the door panel, and it shut.

She kissed him, just a slow peck on the lips. When she looked into his eyes, she was smiling.

"I don't know what this is," she said.

He smiled. "I think you do."

Vase flipped her hair to one side. Her brows were bunched, her eyes slightly narrowed. She was either thinking very critically or she was angry.

"I'm breaking every rule in the book by telling you this, but I think you deserve to know."

Abraham licked his lips. He wanted to kiss her again. It was a huge effort to restrain himself, even with the possibility of insider information she was about to share.

Hell, I don't even know if she wants me to kiss her.

"I'm glad you feel like you can trust me, Vase."

She poked his ribs. It hurt. "I better be able to, or we'll be spending the rest of our career in Terra Sky."

Abraham blinked.

"It's the place where they send really bad people. The most secure prison in space, you could say."

"Oh, right." He laughed.

"Abraham, I'm sorry to say, but this is some serious shit. I don't know any particulars outside of the fact that the Ghosts are real, and they have an agenda. I don't know what that agenda is, but I do know it involves you."

The floor seemed to fall out from under him. He couldn't believe it.

"*Me?* What the hell do they want with me?"

Vase shook her head, forehead wrinkling.

"I don't know. But that's what this particular Ghost came to see me about. He told me to overlook the fact that you're underage. Abraham, he told me to *report your scores to him.*"

"What is this? They want to know about *me*? They want you to *spy* on me for them? Who the hell is this guy?"

Vase grabbed his shoulders. Adrenaline tickled his chest.

"Abraham, you're not listening. I've known the Ghosts were real for almost my entire life. This is the first time I've ever met one. Why do you think that is?"

He shrugged.

"It's because they want you, Abraham."

She hugged him. Her voice floated up tenderly as he held her.

"And I'm determined not to let them have you."

179

The Central Hall was the best accommodations Camp Butler had to offer. At least, the nicest accommodations the recruits were offered. Tall walls, a lot of glass over the ceiling that let the strange orange and purple skies filter in from overhead. They spilled onto the white drywall and stonework that made the hall seem more like a temple than a meeting place. Raven Platoon was gathered in formation, everyone standing stock still, looking sharp and tough.

This was the beginning of the final day of boot camp.

As the stars and fate would have it, it was also Abraham's birthday. He was officially eighteen years old. He had been reminding himself all morning that he was now a legal adult, but he had yet to feel any different from yesterday.

"This is it, fellas. The day to end all days. The battle to end all battles. The ring of fucking fire! You will begin this exercise as recruits, but you will conquer it as Marines! Who here is prepared to earn their stripes today?"

Corporal Johnson's words echoed in the hall. The responding shout from the Ravens nearly tore the roof off the building.

"Yes, Corporal Johnson!"

He smiled, big white teeth almost glimmering in the overhead lighting.

"Hot damn! Hell yes, you are. Some of you may remember when I first brought you here twelve weeks ago. Some of you may have already forgotten." He shot a glance at Abraham. "But one thing is certain. The person you were when you got here is dead. The person you are, the one who leaves here to join the fight across the galaxy…that person is a Marine. There is no greater honor humanity has to offer. After today, you will have earned the title, the distinction, and all the privileges that come with it."

Abraham's heart was racing. He couldn't believe the twelve weeks of basic had gone by so fast. He always heard people say that, but now that he was here at the end, he knew it was true. So much had happened in that time. He would never be the same again.

And he was ready for combat.

Today, the final exercise.

Tomorrow, the Riskar War.

"Mission brief in ten minutes. Raven Platoon, at ease."

Tar punched Juke in the shoulder. "You ready for this shit, man?"

Juke guffawed. "I was born ready for this shit, man!"

Amory's uniform shirt lifted just a bit, showing off her dagger. She was reaching up to ruffle Larry's hair. It had grown back fast and thick. It was almost long enough that she could grab a bunch of it with her fingers and pull him by it. Larry allowed her to muss his hair and wrapped an arm around her waist. His bouncing eyebrows had fully grown back.

"I can't believe it's almost over," Larry said.

Abraham echoed that sentiment but didn't verbalize it.

"Pfft. This is far from over, Larry," said Amory. "Training is over, but this was the easy part. We're graduating school and we're about to walk into the real world. Real combat. This is the part we've been looking forward to."

"I know, Amory." He kissed her. "I'm ready for anything, now."

Amory might as well stab me with that fucking dagger already. Is that what I sound like when I talk to Vase? All drippy and oozie? Blech.

He hoped like hell he sounded at least halfway less squishy than his buddy.

The door opened and in came Ensign Seneca and Staff Sergeant Hinton, Portals in hand. Ensign Seneca took her place at the front of the room. She was in a B-skin, gray and red armor gleaming with a fresh layer of polish. Her rifle was slung across her back, and she eyed her platoon with pride.

"Staff Sergeant, present the scenario," she said.

Hinton got up and pointed at a map of Camp Butler.

"This is where we are, boys and girls. Here, you can see two towers at opposite sides of the main area. This is our tower. That is their tower. If you want stripes, you want the title of Marine, you will capture your enemy's flag and return it to your own. Or eliminate every single one of their combatants. First team to do this…graduates."

Digger raised a hand. "Staff Sergeant, who's the enemy in this exercise?"

Hinton smiled. "How nice of you to ask, Recruit Tachek. The enemy will be played by your worst nightmare. Throughout basic training, you have summarily had your asses kicked nearly without fail by your neighboring platoon. Now, today, you will seize the moment and topple them for good. If you fail, you will start basic training all over again from day one in opposition to a brand new platoon. You will be playing capture the flag against the Eagles' platoon."

A wave of nervous energy pulsed through the formation. Abraham could feel the hesitation in himself and the rest of the recruits.

Digger's chest swelled. He clearly relished the opportunity.

If Digger's ready, I'm ready. Let's do this shit.

They were going to smash faces, melt boots and kick Eagle asses straight out of the corps.

Just a few weeks ago, I would have been pissing my pants. Now, I know my way around a combat zone. I know how to use a laser rifle and a dozen other ways to kill. I know when I see another person in uniform, they know these things, too. We can trust each other with our lives.

Abraham looked at Digger, who was smirking and talking to Piebold about how many Eagle recruits he was going to take out. Even that swaggering douche bag had managed to garner his respect. He may disagree with his methodology, but he knew Digger was the kind of guy who took no shit and would never quit. Amory and Larry, the obnoxious lovebirds who couldn't keep their hands (and the rest of their bodies) off each other, regardless of who was around. Alan Piebold, the imposing giant with a heart of gold and an obsession with conspiracies. Tar, the class clown, and Juke, the village idiot.

And then there was Abraham. He wasn't sure how the others perceived him, but that didn't matter. They accepted him, and that was enough.

We're a ragtag band of kids. And after we kick ass today, we're going to war.

Abraham locked eyes with Ensign Seneca. She was thinking the same thing, he was sure of it. It's all fun and games right now, until the lasers aren't sim rounds, and the wounds aren't temporary. Everything stops being a game, starts being life and death. He wished he could stand next to her right now. The previous night's conversation flickered behind his eyes. Warmed his heart. He realized in that moment, their affection strangled by station and circumstance, what exactly the fire in his chest was.

He had broken one of the military's cardinal rules.

Abraham had fallen in love with his commanding officer.

CHAPTER 23

The drop door opened, revealing a hole in the floor of the aircraft. Gravel and makeshift buildings he had seen a dozen times cruised below at a lazy pace. The early morning sunrise had just begun to stain the land with color. It wasn't the blinding blur he'd come used to seeing in the movies, but it was exhilarating all the same.

Farmboy Abraham could only have dreamed of such a sight. Now, Recruit Abraham had grown so used to it, he was comfortable with a drop from this height. He wondered for a moment about Myles Lannam. Sure, he had been an ensign, had learned to fly a Starfighter, but had he gone through this same sort of training? Or had that small town celebrity been just another cog in the Navy machine?

On Veranda, we all worshipped the kid. The Navy probably just thought of it as another pilot slot filled.

Abraham double-checked the thrusters on his Pulse, the screen on his B-skin's forearm. He was full up, ready to jump. He looked up and down the line, seeing the other Ravens doing the same. Larry and Amory patted each other down, checking clips and status lights, hands familiar with each other. Juke and Tar gruffly patted down plates and slapped helmets together with primal grunts.

Digger grabbed Abraham by the shoulder.

"Hey, Zeeben. We're working together on this one, right?"

Abraham slapped Digger's arm away.

"If you don't use me as a meat shield, I think we can work something out."

Digger said, "This is serious, bro. I'm not getting held back because you wanna fuck up."

Juke leaned in between them. "Ay, come on, man. We really gonna go through this again? Ya boys need to get along!"

Digger headbutted him.

"Back off, prick. Me and Zeeben are having a conversation, here."

Tar slapped the back of Digger's helmet.

"Ay! Knock that shit off, Tachek. Save it for the Eagles, man."

Digger bristled, but he turned his attention to his CLR, fiddling with the strap.

"I bet I'd be in charge if I was the one boning the ensign."

Abraham felt a rush of cool water flood his nerves, his muscles tightening with the sensation. It took everything he had not to grab Digger by the neck and slam his head into the bulkhead.

"We're not boning," he growled.

Amory leaned in, all smiles. "He prefers to call it 'making love'."

Abraham's cheeks lit up, heatwaves crawling down his neck and back. They didn't know. How could they know? He hadn't told a soul about the kiss, and he never would. If the corps found out…it wouldn't be good.

Larry started singing at the top of his lungs, "Ooh, yeah, bay-bee! We make-uh love! We make-uh love sweet looooove!"

Piebold buzzed his lips, starting a percussive beatbox.

Tar got raunchy, rotating his hips.

Juke thrust his crotch and slapped the air as he picked up the harmonies. "Make uh-loooove, man!"

Abraham couldn't help but laugh. "All right, jackasses. It's time to jump."

One by one, they walked to the hole and dropped through. Abraham went last, as he was designated squad leader for their final exercise. It was supposed to be random selection, but Abraham didn't believe it.

The ground rushed up, fast. He popped the thrusters on his armor with a tap on his Pulse. The computer in his helmet calculated a landing trajectory, and they hit dirt about fifty meters from their tower.

Abraham saw the blue light streaks hit around him. Somehow, he had managed to land first. His team hit, forty-one strong, in an array around him. The map on his Pulse showed only one recruit had messed up the jump and landed too far off course to be of any use in this exercise.

That's probably a recycle right there.

"There, coming in hot!" Larry pointed.

Red streaks like meteorites filled the sky three hundred meters away. Abraham saw the field, analyzed it with a practiced eye. The towers were situated about a hundred meters apart, with sparse cover in the area between them. Two single-story buildings were opposite each other, equal distance between the towers. The instructors had set this up specifically to make it as neutral as possible for both platoons.

"What's the word, Zeeben?" Juke asked.

Abraham eyed the field again, trying to think what the Eagles might be planning.

"The longer we sit here with our thumbs up our asses, the less time we're going to have to do shit!" Digger growled.

Abraham knew Digger was right. But he also knew the Eagles were picked by the instructors for a reason. They expected it to be their biggest challenge yet. Since they hadn't beaten them in really anything, he knew they were going to have to think outside the box for this one.

"Hey. Hey!" He shouted, "Listen up! Staff Sergeant Hinton and Ensign Seneca know us. They've been training us this whole time, day in and day out. They know what we need to be tested on. They already know our strengths and weaknesses. This test isn't about beating us into the ground or making things impossible. This is about us overcoming our greatest weakness. If we want to graduate, if we want to become Marines, this is how we do it."

Abraham laid out his plan over the next two minutes. It was daring. It was dangerous. Above all, it was something none of them had ever heard of being tried before.

"Pulling this off is going to require some serious skill," Amory said.

"And perfect timing," Larry added.

Digger puffed his chest up and punched himself.

"I'm volunteering for the point position."

Abraham concealed his surprise with a nod.

"Good. Thank you, Digger. I'll take the other point position. The rest of you know what to do."

Abraham and Digger hit the dirt just outside the perimeter of Raven tower.

"It's going to be impossible to sneak around in this B-skin," Digger scoffed.

Abraham was already working his off. He had the wrist and shoulder pieces off and was working on removing the chest plate. He glanced over at Digger, eyebrow raised.

"You thought we were going to be able to have stealth *and* armor? You've never played a video game before, have you?"

Digger started pulling his gauntlets off.

"This is crazy. Even for you, Zeeben."

"You *like* crazy. It's why you always volunteer for the hardest posts."

"Wrong. I like *honor*. Just so happens the more honor you go after, the crazier shit seems to get."

Both shirked down to their uniforms, B-skin completely abandoned in the gravel and dust. Abraham clipped his magazine belt and slapped his helmet on. He hefted his CLR, scoping around the corner of the building.

"Nothing so far. Eagles are probably confused why we haven't tried rushing their tower yet."

Amory's voice clicked in. "We're in position."

"Okay, here goes nothing," Abraham said. "Larry, give it a go."

"On me! On me! Weapons free!" Larry shouted through the mic.

Abraham watched from his vantage point on the side of the building as Larry led the bulk of Raven Platoon on a sporadic charge through the middle of the field. Thirty-three recruits, rifles raised, war cries on their lips. They lit off several rounds of fire, peppering the base of Eagle tower. A huge laser beam lanced out from the top of the tower, sniping one of their number. The poor guy dropped to his ass, smoke billowing from his chest.

Sim rounds were non-lethal, but that looked like it hurt.

"Okay, Amory, one in the tower like we thought." Abraham continued to scope the terrain. He saw another wide beam rip from the backside of the building opposite him. "And one opposite our position, behind the one-story."

"Copy. Standby."

Digger punched Abraham's shoulder, knocking the scope against his cheekbone.

"What the fuck, Dig?"

Digger pointed. "You're not looking at the right area."

Abraham followed the line-of-sight Digger was pointing at. He saw it.

The Eagles were rushing forward, almost fifty strong, each brandishing a slab of wood. The kind that sim rounds wouldn't penetrate. In effect, they had armored themselves with bulletproof riot shields. Abraham watched, frustrated, as the Ravens' shots chewed at the wooden slabs, but failed to penetrate them.

"Where the hell did they get those?" Digger asked.

Abraham looked close, trying to see just what the hell they were doing. He saw the edges of the wood; jagged, splintered. It popped into his head just as Digger said it aloud.

"They fucking tore down part of their tower? Crazy sons of bitches."

A laser beam ripped from the backside of the Ravens' tower. Abraham saw a trail of smoke curl up from the backside of the Eagle building. Amory had taken her shot.

"One shot, one down." Her smile was audible.

"Damn good shot," Digger said.

"Nice job, Eilson. Climb up to the flag and set up for your second shot," Abraham said.

The Eagles had planted their wood planks into the dirt, creating a wall. The layout of the field had suddenly changed with their maneuver. It was a good plan on their part, to be able to control the layout and flow of the terrain, but Abraham didn't think it changed much on his end.

Digger asked, "When are we making our move? My ass is starting to itch over here."

Abraham waved him down.

"You better scratch it, then. Let's give them another minute or so. I want Amory to take down their other marksman before –"

"Shit!" Larry cried out.

Abraham scoped in just in time to see the Eagles opening a huge salvo of concentrated fire right on the exposed Ravens. They lost a dozen or more as they scrambled for cover. Larry had taken a few hits and was lying on the gravel, slapping his helmet over and over.

"They're getting wasted out there, Zeeben," Digger said through gritted teeth. "This is exactly what I *didn't* want to happen."

Abraham tapped him on the shoulder. "You ready for this? We're up."

Digger nodded. "Hell, yes. Time for some motherfucking payback, bitches."

"In position," Amory called.

Abraham and Digger started their approach to the Eagles' side of the field. They low-crawled across the rocks, skin scratching and tearing, elbows and knees bleeding. They slinked along with nothing more than hushed gasps of pain and gritty determination. As the bulk of Raven Platoon were getting gunned down in the center by the superior Eagle formation, Digger and Abraham worked their way up to the base of the Eagle tower.

Abraham signaled Amory by clicking his mic once, twice.

"Taking the shot."

One meter wide, a blue light lanced out from Amory's position on the Raven tower and chewed through the top of Eagle tower. The marksman toppled off the scaffolding and plummeted three meters down to a hard impact on gravel. Dust billowed up, giving Abraham an idea.

"Amory, weapons free. Digger, go for the flag. I'll keep you covered."

"Opening up a can of whoop-ass!" Amory nearly shouted, and her CLR beamed out several shots.

Abraham started kicking at the gravel at the base of the tower, creating a small dust storm. In a matter of moments, the dust wafted up in lazy swirls. He had reasonably obscured the flag from the Eagles in the center of the field.

Digger slung his rifle and mounted the scaffolding. He scaled the tower as if he'd been climbing trees his whole life, barely pausing to secure his footing before hefting himself up further.

"Hey, guys," Tar's shaky voice came between laser blasts, "I hope whatever the fuck you're doing is working. We've got eight people still standing. I don't think we've even taken out a handful of Eagles yet."

Amory barked, "Less bitching more shooting, Tar!"

Abraham heard a noise, spun to see the Eagles' flag sticking up out of the dirt. Digger slid down the side of the tower, landing with a plume of dust next to the flag. He hefted the flagpole out of the ground, wrapped it in his rifle sling, and waved a hand toward the Ravens' flag.

"Let's get the fuck outta here."

Abraham shook his head. "You go. I'm staying."

Digger shook his head. "Whatever, bro. I'm capturing this thing, and we're graduating."

"Give me your CLR. It's just gonna slow you down."

"Fuck no."

"Digger. Don't make me order you to do it. Just fucking give it to me."

Digger unslung the weapon off his shoulder and threw it to Abraham. "You think you're a real fucking hero, don't you?"

"What the fuck is taking you assholes so long?" Amory cursed. "You can tongue each other's throats later. Bring that fucking flag here. Now, or we're fucked!"

Abraham slung Digger's rifle on his back, next to his own. "Get it home. I'll distract them."

Digger hustled off without another word.

Abraham let the dust settle around him. He climbed up the scaffolding of the Eagle tower, adrenaline making his limbs shake. He knew it was a crazy move, knew it was going to hurt like hell to get hit without any armor, but he also knew it was the only play he had.

The Eagles would be encroaching on the Ravens' flag any moment now. The distraction he provided would be the game-winning move, but he had to play it right.

Once he'd ascended the tower, he slapped two extra heat sinks on his and Digger's CLRs. If he counted right, that meant he had about a hundred and twenty shots per weapon. He flipped the switch on each of them to full auto, then pulled each weapon up to his shoulders. Tendons stretched in his neck from the weight of the added heat sinks.

"Amory, hold your fire until you see them run toward me. I'm cinching it. Right now."

The dust cleared away.

He was looking at the backs of the Eagles, the thirty or so of them that remained. Abraham aimed low and pulled the triggers.

The vibrations shook him to the core, rocked his bones and jiggled his joints until he felt like he was about to break into a million pieces. Shot after shot expelled from his weapons.

He lit the Eagles up, blazing fire right up their asses.

Dozens of kids fell.

He must have taken down two-thirds of their attacking force before they even realized what hit them. Heat sinks fumed on his weapons. They jettisoned just before they would have burned his hands.

There he stood, unarmored and unarmed, awaiting a blaze of hellfire from the remaining fifteen or so Eagles, when he saw Digger climbing the scaffolding of Raven tower. The burly guy handed the flag up to Amory, who slammed it home next to their own flag.

Fifteen rifles swiveled, trained on Abraham. He thought he could hear the clicks of triggers being pulled.

For a solid three seconds, nothing happened.

A siren sounded from overhead.

Blue fireworks erupted from Raven tower.

Ensign Seneca's proud voice floated over the field from a loudspeaker.

"Ravens have captured the flag! Congratulations, Ravens. This is your last day as recruits. Tomorrow will officially be your first day in the Human Marine Corps."

Abraham collapsed, breath exploding out of him. He had fully expected to have broken ribs and punctured lungs from the deathblow of a dozen sim rounds. Now, all he had was a platoon of forty something people that had just graduated basic training.

It was the best birthday of his life.

CHAPTER 24

Sergeant Hinton had been kind enough to drop off a few racks of beer. He even hung out with them for an hour, congratulating the Ravens on their hard-fought victory over their sister platoon. It didn't take long for the recruits to devolve into happy drunks, attitudes overflowing with sentimentality and declarations of undying devotion to each other.

This went on for hours.

The rave energy was finally beginning to slow down with the diminishing sunlight. Someone had dragged a projector into the tent. Juke made a big production about how the only movie they could find was Dark Atlas, a silly film about a guy who practically destroyed an entire planet, but then resurfaced to save it from government corruption thousands of years later. Critics considered it a classic, but casual viewers generally thought it was ridiculous. Juke, who considered himself a cinephile, sided with the critics. Abraham was not a fan of old movies to begin with, but he certainly wasn't going to spend his graduation night watching a boring science fiction movie.

"You're not staying?" Tar asked, his face pinched in disappointment.

Abraham shrugged. "I'm not a movie guy, Tar. You watch it, let me know if it's worth seeing."

Tar crossed his arms.

"Abraham, this movie is the only thing I've been talking about for the last twelve weeks. You know I've seen it before. It's only my favorite damn movie of all time."

"Uh…yeah, Tar…I don't give a fuck."

Abraham gave his buddy a good-natured pat on the back on his way out. He swatted the tent flap out of the way and inhaled the lingering heat of dusty Juno air. He tried to outpace the thoughts running through his head, the emotions swelling up despite the alcohol's efforts to keep them blurry and indistinct. The further he walked, the faster he went, until he was running and panting, his chest burning, his legs aching, but he couldn't escape the feelings.

He collapsed against the fence at the perimeter of the base.

Did I really just run two klicks drunk? What the hell's wrong with me?

"There you are, Recruit."

It was Vase. Abraham hustled himself up, locked himself up to attention and saluted.

"Ma'am."

She saluted back, smiling. Her voice lowered a few decibels.

"Not enjoying the festivities with your platoon?"

Eyeing the surrounding area, Abraham was reasonably sure they were alone. Still, he held a bit of stiff formality in place, just in case there happened to be someone nearby. The last thing he wanted was for both of them to be kicked out for fraternization.

"I was, Ma'am, but...not so much, I guess."

"You've been thinking of your family. That's normal, given the circumstances. You've done your platoon proud, Recruit. You will make a great Marine." She leaned in just a bit, just enough to be heard as she whispered, "My quarters, ten minutes. I want to ask you something."

Abraham nodded and saluted. "Thank you, Ensign."

She saluted back and smiled, a bit too enthusiastically for her public face.

"Carry on, Recruit Zeeben."

Abraham couldn't help it; he had to watch her walk away.

Abraham knocked on the door. Once, twice, then two times quickly.

The door slid open, and she pulled him to her. Her lips met his, and somehow the door managed to slide shut behind him.

Sweet spices he couldn't identify emanated from her, blanketing him with her scent. He pulled her tight, she pulled back, and then broke the embrace.

"Hello," she giggled.

"Hello to you," he whispered, stroking her hair.

"How did this happen, Abraham?" She bit her lip. "How did we end up in this...like this?"

He smiled, and it felt just as good on his face as it did alien. Smiling wasn't something he was used to. "You mean how did you catch my attention? Or how did I convince you to give me yours?"

She stuttered, "I-I mean, this all seems to have happened too easily. I'm interested in you because you confuse me. I know people. I figure them out easy. But you...fascinate me. You're interested in me because...?"

"Because you're the most beautiful girl I've ever seen. And I understand you, Vase. The way you think, the way you feel. We both want the same thing."

"We do?" she asked, eyes narrowing.

"Yes, we do." He cleared his throat. "I've been thinking about you a lot, actually. You know, it's kind of funny, because —"

She backed away from him, her bare feet pattering against the floor on tiptoe, her way of avoiding the cold metal surface. She shut the latrine door behind her. Abraham was left wondering if he was supposed to keep on talking or not.

"Is that what you wanted to ask me?"

A moment passed, then several. His eyes roamed the room, taking in the photographs and memorabilia.

Vase came out, dressed in a flowing blue gown. It was almost mermaid-like. Her hair was down, curled in flowing tresses. Abraham felt a slight breeze moving through his open jaw as he stared at her, unable to blink.

"Do you like it?" She gave an elegant twirl.

Abraham stammered. "I, uh…wow. Vase, you're so much more than your beauty, but you look stunning."

She knelt in front of him, and his heart quickened. She reached under the bed and pulled out a black, rectangular box half the size of a rifle case. It seemed heavy or delicate, the way she slid it across the floor without lifting it.

"What's this?" Abraham asked.

She put her finger to her lips. "Shh. Ensigns aren't allowed luxury items like this, so you have to keep it secret."

Abraham smiled, his cheeks hurting even more. "Of course."

Vase opened the box. She lifted out a violin, the exact one from the picture on her wall. It was brown and black and sturdy. The wood it was made of seemed somehow ancient but not brittle. The smell reminded Abraham of home.

"Slumber My Darling?" she asked, placing the instrument between her chin and her shoulder. She rubbed a piece of rosin back and forth on the strings of the bow with a practiced motion.

"You know it?" Abraham asked.

"I learned it," she said. "After you told me about your mother."

Vase was so many things Abraham couldn't hold together in his mind. Standing before him now, she was a living, breathing statue. Physically perfect. Playing chess showed the intellectual side of herself, adaptable and cunning. Her penchant for psychology led her to be a riveting conversationalist, and this to a guy who grew up with a natural disdain for wasted words.

Tears formed in his eyes. "You're incredible."

Vase's pale fingers gently gripped the bow as she placed it against the strings of the violin. The first note sang out, high, shaky, and sharp. It cut Abraham to his core. He watched her, this beautiful angel for whom he had fallen too hard, too fast. She slung the bow back and forth in lilting song, and he felt himself come undone.

192

Tears wet his cheeks. Memories rose within him. He was six years old, tucked in for bed, and she was there, singing him to sleep. He was at the breakfast nook, holding out his bowl for her to pour milk into his cereal. She was there, tying his shoe for the third time that morning, urging him to gather his things for school, frustration never creeping into her voice.

He was, for the moment, back on Milune, seeing his mother's face clearly for the first time in years. She was walking with them, telling the boys to find a place to sit to watch The Passing. Her golden hair hung down in ringlets, her round face permanently stuck in a smile. The pale light of Dajun played across her white dress, reflected off the pewter of her sash buckle, the light fractured and danced in a million facets under her diamond earrings.

The strings sang beautifully. He watched Vase's gentle intensity, the focus and the passion displayed upon her face as she drew a lifetime's worth of emotion from the instrument. The soothing, somber tones that radiated from her fingers were like tiny kisses to his ears, the sliding of the bow a veil being lifted to spill sunlight into his mind's eye.

Abraham stood and put his arms around her waist, resting his cheek against hers. Her hand worked back and forth, sending off the final note with a reverberating vibrato. When she lowered the violin, her eyes were closed. He knew she was holding back tears herself.

He took a mental snapshot of this moment. He had never been happier.

"Thank you for that." He hugged her tight, emotion squeezing at his chest.

Vase spun in his arms, wiped his tears away with gentle fingers. "I brought you here to ask you something, Abraham, but I figured it out myself."

He took the violin from her and gingerly placed it in the case. When he stood back up, she was looking at a picture on the wall. A picture of herself when she was probably four or five years old, a stuffed animal clutched tight to her chest. It was a donkey with a wilted expression. The background seemed very green. Pastoral.

"That's not Vatican, is it?" Abraham asked.

He could see her shoulder blades move in her open-backed gown when she shrugged. Her chin lowered a bit. Abraham realized it wasn't a shrug, but a sigh. She was experiencing something right now, something heavy. He stood beside her, placed his hand between her shoulder blades, the same spot she had him feel her breathing at the shooting range all those weeks ago.

Unlike target practice, her breathing was shallow. Pained. He could feel her tension under his fingertips, like her muscles were corded or taut. *It must be painful to bear so much stress in a physical way like this.*

"No, it's not Vatican. It's the only place where I have a fractured memory of my mother."

He inhaled more of her scent. His chest tingled with the lovely static skitter across his brain he had come to recognize as an innate reaction to her. It defied all logic, all reasoning, but he couldn't fight it. Even though the rational part of his brain wanted to, even though a large part of him wanted to lock down the feelings, to stifle the emotions and run.

He couldn't do it.

"Vase, you wanted to ask me something, but I want to tell you something."

"Abraham, I —"

He stopped her with a finger on her lips. "No, stop. I want you to hear this, because I'm not going to have the courage to say it again if I don't say it now."

He took a deep breath, slid his finger down to her chin, traced it down her neck, over her collarbone, finally resting it on her hip. She met his eyes, her lower lip curled back.

"I love you."

She looked down, broke the eye contact, and refused to look up. Her voice was small, weak, but a dagger to his heart.

"You need to leave," she said. "Now."

Between heartbeats, Abraham felt like the oxygen had been sucked out of the room. The floor could have opened and swallowed him into an endless pit of darkness. He would have been less shocked than he was at this moment.

"Vase, I —"

She gently removed his hand from her face, walked into the bathroom and shut the door.

"Abraham," she said, "don't make me say it again. Get. Out."

What else could he do? Like a dog with its tail tucked between its legs, Abraham let himself out.

194

CHAPTER 25

If there was one word to describe the atmosphere in the tent, it would be 'hangover.'

The sun spilled its sickly light through the crack in the tent flap, which flitted in the barest semblance of a breeze. Even in the early morning hour, the temperature was climbing high. One by one the recruits woke to groans, gasps, the slapping of bare feet in the latrine, and the occasional crescendo of vomiting and toilet flushing.

Abraham opened his eyes, took in a sharp breath, and retched. A thousand different smells mingled and mixed to create a garlicky miasma of sweat, vomit, piss, and something acidic he couldn't identify. He wished he had been able to stay the night at Vase's. Instead, he'd had to slink back here trailing shreds of ego and heartbreak.

"Oh, shit..." Digger groaned, "this is the worst day ever."

Abraham went to the sink and splashed warm water on his face. He had bags under his eyes, deep purple splotches. On Veranda, these would have been from getting in a fight – probably with Digger – and losing. His last day on Juno, and they were instead from drinking too much.

Never thought I'd say that about myself. Hey, Father, I'm a little tired from spending most of the night with a girl I really like. Oh, and it turns out she hates my guts for some unknown reason.

Abraham scoffed, lathering his face with shaving cream. That was a conversation he would never have with his father. Nor with his brother, either, come to think of it. Even if the Sackbacks hadn't killed him, David wouldn't have looked up from his Portal long enough to feign interest.

He swiped the stubble off his chin with the razor, cleaned up his cheeks and his upper lip, then patted his face down with cool water. Consternation webbed across his emotions when he thought of his family. Thought of them dying at the hands of his most hated enemy.

What happened, exactly? Did they fight, or were they vaporized in a sudden flash of fire? Were they really gone forever, just like that?

That would be shitty if the last thing I said to them was...all that terrible shit I said. Fuck. I hope they made it out somehow.

He never knew he could miss them so much. He had confused the fear he felt on the starship as fear of the unknown. If he were honest with himself, he would have recognized it as a fear of never seeing his family again. Close or not, they were the only human connection he had, until now.

Now he felt close to a group of tough, crude, arrogant badasses.

And he was one of them.

"I hope I get based somewhere far away," Larry was saying to Amory. "I don't want to go anywhere near Veranda any time soon."

Amory was pulling on her Class A pants, looking at herself in the mirror. "Sounds like there isn't much left there, Larry. I'm sorry."

Larry tightened the black laces on his freshly polished boots. It was obvious he was trying to distract himself from emotion. "Not your fault, love."

"Maybe we can check out Probst? Three days with nothing but beach and shade from coconut trees, and me in a bikini at your beck and call." She hugged him from behind, whispering a few words into his ear.

Larry gave a pained smile. "You know I can't say no to my island girl."

Amory patted him on the head. "That's it. Perk up, cowboy."

Abraham laughed behind his hand. Larry and Amory were a pair, that could never be doubted. The more he saw them interact, the less he regretted the fracture in his relationship with Larry. They clearly belonged together. The misgivings Abraham had about Amory were more about her waving her dagger around at everyone than about her intentions toward Larry. He decided at some point to make amends with them.

"Hey, Juke, come check this out, man!" Tar shouted.

"What? What's going on?" The lanky recruit hustled to the tent flap, where Tar was pointing at the skyline.

Abraham and several others hustled over to see what the commotion was about.

Off in the distance but coming in hot was a large spacecraft. Its shape reminded Abraham of a plateau, like a flying mountain with the top cut off. It was a massive ship, the kind that usually didn't enter the atmosphere of most planets for fear of not being able to break through gravity's grip to reenter space.

The insignia of the Human Navy became visible as it approached. Abraham was excited. He had never seen such a grand vessel in his life. The damn thing was so large, it might have been a floating city.

The vessel stopped over Camp Butler, hovering hundreds of kilometers above.

Four clear cylinders sprouted from the bottom and slammed into the gravel below. At first Abraham thought they might be landing gear, but when he saw bodies falling through them and touching down on the ground, he realized they were mobile elevator tubes. Thin plastic that rippled in the wind.

"Wow," he gasped, "this is the coolest damn thing I've ever seen."

Piebold chuckled. "I wonder who that monstrosity belongs to?"

Several murmurs came from the recruits, but no one took a guess.

Amory said, "That's the Admiral of the Navy's ship, the *Victory's Edge*. It's the grandest ship in the Navy's arsenal. It's damn near the size of a small moon."

Digger scoffed. "Unless I'm getting stationed on it, this just means bad news for all of us."

Abraham asked, "How do you arrive at that?"

Digger crossed his arms. "Bigwigs only show up in person to give really bad news. They think their presence is going to somehow cushion the blow to peons like us, but really it's just like pouring salt in a wound. Not only do we gotta hear some shitty news, we gotta hear it in a place where we have to be respectful about it."

"You're an eternal pessimist, aren't you?" said Abraham.

Piebold said, "Admiral of the Navy...that's Admiral Latreaux! I can't wait to tell my dad I got to meet Admiral Latreaux!"

Abraham blinked. The only thing he knew about the Admiral was how much most everyone on Veranda hated him. That, and the few TV spots he'd seen of the gruff man reporting the progress on the Riskar War.

Piebold said, "Maybe it's good news. Maybe we're going straight to the frontlines instead of getting a posting outside the war zone?"

Digger slapped Piebold on the back. "Nah, dummy, they're *promoting* us. The fancy Admiral of All of Fucking Space is here to give us a direct shot at special forces. He's gonna give a big speech about how the Ravens are the baddest motherfuckers since the Frogmen, and we're going straight to Spectre for advanced infantry training."

Corporal Johnson shouted from down the alley, rousing everyone's attention.

"Get your asses in gear, recruits! Our timetable just moved up two hours. No fiddle-fucking around. Get dressed and get in formation or your asses are shipping out to your hometowns as civilians."

Everyone quickly finished changing into their Class As, the fancy version of their uniforms that looked like military business suits. Abraham placed his flight cap on his head, pleased that his returning hair was just enough to hold the hat in place on his head.

This fucking thing's uncomfortable. But damn, I look sharp.

They formed up less than five minutes after Johnson's shouting.

Their formation marched in time to callouts from Sergeant Hinton, who led them up into the front of Camp Butler, right by the entrance to the base. The Eagles' platoon was there, as well as several other platoons that Abraham didn't recognize. All in all, about eight platoons, between forty and sixty or so recruits in each one.

Why are the Eagles here? We beat them. They're supposed to be recycled.

197

The probable answer popped in his mind: the Marines want as many bodies as they can get to fight the war. Maybe they *need* more bodies. It wouldn't be the first time in history that standards and rules had been stretched to swell the ranks.

Sergeant Hinton positioned their platoon next to the Eagles and called them to a halt.

"Parade, rest."

Abraham's body moved on command. Heels parted, wrist clasped behind his back, eyes front. He was in a sea of heat-producing bodies under two very hot suns in the sky and he was not looking forward to the ceremony. The striking of bootsteps near the stage drew his attention. Without turning his head, his eyes swung to the side.

Striding up to a podium which had mysteriously appeared in the middle of the gravel was the man himself – Admiral Latreaux. Abraham was still far away from the podium, but he could see the highest-ranking officer in the Navy with his own eyes. Even from there, he could feel the man's presence.

Latreaux had a certain air about him. It was something like defiance commingled with arrogance. He walked with stiff arms and wide strides, bearing a grin on his face that was somewhere between serious and fantastical. It was like he was trying to play a hero on a bad TV show. Or he was just terrible at facial expressions.

Either way, Abraham felt himself silently agreeing with his Verandan counterparts. Latreaux's first impression was an enigma. It elevated the hair on the back of Abraham's neck.

Captain Pendleton stood at the head of all the platoons, waiting until the Admiral stepped onto the stage to command the platoons to attention. The sea of recruit boots slammed together like crashing thunder.

The large man cleared his throat at the podium, ran a hand down the circle of five stars on his elaborate S-skin and clapped his hands against the podium.

"At ease. At ease, everyone."

There was a long pause of absolute silence. It was so quiet Abraham had to steady his breathing for fear it could be heard all the way up at the podium. Being released from the position of attention, he parted his boot heels and clasped his wrist behind his back. As casually as he could, he glanced around. Every single pair of eyes were fixated on the Admiral of the Navy. Abraham forced himself to stop searching for Vase and return his attention to the stage.

The whole thing was stiff and formal, and continued on with military precision.

The junior officers were marched onto the stage, where they had their ranks pinned onto their uniforms. Admiral Latreaux himself tapped their chests, digital gold bars blooming, but with Ensign Seneca and Ensign Lechero, he tapped twice, creating a silver bar for them.

"I have elected to promote Ensigns Seneca and Lechero from Ensign to First Lieutenants, based on their performance and recommendations from Captain Pendleton," the Admiral explained, face beaming with pride. So much pride, Abraham thought it was a bit misplaced. But then again, he was having a hard time reading the grizzled Admiral at all.

"Well, then, it's good to be back on Juno," Admiral Latreaux barked. A mirthless laugh followed, even though his facial expression stayed the same. "I have to say, I don't frequent this base much. My efforts have been concentrated on The War."

A cloud of unease settled on the scene. Abraham could feel it, almost like it was attached to the words Admiral Latreaux was speaking, like his voice was casting a spell or a pall upon the gathered troops. No need to mention the riskar; the way he said 'the war,' everyone knew what he meant. Abraham suppressed a shiver.

Latreaux continued, pacing now with hands clasped behind his back. "I'm here to congratulate you all on your graduation. I'm here to thank you all for your service. And I'm here to promote the junior officers. Now that I've done all that, I'm going to dispel the rumors that may be circulating amongst you all due to recent developments."

Abraham blinked. *What rumors?*

As far as he knew, the only recent development was the attack on the outer rim planets. His heart hammered against his ribs. Could this be more bad news?

The Admiral stopped pacing with a click of his boots. He drew his shoulders back for a moment, like he was trying to crack his back. He relaxed and scanned each platoon with a hard-nosed look.

It seemed an eternity before Latreaux finally spoke again.

"The Riskar War is over."

CHAPTER 26

After the big speech from Admiral Latreaux, the recruits had to sit through a torturous two-hour promotion ceremony. The only good thing about it was that Abraham got to have his stripes tacked on by Vase.

There was something different about her now, though. Her tight military bearing was unusually formal, even for her. She was very good at wearing the mask – had been wearing it her whole life under her father's in-and-out parenting – Abraham knew from his talks with her. But since he'd said those three words to her, she had been only cold towards him.

"Abraham Zeeben, you are no longer a recruit. I give you now this stripe, this rank of Private. The Human Marines have a history and legacy of valor, honor, and service. Do you swear to uphold these values, to live with the utmost integrity, and to fight for humanity until released from your oath by death or decree?"

Abraham felt a hallowed sense of humility, like the very air around him was constricted. His throat tightened, thinking of the many men and women who had sworn these vows before. Who had died with them written upon their hearts. He was honored beyond measure to join them.

"I swear it." He saluted.

Vase – now First Lieutenant Seneca – velcroed his rank onto his chest, stepped back and fired a crisp salute.

Abraham dropped his salute, spun on his heels, and marched back to his formation to join the rest of the Ravens. He beamed with pride, but part of him stood in consternation at the devastating news from the Admiral of the Navy.

No more riskar War? What the fuck am I supposed to do now?

Once Abraham returned to the formation, the ceremony concluded with a big fanfare of military brass and percussion instruments, trumpeting the Marine Corps theme. Admiral Latreaux offered a farewell salute. Abraham finally heard the words he'd been dying to hear since he'd marched into the field earlier this morning.

Captain Pendleton shouted, "Marines, dismissed!"

Abraham hurried through the platoon to Larry and fist-bumped his old buddy. "Bro, can you believe it? We're fucking Marines!"

Larry slapped his thigh.

"Hot damn, baby! We're combat-coded, fully-automatic alien killers now!"

Amory slapped him on the back of the head.

"Shouldn't we be pissed off that the war's over? I know I am."

Piebold wandered off, muttering curses under his breath. Abraham watched him walk away, wondering if the gentle giant would have transformed into a giant ferocious killing machine if they had made it to the war. Digger was nowhere to be found.

Abraham offered his two cents. "I'm pissed off that the war is over, but that doesn't mean we still can't get cool assignments and fuck shit up. Right?"

Corporal Johnson approached them, his face wrinkled like he smelled something bad.

"Hey, privates, we have a meeting at the chow hall in thirty mike. Let everyone know. We need all hands accounted for."

Larry asked, "What the hell is that about...uh, Corporal?"

Johnson laughed and patted Larry on the back. "You're a Marine now, Poplenko. Cool your shit. Just fucking be there. And bring everybody else, too."

Amory looked up at Larry, eyes heavy.

"What do you think this is, Larry?"

He shrugged. "Hell if I know."

Larry's description couldn't have been more apt, Abraham thought. It was hell. It was worse than hell. It was the worst possible news they could have gotten, and at the worst possible time.

"These are Pulses." Major Fallon, a hawk-faced man with a thick mustache and the senior ranking officer under Captain Pendleton, was conducting the brief. Several junior officers were passing out wrist tablets to each of the new Marines. Abraham took his, wishing he could throw the damn thing over his shoulder.

Fuck. Now even David could have been a Marine.

"These Pulses are going to be your livelihood in the Marine Corps from here on out." The Major cleared his throat. "The Riskar War may be over, ladies and gentlemen, but that does not mean war will not rear its ugly head ever again. However. As this war has taught us, battles are won primarily in space."

Abraham was actually liking the sound of this. So maybe they were going to be pilots instead of infantryman? He could get used to that. He had wanted to fly since he was a little kid.

"The war was costly. We lost many brave men and women who were once pilots. We lost sensory operators and aerial gunners and too many air traffic controllers to count. But we still have our Starfighters, and we still have our Galaxy Cruisers and our Star Fortresses. They may be battle-damaged and weary from war, but fresh Marines like yourselves are up for the challenge, I am sure."

"There is a caveat here. I can smell it," Abraham murmured.

"Nah, that's just Digger shitting his pants 'cuz he ain't going to war no more, man," Juke whispered, slapping Digger's ass cheek.

"Fuck off, Juke," Digger grumbled.

Tar slapped the other cheek. "Shit in ya britches...shit in ya britches..."

"Whatever." Digger crossed his arms, clearly struggling not to strike out at the two.

Major Fallon said, "The Marine Corps of the future has a very limited need for foot soldiers. What we really need is pilots for our spacecraft, but those positions are for officers. The only enlisted positions we really need at this present moment are mechanics."

Groans, moans, and retching sounds erupted from the platoon. Abraham was almost embarrassed hearing the ferocity of the disapproval coming from his comrades. Then again, he felt like the corps had just pulled the rug out from under him.

"Now, now, Marines..." Major Fallon held up his hands, "I know we're all a bunch of bloodthirsty devil-dogs who eat alien intestines like spaghetti for dinner," the platoon cheered at this, "who grind the bones of the enemy to make their bread," another cheer, "who tear new assholes all over this assless universe," the platoon was screaming their fool heads off at this point, "but we are also grown-ass men and women who know how to follow orders."

Silence.

"On your Pulses you will find the manuals for whatever spacecraft you are assigned to work on. You will spend the night reading this manual. You will learn it inside and out. Tomorrow you will be shipped out to Mattox. Once you arrive at Mattox, you will undergo ten months of in-class instruction on what it takes to keep our Air and Space Vehicles flying. You are infantry no more. You are the Marine Corps' newest crew chiefs!"

Abraham felt a little piece of himself die inside. The last thing he ever wanted to be in his life was a mechanic. Hell, he would even prefer slogging out the rest of his days as a nobody on Veranda, shoveling shit and uprooting tobacco under the oppressive glare of his father.

This. Fucking. Sucks.

After the brief, Abraham caught up with Juke and Tar back at their tent to pick their brains about the whole crew chief thing. He knew they were from Aspinos, an industrial planet, so he figured they might have some insight. He caught up with them thirty minutes later, back in the Raven Platoon's tent.

"What do you want to know, my man?" Juke asked.

"Mechanics, and stuff...I don't know?" Abraham stammered.

"It's hard work. Rough on the joints. You're forced to work in all sorts of weather conditions, and it's long hours. Extremely long, painful hours."

Abraham scoffed. "Really? How can you possibly know that?"

Juke's face was blank. He wasn't joking. "Because my older brother was a crew chief, man. He used to send me letters every month bitching about it, until I got a letter from the Navy saying how he died."

Abraham's jaw nearly hit the floor. "Holy shit, Juke, I'm sorry, man, I had no idea."

Juke shrugged. "Don't be. He was a dumbass."

Tar clapped Juke on the back. "Don't be too hard on him, man. He just didn't read the manual as closely as he should have. Anyone could have made that mistake."

Abraham was intrigued, now. Not with a sense of awe and wonder like he had about being an infantryman, but with an increasingly paranoid fear of having his life totally ruined by this forced career change.

"What mistake? If you don't mind my asking."

Juke pulled open the tent flap, letting the other two in. "He hotshotted a tire, and the fucking thing blew up. Cut his ass right in half, guts everywhere. Didn't last long after that."

Abraham was confused. "Hotshotted? What the hell is that?"

Juke scowled and headed to the showers, ripping his uniform off on the way. Tar looked at Abraham with a somber face. "He hates the way his brother died, man. Ya should just read the manual if you want to know what you're doing."

Abraham plopped down on his cot, opened the Pulse and accessed the technical manual. He was greeted with a picture of the S-16 Starfighter. He glanced down at the bottom corner of the page and nearly shit his pants.

"Twenty-six thousand pages? Fuck this."

Abraham left his Pulse on the cot and marched over to the officer's quarters.

He entered through the back, the way he had gone nearly every time he had visited Vase in her quarters. It took him a short ten minutes to get there, to weasel his way into the hallway outside her door where no one save Vase and Lechero would recognize him as an enlisted person without his uniform top on.

He did his customary knock, waited for a response. He waited much longer than usual but heard nothing. He knocked again, just to be sure. Dead silence.

"What the *shit* are you doing over here, Private?"

Abraham's intestines twisted.

Lieutenant Lechero stood with arms crossed, glaring at Abraham. He had murder in his eyes.

A thousand thoughts flew through Abraham's head. There had to be a million ways to worm his way out of this. When he tried to choose one, they all turned to incorporeal dust and left him standing there, stammering.

Lechero leaned in close, his voice barely above a whisper.

"I'm going to give you one-point-five seconds to get the fuck out of here. If I see your fucking face within a thousand meters of this fucking building, I will pull your fucking rank and send your fraternizing ass home. Do not think for one fucking second I am fucking around."

Abraham nodded.

"Now, disappear."

Abraham didn't have to be told twice. He sprinted out of the tent, down the alley and didn't stop until he was sitting on the picnic table outside of the Raven tent. His heart hammered away in his chest. He seethed inside.

What the fuck is Vase's problem? I...shouldn't have told her I love her, huh?

He thought on it, long and hard, but couldn't for the life of him figure her out. Everything with her had been the fulfillment of his wildest dreams. The connection he had with her was concrete. Solid. Nothing on Juno or in space could sever that connection, in his mind.

Up until this moment, he had thought she felt the same.

He saw her, off in the distance by the chow hall. There was a crowd of officers gathered around Admiral Latreaux, who seemed to be telling some kind of story. He was gesturing grandiosely with his hands, but his face seemed more plastic than ever; it never really changed expressions.

She laughed at whatever he was saying. After a few minutes of this, they swapped salutes. The crowd of officers started to head down the alley toward *Victory's Edge*. The Admiral turned to leave, but Vase threw her arms around him, hugged him tight. Her face seemed worried, or maybe conflicted. Abraham didn't know what to make of it.

All right Vase, what kind of game is this you're playing now? You know I'll figure it out. I will make it my mission to figure you out.

204

They were seated in the transport ship, waiting for the next part of their lives to begin. The part they hadn't really signed up for but were all resigned to after Admiral Latreaux's speech. They were issued S-skins. The spacesuit was exciting for Abraham – he was finally getting into space travel as part of his job – but it felt different from the poster he saw in the recruiting office on Veranda. The material was thick and bulky, just this side of unwieldy.

This is going to take some getting used to.

The ship was very different from the planet-hopping craft they'd taken from Veranda to Juno. It was a system-skipper. A long-distance hauler. Abraham thought of it as a whale. The bulk of it was the belly and the tail, where equipment and huge crates of who-knows-what were stacked end to end, wall to wall and nearly floor to ceiling. Beyond this was the trachea section of the whale, or ship, where the walls and ceiling were a series of bulkheads like the ribbed walling of a respiratory tube. Embedded into these bulkheads along the walls and facing the center aisle was the personnel seating. Dim lighting from overhead LEDs cast a blue-gray pall that told the senses it was midnight. The dull thrum of electrical components warred with the running water sound of air being cycled around. The Ravens and the Eagles occupied this vessel. Most of them were trying to lounge in the stiff seats that would be theirs for the week-long trip to Mattox, making small talk or double-checking their duffel bags.

Abraham read aloud from the manual on his Pulse, wishing he were dead.

"The S-16 Starfighter is a single engine, modular Air and Space Vehicle, or ASV for short. It was designed by Luther Mandrake in 9-072. There are several primary, secondary, and tertiary systems that work together to enable this ASV to fly through air, water, and space with no excessive repairs or modifications necessary. The key to the design of the S-16 is redundancy, redundancy, redundancy. Indeed, each system on the Starfighter is triple redundant for emergency purposes, as well as to limit combat vulnerability...holy *shit*, this sucks."

"You realize how much of a demotion this is?" Digger tugged at the collar seal on his S-skin. "We're going to be like squires."

Piebold snickered. "How do you figure that, Dig?"

Digger leaned back against the bulkhead. He had, so far, refused to take his seat. One last act of defiance he seemed to hope would delay the trip and keep him an infantryman for a few more minutes.

"Squires," Digger said, "what did they do? They cleaned the horse, shoveled its shit, made sure it was fed. Cleaned after the knight, dealt with his shit, made sure he was fed. These fucking airplanes and spacecrafts are the horses. The pilots are the knights."

He wrinkled his nose like he smelled something unpleasant. "That makes us the fucking squires."

Abraham couldn't refute his logic. It just made the whole thing sting all the more.

Lieutenant Seneca, Lieutenant Lechero, Staff Sergeant Hinton, Corporal Johnson, and Corporal Nichols threaded their way through the equipment boxes and joined the platoons in the trachea of the whale.

Personnel section, whatever.

"Lieutenant," Abraham greeted Vase.

"Private," Vase greeted Abraham.

The chill on the air was not due to the weather, Abraham noted dismally.

"Damn," Tar muttered, watching the officers go by in their shiny armor, "officers are lucky they get to travel in B-skins, man. That shit is *on point,* ay man?"

Juke snored in his seat, unavailable for a smart-assed reply.

The rest of the Raven and Eagle platoons stopped their conversations, sat up in or took their seats and swivelled to pay attention. In total, they had about seventy Marines and eight officers. It was a full house.

Abraham looked around for a place to sit. For now, it was standing room only. Larry and Amory were already napping under the benchrow closest to him, which was taken up by four Eagles. Abraham shook his head. Eagles or Ravens, it didn't matter. They were all Marines now.

Even though we kicked your asses in the final test, Abraham smirked to himself.

The bravado faded like a match being blown out. It turned out, after thirteen long weeks of harrowing training, of literal blood, sweat and tears being shed day in and day out, there were no winners in the Marine Corps. They were better off than they were before. That was true for most of them, sure. But now they were carried along like leaves in the wind, floating according to the dictation of the powers that be.

Conversation died. The officers and NCOs disappeared in the front of the ship to take their assigned seats. Abraham and the rest of the Ravens ended up finding some open seats of their own. They strapped in and prepared for lift-off.

Abraham stared out the viewport as the massive vessel broke ground. In moments, he was gazing outward at the empty darkness of space. Tears threatened to fall from his eyes. He bit his lip, fighting the emotion that shook his shoulders and raised the hair on his spine. The voyage was going to be a long one. The job he was going to learn was going to be unbearable. He had signed up for a four-year commitment.

Four years of my life, gone. And I'll never get them back.

Sleep did not come, not for many hours. Abraham's eyes glossed over, stars and universes reflected in them as the deep-space craft passed lightspeed, accelerating them at breakneck pace toward Mattox.

It must have been several hours before he realized he'd drifted. When his eyes opened, everything was red. A loud noise warbled over him. He recognized the noise as what had awoken him, but its meaning escaped him. The disorientation dissolved with a cold slap of reality.

It was an alarm. Not just one alarm. *All* of the alarms.

"Holy shit...what is that?" Digger pointed out the viewport.

Abraham hustled past a few Eagles, ignoring their shouts and swats when he bulled his way through their personal space. He leaned over Digger's shoulder to catch a glimpse.

Out there in the white blur of space screaming by at incredible speed, he could see another ship. It was a vessel unlike any he had seen before, in real life or in the classes at basic training. The ship was small. Maybe fifteen people could fit in it comfortably. It was shaped like a sea urchin, a rounded portion in the middle with dozens of jagged spikes sprouting from it. The midsection swelled as if the ship itself were breathing. A red plume emitted from the front of it, giving the appearance it was traveling toward its exhaust trail, rather than away from it.

And just like that, he knew.

"It's a Sackback ship," Abraham said.

Suddenly Larry was next to him, nodding. "It's a *riskar* ship."

Tar asked, "How the hell could you possibly know that?"

"Because I've seen one before. On Milune," his voice quaked, "the night my mother died."

Everyone stared.

"We're in hyperspace," Juke said. "How did they get this close to us?"

It should have been impossible to intercept them traveling at this speed, but the mysterious craft cruised alongside them. It appeared to be getting larger by the minute.

It's coming right at us!

Bright swirls of light collected at the ends of the spikes. It only took a moment.

Amory said, "That's –"

"Helmets on!" Abraham screamed. "Seal your skins!"

The swirls darkened, much like an angry moon he had seen as a child.

Everything went red.

207

A sound like a crashing wave of high tide washed over Abraham. The shriek of warping metal. Then there was no sound at all.

Light blazed so bright he could feel heat in his skull.

His visor blacked out.

Am I dead?

Something hissed inside his suit, tickling his ears.

He blinked. The darkness remained.

The aluminum smell of oxygen made his nose twitch.

You can't breathe if you're dead, dumbass.

He gasped a lungful of air.

A blinking dash appeared in his HUD. Text popped up a moment later:

REBOOT Y/N?

Yes. Fuck yes. Reboot now!

Operating by feel, he slapped the Pulse screen on his wrist.

The visor cleared up. Stars swirled around him. Pebble-sized debris flowed past him. Streamers and tatters like unraveling ropes snaked downward. Stabilizers on his S-skin's joints fired clouds of air at measured intervals. His entire body shook. Panic trickled through him like an electrical charge crawling along his skin.

I'm in space?

Fractured pieces of metal spun wildly below him. Recollection hit with a jolt; it was the transport ship. The deformed metal was covered in sheets of flame.

There's no fire in space…

He tilted his head back to follow the streamers above him.

They were connected to bodies. Bodies that had once been Eagles or Ravens. Some of them had limbs missing or bent and twisted at impossible angles. The body closest to him bore a silver bar on the chest. The helmet was gone. Thin lines leaked from the neck, oddly reminding Abraham of sea sponges on the nature channel Obadiah used to watch.

The streamers were blood.

Body's too big to be Vase, he told himself. Made himself believe it.

Beyond the dead, a vast, bright smear of deep red.

Abraham tried to wipe his eyes. His fingers bounced off his visor. He squinted.

The red smear had a curve to it. He could see landmass above him. His Pulse buzzed:

208

ALTIMETER: 31000 METERS

I'm not floating...I'm falling out of the sky.
His brain started to put the blurry images into some kind of focus. Right side up became upside down as everything shifted in his mind. Vertigo pulled his stomach into his throat. Bile burned his oesophagus.
I'm gonna throw up...
Above was the carnage of the ship.
Beside him, Marines were dead or dying.
Below was a planet's surface.
Something pricked his arm. A cool trickle collected in his gut. His Pulse blinked:

ANTI-NAUSEA DISPENSED

He took a shuddering breath. The knot in his stomach loosened. Abraham slapped his Pulse, opening the control menu for his S-skin.
His readouts showed everything as fully functional. Fine adjustment thrusters spun him around so he could take a better look at what he had thought was a continent.
Trees. Forests. Lakes and rivers.
Okay, don't panic. Don't...fucking...panic.
He was panicking.
The only thing he knew for sure was that he was looking at a planet, and he was caught in its gravitational well. The only way he could go was down.
Down to the surface of a planet he had never seen before. He didn't even know its name or coordinates. Down to a hot, hard landing that he might not survive. Orbital drops hadn't been covered in basic. And certainly not in an S-skin that had never been designed for such a drop.
He crossed his wrists over his chest, locked his ankles, and bore down toward the planet's surface. Red flames crowded around his S-skin, vibrating and blazing.
Sound whipped back inside his skull. It was like the whine of a skiff tearing through the sky above the runway on Milune. It was louder. It was inside his helmet. He could feel the friction inside his suit. Against his skin.
His Pulse chimed:

TERMINAL VELOCITY

If he survived reentry, he would die from impact. *What the fuck happened?* He could hear his heartbeat like a hammer in his skull.

The fear could have been euphoric if he had a moment to dwell on it. Instead, all these feelings flew by him, through him, and then far away from him. He watched the altimeter on the Pulse wrapped around his wrist, ticking down below 10,000 meters. Imminent death became a tangible thing. Something he could feel resting on his shoulder, waiting for the opportunity to reach out and stop his heart if he lost concentration.

The Pulse screamed with a repeating klaxon:

STABILIZE DESCENT Y/N?

Really? You have to ask?

He tapped the button immediately and flung his arms out. Thrusters fired from his wrists and calves. The burn lasted for two agonizing minutes. His rate of descent slowed, but not enough. The red tinge of reentry changed, seeming to paint the inside of his helmet with a gentle glow. The ground rushed up, much faster than he would have liked.

The sky spiraled around him in a blur.

Vegetation exploded as he crashed into the red-leafed canopies of several trees.

His body went numb. Cracks and snaps echoed inside his helmet. He hoped they were branches and twigs instead of his bones. Pain knifed at him. He tumbled and fell until he couldn't orient himself in his mind.

Shadows swept over his vision.

PART 3: DURINGER

All things of the body stream away like a river,
all things of the mind are dreams and delusion;
life is warfare, and a visit to a strange land;
the only lasting fame is oblivion.

- ***Meditations***, **Marcus Aurelius Antoninus**

CHAPTER 27

Abraham swam on a sea of darkness, floating on gentle tides of euphoria. He basked in an absence of light. Weightless, he was as much a part of the dark as the dark was of him. He could think, he could feel, but he couldn't move. It was like his body had dissolved, leaving his soul to float away into the abyss.

A voice spoke to him from the dark. A voice he hadn't heard since he was a boy.

"Son?"

His heart fractured. "Mom?"

"Abraham, baby, you need to wake up."

He could feel his face. It was hot and wet.

He didn't want to wake up. He wanted to sleep in. To go to the store and pick out a toy. Spend the afternoon running around with the other kids on his street. Tackle Father when he came home from the office. Have a family dinner with David and Mom. Maybe go for a walk and get some ice cream after. There was so much he wanted to do, and he knew if he woke up, he couldn't do it.

"Abraham, wake up."

A warm spike of heat bloomed in his chest. He panicked. It felt like something had sucked the breath out of his lungs. Just as suddenly as it hit, the burning subsided enough to let him inhale. His thoughts were murky, like he was underwater.

I'm drowning.

He felt...funny. Like he was wearing a fuzzy blanket.

"No, sweetie, no you're not," his mother seemed to say, "you still have someone to live for."

No, Mom, he groaned. *You don't understaaaaand.*

"So, tell me, son. Why isn't this working? I don't understand."

I left Father and David on Verandaaaaa. They died. *It's my fault.*

His throat tightened. He tried and failed to swallow the emotion. The world inside his head was spinning and throbbing, pulse slowing to match his heartbeat.

"That wasn't your fault, son." Her voice was far away, but soothing.

No, you don't get it. *I'm in love with Vaaaaaase. She's so* pretty. *I dunno what I did to make her hate me so much. I just love her, ya know? Maybe...maybe that's it. Maybe I love her too much? I kissed her. It was greaaaaaat. You think she knows I want to –*

"Commander override!" Mother shouted.

Pain knifed into his arm. His teeth clamped shut. Liquid fire chewed through his arm, snatched onto his heart and squeezed.

213

Abraham gasped, eyes snapping open.

The HUD showed a message from his Pulse:

COMMANDER OVERRIDE: EPINEPHRIN ADMINISTERED

The visor on his helmet caught a glare of sunlight.

Vase stood over him, her polished B-skin armor gleaming with hints of red light. She was shaking him by the neck of his armor. The wet heat on his face was sweat. There was a smudge on his visor the size of Vase's palm. Abraham was wide awake, his vision sharper than it had ever been.

"Oh, it's you!" He smiled big, cheeks stretching as he fumbled for his helmet release latch.

Vase slapped his hand away. "Stop that. We don't know if this atmosphere is breathable yet."

"Come here, you..." he said, wrapping his arms around her.

Vase grabbed his hands and pulled them off her. "Private! Knock it off." She looked around as if she had just heard something. "Look, Abraham. You need to pull it together. We're in hostile territory and I need you to be functioning."

"Oh, Vase, I loooove yew," he drawled as the heat billowed in his veins. "I think you looooove me, too." A thought occurred to him in a flash, like a solar flare. "Hey, if we're in love, which we definitely aaaare, you should stay the niiiiight."

He smiled so big his cheeks cramped.

"Oh, hell," Vase said, tapping at her Pulse.

"What's wrong? You don't want to?" He giggled. "That's a *lie*."

"Dammit," she growled, slapping at her wrist. "There it is."

COMMANDER OVERRIDE: MORPHINE DRIP TERMINATED

The heat in his chest dissolved.

Abraham tried to rub a hand on his head, but his fingers bounced off the visor. There would be no relief for the sudden itching he felt come on. He had never been more confused.

"What is...what're you doooing?"

Vase helped him up to his feet. She slung his arm over her shoulder. "Walk it off, Marine."

When he had regained his composure, Abraham noticed they were alone.

"Where is everybody?"

"We were attacked. I'm not sure how they found us so quick, but they did. And they shot us down. Our vessel is in pieces. We sent the SOS just before the transport came apart. I'm not sure if anyone picked it up. There's no other human craft on this planet."

He glanced around at the alien environment. It was little more than a clearing of tall red grass and an endless forest of red-leaved trees.

Abraham said, "So, you're saying –"

"Until we get word that someone received our distress call," her voice cracked, "we're stranded."

"I thought the war was over?"

She locked eyes with him. Her hair obscured by her helmet, she was now just a pretty face with an expression that said, *stop fucking around.*

"The war *is* over."

Abraham blinked. "You said *they* found us. That implies *they* were looking for us. We just got shot down by a *Sackback ship.* The war isn't over, Vase."

She slapped the top of his helmet. "In the military we call them riskar." She bit her lip for a moment. "And I'm Lieutenant Seneca, Abraham...Private Zeeben!"

She growled in frustration.

"What's going on, *Lieutenant?* Seriously, you've been acting weird ever since..." She eyed him dangerously, and he chose his next words more carefully, "...uh, ever since the other night."

"We don't have time to talk about this shit. Our ship is destroyed. I'm only getting pings on twenty-three transponders."

Abraham bristled. The last few minutes were a haze, but he felt something crawling up into his awareness.

Was I gushing over her, or was that a dream? She didn't hear all that, did she?

"Was I, uh...rambling just now?"

She tapped at her Pulse, ignoring him. "Okay, that's better than nothing. Looks like eighteen Eagles and ten Ravens are on the planet's surface."

"Vase."

She glared at him. "I didn't know how well you handled the drop, since it wasn't covered in basic. When I couldn't wake you up, I gave you pain meds and adrenaline. You're functioning now, so I need you to pull your head out of your ass and help me get control of this situation."

Her words snapped him out of his spiraling train of thought. Her voice was different. Terse. The only time he remembered hearing her like this was when the Ghost had visited her.

She's scared. She should be. People are dead. We have no idea where we are. We have no weapons. Why am I not scared?

Abraham surveyed the area. Red trees in thick clusters surrounded by tall thin reeds like grass, and a pale yellow sky overhead. He had no idea where they were, and that unsettled him. Gravity seemed slightly lighter than he was used to. His Pulse marked it at just under three-quarters of a G. He patted his side, searching for the CLR that had hung on his shoulder every day for the last thirteen weeks.

It was missing.

Apparently, since the 'war was over', Marines didn't travel with weapons anymore.

Vase, seeing him fumble for a rifle that wasn't there, tapped her B-skin's thigh panel. It slid open, revealing an L-pistol.

She smiled sheepishly. "My father gave it to me. I'm probably the only one on this planet with a weapon. The only human, at least."

"So, you're saying that's not standard issue?" he asked.

She closed the panel without responding.

"We need to rally with the others," Abraham muttered.

Vase sighed. "No, they need to rally with *us*. Based on the transponders still up, I'm the commanding officer."

The helmet was gone, red tatters streaming from the neck, a silver bar on the chest...

"Yeah...Lechero didn't make it. This is fucked."

Vase kept tapping at her Pulse, not even bothering to look up.

"You're not paid to share your thoughts. You're paid to obey my orders."

"You mean I'm not paid to share my thoughts *anymore*. And believe me, I'm gonna do what you tell me to do, that's not going to change. But I still think you're acting like an entitled bitch."

She stared at him, or a thousand kilometers past him, looking right through him. He could feel it, the hurt in those beautiful eyes. He knew he had taken it too far. Somehow, she was able to ignore him and act like she had lost interest in him, suddenly denying the feelings for him she had confessed just over twenty-four hours ago, but he was an asshole for telling her how she was behaving?

"Vase, I –"

"Stop." Her voice cracked. She sounded hoarse. "We're going into that forest over there. It's the only cover I see within walking distance."

Abraham agreed.

She pulled a Sky Eye out of her drop bag and chucked it into the air. The little disc unfolded its wings and buzzed off like an overgrown insect.

It soared upward, a tiny corona lighting its underside. Abraham watched until it was so small it disappeared.

Vase tapped her Pulse, placed it next to Abraham's, and swiped to mirror the feed on his device.

The view from above showed Abraham and Vase standing in a small clearing, a lake to the south and a dense cluster of trees to the west. The forestry was thick, concealing most of the landscape under overlapping canopies of red and orange and yellow leaves. Up to the north, about three hundred meters away, Abraham saw the first signs of life – a spire.

The thing was made of trees wrapped around each other, creating a spiral cord that stabbed upward maybe a hundred meters or so. At the top of the tower rested a massive boulder. It looked like an optical illusion. How could such a huge rock balance on such a tenuous point?

"I'm sending a rally signal on the Pulse net," Vase said, still tapping the device. "Do you have something?"

Abraham entered the forest, stomping through waist high foliage, and held out his wrist to show her. She grabbed his hand then let go of it, coughing uncomfortably.

"What the hell is that?" she asked.

Abraham shrugged. "It looks like a spire of some kind. Not really sure what it does. Or who it belongs to."

They cleared the thicker section of the reeds and entered a small ravine near the base of the tower. The stone was about the size of a skiff, perfectly rectangular and smooth. Besides the gravity-defying perch on which it rested, the thing also looked polished.

"How the hell did somebody get that big ass thing up that high?"

Vase shrugged. "Anti-gravity, I guess."

The stone shifted. A thunderclap reverberated through the air as it started rotating atop the twisted trees. It blurred with speed until it began to glow a bright, bright orange. Abraham realized what it was a moment later.

The siren began wailing. Abraham and Vase shared the same look: *This isn't good.*

Up until this point, Abraham had never actually shit his pants. He'd been scared out of his mind, thought he was going to die, thought a fucking moon was going to crush him into oblivion, but somehow he always managed to internalize the fear.

This was something new to him, and no amount of basic training or schoolyard brawls could have prepared him for it.

Vase dragged him to the ground with a thud. They crawled under thick, heavy roots, scraping up loose soil to cover themselves. Through the helmet filters he got a scent of something like chamomile tea and copper. Abraham rolled over onto his belly so he could see his Pulse without leaving his place of concealment.

It started off as little trails of movement. The shake of a tree. A few snapping twigs. It could have been a breeze or a small animal making its way through the jungle. Except the movements multiplied. It was now a dozen trees swaying. Thirty twigs snapping.

Adrenaline chewed at his gut.

They were being *hunted*.

The siren continued to wail. The whirling stone emitted black smoke that billowed up into the sky. It seemed such a primitive technology, but Abraham still couldn't understand the physics at work.

He was about to shift to his other elbow when he sensed movement.

A stomp shook the earth barely a meter in front of him. He saw a foot, roughly human in shape, but with thick black talons like those of a hawk. There was a strange sort of sandal on the foot that covered the non-talon portion. A glint of light caught it at just the right angle.

It was armor.

A stream of guttural barking filled the air.

The owner of the foot seemed to be instigating something, calling out to his buddies. Abraham stole away a second to glance at his Pulse, where the translation appeared in small letters.

TRANSLATION: RISKAR
TAKE ONE ALIVE, KILL THE REST

Several more barks came back. Abraham read the translation.

RICTOR REIGNS! RICTOR REIGNS!

No fucking way, Abraham thought, a sudden swell of excitement flooding his veins. *If that's Rictor, I'm the luckiest bastard in the universe. I'll kill him with my bare hands.*

It would, of course, be impossible. No, not impossible...just a suicide mission.

I'm comfortable with that.

After everything he had been through, he never imagined he would get this opportunity. He was coiled underneath the roots of a decaying tree on an alien planet whose name he didn't know. He was next to the woman he loved, a woman who infuriated just as much as fascinated him.

218

A woman he would die to protect. He was possibly one meter away from the very person responsible for ruining his life. For killing his family.

He would be an idiot *not* to take the opportunity when it was right in front of him. Abraham shifted his weight to his knees, hand creeping toward Vase's thigh.

Vase pressed his hand onto her thigh and held it. He looked into her eyes. She shook her head inside her helmet, eyes piercing. She tapped at her wrist with deft fingers. His Pulse blinked.

MESSAGE: LIEUTENANT SENECA
DO NOT MOVE. WE NEED INTEL MORE THAN WE NEED HIM DEAD.

Abraham gritted his teeth but nodded. Vengeance would have to wait. But he silently vowed not to leave this planet without killing Rictor. Hours passed. His legs were cramping. He had to piss. His throat was dry and scratchy. The oxygen in his suit was running low. He tapped his Pulse, pulling up the environment scan report.

ESR: ATMOSPHERE HUMAN-BREATHABLE

He smiled to himself. *Helmet's gonna have to come off soon.*

The taloned feet of the riskar disappeared into the darkening foliage, leaving Abraham and Vase alone in the woods.

Oxygen ran out hours ago. They carried their helmets as they moved, trying to make as little noise as possible. Abraham and Vase talked about the rank humidity, the smell of ammonia and loamy earth. They still had no idea where they were. The Pulse net didn't have this topography loaded in the database, but that wasn't unusual. Space was a big place.

The moon was dark yellow, almost orange. It was huge in the sky, so big it reminded Abraham of Dajun. Dajun, the moon that had taken his mother from him all those years ago.

He hated it, tried not to look at it, but he couldn't help glancing up every now and then just to remind himself it wasn't getting bigger.

A few hours later, they linked up with the survivors at a makeshift camp in a cluster of trees.

Abraham crushed Larry in a bear hug. He even gave Amory a one-armed side-hug. He was just grateful they were alive. Piebold and Digger, Tar and Juke, they had all made it. Staff Sergeant Hinton, Corporal

Nichols and Corporal Johnson. A few other Ravens and the rest were Eagles, for a total of twenty-two Marines.

Vase found Hinton and asked, "Sitrep, Sergeant?"

Hinton's face was flat and emotionless as he reported to Vase.

"Lieutenant," he said, twitching with an itch to salute but refraining at the last moment, "we have twenty-six total transponders active. Twenty-two here at camp. Privates Miran and Schuster will not last the night without medevac. Three more with broken bones, two with sprained knees or ankles."

Vase started working at her Pulse.

"Recommendations?"

Hinton cleared his throat. "Ma'am, we need to leave a few Marines here to keep an eye on the wounded. The rest of us need to verify the status on the four stray transponders."

"I agree," she said.

"Ma'am," Corporal Johnson approached her.

"Go ahead, Corporal."

He tugged at his S-skin. "We gonna need to shirk these noisemakers if we don't wanna announce ourselves to the enemy."

Abraham didn't need to hear that twice. He ripped the thing off immediately.

The situation ran through his mind – out of fifty or more on the transport, they were now down to twenty-six, seven injured. Marooned on an unknown planet with no weapons except Vase's secret pistol. To top it off, they had no means of off-world communication on a planet crawling with riskar militants actively searching for them with the intent of killing all but one.

He added his S-skin to the pile by the helmets. The humidity made the sweat spots under his arms feel cold. He felt like an idiot wearing combat boots and a black, skin-tight undersuit. He pulled at the fabric where it rode up by his groin.

Never imagined I'd fight a war half-naked.

Abraham's Pulse vibrated on his wrist:

TACTICAL MAP UPDATED

Abraham got up to join Vase and Sergeant Hinton. Digger and Larry came over, followed by Amory and Piebold, Tar, Juke and three other Ravens. The lack of illumination, in addition to everyone's black undersuits, made for an awkward huddle.

"All right, listen up," Hinton said, "we're in the shit now. What do Marines do when the shit hits?"

"Get to shoveling," Amory said.

The big Marine nodded emphatically.

"That's fucking right. We've got four friendly transponders spread out to the west and the north. We're operating as search and rescue in hostile territory. So, battlefield tactics question: what do you do when your enemy has weapons superiority and the homefield advantage?"

Digger said, "You go primitive. Guerrilla warfare."

"Hot damn, Tachek, you just gave me a hard-on. *Fuck yes* you get primitive. Cover yourselves in the terrain. Blend into the environment. Fashion weapons out of whatever you can get your hands on. We're leaving in twenty mike."

Abraham removed the emergency knife from his S-skin's drop bag. Blade to hilt was ten centimeters of hardened tungsten. Sturdy enough to do damage, but not worth much against enemies with long range weapons.

It's just like Staff Sergeant Hinton said. The Marine Corps is used to dealing with defunct equipment. Here I am in my first real-world action and the first thing we do is make spears out of sticks and survival knives.

Behind him, someone was gasping.

Abraham turned to check on the wounded when he saw Digger with his back turned to him.

Is he crying?

At Digger's feet, Schuster lay against a tree root, holding his chest. Folds of torn S-skin were parted over a gaping wound. Every few seconds his chest would rise and shudder. That was the source of the gasping he'd heard.

"Dad?" Schuster whispered.

Digger knelt and grabbed his hand. "I'm here, son," he said in a hushed tone.

"Dad...I'm suh-sorry."

Digger ran his fingers through Schuster's hair.

"Nothing to be sorry about, Lucas. You've done us all proud. Rest up, now."

Schuster shuddered, lips quivering.

The gasps weren't coming from the Marine's throat, Abraham realized. They were coming from the wound.

And then they weren't.

A faint crackle followed by a long exhale escaped his lips. He didn't shudder again.

The stillness of his body matched the silence in the air, like this moment belonged to him.

This guy gave me my first beer. Now he's dead.

Digger gently closed his eyes with a hand. He wiped his face and stood.

"The fuck you looking at, Zeeben?" He walked off.

"I don't know," Abraham said to Digger's back.

The Staff Sergeant went around the circle, patting everyone on the shoulder. He gave the signal for patrol formation, taking point. Vase took her position at the rear. Abraham saw the Eagles doing the same, with Corporal Nichols in the rear. An Eagle Abraham didn't know by name took point, and they led the way, staying about a hundred meters ahead of the Ravens.

I thought my first patrol would be just like in basic...when we had rifles. This is suicide. If we get caught, we're going to get shot to pieces.

He didn't like the feeling of helplessness that came over him. He didn't like how desperate he was to feel the weight of a CLR in his hands. Abraham started his march, keeping in pace to maintain his position in the column of Ravens. He also didn't like how every odd-shaped branch, every crack of a twig or rustle of a leaf sent his senses screaming.

His heart raced like every step was going to be his last.

They slinked through the overgrown brush, moving at a snail's pace. The idea was to be silent and stealthy, to avoid unwittingly stumbling on an enemy position.

An hour went by. The smells ranged from damp grass to full-on methane gas. It was unpleasant, but the Pulse report showed benign toxicity levels. Abraham's shoulders and legs were burning with fatigue. It was hard work scrambling through the tall fronds of brush, carefully parting the strands to minimize noise. Each step was like ambling over a fence, stretching leg muscles in a way he hadn't really used them before.

They were creeping up on two hours when they finally reached another clearing of low-cut grass. It was more mulch-like the further it stretched, right up to the bank of a slow-moving river. A sliver of golden moonlight emanated from above. Two figures walked along the riverbank.

Abraham's breath caught in his chest.

They were humanoid. One tall and thin, the other shorter and a bit wider. The moon began to fall below the horizon, stealing the light. It was hard to define exactly what species they were looking at. The two beings walked along the river side by side at a slow, meandering clip.

The Ravens watched them from the relative safety of the dark.

Hinton tapped Digger on the shoulder, starting a chain of hand motions down the line. Finally, Amory patted Larry, and Larry patted Abraham twice on his right shoulder and pointed to the clearing.

Eagles are pressing toward the transponders. We're going to the river.

Abraham nodded, turned and patted Vase the same way. She nodded back.

One by one, the Ravens slinked out into the clearing, staying within arm's reach of the forest. They stalked along, right up to the river's edge, where Sergeant Hinton produced a vial from his drop bag. He plunged it into the river, collected a few drops of the liquid and dripped them onto his Pulse.

The moon disappeared completely. There wasn't a single star in the sky as far as Abraham could see. For some reason, the thought brought a sense of dread. Suddenly, dying on *this* alien planet didn't seem as good an idea as a lifetime of work on the Veranda farm.

Text popped up on Abraham's Pulse.

MESSAGE: STAFF SERGEANT HINTON
RIVER IS PRIMARILY DIHYDROGEN MONOXIDE. HIGH SALT CONTENT, BUT IT'S WATER. RECOMMEND REGROUP WITH EAGLE PLATOON.

Abraham fiddled with the survival knife at his belt. He took in a sharp lungful of wet grass. The moisture from the river felt like a cold breath on his face. He leaned over it and took in a deeper breath.

The stench was so bad he almost coughed. A rush of something like ammonia and rank mildew filled his sinuses. It made his eyes water.

MESSAGE: LIEUTENANCE SENECA
RETURN TO RECON ROUTE

He tore through the brush and ended up in a rolling patch of short grass. The river bent to the north where it disappeared on the horizon. The skeleton of a strange fish broke the surface of the water, hovering a full two seconds before plunging back down.

Larry and Amory appeared beside him, panting.

Larry shoved him and whispered, "What the fuck, bro?"

Amory pointed to the south. "Guys…what is that?"

Abraham followed her finger, back to where he had estimated that the small explosion had taken place. Something pulled him there. A feeling like a belt being cinched too tightly around his gut. He thought he knew what he was going to find, but he had to see for himself.

It was a blackened circle in the field, white smoke rising from it like fog. Two bodies lay in the center, one taller than the other. Neither of them wore armor. Neither carried weapons.

"Private Zeeben, what the hell are you doing?" Sergeant Hinton shouted hoarsely.

Abraham stared down at the bodies. His brain felt fuzzy. They each had three eyes, stuck open and glazed over. Bits of flesh were crisped and flaking. The abdomens were caved in. These aliens were thin and delicate without their armor. Severed tubes wilted at their necks.

He was looking at the two beings he had seen walking by the river.

He should have been elated, but this was…different. They had not been wearing armor, weren't carrying weapons. These were not soldiers.

And one of them had been a child.

CHAPTER 28

Abraham, surrounded by the rest of his platoon, looked down at the grisly sight.

Amory stepped into the debris field, shrugging off Larry's attempt to keep her close.

"Fuck off," she growled.

All at once, the Ravens lowered their makeshift spears or sheathed their knives. Abraham wasn't sure if it was a conciliatory gesture to the fallen or if they all just wanted a moment to rest. Vase stepped forward and heaved a sigh.

"Ravens, listen up," she said.

All eyes were on Amory. She kneeled by the bodies, even as Vase continued speaking.

"We've gone off course here. The Eagles are almost to the first two transponders, and we don't know what they could run into. We need to link back up with them."

Corporal Nichols asked, "What the hell was this? Did they try to drop an airstrike on us and missed, or do they make a habit of taking out their own people for the fuck of it?"

Amory reached a hand down and gently closed the eyes of both victims. Her lips moved, mumbling phrases that sounded like prayers. Her right hand rested at her waist, brushing at her belt.

Vase, unaware of Amory behind her, said, "Our primary objective hasn't changed. We need to acquire transport and escape. To do that, we need to make sure we aren't leaving anyone behind and then get our asses in gear. The longer we're here, the more likely we're going to be discovered."

Amory slung her dagger from her belt and stabbed the adult in the skull.

Abraham blanched. *They're already dead.*

She muttered under her breath, "Your soul is safe with me."

His Pulse vibrated, but he couldn't take his eyes off Amory. Revulsion coursed through him as she knelt beside the child, raising the dagger again.

Abraham reached out and grabbed her wrist.

"What the fuck are you doing? They're already dead!"

Amory shoved him off her. "Back off, prick. I'm honoring them."

Larry grabbed Abraham under his arms, holding him back.

Amory rubbed a hand over her very short hair, raised the bloody dagger and plunged it into the skull of the child.

Abraham felt the impact, the crunch inside his own skull.

She said another prayer.

Why am I having such a strong reaction to her mutilating Sackback corpses?

Abraham's Pulse vibrated.

TRANSLATION: RISKAR
YOUR SOUL IS SAFE WITH ME.

Horrified at the barbaric display, Abraham shrugged Larry off and rejoined the rest of his platoon. He took a deep breath, trying to delete the memory from his mind. Amory's dagger, covered in a substance like a mix between motor oil and stone-ground mustard. He knew it was riskar blood; nothing like that could ever come out of a human. That blade, the very one she had held against his ribs a few weeks ago, had just been used to mutilate two corpses. And one of them a fucking child.

Sergeant Hinton rested a hand on his shoulder and gently bumped foreheads with him.

"You know, Private, there's all kinds of life out there. Some is nice, some is mean. But they all have homes, families, you name it. Some people feel like they're not all that different from us. They'd be wrong."

Abraham glanced back at the scene for a moment, curious at the sudden silence. They were staring not in his direction, but at Amory, like she was some kind of monster.

"I don't know how to feel about this, Staff Sergeant. I hate the Sackbacks. They killed my mother. They killed my father and my brother, too. But these were...just a father and son."

"Daughter," Amory said. She rubbed the dagger against her Pulse, adding the riskar DNA to the database. "These riskar were Anktala. Just workers."

Piebold crossed his arms and asked, "How do you know that?"

Amory tapped at her Pulse. "They have a lower concentration of Moscovium in their blood. My parents...my adopted parents, they were Ekpitala. Outcasts."

Abraham shook his head. None of this made sense.

Hinton placed a large hand on his shoulder.

"Now you see the dilemma of war for the first time with your own eyes, Private. There are no winners in war, just those who lose less. When the fog of war settles and the fighting is done, winner and loser alike count their losses and rebuild."

"Yes, Staff Sergeant. I'm just not sure how I feel about it all."

Vase shouldered her way into the conversation.

"That's because you're not meant to, Private Zeeben. A good Marine keeps his focus on the here and now."

Abraham rolled his eyes, but decided he was going to let that one go without a response. Here she was in her role as commander of the platoon, and she was going out of her way to be petty to him. He realized in that moment that he was doomed to a miserable career if he couldn't figure Vase out.

Or, he thought, *maybe just a broken heart.*

"Hey, Staff Sergeant, check this shit out," Digger called.

Everyone rushed over to Digger's position, about five meters from the bodies. It was right in the center of burnt field, the impact site of whatever killed the two riskar. The burly man was standing in front of a silver-covered depression in the ground, like a two-meter-wide manhole cover. It looked heavy.

"This isn't a natural formation," Piebold said.

"No shit, Piebold," Abraham said. "When's the last time you saw a manhole in the ground with red light coming out of it?"

"Abraham," Larry said. "What the fuck are you talking about?"

All eyes were on him. No one spoke.

"What?" he asked.

Vase moved up to him and patted his shoulder.

"Are you all right?"

His stomach felt queasy. As much as he didn't want to, he knew he had to ask. "You guys don't see it? Really?"

The silence and baffled looks he got from everyone were enough.

"Abraham," she whispered, "as soon as we get to a decent medical facility, I'm getting you evaluated for a TBI."

He scoffed. *I'll show you.*

"Get outta the way."

He stepped through a few people, got right up to the oversized manhole and knelt beside it. Upon closer inspection, he could see it was metal of some kind, clear of brush and dirt. It looked polished. A crimson ring of light lit the circumference. Apparently, a light only he could see. He placed his hand on it to try to lift it by the edge.

His hand hurt. It felt like a pinch, or a pierce through his palm and out the back of his hand. Like he'd been stabbed. It reminded him of slamming a metal rod against the ground, vibrations jostling his bones. His right arm from wrist to elbow went numb, tingles racing up and down it.

What the fuck?

The circle rotated with a sharp hiss.

Abraham stepped back, holding his injured arm.

The metal spun a few more times. A crack of red light spread two meters out to either side where the earth began to separate.

The ground tremored.

"Be ready for anything, Marines!" Vase said, drawing her pistol.

A pneumatic squeal spewed debris as the crack widened. Abraham stumbled back.

The ground opened up, two large doors swinging open with massive force. Corporal Johnson was flung back a few meters, shouting. He slammed into the grass a meter back. Where the corporal had stood was now a dark, square hole in the ground.

"What the –"

Flickering floodlights from the hole cut off the corporal's question. The light stabilized. Abraham leaned over the edge of the hole.

Inside were equipment racks. CLRs, rocket launcher attachments, magazines and heat sinks, grenades and Sky Eyes, a few B-skins, even some MREs. Enough equipment to supply a small platoon.

It took half a second before they rushed the pod, bowling Abraham into it and slamming his head against the CLRs. He quickly grabbed what he could and got out of there. Something about the tight space packed with bodies grated on his nerves.

In a matter of moments, the Marines were double-checking their new equipment with a series of clicks and clacks that dissipated in the jungle fronds and leaves. There were enough B-skins for everyone.

Abraham stepped into the armor-plating and yanked it up. Gears clicked. Servos whined. He slid the helmet on. The internal HUD sparked to life, syncing with his Pulse. A small tactical map floated in the lower right field of the visor.

I'm ready for war now.

Beside him, Amory slid a few grenades onto her belt and passed a few more to Tar and Juke. Larry and Piebold were chowing down on the food rations.

Abraham felt safer inside the B-skin, but he still felt naked without a CLR. He scanned the rack, grateful to find two that hadn't been claimed yet. He clipped it onto his shoulder sling and reached over Digger's head to grab four heat sinks and four magazines, then stepped back to let the rest of his platoon take their pick.

It took him another thirty seconds to look over his gear, slide the sinks and mags onto his belt, and finally load a heat sink onto his rifle. He heaved a sigh of relief. He felt just a little more in control of his life, now.

This is too convenient.

He waited another minute, watching his teammates elated to have fresh equipment. They may not have the numbers, but now that they had weapons and equipment, they stood a fighting chance. He decided to get the burning question off his chest.

"How did this get here? Did anyone see this pod on our ship before we crashed?"

"No wonder you're still a virgin," Digger glared at him. "You really know how to ruin a mood, don't you, Zeeben?"

"I'm just saying," Abraham shrugged, "this is standard issue Marine equipment, but I don't remember seeing any of this stuff on our ship. Not the pod, either."

Larry was already chewing on something he'd dug out of an MRE. He said between bites, "So what're you saying, Abraham? You think this stuff is poisoned or something?"

"No, I'm saying *how did it get here?*"

Vase and Hinton shared a look. Hinton started frantically typing on his Pulse. Vase put her hands on her hips and sighed.

"We need to rendezvous with the Eagles. Once we're there, we can look at our options for finding temporary shelter. Some place to gather ourselves and catch our breath before we proceed with our escape plan."

"Ma'am," Hinton mumbled, his face dour, "I can't raise the Eagles on the Pulse net."

It was daylight when they found the transponders.

Two G-seats from the transport ship rested on their sides, shorn at the edges. Two bodies were still strapped in, limp arms draped toward the ground. The S-skins were blackened and shriveled. Glass shards protruded from them at odd angles.

They couldn't have survived the impact, Abraham thought. *Sackbacks lit them up anyway.*

"Sergeant," Vase whispered, "are you getting anything?"

Hinton tapped his Pulse. He locked eyes with her and shook his head.

"If the transponders are still pinging," Amory whispered, "where are the Eagles?"

Larry swallowed noisily. "Are the riskar smart enough to set a trap?"

Amory scoffed. "Of course they...oh. *Oh.*"

The tree line exploded.

They charged into the clearing like lions.

Guttural bellows, throaty roars, bony limbs raised with stony knuckles curled into fists.

Their armor was polished to a perfect shine, varying in colors from blue and red to something like copper. The faces of the enemy were the most disturbing; three eyes above a mandible like the upper teeth of a human skull. Finger-like claws where their chins should be. Puffed sacks dangled from tubes on either side of their necks that swelled with respiration. They looked like bicep muscles with the skin torn off.

Abraham had paid very close attention in the classes on alien anatomy at basic training. There had been several on the riskar. He recognized the neck-sacks as lungs, the most vulnerable part of the aliens' bodies. This was where he chose to aim when he slammed his CLR into his shoulder.

The thump in his shoulder, the laser blasts screaming through the air, the smoke and crackle of free-flying death...it was almost like being at the firing range, except for the incoming fire.

The forestry was so thick it was hard to see, but he did his best to follow Vase's advice from training.

Aim, breathe, squeeze. Repeat.

One riskar, more brazen than the rest, outdistanced his counterparts. He bellowed from the sides of his neck and raised his spiked rifle over his head.

Abraham put his crosshairs over the neck, slowly releasing a breath and squeezing the trigger at the same time.

Pop-pop!

The lungs deflated. The alien dropped its weapon, clawed hands flying to its shoulders. It reminded Abraham of an old image David had shown him years ago; an ancient mummy laid to rest in a sarcophagus.

Laser blasts bit into its torso, scorching armor until it collapsed in a smoking heap.

I just killed for the first time and now *my brain starts remembering history? What is wrong with me?*

"Frag out!" Juke shouted.

The grenade sailed into the field. Abraham felt the detonation in his knees.

Fragments of riskar rode a fountain of dirt a meter high.

"Nice one, bubby," Juke called out. "Tree for one!"

Vase slammed into the tree root right beside Abraham, her shoulder brushing against his. She slid her CLR over the moss and decay, lit off a few shots and ducked back down.

"What're you staring at?" she growled.

Abraham couldn't stop himself. He smiled. "You look beautiful, Ma'am."

She scowled. "Shoot back or shut the fuck up."

Abraham nodded, returning to combat, but he did not stop smiling.

Not until he took a round to the shoulder.

The impact spun him off his heels. He dropped to the forest floor before he knew what hit him. A tiny plume of smoke wafted up from his left shoulder. He reached over to try to feel it, to see if his arm was still attached, when he felt pain bite into his fingers.

He pulled them back, seeing blood trickle from them. Waving his hand in front of the smoke, he got it to clear enough that he could see the wound. A jagged piece of glass the size of his fist had pierced clean through his B-skin and into his deltoid. The round, a blue glass-like projectile, was so sharp he had sliced deep into two of his gloved fingers just by touching it.

"I'm hit," he said into his mic. "Not bad, though. I'll live."

Vase was there, reaching for the glass piece.

"No, stop." He swatted her hand away. "Use your weapon to knock it out."

"Abraham, you're in shock. That's not going to work."

He showed her his bleeding fingers.

Vase did as he asked, slamming the butt of her CLR against the glass piece.

Abraham screamed. The piece shattered, leaving hundreds of tiny shards embedded in his shoulder.

"I'm sorry! Holy shit, Abraham, I'm sorry!" Vase blanched.

He resisted the very strong urge to rub the wound, which now felt like a gunshot wound infected with chicken pox. It took everything he had to pick up his rifle and shrug his shoulders.

Text materialized in his HUD.

PAIN MANAGEMENT SUITE ACTIVE

He felt the prick on his arm. Ice trickled through his vein. He sighed. It wasn't enough to make him hazy, but it took the edge off.

"I'm fine. What do we do now?"

Vase shook her head. "We're fucked. We need to retreat. We've got the whole fucking planet alerted to our location now."

Abraham glanced at the Sky Eye feed in his HUD. The drone was still circling overhead, giving him a clear view of their predicament. They were boxed in. More riskar than he could count were encroaching on their position from just about every side. There was a slight break at the east, but that was due to the start of a mountain range that made for some tough terrain.

Which is probably our only shot.

"Lieutenant, we have to go east. There might be a crevice in the mountainside we can hole up in. It's our only shot."

231

Vase repeated his words on the platoon-wide com channel.

The battle raged on. Humans fired lasers. Riskar fired white-hot shards of glass and metal. The riskar splintered into pieces when they took a direct hit. Humans fell bleeding and screaming, only to be dragged off into the jungle by the aliens.

Abraham held the trigger, firing off dozens of shots in a matter of seconds. The advancing line of riskar fell, missing limbs and lungs. More appeared through the trees, their weapons glowing. The sky was filled with glass and smoke and the crackling of flame.

Abraham's heat sink started smoking. He thumbed the release, dropping it to the ground while simultaneously reaching for another on his belt. He slid it across the receiver, slapped it to lock it in place, charged the handle, shouldered his weapon, and opened up with another salvo. He was thankful for the endless drills in basic. He didn't even have to think. His body just knew what to do, like a robot programmed to shoot, reload, repeat.

"Ravens, retreat! Fall back to the mountainside, let's go!"

Vase exited her cover, firing on automatic. Once she had the attention of the riskar, she disappeared into the jungle.

Abraham mimicked her move, firing off a few shots, splintering a few more riskar before turning tail and sprinting into the jungle. He held his left arm against his side, fighting the dull pain in his shoulder with every step. The Sky Eye showed he was right on course for the near side of the mountain. Several blue arrows that indicated his teammates were swiveling to follow him.

Piebold and Digger were right behind him. Tar and Juke passed him, drawing closer to Vase. She fired a few shots from her CLR to burn down the excessive foliage that threatened to slow their escape.

Vase stepped through a wall of fire that she had made, then held up a closed fist.

Stop.

The enemy fire was still screaming at their backs. Abraham knew if they stopped, they'd be dead. He kept on going, rushing through the wall of fire, prepared for anything.

Anything except a sheer cliff and the ravine below.

CHAPTER 29

He tumbled right over the edge, vision spiraling. Head over heels he plummeted, taking hits against rocks and tough tree roots the size of his thigh. He rolled so fast, so hard, he couldn't tell up from down until his helmet careened face first into a jagged boulder.

His visor cracked.

It took a moment for him to breathe again. Without moving, he tried to assess if he had broken anything.

Left shoulder hurt like hell. Right knee was banged up from a gnarly tree root or a rock, he didn't remember which. All in all, he felt okay. No broken ribs that he could tell. And he hadn't snapped his neck during the fall.

He looked up, up, up.

About ten meters up he saw Piebold and Vase waving their hands. Glass shards whizzed between them. Vase shoved Piebold back and ducked into the forest. Abraham looked around, but the only way back up was to climb a sheer rock face at a ninety-degree angle.

"What the fuck, Zeeben? You didn't see the lieutenant with her hand up, or what?"

The voice came from somewhere behind him. He turned to see Digger.

Abraham sighed. He was separated from his platoon and that was bad enough. Now, he had to be separated from his platoon *and* stuck with Digger. Part of him was relieved not to be alone.

"Hey, I'm talking to you!" Digger shoved him. "The fuck's your problem?"

Pain stung his shoulder. It was a small pain, Abraham had to admit, but it was there.

"Look, it was keep moving or get shot in the back. I didn't have time to think."

Digger guffawed. "Ha! Yeah, like that's gonna fly. We're in fucking *war*, bro. You have time to think. You just only get one chance to do it. And you chose fucking wrong, Zeeben. Now we're royally fucked."

A rapid increase in glass shards tore through the thickets up on the ledge. Sergeant Hinton tumbled out of the foliage, glass fragments sticking out of him like spines on a porcupine. He bellowed into the com frequency, CLR blazing as he fell backward down the ten-meter drop toward a grotto at the base of the cliff.

Abraham and Digger shared a look.

They both nodded to each other and made a mad dash for him.

Once they arrived at the grotto, they started picking through fallen fronds and leaves the size of human bodies. They searched, but both came up empty-handed.

The tree next to Abraham erupted in fragments. Sturdy wood pieces bent and wilted, glass shards tearing into it.

K-TOOM! K-TOOM! K-TOOM!

Abraham recognized that sound. A CLR firing in scattershot.

He spun toward the source of the shots, weapon up.

Sergeant Hinton stood before them, larger than life. Glass shards a quarter meter long protruded from his body at random angles. Blood spattered his cracked B-skin, his compacted CLR, his face. His normally chaotic energy was suddenly focused.

Behind the tree, Abraham saw four smoking ruins of riskar bodies. They must have followed Hinton over the cliff. Abraham cursed himself for not being observant enough to see them. They could have killed him and Digger. Probably would have if Sergeant Hinton hadn't gotten them first.

Hinton fell to his knees, groaning. His CLR hit the forest floor. He leaned back on his ankles. Blood trickled from the corner of his mouth.

"Sergeant, we gotta get you the hell out of here!" Digger shouted.

Hinton shook his head.

Abraham let his rifle dangle from his sling. He grabbed his own wrist with one hand and held out the other to Digger.

"C'mon, let's make him a chair and get a move on!"

Digger copied Abraham's gesture. They linked hands, creating a chair with their arms, and slid it under their former drill instructor, careful to avoid the embedded glass rounds. He rested an arm on each of their shoulders. Abraham grimaced at the weight; his old instructor probably weighed two hundred and eighty pounds.

They hustled through the forest, kicking red leaves, stomping through coiled brush. Adrenaline pumped through Abraham's veins. He felt like he was on fire inside. The only thing he could think of was getting Hinton to a safe place away from the enemy. He just wanted a minute to catch his breath, to knock these glass shards out of Hinton's body, anything that could possibly keep the man alive long enough to get proper medical attention.

We don't have any medical attention.

He didn't want to think about that.

Hinton's head swayed. He moaned.

Digger said, "Zeeben! He's not gonna make it."

Abraham refused to hear it. "He's making it, Dig, just keep going. We're almost there."

"Almost where?"

The underbrush was tricky to maneuver over. Everywhere he looked was red. Red leaves, red blood, red berries on red bushes. Abraham didn't see anything that would count as a hideaway spot. Digger was right – there was absolutely nowhere to go.

"We're going to have to make something!" Abraham grunted into the mic. "Put him down here."

They deposited Hinton on a soft bed of foliage at the base of a large tree. Abraham loaded a fresh sink, slapped it home and charged his rifle. He lit up the canopy above, trying to concentrate the fire as close to the center as possible. Huge, thick fronds began to drift and crash down around them. The report of the rifle was deafening.

It took half of his heat sink and about twenty seconds before they were blanketed under the stuff. Abraham crouched down, grabbed fistfuls of the brown stuff, the coiled underbrush, and spread it over Hinton. Digger stood guard behind him, weapon raised.

Hinton effectively hidden under the stringy brown jungle moss, Abraham patted Digger on the back.

"Cover!"

The two jumped into a cluster of bushes a few meters from Hinton and waited.

They waited for a long time. It had to be an hour or more that they waited. Abraham kept his eyes glued to his Pulse the whole time, waiting for a message from one of the Ravens, or for something to change on the view from the Sky Eye. The minutes passed by slowly.

Every minute or so he would hear Hinton cough or gurgle. Brush rubbed against brush as he made minor adjustments in his seated position.

Abraham knew the riskar were coming, he just didn't know when. He needed them to come, check this area out, and then give up. Only then would it be safe to get Hinton up and move him to a better location.

There isn't *a better location.*

Anywhere's better than here. He had to believe that.

Around the hour and a half mark the bushes began to shake. He could feel sweat on his palms. Hunters in the heart of their home territory, the riskar slinked along, neck sacks swelling and shrinking, armor pieces clinking like knives scraping against each other.

Abraham realized Hinton's breathing was going to give them away. There was nothing he could do about it at this point.

The barking started up.

"I hear one of them. The tracks were for two. Perhaps one did not survive the fall."

235

"No. One is here, abandoned by the other. One is far from here, has left his comrade behind like the coward all humans are. There is no honor among this species."

"Very little, General."

"Over here, General."

One of the aliens kicked aside the brush covering Sergeant Hinton. He was a broken man. Abraham hated seeing him like this. Hated that he was just as scared for himself as he was for his mentor. Hinton was sitting and bleeding. Exposed in front of the enemy.

Abraham's Pulse buzzed.

MESSAGE: STAFF SERGEANT HINTON
LEAVE NOW

Abraham was going to send a message back but decided against it. He wasn't about to leave, either. Marines did not leave anyone behind. He looked at Digger, and they both shook their heads together.

Some of the glass shards had fragmented, collecting into tiny pieces of sand that Hinton was rifling through with his hands. His face was stretched in pain, his left leg twitching. A vein in his neck throbbed. Sweat coated his bald forehead. Blood ran from his shoulders and chest, collecting around his abdominal wounds and pooling by his waist.

General Rictor stepped into full view, his back to Abraham and Digger's position. Abraham breathed deeply, trying to keep himself absolutely still with every fiber of his being. The stench of humidity commingled with the sweet, earthy tea fragrance of the dirt.

"Human," Rictor's voice wavered. "How did you find this place?"

Hinton smirked and spat. "Da fuck do I look like to you, a fuckin' navigator?"

Rictor leaned down, his hand hovering over a glass shard in Hinton's shoulder.

"Speak the truth and live. Lie and you shall surely die."

The riskar General's fingers wrapped around the glass and yanked. Blood and glass slivers flew out of Hinton's wound, pattered onto Rictor's leg armor.

The normally boisterous Staff Sergeant screamed. His hand flew up to the wound, possibly to try to staunch the blood flow or protect it from further injury. He pulled it away, screaming harder, dozens of fibrous glass filaments protruding from it.

Abraham flinched at each scream, winced at each shuddering breath. Beside him, Digger was gritting his teeth. Sweat collected at the tip of his nose.

"The Slinger is one of our modern takes on weaponry," Rictor said, showing Hinton his weapon. It looked like a combination of a belt sander and a pistol from an old western movie. Resting atop the belt were small bricks of sand. A tiny flame at the tip of the weapon came to life once it left the holster.

"The Mighty riskar are known for gravity control, while humans are known for their weapons of war. It will amuse me, human, to use this, a primitive weapon by your standards, to expose your insides. I will kill you where you sit. If you would like the honor of an honest fighter's death, you must tell me...how did your kind find this place?"

Hinton brushed his left hand over his wounds. He screamed again, but when he looked down at both of his hands covered in glass needles, he started laughing.

"I'm dying here," Hinton said between shudders. "Ain't nothing changing that."

Rictor stepped on the wounded Marine's leg. The talon sank in with a bone-breaking crunch.

Hinton groaned and whined. He took sharp breaths, oddly reminding Abraham of a woman in labor.

Abraham looked down at his Pulse. There was a sea of red dots all around them. It had to be over a hundred riskar soldiers. Zero chance for him and Digger to take them on and successfully destroy the communications tower. They had to play the waiting game.

Only it wasn't a game. This was a man's life, and he could do nothing to save it.

Rictor made a sound like an animal choking. Abraham realized it was a laugh. He couldn't take his eyes away from the grisly scene in front of him.

"I cannot grant you an honest death, human. Not when you waste away so pitifully before your enemy. You should still consider yourself blessed. For today, you die on Duringer, the holy land of the Mighty riskar."

Rictor pointed his Slinger at Hinton's head and pulled the trigger.

Flame swelled at the tip of the weapon. The belt whined, slinging a sandbag into the fire. The wheel spun, launching a splash of orange liquid an instant before it expanded into a large shard of glass.

The glass pierced Hinton's forehead. Cracked through his skull. Air rushed out of his lungs. It sounded like relief.

The toughest Marine Abraham knew fell forward.

Dead.

Rictor raised a fist and barked. "Humans desecrate our holy land. Find them! Kill them! But save one for your General. I will break one like the bone of a Flipper Fish. They will know our pain!"

Hoots and barks sounded from all around. The riskar militants sounded like a high school sports team. Abraham couldn't believe the similarity.

Just as quickly as they had come, the riskar slinked off into the jungle. They disappeared into the foliage. A few moments passed with rustling leaves and the low buzzing of insects reclaiming their territory.

The aliens left a resounding silence in their wake.

Abraham didn't move for a full ten minutes. Now that the riskar were tracked by the Pulse with some accuracy, he watched the screen like a hawk, never taking his eye off it. He looked up after the red dots had gone a considerable distance.

Digger was staring at Hinton's body.

"Dig." Abraham patted him on the shoulder. "You all right?"

Digger swatted his hand away. "That's a dumb fucking question, Zeeben."

Abraham knew it was. He just didn't know what else to say. "It's going to be a hike. I'm not sure we can carry him."

Digger spat. The loogie splattered against his visor. He cursed.

"I know. Let's just go."

Abraham and Digger weren't friends, but they were comrades. They had been through basic training together, and now they had both seen the death of their drill instructor. They walked the frontier of loss together, their position precarious. The path ahead was filled with impossible odds and probably ended in death. The path behind was nothing but certain death. These were their only choices.

It was a brief moment of silence, mourning the loss.

The decision they made was the only one they *could* make.

War. I can't believe I ever wanted this, Abraham thought, following Digger toward the northeast.

CHAPTER 30

Crackling started in both their ears. *"Abraham, you come in?"*

"I read you, Lieutenant."

Static for a moment. *"...team Bravo. Get to the com hub."*

Abraham tried to put his hand to his ear. The helmet couldn't press any harder against his head. He could barely hear her over the sounds of war.

"Say again, Lieutenant. Your transmission was broken."

"You're closer than we...destroy it...we'll get the ship."

MESSAGE: LIEUTENANCE SENECA
TACTICAL MAP SHOWS RISKAR OFF-WORLD COMMUNICATION HUB AT LOCATION NOVEMBER. DESTROY IT AND WE WILL PROVIDE EVAC. STAND BY FOR COORDINATES UPLOAD.

Abraham understood. Digger and he were now designated Bravo team and would be going to destroy the communications tower. That made Vase and the rest of the Ravens Alpha team. They would steal a ship, the only ticket off world at this point.

They must have given the Sackbacks some hell.

The sun had set and come up again since the firefight. Another fourteen-hour day and night. Abraham hated every minute of it. It was hard not to think of it as a punitive kind of camping trip. Listening to Digger grumble to himself, chomp ration bars like a sawmill, and rip ass every fifteen minutes was close to the worst kind of torture he could imagine.

The reality was far bleaker. They were stuck in a seemingly impossible situation. Maybe with the distraction of Alpha team's open warfare up the mountain, Bravo team would stand a chance at sneaking off undetected. Either way, they were definitely going to lose more people before they escaped. If they escaped.

He sipped several gulps of water from his helmet straw.

"What're we doing here, Zeeben?" Digger asked.

Abraham checked himself, patting down his S-skin and looking over his CLR. He looked Digger over, noticing nothing more damaged than some heat wash on his B-skin plates. Other than Abraham's injury, the pain of which was being managed by his B-skin's medical suite, they were basically scot-free at this point.

"Vase wants...uh, Lieutenant Seneca wants us to destroy the off-world communications building while they hijack a spacecraft that can get us out of here. This is the only way we can get off world. It's going to be me and you now, instead of a team of five or six."

239

"Oh, that's just great." Digger slapped his leg. "I'm never getting out of this alive, now."

Abraham bristled at that. "Digger, I don't know why you insist on having a problem with me. I've proven myself to be loyal to our platoon. I'm just trying to figure out the best way to do this. Why don't we start heading toward where we need to go, and you can bitch about it on the way?"

Abraham started wading through the thick foliage, stepping over waist-high bundles and clobbering the stubborn stalks of plants that sprouted from the jungle floor. His muscles ached like he'd been working out for the last few hours. Which he kind of had been. The stale smell of stagnant saltwater hung rancid in the air. There was nothing about this place that was familiar. Nothing comforting. One thought kept nagging at him, like an aggravated wound he couldn't stop itching.

Rictor said this was the home of the Mighty riskar. If this is Duringer...how did a planet move halfway across the galaxy?

Abraham and Digger crested the hill at Duringer's equivalent of high noon.

The last night had gone by in a blur of humidity, sweat, bad breath and slow movements. It was the third day since the crash. The green and blue gas giant that filtered the yellow lighting of the sun called Arinth was visible in the sky today. It looked like a broken candy jawbreaker. The heat ratcheted up to well beyond unbearable.

"How close are we, Zeeben?" Digger huffed.

"We're nearly there." Abraham checked the map on his HUD.

They were less than a thousand meters from the building. Through the tangled foliage at the top of the hill, he could see the black spire that rose from it. Several rocks spun and glowed different colors up the length of it. The base looked like an enormous ribcage spread over the top of an adjacent hill. Several riskar were inside the structure, working at keypads or barking into communicators. One was seated on a hollowed tree stump outside the structure, a pile of apple-sized cartridges collecting at its feet; Abraham realized it was taking a shit right out in the open.

Sick bastard.

Abraham did a quick double-check of his equipment. He had two magazines, two heat sinks, one rocket launcher attachment. Digger was doing the same, making a little noise as he jostled his CLR against the plates of his B-skin. The sweltering heat reminded Abraham of Veranda, the intensity of it causing him to momentarily slip into a different reality. Some odd light years away, he wondered if his father and brother were sweating in heat like this, too, working the earth. The other reality dissolved as quickly as it had come. He now wondered if they were buried under the very earth they had worked for so long. It was still hard to think of them as dead.

"Okay, how're we gonna do this?" Abraham asked Digger.

Digger said, "You're the brains of this operation, Zeeben. I'm just here to kick ass and kill Sackbacks. Whatever you think, that's what we'll do."

Abraham blinked. "You serious?"

Digger stared. "Yeah." He considered for a moment. "Unless your plan is fucking stupid. Then I'm not doing it."

Abraham shrugged. "Can't fight that logic."

He looked out at the building. It was an interwoven mess of bark and bent trees. The branches overlapped and weaved between each other like a crisscrossed ball of yarn. The surrounding jungle receded a good thirty meters from the base. Tactically speaking, it was a secure position that would be difficult to attack effectively.

Abraham had seen a whole lot of nature on this planet, but very little technology. Even the technology he had seen, the siren made of stone and a tree, was constructed from nature. The idea came to him in a flash.

Fire.

"You get any bright ideas?" Digger asked.

Abraham smiled. "Yeah. We're gonna burn the fucker down."

Digger smiled. "Can't fight that logic."

They were in position, just waiting for the call from Vase. After three and a half days, his helmet was starting to feel clouded with the funk of his own breath. He was getting more and more antsy as the hours wore on. By the timer on his Pulse, they only had four hours of daylight left.

Still, Abraham didn't want to jump the gun. This wasn't training. It wasn't a simulation. They had already lost people. There was only one chance to get this right, and it was absolutely critical that they get it right. Abraham and Digger's lives depended on it, just as much as the rest of the Ravens. The riskar would kill them in a heartbeat if they had the opportunity. If this didn't work exactly as planned…

Don't think about that.

Digger clicked his mic. "We doing this, or what?"

Abraham sighed. "You know the plan. Do I need to repeat it?"

"I've been sitting here so long my ass is starting to itch," Digger laughed.

Abraham recognized the laugh as Digger releasing his nerves.

Abraham sighted in on the base of the tower. A small contingent of riskar were gathering there, weapons drawn. They barked at each other, traded pats on the back and even smacked foreheads together. And they were getting ready to head out.

"I'm moving," Digger said.

"No, Digger, wait!" Abraham called after him, shouting over the frequency.

The stout man ignored him.

Abraham exhaled slowly, letting anticipation wash off his shoulders. He kept his weapon sighted in on the patrol. They were starting to spread out a few paces away from each other. In another few seconds the overgrown jungle would completely envelop them, obscuring them from any shots Abraham could throw at them.

Digger angled himself toward the east and disappeared into the brush. Leaves rustled, twigs snapped. It was such a racket Abraham knew the riskar would hear him and alert on his position at any moment.

The rocket launcher slid under his CLR and clicked. The targeting reticule popped up in his HUD. The sightlines rested just at the base of the tower. *The rocket should be enough to clear out the bottom floor of enemies and make a path for Digger to storm the tower.* It wasn't the best plan, but it was the only one they could come up with in a hurry.

He pulled the trigger. It clicked. Almost a full second of delay –

WHOOMPF!

The kickback was extremely satisfying.

The rocket slammed into the base of the tower.

Right on target, Abraham smirked.

The earth shook. Smoke spewed. Woven trees burned like struck matches. Green-gray bark turned black and began to peel.

Flaming riskar bodies fell, twitching. The aliens' carapace armor darkened like shelled nuts baking in an oven. Abraham leaned his back against a tree trunk, dumped the rocket launcher attachment and telescoped the CLR's barrel to marksman mode. The weapon whined as it automatically dialed up the laser intensity.

"Nice hit, Zeeben!" Digger cheered through the radio.

He dialed down the rate of fire to single shot just as the riskar opened fire.

Yellow flashes lit off in the forest. Abraham watched red leaves turn into purple smoke. The enemy sent round after round in random directions, probably convinced there was a contingent of human soldiers encroaching on their territory.

Abraham would have laughed if it hadn't been real war. If he hadn't seen Lechero's headless corpse. Or Sergeant Hinton with a jagged piece of glass in his forehead. Even the corpses of the unarmed riskar father and daughter nagged at him. The old him, just a few hours ago, would have laughed and jeered like a rowdy cowboy over the deaths he'd just caused.

Now, I just want to accomplish this mission and get the fuck off this planet.

"Woah, what the hell is this?" Digger said.

Adrenaline coursed through Abraham's nerves.

"What? You good? What's going on?"

Digger appeared up on the knoll at the base of the tower. Abraham watched him through his scope, trying to keep a view of the field as well as on his comrade. He wasn't about to let Digger get killed by the Sackbacks. They had taken too many of his friends and family already.

"You hear that?" Digger growled.

Abraham heard it through the helmet frequency. It sounded like someone stepping on bubble wrap.

Pop...pop-pop...sizzle...

"What the fuck is that?" Abraham asked.

A riskar soldier tumbled down the stairs, skin ablaze. Digger swatted at the head with the butt of his rifle, knocking it back. He kicked it in the chest, sending it spiraling down the hill. As it fell, the armor carapace around the abdomen ripped open, spilling charred innards like oil-covered confetti.

"Digger, it's the riskar. The noise, it's not a bomb or anything, it's just...them."

Digger opened fire, roasting two more aliens that tried to ascend the hill. "Fuck yeah!" he whooped.

Through the scope, Abraham could see the zeal in Digger's eyes, his wide grin bordering on maniacal. "Let 'em cook, Zeeben. I'm going up to the control room."

Three riskar emerged from the jungle, hooting and chittering like wild animals. They scaled the hill with a blur of speed. Clawed hands reached into the communication building, slashing wildly.

Abraham sighted in. Held his breath. Pulled the trigger.

The rifle screamed.

Through the scope, he saw the lead riskar's head melt like a wax candle. The smoking body dropped to its knees and rolled into the flames, lungs popping.

243

One soldier turned to look in his direction. Abraham pulled the trigger. The soldier pointed and shouted as his chest caved in. Abraham scored another direct hit.

Two shots, two kills.

The third soldier ducked, finally catching on that he was exposed. Abraham sighted in, but the Sackback was too fast. He zipped right up into the building. Abraham pulled the trigger.

The beam dissipated against the hardened structure of the building.

"Digger, one coming up. And he's pissed off."

Digger huffed, his voice grating, "I don't know what the fuck I'm looking at. What does a Sackback com array even *look like?* Pulse doesn't know what to make of it, either. It keeps showing me a schematic of a ship."

"A ship?" Abraham asked.

"Fuck it," Digger said. The frequency filled with automatic CLR fire.

Digger can't use the computers, so he's shooting them up. I picked the wrong role, here...

Purple smoke plumed in front of him. Through the filters in his helmet, he could smell burning foliage. He didn't have time to talk with Digger.

Abraham hit the ground, flat, rifle stock in his deltoid. His wound burned. Stars glimmered before his eyes. He held his breath against the pain.

Damn, this shit hurts.

Slivers of glass embedded in the wound felt like scissors sawing on his flesh.

PAIN MEDICATION DEPLETED

"Great."

RESUPPLY RECOMMENDED

No shit.

His left eye stung so bad it went blurry with tears.

I'm a Marine, dammit! I can't quit. Can't leave Dig out there alone.

The riskar emerged from the brush, armored demons with flaming glass scorching the air before them.

Abraham grabbed the front of his weapon and yanked it back, collapsing it to rifle mode. He spun the dial selector to automatic. If the Sackbacks wanted to throw fire, he was going to fight it with fire of his own.

He aimed low and held the trigger, sweeping his weapon slowly from side to side. The shots tore out, biting and chewing their way through the riskar, buckling them at the knees, tearing away feet and ankles, dropping them into each other, causing a pile-up of wounded, but few dead.

The heat sink popped off with a huff of white smoke. He kicked it toward the enemy and rolled onto his back. With a shout of pain, he jumped up onto his feet and ran for the only cover he could see.

A crevice in the side of the hill.

Abraham dove for it, arms wide.

He landed belly-first.

The impact shook his brain against his skull. He thudded like a kid falling down the stairs, voice and breath forced from his lungs. He slid down his backside over a collection of pale, smooth rocks.

In the span of a heartbeat, confusion swirled in his mind.

I haven't seen rocks like this since...Leona Lake.

He managed to cling to a broken tree stump at the edge of a precipice. As he stood, his rifle strap snapped. Abraham watched his CLR tumble over the edge and splash into the white rapids of a river. He heard the rolling roar of the water below and decided he'd reached a dead end.

The riskar were right on his heels. He couldn't turn back, either.

The side of the hill exploded. He fell.

The churning rapids swallowed him.

His body jerked. The current tugged at him. White noise filled his helmet.

An icy stab at his neck.

His body wasn't moving, but inside his skull his brain still spun.

A drip of sweat hit his upper lip.

Abraham looked down at his shoulder. A frayed string was all that remained of his rifle strap. The tattered end lifted off his chest, swaying slightly. A cloud of bubbles ran across his B-skin plates, rushing up over his cracked visor. Sunlight rippled above him.

Glass rounds from the riskar zipped into the rippling sunlight and floated, reflecting the light like a handful of diamonds before drifting slowly away.

Water pooled inside his helmet, the level rising to the bottom of his chin. *Holy shit–I'm drowning.*

Panic blared like an alarm in his mind.

Fields of air bubbles bloomed beneath him, rushing to the surface at a forty-five-degree angle.

A steady trickle of water worked its way through his visor. Cold fingers pressed at his neck as it slithered under his B-skin plates. He felt himself sinking.

Abraham flailed his arms and legs. He was too scared to scream. He fumbled at the release latch for his helmet. Pressure shoved him down like a wave crashing against the shore.

White and brown shrapnel peppered the surface. Flames danced across the ripples, dissipating as the wreckage sank. The jagged debris was too large to be riskar carapaces.

His stomach leapt into his throat.

Digger.

The explosion had come from the tower. Digger was in the tower just a moment ago.

His visor buckled under the water pressure. Saltwater spewed into his face. Instinct kicked in. He took a deep breath –

– of water. It stabbed his lungs like an ice pick.

He coughed in a frenzy, desperate for air. His vision narrowed. Thoughts passed through his head like intermittent sparks.

Pulled the release latch. Helmet floated away.

The unlock on his B-skin. Found it. Yanked it.

Thrashing on the rocks. A murky cloud enveloped him.

I can't see. I can't see! Ican'tseeIcan'tsee!

Hiss. Thunk.

Ice flowed over his undersuit. Chill in his bones.

Go!

Kicked off the floor. Pain in foot.

Contorted body like jellyfish.

He broke the surface with an explosive exhale.

Purple and black spots bloomed and blinked in his vision. Through the gaps, he could see smooth rocks ahead. Too far away. His lungs felt like they were cracked.

He couldn't fight it. The current swept him away.

CHAPTER 31

It was Vase standing over him. She was beautiful.

Her dress was midnight blue. Her hair was down, the blonde and brown sides equally captivating as she danced, silk dress swirling about her person.

She was like a ballerina dancing through a melodious run of strings that sang through space. The rushing vibrations through the violin, controlled by delicate but precise fingers, dictated her movements, her swirls and pirouettes and the tiny pauses on tiptoe, but never did her expression change.

It was passion. Concentrated, serious, unbreakable passion. And it was chiseled to perfection on a canvas of beauty. He watched her, lost in the dance. The swaying of his heartbeat was a visible pulse of purple light that glowed in her delicate hands.

All at once, the dance ended. The wind stopped. Her hair whipped and clung to her cheeks, immobilized. The violin was gone. It had never existed.

She held it out to him. The heart. The central cortex of his being. She opened her eyes. Limitless depths of shimmering blue pulled him in. He wanted to speak, to tell her he wouldn't fail her like he'd failed his mother.

He choked.

"I'm not going to accept this from you, Abraham," she said. Her voice sounded like his mother.

"I'm not giving it to you, Mom," he said, confused. "I'm just trying to remember you."

Vase looked at him, really looked into his eyes. Eye contact was a connection, a direct link between souls. It was something he did not like to share with most people. These thoughts made perfect sense here, in whatever realm this was, but they couldn't remain corporeal outside of it. He didn't have time to think that through.

"Am I dreaming?"

"That's for you to decide, Abraham." It was Vase using her own voice. It must have been a trick of the delirium, a trapping of the dream that had him hearing his mother's voice for the second time in fifteen years.

"I must be dying," he said.

Vase smiled. It was a warm, knowing smile. "You're far from dead, Abraham."

He frowned. The euphoria around him felt like morphine in his veins. It made him float. His insides were fuzzy. Warm.

"If I'm not dead, then this is a dream."

Her smile deepened. He saw her perfect white teeth. Smelled the welcome freshness of her breath. She had somehow drawn closer to him, her nose nearly touching his. Her body was just inches away. He could reach out and touch her, draw her close, draw on the comfort of her presence if he only –

– woke up laying on a cluster of river rocks.

His helmet was off. He was in his undersuit.

How did this happen?

The smell of burning foliage slapped his brain. Blinking from the assault, his eyes caught flashes of orange light and purple smoke. The crash of shattered glass echoed inside his head.

Oh, he remembered. *I'm in a war right now.*

"Private Zeeben, this is Lieutenant Seneca. Come in. Right fucking now!"

Her voice was far away…his earpiece was missing.

The frequency crackled. "Abraham…it's Vase," her voice sounded strained. "If you can hear me, please talk to me."

Piebold's voice came in, "His transponder's still up, ma'am."

He rolled onto his back. The night sky was full of foreign stars. He didn't recognize a single constellation.

It's still kind of pretty, though.

He felt a pinch at his throat. His chest seethed with pain. No, it was his shoulder. He looked down and fought the urge to vomit.

A two-inch puncture in his deltoid, deep enough he could see the smooth paleness of part of his clavicle. The edges were an angry, festering red with slivers of glass surrounded by pockets of pus. Seeing it with his own eyes made the pain worse.

The Pulse on his wrist was cracked, half the screen black, but he could still make out part of the map.

The blinking part where Vase and the rest of his platoon were…they were twelve kilometers away. That couldn't be right, location November was supposed to be twice that distance from…

His head hurt. He couldn't remember.

The water. *Digger…*

"Private Zeeben. Are. You. Alive?" Vase's voice came from his Pulse.

He fumbled for the earpiece. He rolled onto his side, found it between a couple of rocks and jammed it in his ear. "Digger, come in," Abraham radioed.

"Abraham!" Vase shouted. "Rendezvous on my position, now. If you can. Are you injured? I need a sitrep."

Standing on shaky legs, Abraham reached for his rifle on his shoulder sling, but it was broken. He didn't remember that happening. He had to be suffering from a concussion. He just hoped he wasn't forgetting anything important.

"Digger, come in, bro. Where the fuck are you?"

"Abraham." It was Larry. "We gotta get out of here. Now, man. The entire riskar fleet is gonna be crawling up our asses any second."

"Larry," Abraham laughed, because he didn't want to cry. The relief he felt, knowing his people were still alive, was a suitable substitute for anesthetic.

He tapped his Pulse, trying to read the entire map, but half the screen was black.

A roar sounded from above. Pebbles smacked against rocks and red grass as they tumbled down the mountainside. The earth shook violently beneath his feet, almost knocking him to his ass. Abraham threw out a hand to steady himself. He looked around but couldn't see the source of the rattling.

The snapping of bark drew his eye up the hill.

A red line was zipping across the sky like a slow-moving laser.

A riskar starfighter screamed overhead, swallowing up the light. Abraham dropped to his stomach and covered his ears. The trees dipped down, almost like a bow, as he watched the black and red craft soar over the mountain range and out of his line of sight. Tree bark creaked as the foliage straightened back up.

"Did you guys get a ship?"

Vase said, "No, we didn't. Any craft you see are *not* us. Rally up with us ASAP."

That woke him up. *Now I have to worry about air patrols. Great.*

He tapped the working half of his Pulse.

"Okay, looks like I can make it to your position if I walk all night."

"There," Vase said into the radio. "We'll set up a perimeter by this waterfall. See you in the morning, Abraham."

"Sure," he said, kicking at the dirt with his bare feet.

Nothing like a twelve-klick hike in just a B-skin undersuit. I hope the boot liners last.

It all hit him like a lead weight. *Digger's gone. He needed me, and I let him down.*

He didn't know which was worse – the festering in his shoulder or the festering in his mind. If he survived, the shoulder would heal.

He wasn't sure about anything else.

CHAPTER 32

"Abraham! Over here." Larry's hoarse shout came from somewhere between the trees.

Abraham hustled through the red jungle, trying to be fast and quiet. It was a skill he knew he'd never master. Several twigs cracked under his boots as he closed in on the Ravens' makeshift camp.

He was about to clear a line of thickets when lasers tore through the wall. He had to hit the deck to avoid catching fire.

"Whoa, hold your fucking fire, boys! What the hell?" Abraham shouted.

"Cease fire!" Amory shouted. "Zeeben, is that you?"

Abraham scoffed, rubbing brush and carbon debris off his face. "Of course it's fucking me! You think your boyfriend would mistake a Sackback for me?"

Piebold and Larry helped him up, clapping him on the back. Abraham felt a pinch on his back and cried out. "What the hell, bro?"

Piebold held up a severed riskar claw. Dried blood stained the chest plates on his B-skin. "Sorry, Ham. You walk around with this thing dangling off you like a tail, the Pulse sniffer is going to think you're one of them," he said. "Where's Digger?"

"Piebold, were you hit?" Abraham dodged the question, gesturing at the mess on his armor.

The big man shook his head. "Not me."

Amory glanced down at her Pulse, frowning.

Larry laughed. "Where's your B-skin, Abraham? Your boots, at least?"

"It's a long story," Abraham said, waving his buddies down. "Where's Va– the lieutenant?"

Heartbeat started racing. He scanned the ranks but he did not see her. Just a bunch of gruff Marines, covered in soot and debris, chomping down ration bars or taking pisses with their backs turned. Tar and Juke stood perimeter guard, serious expressions looking out of place for the usual jokesters.

"Where is she?" Abraham demanded.

Amory rolled her eyes and heaved a sigh. "The lieutenant is bathing naked in the waterfall behind that tree line, lover boy."

Abraham rushed to the tree line, face red. It wasn't that he wanted to catch her in such an ideal situation, he told himself. He just wanted to lay eyes on her and make sure she was okay. After losing the Eagles and Digger, Abraham wouldn't trust anything but seeing her with his own eyes.

He swatted the brush aside to gaze down into an empty valley. Uproarious laughter ensued behind him. Tar fell on his ass. Juke rolled around on his back. The rest of the Ravens slapped hands. Larry had tears rolling down his face, guffawing loudly.

The heat returned to Abraham's cheeks, hotter than ever. "You know what? Fuck you guys."

Amory strolled up to him, her shoulders squared. She looked intimidating for such a small girl, with her B-skin that was two sizes too big and her diamond-pommeled dagger hanging out on her belt. She hefted her CLR over her shoulder like it was a toy gun. Her hair-tie had broken at some point; it was frizzy and down to the nape of her neck. She looked like she'd been through hell, just the same as Abraham.

"No, fuck *you*," she spat. "What the fuck happened to destroying the off-world com hub?"

"What're you talking about? I was trying to cover Digger, but I got rushed by a shitload of Sackbacks. I did what I could, but I fell into a river. Digger...he destroyed it. Look at me, I'm all beat to shit."

Abraham knew he was a mess. His undersuit, supposedly made of highly durable material, was cut and frayed at the knees and elbows, covered in grime and dirt all over. His face was just about the same. He had a bruise he could feel heat radiating from on the back of his head, and his neck piece was cracked where his helmet had been forcibly removed. His body odor was briny from the dip in the river.

"Abraham," Amory said, eyes narrowing, "you didn't destroy the com hub. That was still another three clicks to the north." She showed him her Pulse, which was fully intact, unlike his. "You took out something else."

Abraham saw the map. The layout of the riskar infrastructure made no sense. There were a few solitary buildings isolated every couple of klicks. Occasionally, a small cluster of two or three. Not enough accumulation to be called a city. If this was their home planet, why didn't they congregate mass populations into closer areas like most advanced civilizations?

"What the hell was the satellite for, then? I saw a spire at the top of the building, before Digger stormed inside and..."

Silence fell like a heavy storm cloud on the group. Several Marines shook their heads, a few kept glassy eyes and stern stares. Piebold stiffened, but his expression didn't change.

Movement from behind him drew his attention.

Vase strode into the camp, looking distraught. A blonde lock of hair had broken free of her braids and clung to her forehead. She was almost storming into the camp, boots stomping, making a lot of noise for a group of people who were trying to remain concealed. She stopped in her tracks when she saw him.

"Private Zeeben." Her voice softened, just a bit. "Good of you to grace us with your presence."

Abraham went to salute, but remembered they were in a combat zone. Only people who wanted their officers to have their heads blown off by snipers offered salutes in enemy territory.

"Ma'am," he offered, "it's good to be back."

Everyone in the camp instinctually turned at the sound of the commanding officer's voice. Tar even paused chewing his ration bar.

Vase cleared her throat. "I was able to get in contact with a human ship. It's just a civilian science team doing remote sample gathering, but they were able to relay a message for us. The Navy is going to find out about this situation shortly. They'll send a rescue team for us."

"So, we know where we are now?" Piebold asked.

Vase smiled. "We do. And so does the Navy. It won't be long before evac arrives. Maybe another day."

Sighs of relief passed through the camp like a sharp wind. Everyone looked at each other, smiling and nodding. The idea of getting rescued from a hotbed of hostile riskar sounded great to everyone.

"There is one problem, though, and it's kind of a big one."

Abraham held his breath.

Vase plopped down on a broken tree stump, tapped her Pulse a few times. Intensity poured from her eyes as she looked at each of them before she made her declaration.

"There was no way to send the message without it being intercepted. The riskar Royal Fleet will be on its way, which means the Navy will be playing chase. I'm saying all this to say…the war isn't over. But it's about to be. Everything's going to be decided here in just a few hours."

Abraham's breath slipped out, and with it, the little piece of comfort he had knowing that Vase was alive.

We're fucked.

"So how come you didn't get a ship, then?" Abraham asked later that night.

The buzz bugs were slicing the night air with a low rumbling serenade. The gas giant in the night sky looked pretty close to an aurora. The groupings of stars were unfamiliar, but their presence was just close enough to normal that Abraham felt like he could have been having this conversation on the porch of the Zeeben homestead, when the tobacco plants were in full bloom and the Verandan humidity was at its peak. Instead of fertilizer and tobacco, he smelled vanilla, honeydew, and something like eucalyptus.

Vase moved a lock of hair from her forehead and swatted at a wingless bug that kept buzzing by her head. What made it buzz, Abraham couldn't tell.

She made a sour face. "The spaceport is further than I expected. The map we got from the Sky Eye was only so accurate."

Abraham nodded. "I didn't appreciate getting shot at when I finally managed to find this place."

Vase locked eyes with him. "Private Poplenko said he dug a riskar claw out of your back. You're lucky to be alive."

Abraham pivoted to show the tear mark in his undersuit. "I don't even know how it got there. I just wish Digger..." he choked on a lump in his throat. "Being alive doesn't take the sting out of it."

Vase chuckled. "I'm glad you didn't die, but I'm also pissed off that the com hub is still up and running."

Abraham asked, "What the hell did Digger and I destroy? He...he fucking died taking it out, I just want it..."

She put a hand on his shoulder. "You want his sacrifice to mean something. I do, too, Abraham. I'm not sure what that building was, but it must have been important if the enemy presence escalated once you started your assault. Maybe they didn't expect us to strike there. It was a vulnerability they didn't know they had."

He nodded, kicking at a root. "Yeah, maybe they were hiding it in plain sight, like they've done with this planet the entire war. It was always charted in the Echoplex sector, but here we are standing on it, and we were travelling through the Down Space sector. I still don't know how they managed that."

"Castle," she smiled.

His brow wrinkled.

She turned her head slightly. It was a friendly gesture that, for the moment, felt like they were back in her office on Juno. Just another late-night conversation over the ancient wooden chessboard.

"They castled an *entire planet*?"

Vase shrugged, looking off into the distance.

"Sure looks that way, doesn't it? All I know is, I want to get off this shithole as soon as possible."

She locked her gaze on some distant object. The slightest motion rippled her shoulders for a minute, a motion Abraham caught instantly. It was a shiver.

"It's not your fault that we lost people. You know that, right, Vase?"

"Lieutenant," she mumbled. He felt the friendly vibes beginning to die.

Abraham put his hands on her shoulders. "Vase, stop. This is war. No one cares if I call you by your rank." He took a deep breath. "Or if we do anything else."

She shrugged him off but didn't turn away. "I care. We're in the fucking military, Abraham. Just respect my rank. Follow my lead. Don't second guess my decisions and we won't have any problems."

He nodded, cheeks red and ego crumpled up like a cheap soda can. He joined her in staring at the red and yellow tree line.

Several minutes passed in silence. He enjoyed just being with her, knowing that she was safe. That she wasn't totally repulsed by his presence. That perhaps, based on how she'd paused when she saw him in the camp, she might actually still feel something for him. He decided to bury his shame and try again.

"Vase," he said, voice low, "I love you. I don't care if you feel the same way or not. I mean, I do. I want you to feel the same way. I hope that you do. I'm, uh...I just don't know how this is going to shake out, and I want you to know it. Know how I feel about you...you know?"

She smiled. She looked at him with her big blue eyes, in which the power of life and death over his heart dwelled. A ray of thin red light caught her just right, and for a moment, the dream of her dancing with her violin flitted up in his mind. His chest swelled. Before he could stop and think about it, he leaned in to kiss her.

She turned at the last second. His lips touched her cheek.

All she said was, "Thank you."

A chime sounded. She held up her Pulse so they could both read the message.

MESSAGE: NAVCOM WAR DEPARTMENT
ATTN: 1st LT VASE SENECA.
NAVCOM ETA: STANDBY.
RRF ETA: 3 HOURS.
INTEL: 1EA HYDRA DETECTED ON-WORLD.
MISSION UPDATE: DISABLE HYDRA BY
1) LOCKING LAUNCH HANGAR DOORS
2) CUTTING FUEL SUPPLY LINES
SCHEMATIC DIAGRAM TO FOLLOW.
REPLY ONLY WITH CONFIRMATION OF MISSION COMPLETE.

"What the fuck is a HYDRA?" Abraham asked.

Vase sighed. "We have no time. We need to formulate a plan. Now."

"Why is the Navy on standby? I thought you said they were coming here, too. To end the war."

Vase shook her head. "I thought they would. Now, it's just us. They won't send the fleet until we disable this HYDRA weapon."

Her Pulse chimed. A schematic came through, showing the object in question.

It was shaped like a rocket ship from a cartoon, spikes and weird angled parts jutting out from it at odd points. The part that really caught his eye was a line of writing at the bottom: YIELD = 1.125 AU.

He knew that abbreviation very well. David had used it several times when reciting articles on space affairs for years.

"Vase...AU is for Astronomical Units."

"I know, Abraham."

"That means this weapon can destroy a small solar system."

"I know, Abraham."

"We have to disable this thing ASAP."

"I fucking know, Abraham!" she screamed. "Fuck, you really know how to drive a girl batshit crazy!"

He smirked. "I thought I'd never hear you say that again."

CHAPTER 33

The Pulse threat detector was not on the fritz, so when it indicated upwards of three hundred moving bodies around their destination, it killed morale.

The consensus was that they were all going to die unless they were somehow able to disable the weapon. After more than four days on Duringer, there wasn't a soul among them who wasn't looking forward to being rescued, leaving the stinking waste pits and the imminent threat of death behind. The words 'suicide mission' didn't have to be spoken. They hung over them like an ominous cloud.

Abraham hated his new boots. They were too small, but that wasn't the only reason he hated them. They had belonged to Corporal Nichols, before the riskar had buried a slab of glass in her neck. She bled out in Piebold's arms during their escape. Now her body was covered in leaves and brush at the south side of camp. He couldn't bring himself to remove the rest of her B-skin. If the boots were any indication, the female variant wouldn't fit him right, anyway.

He hated these boots. His bruised foot throbbed with every heartbeat. He could feel his socks like mushy sandpaper against his skin. He longed for a shower, a toothbrush, a fucking *steak*. The thought of summer holiday on Veranda, his father grilling steaks under the blazing sun...his mouth watered.

Rain fell in a slow cascade. It wasn't the pitter patter he was used to. Fist-sized drops crashed against jungle foliage with impacts like water balloons. A direct hit by one of these drops was like having a bucket dumped on your head. Larry had compared it to feeling like catching a towel snap from the jocks in the locker room, like Digger used to do. That killed the mood for a few minutes as they all geared up for one last mission.

Abraham made up his mind as he locked and loaded Nichols' CLR. He was going to die on this one, there was no other way about it. His only objective at this point was to make sure Vase lived to see better days. He wanted Larry and Amory to leave this shithole behind, to live to fight and fuck another day. It was something Digger would have said.

Damn. Digger's been on my mind constantly. I never knew I cared about the guy so much. I can't believe he's fucking dead. I can't believe I couldn't keep him alive.

The march to the waypoint in Vase's Pulse took almost an hour. The torrential downpour that had started out of nowhere gave them plenty of sound cover, so they were able to practically sprint through the endless forest until they were a few hundred meters from the site. With no more Sky Eyes at their disposal, they were going in blind.

But their fate, and the outcome of the Riskar War, rested on their shoulders.

Abraham wasn't about to let that one go.

They stopped where the forest ended. A squared bunker was wedged into the base of a sizeable hill. It was a glorified garage door with grass on the roof, surrounded by trees thicker and taller than redwoods. It almost looked like a spacecraft had crash-landed here, buried itself halfway into the surface, and had been forgotten for years. Vines and creepers stretched over it like tentacles. It reminded Abraham of the entrance to a mining cave.

The launch door for the HYDRA was visible under the sparse grass in the open clearing, like the closed eye of a sleeping giant.

Vase charged her CLR. She stood at the head of the pack, her jaw set. She wasn't a large woman, but her trim physique and air of grim determination gave her an ethereal presence. She emanated a sense of strength that was palpable.

At least, that was Abraham's perspective. He might have been a little biased.

"This is it, Ravens. I'm taking point. We're going to storm the bunker, take out anything that moves, and try to find their computer systems. Once we do, we're going to lock down the launch door. Anyone left standing is going for the HYDRA. The primary fuel supply line is at the nose, next to the reservoir near the top of the missile. The secondary is two lines from the accumulators on either side. Everybody got that?"

They all nodded. No one expected them to get that far.

Amory leaned back and kissed Larry over her shoulder.

"We got this, babe," he told her.

Abraham leaned in to Vase and whispered, "I love you."

She nodded.

"You gonna say it back? We're about to die, Vase."

She nodded.

It was all the confirmation he was going to get. For now, it was enough.

Arinth had been steadily rising for an hour. The darkness of night gave way to the sixth day, the day that was to be their last on Duringer. Probably the last day of their lives.

They charged their weapons, safeties off.

Vase rushed out into the clearing first, war cry on her lips.

Abraham, Piebold, Larry and Amory followed. Corporal Johnson, Tar and Juke were right behind. The remaining three Ravens followed, war cries on their lips, weapons raised.

The surrounding jungle was silent.

Confusion shook Abraham to his core. His boots crimped the grass in the open field, pounded hard across the launch door, turned metallic at the entrance to the bunker. They cleared the two-hundred-meter sprint without so much as a raised alarm or the bark of an alerted enemy.

"This doesn't feel right," Amory panted.

Larry, his back against the doorway, his rifle pointed into the jungle, tremored visibly. "I know. We just raised a fucking racket and there's no sign of anything. It doesn't make sense."

"If they aren't here, where are they?" Piebold asked.

Vase was coaching Juke on how to try to interface his Pulse with the terminal. It was a hand port of some kind with a screen that glowed a dull green. It didn't look like any computer terminal Abraham had ever seen, but he had been so focused on hating the riskar all these years he hadn't taken the time to learn what their technology looked like.

"That's the prompt you're looking for," Vase patted Juke's shoulder, her tone encouraging. "Open the troubleshooting suite once you're in and let the program run its interface mode. It'll find a way to crack the system."

"And if it doesn't, what do we do then, Ma'am?" Juke asked. Sweat gathered at his bushy eyebrows, and he licked his dry lips. It was the most nervous Abraham had ever seen him.

"Here," she said, "use mine. If that doesn't work, we'll find a way to get them to come out."

Juke hooked up the lieutenant's Pulse into the terminal and tapped at it feverishly. Tar was next to him, alternating between eyeing the forest and casting glances at his buddy. He kept his teeth locked together.

We're all nervous.

Static emitted from all around them. It was like suddenly stepping into the midst of a thunderstorm or a wind tunnel. The sound was deafening in his earpiece.

Juke shakily held up his Pulse.

It was the face of a riskar. Not just any riskar.

General Rictor.

The Sackbacks did not exhibit facial expressions in any recognizable form to humans, but Abraham could tell the general was fuming. The lung sacs at his neck pumped like racing heartbeats.

"Salutations, humans." His mandibles flexed momentarily. Maybe a gesture of anger? "Enjoying your stay on Duringer? I invite you into our inner sanctum."

The bunker emitted a weak hiss. The jungle door began sliding into the dirt floor, revealing a long tunnel of darkness.

Rictor coughed, the riskar version of a laugh. "Or turn back now like the cowards you are."

Vase opened her mouth to speak, but Abraham stepped in, close to the Pulse. "My name is Abraham Zeeben, and I'm going to kill you for what you did to Milune!"

Rictor's three eyes blinked from left to right. "Pathetic! The Honorable and Mighty riskar would never have desecrated such an unworthy society. Humans are an unthinking majority that march faithfully to their own demise at the siren call of an unworthy leader."

Vase tried to step in, but Abraham held her back. "We're going to end this war right now. If the riskar are supposed to be so honorable, then why don't you fight *me*? One Sackback, one human. Fight to the death."

Rictor stepped back and waved a hand. "Honor must be tested, pathetic Zeeben."

Two riskar entered the frame, carrying a body.

A human body.

The B-skin plates were cracked and charred, barely holding together. Abraham recognized the burly man instantly, even before Rictor lifted his chin to expose his face.

"My offer of benevolence still stands, human. I will let one of you live. If you wish it to be this one, then you must enter and sacrifice yourselves. If not," he hefted his weapon, touching it to Digger's temple, "I understand."

Digger gritted his teeth into a pain-filled smile. "Kill this fucker and go home."

Abraham looked at Vase. She looked at him. There was only one choice to make.

"All right, Rictor. We're coming in," she said.

"Coming in to kick your fucking ass!" Tar shouted.

"Ugly ass bitch," Juke added.

"Hang in there, brother," Piebold said. "We're coming for you."

Rictor slapped Digger's face, drawing two lines of blood across it. "Take this one away. Let them come for him." He turned to face the camera. "You have made your choice, humans. Now, enter your grave."

CHAPTER 34

The revelation that Digger was alive lifted a huge weight off Abraham's conscience. It doubled his resolve to get his old archenemy out of the clutches of the riskar. The list of casualties and precious lives the Sackbacks had taken from him played through his mind as he entered the bunker, leaving the light of day behind for what he knew would be the last time.

Rictor called this our grave, he thought. *I'll make it his grave, too.*

The hallway was straight and narrow. The darkness hung heavy around them, playing on their paranoia. Abraham had to duck at some points just to fit through. A minute later, he started feeling disoriented. In total darkness, they had to make do with tiny beams of light from their B-skins or rifles.

The whole thing had a feel like the cheesy horror movies Abraham had seen at Larry's house growing up. The kind of movies they watched when Larry's grandparents were asleep and David was so engrossed in his Portal he wasn't paying any attention to what they were doing. The kind of movies that Abraham felt like he was living in now.

The death and destruction he'd seen in less than a week was enough for a lifetime. As he and the rest of his team stalked through the darkness, he wondered if he'd ever watch anything like that again. Would video games even be of interest to him after experiencing real war?

I fucking doubt it. I never want to see another living thing killed again. After this, I'm joining the Human Collective…'peace through nature', right?

"Keep tight. We don't know what we're walking into," Vase said.

Abraham regretted not taking Corporal Nichols's B-skin. One good shot to the head and he'd be dead. Dying before he could kill Rictor, the one person he hated more than anyone else in the galaxy, was not an option.

Sackback, not person, he corrected himself. The father and daughter were innocent, but Rictor and the other riskar warriors…they were worse than dogs.

And I will slaughter them like dogs.

"How far down does this fucking thing go?" Larry muttered.

"Why ain't we seen a walking ballsack yet?" Juke asked.

This devolved into nervous chatter amongst themselves. Amory, however, remained quiet. Abraham wondered if she was starting to feel conflicted about killing the same kind of aliens that had raised her. This thought surfaced for only a moment before he recalled her gung-ho spirit in basic. No, he thought, it must be something else. Maybe it was something as simple as the fear of combat, or the fear of certain death. Both things they drew closer to with every step.

"I'm detecting ripple signatures." Amory was glancing at her Pulse. "Looks like they're moving."

The unbroken half of Abraham's Pulse showed a dozen riskar vessels sliding into orbit. The way their fleets traveled, it would be a matter of minutes before dozens became hundreds. The blockade of Duringer had begun, and with it was gone the only chance Raven Platoon had to escape.

"Fleet's arriving now," he said.

Tar snorted. "We were never getting outta here alive anyhow, man."

"We can still save Dig and kill the ugly-ass general, man," Juke said.

A resolved silence descended on the group.

The corridor stretched onward, winding and weaving, but always at a slight decline. The air started to moisturize. Abraham could feel it on his skin, the humidity like a tiny electrical charge at the tip of his nose, collecting at the base of his neck. His hair had grown out just enough to prevent sweat from pouring down his forehead. The ration bar he'd eaten a few hours ago sat in his stomach like a greasy brick.

"Anybody see anything?" Tar asked, light from his CLR sweeping the darkness.

Several negatives were issued. Flashlights continued to rove back and forth. Boots clicked on the hard floor. Deeper still they marched on, surrounded by shadows, twitching at imagined movements in the oppressive dark that swallowed them up meter by meter.

"Up ahead." Abraham double-checked his safety was off. The hair on the back of his neck stood on end.

The tunnel widened ahead. There was no telling what lay deeper in the shadows.

"Forward," Vase said. "We can't go back."

Abraham was sure she meant it as an explanation, but it sounded a lot more like justification. Like Vase wasn't sure she was making the right decision. Or she thought she could be making the wrong one.

He was mulling over the implications when the lights came on in a blinding blaze.

The tunnel ended ten meters ahead. There was nothing but a smooth cave wall that ran up to the ceiling a dozen meters overhead. Spaced every five meters was a series of girders that held up the walls and ceiling.

It was a dead end.

A kill-box.

Abraham spun on his heels, finger on the trigger.

Corporal Johnson said, "Holy shit, we've got incoming."

Hustling down the corridor were dozens of riskar soldiers in bulky armor, their strange weapons raised aggressively, mandibles scraping back and forth like hungry hands rubbing together before a meal.

It sounded like pouring rain.

How the hell did they sneak up on us?

"All right, Ravens," Vase said through gritted teeth. "This is what we signed up for. Make sure not to overlap your fire lanes, and stay out of each other's way. We're going weapons free in three…"

The riskar, as one, took a step forward. It sounded like thunder.

"…two…" Her voice quaked.

The combat had worn them physically. The losses weighed on their hearts. The one thing they had control over was their mental state.

In this pivotal moment, it was razor sharp.

As one, the battle-weary Marines shouldered their weapons. It, too, sounded like thunder.

"…one…" Her voice a whisper.

Abraham could hear her tears through her choked voice. He felt them in his own. He gritted his teeth and flexed his jaw. If this was the end, he was going to burn through these fuckers until he got to Rictor. Nothing less than Rictor's head on a pike would satisfy him.

"Weapons free!" Vase shouted.

Laser blasts and glass shards tore through the corridor like chain lightning.

Abraham saw a flash of red rain spray onto the wall next to him. He didn't know what to make of it at first. Not until he saw Amory collapse against the wall, behind a structural girder. Her face was shocked. Her hand pressed into her side. Abraham could see her ribs between her fingers. Blood spilled around them. The B-skin plates were too big; they had left her exposed. Glass fragments cracked under her boots as she stumbled, smearing the wall with a bloody handprint.

Larry screamed, "Amory!" He shoved Abraham out of the way.

Right toward the incoming fire.

Glass rounds shattered against the wall beside his head. It was like a chandelier exploding.

Abraham ducked and opened up with his weapon, trying to give Larry time to assess her condition. The whine of the laser weapon discharging felt good.

"No, I won't…I can't do it, baby, I'm not…you're not dying!" Larry blithered, sobbing.

Amory screamed.

Abraham risked a momentary glance.

Larry's hand rested on her ribs. Blood flowed through his fingers, pooling on the ground. Amory's chest huffed rapidly. She raised her hand weakly to touch Larry's face.

Abraham's chest grew heavy. This one was going to hurt worse than Digger. The fact that Amory was so important to Larry made her important to Abraham. The heat of the firefight stole the time that should have been available for mourning. The shock hadn't fully hit Abraham. He knew he had to keep Larry's head in the fight.

"Larry, you good?"

Larry's eyes bulged and flickered. He was looking for a solution he knew didn't exist. Abraham could feel the desperation in his friend's gaze.

"Nah, man, she's dying!"

Abraham dropped a smoking heat sink, slid a new one onto his CLR and locked it down. He sidled back up against the wall. Tar shoved him back toward the pair, nearly cracking his skull on the girder. Juke took Abraham's spot at the front of the formation. Both of their weapons screamed with non-stop laser fire.

A closer look at the injury showed her glass-pierced lung, visible where the skin had been torn completely away. Even in a hospital with doctors and the best equipment, Abraham doubted she could last more than a few minutes.

He did the hardest thing he ever had to do. He grabbed his friend by the shoulder and shook him. "She's gone, Larry. Kiss her goodbye. Pick up your weapon and fight, Marine!"

Amory's bloody fingers held out her knife, the diamond pommel glittering like a disco ball, casting wisps of light over her pale form.

Larry shook his head. "No, baby, I can't do that to you. I know you want me to, but I just..."

A Raven fell up ahead, glass shard sticking through his forehead. Juke dropped and pressed his fingers to the guy's neck. He shook his head, swapped heat sinks on his rifle and sent a volley of laser blasts down the corridor.

They were losing. They needed every gun they had in the fight.

Abraham snatched the dagger from Amory's hand and held it up to her face. She locked eyes with him, blood coloring her pale lips. She nodded. She tried to mouth something, but her motor functions were already shutting down.

"No!" Larry shouted. Piebold grabbed him under the arms, holding him back.

Abraham pierced her, right in the forehead.

"Gah!" Larry shouted.

263

"I'll keep your soul safe, Amory. Rest in piece." Abraham removed the knife and shoved it in his belt.

Larry stared at him, equal parts confusion and revulsion. Something in his expression darkened.

He shook himself loose of Piebold's grip and charged his rifle. He turned toward the riskar with a face like wet stone.

"Give 'em hell, Marine." Abraham patted him on the back.

"I'm never forgiving you for this, Abraham. Never."

Larry popped out of cover, rifle blazing.

CHAPTER 35

The riskar fell two and three at a time, laser blasts cutting through their armor like knives through butter. They raised fists and barked at each other. Glass rounds ricocheted off the walls. Shrapnel and shards ricocheted around them. Fire and laser bolts lit the striated dirt and rock of the tunnel walls in flashes as the Marines advanced a few paces from the dead end at their backs.

Burning cordite hung in the air. Larry, tucked behind a girder a few meters in front of Abraham, loaded a fresh sink and fired on full auto. In the blast of light, Abraham saw something up ahead.

The tunnel split into a fork. He didn't have time to think about how they'd missed that on the way in; covered by a bulge in the cave wall, he glanced at his tactical map. The left fork was the way they'd come. The right fork curved deeper into the underground before narrowing into a stretch that ended in a perfect circle. The HYDRA's launch chamber.

A scream pulled his eyes off the map. At the wall opposite him, a Marine took a cluster of glass shards to the side of the face. He flinched, stumbling out from behind the cover of the cave wall.

Abraham stepped out of cover. Three riskar entered his sight picture. He fired, fired, fired.

In his periphery, he saw broken glass slice open the man's B-skin plates, piercing his abdomen. Blood spilled. He fell to the ground, screaming and bleeding at Abraham's feet.

Abraham knelt but never stopped squeezing the trigger. His rifle screamed like a banshee, laser bolts sizzling through the riskar. By the time he was able to drag the Marine back into cover, he was no longer screaming. The pool of blood left a thick skid mark on the floor. Abraham knew he couldn't do anything for him.

"Fire in the hole!" Tar shouted, yanking the pin out of his grenade.

"No!" Juke shouted. "You'll bring down the whole fucking tunnel!"

"We're dead already!" Tar hurled the grenade down the hall.

It bounced twice and rolled right into the center of the riskar ranks.

A half second later it detonated.

Shockwaves buckled Abraham's knees. A gust of hot air buffeted him. The barks and hoots stopped.

Cracked carapace parts flew, edges glowing white-hot. Riskar innards and armor pieces clattered against the walls and slid across the floor. The clamor was like a kitchen full of pots and pans overturned on the floor, followed by the shrill whine of high decibel-induced hearing loss.

Somehow, the tunnel held.

Abraham checked his CLR. He had maybe ten shots left in his heat sink.

He scrambled over to Amory's body, tried not to look at what he'd done to her. He appropriated two magazines from her B-skin, checked to make sure they were full.

Sixty rounds. It wasn't enough.

It all comes down to this.

He looked down the gore spattered hallway, stomach clenching. The odor of death and burnt flesh was starting to become familiar to him.

They were all squeezed to the sides of the tunnel, backs against the wall. Directly across from him, Vase swapped sinks on her rifle and glanced at her Pulse. She made eye contact with him. She must have seen something in his gaze because she shook her head.

"They're here. With the fleet in system, they're not going to launch the weapon. They'd destroy their planet if they detonated it this close. We'll clear this tunnel and get a ship. We can still make an escape. One last push, Marines."

Abraham said, "I'm going for the HYDRA. If nothing else, it'll draw some of them away from you."

Vase looked at him. Looked *through* him. Her mouth opened, but she didn't speak.

I'm not waiting for you to give me the okay, he thought.

He dropped the heat sink to the floor, slid the mag into his CLR and slapped it home. Yanked the charging handle to load a round in the chamber.

He stepped out from cover and said, "I'll see you topside."

Behind him, he heard the shakiness in Vase's voice.

"We'll get you out, Abraham."

"I know," he said.

He charged down the tunnel and took the right fork.

A chorus of guttural shouts sounded from behind him.

If they get control of a ship...I don't know how the hell they'll manage it, but if they do...there's no way I'll get out in time.

That was the look Vase had given him, he decided. She knew it, too.

It's a one-way trip.

Further down the dark path, he could hear the riskar chittering to each other. Every five meters a structural ring jutted from crags in the rocky earth, the same as the rest of the tunnel. Except now he was alone, and any number of the enemy could be hiding behind him, waiting to put jagged glass rounds in his back.

Running and gunning wasn't an option. He slowed to a walk, rifle stock in his shoulder. One of the soldiers peeked his head out from cover.

266

Abraham pulled the trigger.

Kickback slammed into his shoulder.

The report of the rifle echoed up and down the walls. An electric pop in his ear became a droning whistle.

The force of the kinetic round caved in the skull and popped off several chin mandibles.

That's for Milune, Abraham thought. *For Amory. And Digger.*

He stepped over the twitching body. Rage seethed in his veins. *This is why I joined,* he thought with a grim smile. *Revenge.*

The overwhelming surge of emotion boiled inside him.

He saw red. It could have been the glow of emergency lighting, or an alarm. It filled the tunnel, illuminating a twenty-five-meter-long corridor. He could see everything with stark clarity. Lungs bounced in the air as the enemy swarmed. Chin mandibles clicked. Clawed feet scraped against the floor. So many he couldn't count.

His chest swelled. Rifle in hand, he kept his march steady.

Slingers sighted in on him. Fire and glass flew.

Adrenaline spiked in his chest. Sound became non-existent.

This moment was a black hole. It stretched his whole life out before him and sucked it in, devouring it until the only thing he knew was his rifle and the enemy in front of him. His brain regressed into a primal state of function. There was no thought, no emotion.

There was a boy who had become a man. There was a rifle in his hand. Abraham smiled. He pulled the trigger.

A riskar chest bowed in, tiny armor fragments spiraling like splintered wood. Glass shards slammed against the walls around him.

He pulled the trigger.

A clawed arm separated at the shoulder joint, trailing blood. Glass shards fell to the ground in front of him.

He pulled the trigger.

A gaping hole the size of his fist punched through another alien and knocked it off its feet. Armor bloomed like an opening flower.

Glass crunched under his boots.

Abraham kept his march steady. He took his shots. In front of him, riskar fell. Inside of him, something rose.

He pulled the trigger.

Click.

He sidled against the wall, dropped the empty mag.

Click. Slap. Slick-slack.

Abraham stepped out again, firing indiscriminately. Everything was red. He hadn't taken a hit yet, but everything was red.

Kickback.

riskar fell, clutching holes and missing limbs.

Kickback.

They charged him, and he shot them at point blank.

The blood of his enemies was the only thing that touched him. He pounded across the floor, claws cracking under his boots. One of them got close. He shot it in the stomach. Stringy viscera erupted from the back like a parachute. He kicked it down. Fired three more rounds. Three bodies hit the floor.

A lung deflated under his boot.

He slammed the barrel of his weapon forward, pinning a riskar to the wall.

He pulled the trigger. Carapace armor cracked, fountaining blood. The creature slid down the wall. He jammed the barrel into the middle eye and fired.

Pale gray brain matter and viscera painted the wall. Hot blood flecked his face. Abraham scanned the area, breathing deep.

He glanced up at the hallway behind him. It was littered with bodies and fragments of bodies. The carnage was worse than the aftermath of Tar's grenade.

He was alone. He ran a hand down his chest and stomach. No human blood. No injuries. It was impossible.

He checked his magazine. Three bullets left.

Another corridor ran to the right. Its walls pulsed with a green glow. The HYDRA.

There was still time.

He had left the rest of the Ravens behind in his suicidal march. He hadn't expected to make it this far. Still didn't understand how he was alive.

"Ravens, Private Zeeben. Do you have a ship?"

"Abraham?" Vase asked, relief evident in her tone.

"According to my Pulse, I'm close to the HYDRA. I'm continuing with the mission."

He turned right, following the green light.

"Copy," Vase said. "We made it out, but we're still waiting for an opportunity."

Relief flooded his chest. "Good. I'll see you soon."

He switched his radio off.

The riskar weapon lay ahead. He could feel it. If he knew anything about General Rictor, it was that he left nothing to chance. He would be near the weapon, wanting to push the button himself.

Abraham was going to make sure he didn't get that chance.

He followed the tunnel through a massive open access door that gave way to a walkway made of material not unlike the riskar carapaces. His boots were also extremely loud against it. Stealth wasn't going to be an option from here on out, he surmised. Something caught his attention. He paused and listened.

It sounded like rushing water.

There was a river underneath the walkway.

It smelled profusely like ammonia. He felt lightheaded. Abraham wished he had his helmet to filter it. If not for safety's sake, just as a screen against the stench. It could have been a flowing stream of riskar shit for all he knew. It made his lungs feel itchy and tight.

I gotta get the fuck out of here.

The tunnel constricted as he walked further in. The plating underfoot started to become less and less formed, until he could see actual hardened earth. Had the aliens not built structures this far in?

The green light was brighter here. Abraham sprinted with thunderous boot stomps, the excitement getting the better of him.

The walkway spilled out into a large chasm. The entire space was about the size of a sports arena, maybe a hundred meters in diameter. There in the center of the room, standing like a towering behemoth from hell, was a titanic black spire. Lines of green glow traced up and down the thing, pulsing. The base was wide with bulbous nacelles, large enough to be neutron engines. Abraham counted four he could see from where he was standing.

This HYDRA was definitely meant as a genocidal weapon. It was a weapon that could put a sizeable hole in a galaxy. How long had the riskar been developing this? Did they originally intend to use it against humanity?

Abraham thought of the implications. Destroying an entire solar system.

The riskar Royal Fleet was cocooning Duringer like an iron curtain. Even if he disabled this weapon, nothing would be allowed off world.

Nothing is getting off world...except for the HYDRA.

Abraham smiled, seeing the weapon in an entirely new light.

He moved onto the railing and entered the chasm.

Ascending stairs wound up the side of the cave to a three-story structure near the top. Downward, there was the launchpad. The cave was empty of any living thing. Abraham surmised this was due to the blast-off effect of concentrated smoke and flames, which would preclude any normal person from loitering in the area.

269

Abraham climbed up the stairs. He couldn't believe his luck. There was no resistance. No enemies jumping off the walls or creeping in the shadows. He walked right up to the lower tier of the hardened structure and pulled the door open.

Inside was a different story.

Several riskar in flowing white gowns were stationed at various terminals. They turned to look at him all at once. Their clawed hands were covered in fuzzy blue material. A thin layer of glass sealed the gaps in their carapaces, including a closed-top tube over their heads.

They're scientists, he thought in disgust. *Who knows what kind of weaponry they could be cooking up in here?*

"Nobody move and nobody has to get hurt." He brandished his CLR, trying to look threatening without also coming across as unhinged.

The scientists glanced at each other, then back at him. Almost in perfect unison, their fuzzy blue claws came straight out from their bodies, claws spread.

Close enough to hands up for me.

"Okay, good." Abraham looked around, suddenly panicked. He didn't expect this to go so easily. Didn't have a plan for this. He might have gotten himself in over his head. Reaching a finger into the neckpiece of his S-skin, he switched his radio back on.

"-ham, where the fuck are you?"

"Vase, it's Abraham. I've got the scientists at gunpoint in the bunker. How do I disable the HYDRA?"

"Holy shit, really?"

"Yes, really. No one else has to die. Just tell me how to disable this thing."

"Abraham...you can't do this by yourself." He could hear a certain edge creeping into her voice.

"I know," he muttered. "So, help me. How do I stop it?"

"You have to –" Laser fire erupted so loud he jerked his earpiece out and left it dangling.

Abraham turned his attention back to the scientists. He sighted in on a feeble looking one and dragged him to the front of the room. The oldest looking one was probably the senior scientist, right?

"All right, here's the deal. If you don't..." He had a moment of consternation. He wasn't sure what to do. He had two choices. Both with potentially disastrous consequences. Both high risk, high reward. One was what he was ordered to do, the other...seemed right.

He went with his gut.

"If you don't launch this fucking weapon, right the fuck now, I'm killing all of you. Starting with Einstein here." He jabbed the barrel of his rifle against the glass of the alien's tube helmet.

Fuck. Even these assholes have helmets. I'm definitely getting some alien disease if I survive this.

The riskar gathered up in a huddle, barking and jeering at each other. Abraham didn't like that, so he fired a warning shot at the ceiling. That got them scattered like overgrown roaches, hustling to their computer stations, slapping clawed fingers against organic yet complex technology. Abraham didn't understand a single thing about it, but he did respect that it was the riskar version of advanced tech.

He shouldered into the riskar next to him. "Hey, Einstein, you know how to get the speakers on in this piece? I got a message for the general."

He stuffed his earpiece back in.

"Vase, it's Abraham. Listen up. I have one final request. It's important, so I need you to promise."

In between bursts of gunfire and screams of war, she replied, "Do you have...shut down yet?"

Abraham smiled. "Message the Navy and tell them to stand by."

The frequency squelched. "...disabled yet?"

"Vase, you're not listening. Tell the Navy if they send in any ships, they're not getting them back. I'm not disabling the HYDRA. I'm *launching* it."

"Are you fucking *crazy*? Abraham, don't! I will personally have you court martialed! You will be rotting in a cell at Terra Sky for the rest of your miserable fucking life!"

He yanked the earpiece out mid-scream. She wasn't happy about it, but then, when *was* she happy, anymore? Ever since he had told her he loved her, ever since the Admiral of the Navy came to visit, she had been on edge, and he was over it.

The thoughts that run through your head when you're trying to launch an intergalactic super weapon.

A loud bark sounded from the back of the room, followed by a thud.

All movement in the room ceased. Sound quieted. Someone groaned. It was a human groan.

CHAPTER 36

Abraham spun on his heel.

Ten meters away, Digger rolled across the floor, covered in mud. He was soaked head to toe, as if he had been submerged in a swamp for hours. He coughed up phlegm, mud, and red grass. His hands were tied with vines behind his back. When he was shoved or thrown, he fell over in the tangled mass of riskar scientists, who barely managed to step over him.

"Impressive, human Zeeben."

General Rictor stood on the opposite side of the structure. Ornate carapace armor shone in the light. He was tall, for a riskar.

Abraham eyed his enemy, fear and anger dancing inside his stomach.

Rictor was a solid meter taller than Abraham. As far as the riskar went, their general was a stand-out specimen. His armor was rounded and bulbous, carved with ornate inscriptions; the design fit his abnormally large musculature. Three red eyes beamed over scratching chin mandibles that never stopped moving.

The armor was black and green, the edges of each plate silver and striated. Abraham recognized this from anatomy class at basic; they were sharpened on purpose, like knives. He made a mental note not to go close quarters with him; he'd be shredded in moments.

"You have managed to do the impossible, human. Commendable." Rictor's neck-lungs billowed for a moment, left then right, almost like a sigh. "You speak the tongue of the riskar. You wear the Pontcha on your belt. For that, I offer you a warrior's death. I will let this one live if you lay down your life for him."

His English is really good, Abraham thought. *He's playing mind games with me.*

Abraham laughed.

Spit flew from his teeth as he shouted, "You think I'm letting you *live*, asshole? You killed my family, Rictor. My friends. My whole life, every decision I've made up to this point, has been for Milune."

Digger wriggled up against a gnarled tree root, a riskar desk, until he was seated. Blood trickled down his bald head, covering one eye. He tried to shake his head to clear it, but it had no effect. He cleared his throat with another cough.

"Stop talking shit and kill him already," Digger muttered.

"Digger, you good?" Abraham took a step closer to Rictor.

"No thanks to you. I'm fine." He shook his head. "The only guy who did his fucking job." He spat a stream of blood. "And this is the thanks I get."

"I'm getting you out of here. Just stay awake."

Digger chuckled, but his voice was weak. Eyelids drifted shut.

Rictor stepped forward, clawed feet clinking against the floor.

"Human Zeeben, you have lost. There is no fight left. My fleet is already here. Even now, they are preparing to guard Holy Duringer from your Navy. All I require of you is a message to be sent to your admiral. If you do this, I will let your friend live, but you and the rest of your interlopers will die."

Abraham didn't have to think about that for long.

"No deal. I send the message and you'll kill us all anyway."

"Human Zeeben, really. I have allowed you to keep that weapon pointed at me during this discussion. Do I seem so human-like, incapable of making and keeping an honest oath?"

Abraham checked his belt, just barely flicking his eyes downward. He had Amory's dagger. One pistol. Two rounds left in his CLR. If he missed, he was going to have to go close quarters with Rictor, where he would invariably be skinned to death. Digger had always been a better shot, but Abraham didn't know what kind of state he was in.

"Digger, you still with me?"

He moaned.

"I want you to do something for me, okay? I'm going to surrender to the general, here, but I want you to give a message to Vase. She's the only thing I've got left."

"Zeeben?" His eye drifted open.

Good, he's still coherent...

Abraham took a step closer. He was now a meter from Digger, five meters from Rictor. He made eye contact with Digger for the briefest span.

"We never got along, but I didn't realize how much I hated you until our first training exercise. You ever do something like that again, I won't be making it back to her alive. And she'll know it's all your fault."

Recognition illuminated Digger's face. His good eye popped open. He showed his hands, no longer bound but still tucked behind his back. He had somehow broken the restraints. Blood patches tipped his fingers; the nails were missing.

Abraham's skin crawled. That looked painful.

"Throw down the weapon, human Zeeben. I will not ask again."

Abraham nodded, held his weapon out, offering it to Rictor.

273

The general took a step forward, stretched his arm out to take the weapon.

It fell from Abraham's grip. Digger rolled forward with a yell, caught the weapon, and fired.

The bullet blew through Rictor's shoulder. The armor fractured, piercing tan and gray flesh. Shrapnel radiated in a cloud of grainy yellow blood.

Abraham ripped his pistol from his belt and aimed.

The alien roared, his lung sacs shaking violently. One clawed foot slammed Digger into Abraham, toppling them. He fell, squeezing the trigger as fast as he could. All his shots missed.

Abraham's head hit the deck. He saw stars.

Digger pushed against him. "Lemme up!"

Rictor pounced, pinning the two against the floor. Digger's elbow pressed into Abraham's gut. He felt the wind squeeze out of his lungs.

"Dig!" he wheezed. "G...et...uh...up!"

Rictor's claw reared back. It swiped fast as lightning. Blood sprayed from Digger's face. Hot and sticky, it flecked onto Abraham's cheek and chin.

Abraham tried bridging his back, but the weight was too much. He folded himself at the waist, legs flying up. His boot slammed into Rictor's knee joint, drawing a shriek from the alien.

It was enough.

Digger rolled off him.

Abraham rolled the other direction, frantic.

Terminals were blinking, left unattended. Sirens blared. Thin smoke trails wafted in through the doorway behind Rictor. No other signs of the weapon preparing for launch. Not a scientist in sight.

Abraham levelled his pistol. Rictor and Digger were scuffling; if he fired, he could hit Digger just as likely as he could hit Rictor.

Fuck it.

He dove into the fray.

Rictor's armor was sharp angles, serrated on his limbs. Abraham wished he still had the B-skin plates like Digger. The bulky armor was the only reason he was still alive.

Rictor pummeled and scratched at Digger relentlessly. Sparks flew from each impact with a sound like knives on whetstone. Digger dropped to one knee and crossed his forearms over his face, screaming.

Abraham jumped and kicked. His boot connected with Rictor, but his weight slammed into Digger. They collapsed to the ground.

Rictor howled, launching himself at Abraham.

Abraham got to his knees as the riskar slammed into him.

Human and alien bowled into the terminals. Elbows and knees clattered across buttons, tore through roots, sent sparks flying. Abraham watched the room spin end over end, struggling to get a good grip on his enemy. He latched onto the rib cage area only to have the armor nearly slice his fingers clean off. He pulled back a bloody hand just before the segments clamped down completely.

"I'll kill you!" Abraham screamed.

He slammed his fist into the general's neck.

"You die!" Rictor slashed Abraham upside the head.

Pain lines burned his scalp. Shadows and stars swirled in his eyes. He felt heat trickling down the back of his neck. Knew it was blood.

They traded punches and kicks. Each time Abraham made contact, he ended up lacerated, bleeding, inching closer to blacking out. He could feel the impact of his own punches coruscating up his arms.

Digger was there, growling, blood flecking between his teeth. He had Abraham's CLR in his hands, swinging it like a club.

Rictor dropped to his back and kicked.

Digger fell right into the claws of Rictor's foot. If not for his B-skin plates, he would have been eviscerated.

Rictor bucked his hips. Digger flew.

Abraham heard the crash, the meaty thud. He did not hear Digger moan or cry out. There wasn't time to check on his friend. He grasped a gnarled root, pulled himself to his feet.

A new alarm rang out, loud and sharp. A symbol popped up on one of the screens: an upside-down flame.

Rictor and Abraham locked eyes, the alien's three to Abraham's two.

"I guess that means blast-off, huh?" Abraham asked.

Rictor said, "I speak truth. You can't hear it. Riskar are children of Apocalypse, stewards of gravity. We see it with our eyes, sense it with our bodies, manipulate it with our minds. Humans want…and now, have stolen. We fight…to get it back."

"We didn't start shit with you."

Rictor coughed. "You know nothing of politics and war. Your human treachery will be punished."

Rictor limped closer, steadying himself with a clawed hand on the wrecked, sparking terminals. Yellow, grainy blood streamed from his shoulder. It ran through the gaps in his armor plates and dripped on the floor.

He gurgled, "The Mighty riskar will always defend our power."

"Defend? You destroyed…Milune. Somehow…pushed Dajun into it. Crashed the…fucking moon down on us!"

Rictor's eyes were half-moons.

"No," the alien's voice sounded like a skiff engine at low RPM. "Riskar stealth ships could not do this. It would take our *entire fleet.*"

"This weapon's going off no matter what, Rictor. I'm gonna die, and you're going with me. Just *admit it!*"

Abraham unsheathed Amory's knife from his belt, holding it in a reverse grip. The diamond-pommeled dagger glinted in the light. The surface of the blade was mirror clean. He didn't remember wiping Amory's blood from it. Out the window, he could see the riskar's superweapon preparing for launch.

That's it. We're all dead.

He smiled, turning his back to the glass window to face Rictor.

"Vase Seneca. Larry Poplenko. Alan Piebold and Digger Tachek. Amory Eilson. The Eagles and the Ravens."

Rictor stumbled with a choking laugh. He was just a few meters away.

"David and Obadiah Zeeben. Myles Lannam."

Rictor was close now, almost within arm's reach.

Abraham blinked away tears. "Kellina Zeeben. And two billion other innocent lives on Milune."

Rictor lunged, chin mandibles flexed, blades on his armor open and pointed at Abraham.

Abraham stood tall and opened his arms, dagger blade down and out.

Impact.

Rictor slammed into him. Blades bit into his skin. Pressed against his ribs. A hailstorm of glass surrounded them as they fell out the window. Down they fell, toward rising clouds and a floor of fire.

Abraham's left hand flailed, grasping for something, anything to hold onto. He held the dagger tight in his right hand.

He found it. A thick cord. A jungle vine that had grown over the HYDRA after years of storage. He snagged it. Friction scalded the soft tissue of his palm. Ligaments tweaked inside his elbow. Something popped in his left shoulder.

He held on.

Rictor slid, blades peeling layers of Abraham's S-skin as he dropped. Abraham shook himself, kicked, tried anything to get the alien off him, to drop him down to the fiery death he deserved.

"Zeeben!" Rictor howled, both arms thrown out wide.

The alien wrapped himself around Abraham in a crushing bearhug. Abraham screamed.

The serrated portions of the carapace armor sliced into him, grinding against his forearm bones and his shins. The darkness swirled, nearly obscuring his vision completely. He could feel his skin being shaved and peeled.

A blast of red lit his eyelids. It was the fires of ignition.

Flames roared to life under them. Abraham and Rictor glanced up to see the hangar door opening, letting in a steadily growing view of the bright daylight sky.

Who opened the doors?

As the HYDRA rose into the sky, it passed by the structure from which they'd fallen. Abraham saw him there, a blood-covered statue offering a crisp salute.

Digger.

The exhaust from the superweapon crawled over the cave walls, rising like a geyser.

Flames billowed into the open window.

Digger didn't flinch. The wall of fire consumed him.

The Marine sacrificed himself to ensure the success of Abraham's plan. It was the greatest act of heroism he had ever seen.

His chest burned with pride and regret.

Rictor struggled against him, trying to leverage his weight to dig the sharp edges further in. Tiny blades wriggled between his ribs, trying to penetrate the soft flesh beneath.

"No!" Abraham growled.

Rictor barked in his face. "Milune was not riskar, Zeeben. *You* attacked *us* first. We are merely defenders!"

Abraham let himself go limp. He lost his grip on the vine. He clutched Amory's dagger like his life depended on it.

Rictor roared. He slammed both claws into the side of the riskar superweapon, puncturing it.

Abraham tried to breathe. His vision swam. He was pinned between Rictor and the HYDRA. The ground was racing away. Fast. He cast a quick glance up. The riskar Royal Fleet.

Hundreds of ships, large and imposing, dominated the sky. The sea of red plumes pointed down. They rode the current of their reverse propulsion system elegantly. Gathered like this, they seemed an insurmountable wall of alien power. It was just as beautiful as it was intimidating.

The HYDRA soared into the sky.

Abraham tried to blink away the flashing glimmers of hypoxia. Vibrations coruscated through Rictor's armor, shaking the blades that punctured Abraham. It was like sandpaper on a third-degree burn. He didn't have enough air to scream.

Rictor coughed. One lung sac was deflated completely. The other was withering.

Abraham closed his eyes. The rushing of the air as it started to thin. The weapon would detonate any moment now. This entire arm of the galaxy would vaporize in moments.

Rictor looked up at him with one eye half-open.

He shouted over the passing airstream.

"Grant me an honest soldier's death, Zeeben. You have the Pontcha. You are a worthy warrior. Take my soul. Bear it in safety...and...honor!"

Abraham hesitated. He wanted to kill Rictor, but giving him the death he wanted?

Amory flashed through his mind. Digger. His family. His mother. Larry. Vase.

He realized then that he was more than himself. He was a Marine. His actions were more than just the decisions made by a tobacco farmer on a backwater planet. He was, in this moment, a steward of humanity. A beacon of hope. The bearer of the freedom flag.

Abraham stabbed the blade into Rictor's head. It crunched.

He tried to remember what Amory had said, but the riskar language fell from his lips without a thought. He heard the words coming from his throat, but it took a moment to realize the truth.

He *had* been speaking riskar. That's why he understood Amory when no one else could.

"Rictor, your soul is safe with me."

He ripped the blood-stained blade out.

General Rictor's eyes shut. He went limp. He hung, affixed to the weapon by his claws.

Abraham dug his earpiece out of his neck flap and put it in. In all the commotion, he'd forgotten it was off.

"Vase, you there?" he asked.

"Zeeben? Abraham? Is that you? I can barely hear you. Where *are* you?"

She couldn't hear him. There was no point in making a dying declaration if she couldn't hear him.

A jolt of claustrophobia ran through him. Rictor's armor had pierced his body in several places; he couldn't get the much larger being off him.

Abraham took a deep breath. *I don't have time for this.*

He swung the Pontcha, slicing through Rictor's wrist.

It happened all at once. Rictor's arm separated from his clawed hand. The barbed protrusions of his armor squelched out of Abraham's abdomen, trailing red. His scream was drowned out by the airstream. A black ring appeared in his vision growing larger by the second, but he fought it.

Don't pass out now.

He kicked off the surface of the weapon, separating himself from the danger of the white-hot exhaust plume. The HYDRA blasted off toward the wall of riskar ships, their dead general dangling on its side.

Air whipping over his face, eyelids peeled back from the force of his freefall, Abraham looked down on Duringer. The red jungle. Huge swathes of red-leafed forest. Crystal clear streams that ran through them. Glaciers instead of clouds that sailed through the sky on mysterious red winds. Down there somewhere, more fathers and mothers. More sons and daughters.

He knew the HYDRA would be the last thing they saw.

He was the harbinger of another Collision to a young riskar, staring at the sky right now. There was no escape, now. The entire planet was about to go up in atomic flames.

"Abraham, are you listening? We have a ship. Where *are* you?"

He tapped his belt, firing off his homing beacon.

"Holy shit, I've got him!" Larry called over the radio.

Tar said, "We'll be caught in the blast if we don't break atmosphere!"

"We're not leaving him," Vase said.

"Riskar ships can jump in atmo, but we don't have time to get to him!" Juke shouted. "The HYDRA's detonating any second!"

"Stop wasting time and pull up under him!" Piebold barked.

Abraham felt the tears being ripped from his eyes as he hit terminal velocity. It was a beautiful sight, the planet below. Even though he'd lost friends, killed and nearly been killed by aliens, it was still a beautiful sight.

Duringer was a beautiful planet to die on.

A searing flash of red light blinded him, stealing the beautiful vista from him.

The thud of impact squeezed his breath away. The deafening roar of his descent fell silent. His stomach churned. He breathed.

Abraham opened his eyes.

He was floating on a red cloud.

CHAPTER 37

"I see him," Piebold's voice crackled over the radio.

A strange ship zoomed across an even stranger sky. Vase and Larry were at the helm. "Abraham," Vase breathed, evidently relieved, "what are you doing?"

He looked down at himself. He was lying on his stomach, floating on a red screen. It wasn't a cloud, but a solid disc of red light. He barely had the strength to lift his head up enough to see it. Blood dripped from his wounds, collecting on it.

It was impossible to guess how thick it was, but when he looked through it, he could see tree canopies several kilometers below. "Uh, Vase…" he coughed, "are you doing this with your ship?"

"No," she said with a shaky voice. "I'm not."

"Detonation!" Tar came in on the radio, screaming at the top of his lungs. "Get your ass inside, Zeeben. *Now*, or we're atomized!"

Abraham rolled onto his back.

Up in the sky, the riskar Royal Fleet was bearing away from their position. The red plumes now angled away from Duringer. The HYDRA was a giant flashing swirl of energy, a ball of liquid lightning bolts, swelling like the great wave of a tsunami. Abraham was about to remark on the lack of sound when the blast wave hit. He fell through his floating platform.

He tumbled through the air a few meters before slamming into the open hatch of the pirated vessel. Cheers reached his ears. He was surrounded by the voices of his friends.

Relief flooded Abraham's chest.

He hoped that would be enough to fill in the gaps where he had bled out.

Vase's face came into view. Her lips touched his, and he drifted off.

The darkness was cold. He felt naked in its grip.

Shivering, he struggled against it. There was unfamiliarity on the air, something that…smelled. It was vanilla. A faint aroma of honeydew.

"Abraham." It was the sweetest voice he'd ever…

He opened his eyes, too scared to move.

The bedding under him felt like a cold slab of marble.

Am I in a morgue?

The ceiling was white. The walls were gray. The light was just a little too bright. It felt like the sting of fingertips touching his pupils. Standing over him was his commanding officer, Lieutenant Vase Seneca.

"Hello," he said with a weak smile.

"You're awake." She laughed. A mellifluous sound. A caress on the cheek.

He felt numb from the neck down. Slowly, he craned his neck to look at himself. A blue cotton sheet covered his body. From the general shape of it, it appeared he still had all his appendages attached.

"What happened?"

She kissed him, held his head in her hands. "We survived."

He frowned. "We did? I thought I saw..."

She nodded, her smile failing. "We lost some people. A lot of people. We were shot down, crash-landed on the riskar's home planet. Abraham...remember the chess move you taught me?" She quieted her voice and glanced around conspiratorially. "Castling! The riskar did it. They castled their home planet."

"How?"

Vase shook her head. "We still don't know. It's gone, anyway. Eight percent of Sector Twelve is...just a hole, now. But there's something else, Abraham. Something more."

He licked his dry, cracked lips. "What?"

"*You*, Abraham. I knew there was something different about you. It's why I was so interested in studying your psychology. Beyond that, there's actually something going on with you. And..." she looked around again, "...there's someone here to see you."

Her eyes narrowed, tears suddenly sheeting over them.

"What?"

He remembered. The red disc. Riskar words from his mouth.

"I don't care about that. I...I want you here, Vase. By my side."

She smiled. "I know, Abraham. But right now, I have to go."

She kissed him.

The elation he should have felt didn't come.

Tension wracked his body.

The electric tingles of nerve pain knifed into him, tracing laser lines of heat all over. He flinched and hissed. Tried to slow his breathing. Everything hurt. His bones, his muscles, his brain. The confusion was worse.

She walked away and his heart broke. Hot tears ran past his jawline. A groan escaped his lips. As long as he lived, he never wanted to see her walk away from him again.

The door opened. She left, and someone else entered.

Cold ice spread through Abraham's gut. He felt like he'd had his breath sucked out of his lungs by a vacuum. Fear chewed at his chest. The man entered as a shadow, his heels clicking sharply with each step. He stopped at Abraham's bedside and pivoted his shoulder. A sliver of light spilled through the window, illuminating his face. Most of his face.

A black bar hovered over his eyes. His skin was dark, his scalp covered in short white prickles of hair, his face freshly shaved. When he smiled, his white teeth seemed to be floating in a dark cloud all their own.

"Private Abraham Zeeben," his voice was breathy and high. "I am Operative Smithers of the Ghost Society."

With all the crispness of a proper military salute, Smithers offered his hand.

Abraham stretched himself, painfully, to shake it. It was like grabbing a metal door handle. He shook it quickly and collapsed to his back, exhaling through the pain.

"Do you know why I am here?"

Abraham laughed. "No fucking idea."

Smithers smiled, wider this time. "I wonder if you are aware of your unique situation, and why the Society is interested in you."

"I ended the war. That not enough for you?"

"Actually, quite the opposite." Smithers steepled his fingers. "You have outperformed all of our expectations."

Abraham's blood froze. "Expectations?"

Smithers nodded. "You are the son of Obadiah Zeeben, are you not?"

He nodded.

"Then the old man must not have told you. Abraham, have you ever had your DNA tested before?"

"Of course. When I signed up for the corps, on Veranda."

"And the results?"

"Nobody told me anything. It was just a routine sample."

Smithers shook his head. "No, Abraham. Your DNA is unique. According to our testing, which has been extensive, you are not entirely human."

Abraham's head swam. Panic wrapped his body in a cold sweat.

Stop. Don't say it.

"You're full of shit."

"I'm full of *facts*. A big one you are overlooking here is that your DNA is, at least partially, *Nephropidae Pulmonis Volitare*."

Abraham blinked.

"Abraham, you are part riskar."

His brain stopped. He struggled to breathe. "How is that possible?" he croaked. "I have a human mother and father! A human brother! I'm not part...alien anything!"

He felt like he had bugs crawling under his skin. Or his skin was made of chitin, like insect carapaces. His body suddenly felt much less safe to be in. He wished he were just dead instead of anything other than human.

"How many times have you floated in mid-air before?" Smithers cackled. "You're not human, Abraham. Not completely. The riskar can manipulate gravity. Control it, essentially. It appears that you can, too."

"But, how..."

The conversation with his father...

You saw the red?

The red.

He knew something. Abraham's father had known something and kept it a secret from him. And now that he was dead, he would never know the truth. The betrayal tasted foul, like wet copper in his throat.

It came to him like a whisper inside his head. A secret his subconscious had been keeping from him, but now took a perverse sense of pleasure in revealing to him.

The disc that had appeared out of nowhere to prevent him falling to his death on Duringer. It wasn't magic. It wasn't something from the riskar ship.

It had come from *him.*

Somehow, *he* had done that.

He charged through a storm of fire in the hallway on Duringer, never taking a single hit.

The supply pod embedded in the ground that responded only to his touch.

The red wrapped around David, saving him from the bonfire.

He had done it all.

He croaked the answer out before he knew he was speaking.

"I can see gravity."

Smithers clapped his hands and held them together. "You are the only human who can. Part human, at least." He cleared his throat. "We're hoping you take us up on an offer that, frankly, I doubt you can refuse."

Abraham cried. He couldn't hold it back any longer. His entire family was dead *and* he wasn't human? His whole life was unraveling. He didn't know what to think or believe anymore.

Smithers said, "If you come and work with us, we will provide two things that you desperately want. The first is financial compensation. The second is something a little...closer to home."

"Closer to home?" Abraham stammered.

283

"Yes. I will explain more, but only after I have your word that you will answer our call."

Abraham wiped the tears and mucus from his face. He rubbed it off on his blanket.

"Okay. Okay." He took a deep breath. "Can I have some time to think about it?"

Smithers smiled. "We will give you some time."

He turned to leave.

"Wait," Abraham said, "how do I get in contact with you?"

Smithers never stopped walking, never turned around. He opened the door and said over his shoulder, "You do not contact the Society. If we want you, we will get you."

The door shut, leaving Abraham shuddering in the silence.

CHAPTER 38

The weeks went by slowly. It was agonizing. Chock full of boredom and long periods of waiting alone in quiet rooms. Abraham was thankful when he was finally cleared to leave the medical station. At least he was allowed to walk the corridors of the ship.

It wasn't until his third day of mobility that he realized he wasn't on a ship; he was in a building. The tallest building he'd ever heard of. His room was on floor 465, and there were many floors above him. The only planet he knew with buildings that tall was Vatican, the human capitol.

He was finishing setting up the chessboard in the waiting area when Vase came to see him. She had been visiting every day at lunch. They ate and talked. They went back to Abraham's room for some private conversation. He stole a few kisses from her. They both carefully avoided talking about the revelation from the Ghost, a revelation he didn't entirely believe. They went back and forth on the mysterious red disc that had saved his life, not sure what that was or how it happened. Abraham talked past that as quickly as he could; he didn't want to think about Duringer anymore.

They would eventually get to a place where they had talked themselves out. Abraham was groggy and tired from the medicine. Vase was tired from thinking about the bureaucracy that was her life as an officer in the corps. The conversation would die, and they would be reduced to sitting and staring. Just watching each other breathe.

"The services are tomorrow," she said, solemn.

"I know," he replied. "I'm surprised they waited this long."

Vase played with her hair, twirling one brown and one blonde lock together. "You know he's been wanting to see you. It'll be good to see him before…you know."

Abraham stiffened. She could only mean Larry. His best friend up until Duringer. A lifetime ago, now. They had both been different people.

"I'll see him tomorrow."

The breathing and staring resumed. A minute passed, Abraham searching Vase as she searched him. He felt like they were looking for something in each other, something deeper than the words they shared. Was the silence a sign that they hadn't found it yet? Or did it mean they hadn't worked up to openly acknowledging it?

"I had your uniform authorized. You made rank. Private First Class."

It was a bad joke, Abraham thought. That was unlike Vase, really. "Are you avoiding telling me something?" he asked.

She shook her head. "No, why would you think that?"

Abraham shrugged it off. "I don't know."

Vase hefted up his new C-skin, the mess dress uniform of the Marine Corps. Abraham noticed the two chevrons on the chest, standing proudly over a shifting field of red and black and gray triangles. When he graduated basic, there had just been one, sewn into a fabric uniform. He hadn't expected to make rank within a week of graduating. Then again, he hadn't expected to be thrown straight into a war.

He hadn't expected to lose so many of his friends, or to kill so many riskar. Come to think of it, he hadn't expected to survive the fucking war. Now it was truly over. A ten-year war, ended in a week. Rictor was dead, Duringer was gone, and so was everyone he cared about. Except Vase. It might have been the medication, or just his increased comfort in her presence, but he felt his gut swimming with emotion.

"We lost so many good people," he whispered.

"I know. If I had known it was going to be like this...I don't know if I would have joined the corps."

Abraham nodded. "I was young and stupid. I couldn't have been talked out of it. Vase," he held her hand, "I can't lose you. No matter what, as long as you love me, I'm going to be okay."

Her face lit up. "You sure you're going to be okay?"

He smiled. "I am. We're going to get through the next four years without a hitch."

Vase's eyebrows narrowed. "Without a hitch?"

He laughed. "Well, maybe we'll get hitched. We've ended the war. There isn't any reason to think differently, is there?"

The laughter died. The smiles faded.

"I don't think so. But, if I'm honest, Abraham...I'm scared."

He hugged her. Feeling her body against his, smelling her intoxicating scent...he just breathed in deep the sensation of her.

She was trembling, as was he.

"Whatever comes our way, we'll conquer it together."

She nodded in agreement, spreading her tears against his cheek.

He kissed her, gently pulled her hip until she wrapped her legs around his waist. Her kisses were intense, more intense than anything she had shared with him up until now, and salty with her tears. He could feel the tension in her body as she pressed herself against him, caressed his hair, each breath a shudder against him.

They fell onto the bed, wrapped in each other's arms.

Between kisses, she said, "I love you, Abraham."

A supernova bloomed in his chest.

For the first time since they'd started their romance, Vase stayed the night.

A hundred formations of military men and women from all branches of service were stationed at regular intervals on either side of a wide red carpet.

The assembly hall was the kind of space that was so large it didn't have a smell. Polished titanium pillars held up floor-to-ceiling glass panes that stretched for three or four stories straight up. The ceiling was four large windows through which the assembled men and women gazed upon the unending darkness of space and the innumerable stars beyond.

Abraham wanted the whole thing to be over. An award ceremony and a funeral at the same time seemed crass.

Admiral Latreaux spoke from the podium. "This is the Hall of Heroes. All who enter here stand on hallowed ground. This is not a ceremony to honor the living, but a ceremony to honor the dead. It is by the shedding of their blood and the sacrifice of their flesh that we are restored. We are made whole, made new, made perfect by the ultimate sacrifice made by these brave men and women. Today, we honor them."

He read the names, held each medal aloft for all to see, then rested it on their pine box. One of the surviving Marines would march to the pine box and punch or press the medal into the box, salute, then march back to their place in line. Every thud of a medal being pinned drew tears from the small section at the front where the family members were gathered.

"First Lieutenant Eduardo Jiminez Lechero. Twenty years old, hailing from the First Ward, Destin. He is laid to rest with the Bronze Star with Ribbon of Valor."

Vase pressed the medal into the box, saluted and quickly returned to the line.

"Staff Sergeant Demarius Hinton. Twenty-six years old, hailing from Lower Level Three, Mattox. For actions that far exceeded the call of normal duty, and for providing the training which ultimately enabled the success of the Marines that stand before us now, he is laid to rest with the Silver Star with Ribbon of Valor."

Abraham was about to march forward, but Piebold beat him to it. When he punched the medal into the wooden box, it crunched. He fired a sharp salute and quickly marched back to the line.

"Private Amory Eilson. Eighteen years old, hailing from Ipthus, Halzenti." The Admiral held her medal aloft, a silver oak leaf cluster adorned with several stars, and a flowing red and black ribbon. He placed it atop the empty box and said, "Private Eilson exemplified the commitment and dedication of a true Marine, even in the face of overwhelming enemy fire. The actions of Private Eilson reflect great credit upon herself and the Human Marine Corps. She is laid to rest with the Marine Corps' highest honor, the Silver Supernova with Ribbon of Valor."

Larry took to the stage, placed his hand on the medal and pushed. The pins clicked into the box, affixing the medal to it. He saluted, held it for a moment, then marched back to the line and stood at attention.

"Private Denton 'Digger' Tachek. Nineteen years old, hailing from Stony Ridge, Veranda."

Latreaux held out a shimmering medal the size of a dinner plate. It was trimmed with blue and white flowing ribbons. He laid it on the box next to Amory's.

"The selfless actions of Private Tachek enabled the rest of the Raven Platoon to escape with their lives, but more than that, they ensured the successful deployment of the riskar's own superweapon, destroying the majority of their naval fleet and effectively ending the Riskar War. Private Tachek's valorous actions reflect great credit upon himself and the Human Marine Corps. He is laid to rest with the highest military honor, the Navy's Medal of Honor."

Abraham marched up to the medal and punched it into the box. His knuckle split against the rippled edge. He saluted, a trickle of blood running down his hand. Digger saluted him behind a wall of fire in his mind's eye.

It's not the same when you can't hit back, Dig.

He returned to his spot in the line, throat and chest burning.

After the rest of the names were read, Latreaux gave a salute and dismissed the formations. Hundreds of men and women marched, sounding like a retreating thunderstorm as they filed out. The informal ceremony began when it was just family and friends remaining.

Larry Poplenko took to the stage, guitar in hand. He slung the strap over his shoulder and turned his back to the front row, eyes only for Amory's photograph above a rectangular box that was supposed to be her remains but was just empty. The Silver Supernova medal shimmered.

Larry strummed his guitar, slow and sad single plucks like raindrops. Words fell from his lips, just barely above a whisper, as he recited the song he wrote for his fallen lover:

I buried myself on Duringer
Far from home.
When I dug myself out
Of the grave I made
Fragile flesh escaped
But not unscathed.

They say, some of them say it to this day
The bones remain
I'll never know
Because you're in a place
A place, a place I cannot go.
I hope it feels like home
Cause one day I'll join you.
One day I'll find you at home,
We'll make it our home
Beneath the loam.
But 'till then, I'll roam
Just another ghost,
A spirit without form.

Larry lowered his guitar. The air was thin. The silence was painful. Abraham smiled. He walked up and put a hand on Larry's shoulder. "Back in that Navy office on Veranda...we didn't have a clue what we were getting into, did we?" Abraham asked.

"Fuck off, Abraham." Larry shrugged his hand off and stomped away.

Abraham deflated. "Sure, man."

His reply was lost in the widening gap between him and his best friend.

Vase slipped her fingers into his. She pulled him back into the antechamber, away from everyone. "Everything okay?"

He tensed. Her grip tightened on his hand.

"No. I don't think things will be okay for a while."

She blinked. "What's this about?"

He pulled her to his chest and wrapped his arms around her. He stood there for a moment, holding her.

"Rictor," he cleared his throat, "before he...after I..."

Abraham felt heavy. Emotion bled through his pores. He had gone as far away from home as he could, but he had not outrun The Collision. He knew now that he never could. Something happened that day that led him here. Something he still didn't understand.

I'm different, now. I'll never be the same.

He didn't want to bring it up, but he knew he had to. Vase and he did not keep secrets from each other. He tried to speak but the words got caught in his throat. Vase put a hand on the back of his neck. He took a deep breath and tried again.

"Rictor said the riskar weren't responsible for The Collision."

Her nails pressed on his neck.

"If they aren't," she asked, searching his eyes for the answer, "then who is?"

Abraham said, "I don't know yet."

EPILOGUE

David rushed out of the house, fuming. "I'm not taking this shit anymore, Father!" He threw the Portal on the ground and stepped on it. His shoe slid off the slick surface and he fell on his ass.

The device simply collected dust in the shape of his shoe print. David growled. Everything, everything lately was pushing him over the edge. Ever since Abraham left, he was the one getting screwed over. It wasn't fair!

"David, son, you get your ass back in here. Finish your dinner and get some sleep. We got our final day of harvest tomorrow, and then you can take a couple weeks off."

Obadiah Zeeben stood in the doorway with his pipe, gently exhaling a cloud of smoke over the porch steps. He wasn't wearing his field hat. Long wisps of silver hair drifted in the breeze, like stray cobwebs.

The harsh sun stung David's already sunburned skin, but he didn't care. If Abraham could run out when things got hard, he could, too. He stood and brushed his pants off.

"I'm going, just like Abraham. I'm not working anymore!"

Obadiah nodded. "All right, then. I'll be here when you come back."

The screen door shut. David huffed and stomped away from the homestead. He went about ten steps before turning around to retrieve the Portal. His beloved device in hand, he turned and headed into the city.

He hadn't been in the downtown section of Veranda in a long time, but he still knew the way. It wasn't like strolling through the downtown section of a big city planet like Milune.

Milune...the year 10-006, at approximately 2000 hours, what would have been the two hundred and fortieth Passing recorded. Milune...former population 2.12 billion souls, pre-Collision. Post-Collision: thirty-three survivors.

David slapped his head. *Too much information. Too much. Calm down.*

He slapped himself again, trying to calm the torrent of data that seemingly flexed with a will of its own inside his head.

"Hey there, you lost, kid?"

David turned to look at a fat man with a suspicious mustache in a surplus-store version of military camouflage. A half full bottle of brown liquid sloshed in his hand. He was standing at the entrance of a rather large house.

"Uh, no, thank you." He turned his nose up at the man and kept walking.

"Fucking kids are assholes." The fat man slammed the bottle of liquor on the porch, sending glass shards everywhere. He screamed for two boys to come sweep it up, and they did, hustling about like little soldiers.

David shook his head. *Don't remember seeing that last time I was here.*

He was about to turn a corner when he heard a noise like change rattling in a purse. Curious, David turned and headed down the alley, fixated on the sound. The further down the alley he got, the louder the sound became. The brick walls of the buildings on either side seemed to draw closer together as he walked.

A door slammed shut. The rattling stopped.

His eyes adjusted. Someone was standing in the alley.

"Hello, David."

He froze. *I shouldn't be here.*

Panic pressed at every square centimeter of his skin all at once. "H-h-how do y-you know me?"

The man grabbed him by the shoulders and whispered, "I'm a big fan of your brother."

His Portal slipped through his fingers. Glass broke at his feet. Strong arms bearhugged him.

Before David could react, just as the plasma began to rain from the sky and Veranda began to burn…

David and the Shadow Man disappeared in a flash of red light.

Acknowledgements

The author would like to thank many close friends, dear family members, and even hated enemies for the strength and inspiration to complete this work. In fact, this book has been rewritten several times, and in each version, it drifted further and further from its original idea.

The initial idea: what if Indiana Jones became a Jedi?

Obviously, that's not the book you just read, nor will future books in this series be heading in that direction. The creative process is a maelstrom. A natural process subject to unnatural disasters, only survived by supernatural perseverance, for which the writer cannot (if he's honest) claim total responsibility.

The following names are the people whom the author would like to recognize as having helped; frequent family pep talks, ball-busting brainstorms with buddies; beta readers and evil editors...to name a few:

Trevor Acor, Alex Acree, Michael Altazin, Sir William Belkofer, Eric Burnworth, Kelly Burnworth, Kyle Bryant, Randy Carrasco, Tiffany Carrasco, Sebastian Hidalgo, Donnie Jenkins, Peter Marsh, Kirk "Red" Nelson, Ricky Samilton, Bill Scheve, Louise Scheve

APOGEE

PROLOGUE

"He's not dead," Vase said over her iced macchiato. Ice clattered against the glass as she stirred her straw, blending milk and coffee in a swirl. "I don't care what anyone says. I know him."

Longarm Detective Djet Rincon frowned across the mirrored surface of the table. She took a sip of foam from her own simple brew, exposing a small half circle of espresso the color of her skin. The shape trembled when she set it down. The turbulence on the surface of the espresso held her eye as she thought.

She had intentionally chosen the seat with her back to the sprawling Dominicus Dorsi district of Vatican. The interconnected towers and constant air traffic blazing lines of light across the sky would have distracted her. And right now, she needed to focus. Vase requested this meeting off the record. It didn't matter that they were friends, or that they had history. The important thing was that Vase had a missing person's case, and she knew a detective she could ask for a personal favor. A nondescript coffee house near the spaceport, filled with patrons from every corner of the galaxy that kept the ambience at a dull roar, provided enough cover to keep their conversation private.

Coffee is deeply personal, she thought. *You can tell a lot about a person by the way they order it.*

Her eyes flipped up to Vase's cup, held loosely in her pale, delicate fingers. Fingers with clear-coat nail polish, perfectly shaped, but not the work of a salon. *Vase may be a commander now, but she's still very conscious of her appearance.* Scrawled across the side of the cup in thin silver markings only legible to the person who made them were the modifications made to the coffee. An order that specific could only be made by one of two people – an uppity coffee snob, or a control freak.

Djet tapped her fingers against her cup. Her accent was a stealthy mix of Irish and Jamaican, and just like the coffee they drank, it could be traced back thousands of years to Earth. If you believed the stories about humanity's dark past.

Djet said, "Okay, so ya know him. How well do ya know him, really?"

Vase's face remained frozen, but she blinked several times. "What do you mean?"

Djet pulled her hair back into a tight ponytail. So doing, she transitioned from 'best friend once upon a time' to hard-nosed detective.

"If ya want him found, I need to ask some questions. The usual questions detectives ask in a missing person's case. Ya need to answer honestly if ya actually want him found."

A sigh escaped her lips. She leaned back in her chair, eyes watching the air and space traffic for a few moments before she replied.

"Of course," she said, like it was the most obvious thing in the world. "I don't have anything to hide. You know that, Djet."

Djet slid her espresso forward and planted her elbows on the table. It was a tactic she used to capture a suspect's undivided attention. Close proximity and eye contact upped the pressure. It broadcasted loud and clear: *if you lie, I'll see right through it. I already know the answer to the question I'm asking, so do yourself a favor, and just come out with the truth.* She did not relish using these tactics on her closest friend, but Vase was an uncharacteristically hard person to read.

"On the contrary, Commander Seneca. I think ya have been collecting secrets since the last time I saw ya. Intelligence is a game of smoke and mirrors. I need honesty if I'm going to be any help to ya. How long have ya known him?"

"Three years."

"What was the nature of your relationship?"

Vase blinked twice. "We were lovers."

Djet nodded, just a bit. "Ya were intimate."

Vase broke eye contact, looking up and to the left. "Yes. Not that you need to know that."

"Oh, I do." Djet smiled. "I need to know everyting, Vase. Every little detail helps."

Vase snapped her eyes back to Djet's. They were shiny now, covered in a thin layer of tears. Her lower lip trembled as her words squeezed out through clenched teeth. "Do you need to know how big his dick is, too?"

A pang of regret hit Djet in the stomach, but she held the smile on her face, refusing to blink. She wouldn't let Vase put her on the defensive. Not when she was the one asking for a favor this time.

"Ya mentioned in your message that he stormed off the last time ya saw him. That means he was upset with ya, which could give me an idea of where he went. Why he was mad at ya makes the difference between him hitting the nearest strip club or going off-world with no intent of returning."

Vase scooted her chair out from under the table, metal on marble grinding obnoxiously. She flipped a dial on her belt, changing her C-skin pattern from an ambient white to the red and black cascade of Marine

Corps camo. "I'm late for work. If you didn't want to help, Djet, you could have just said so."

"No." Djet leaned back in her chair until it creaked. "You're scared."

Vase flicked a lock of blonde hair from her forehead. She checked the braids on the brown side as her eyes looked anywhere but at Djet.

Djet's smile faded. Vase's behavior was strange. She was stressed, that much was obvious. But she seemed different. Three years ago, the last time Djet had seen her, she was stressed but optimistic. Now, she seemed...agitated. Something in her gut told her it wasn't simply because this boyfriend had disappeared.

Vase snapped, "I'm not scared. I'm worried. There's a difference."

Djet sipped her espresso, careful not to singe her tongue. She inhaled the wafting steam, basking in the pleasant aroma. This wasn't much to go on, but that was normal for missing person's cases. It was why she hated working them more than just about anything else. It was anyone's guess whether the man in question was dead or alive; if he had run into the wrong kind of people – which happened a lot on Vatican – or if he had skipped off this rock to get away from a bad breakup.

Vase finally looked at her with a deep, shuddering inhale.

"What did he do to ya, Vase?" Djet asked, allowing her concern to bleed into her tone.

Commander Vase picked up her coffee and turned to leave. Her flippant reply cut the cord on the conversation with no room for debate.

"Let me know if you find anything."

ΛPOGEE, BOOK 2 OF BY BLOOD OR BY STAR
COMING IN 2022

Printed in Great Britain
by Amazon

76836483R00180